RIMWARD
STARS

BOOK FIVE
OF THE CASTLE FEDERATION SERIES

RIMWARD STARS

BOOK FIVE
OF THE CASTLE FEDERATION SERIES

GLYNN STEWART

FAOLAN'S PEN
PUBLISHING
faolanspen.com

This edition published in 2018 by:

Faolan's Pen Publishing Inc.

22 King St. S, Suite 300

Waterloo, Ontario

N2J 1N8 Canada

ISBN-13: 978-1-988035-53-6 (print)

A record of this book is available from Library and Archives Canada.

Printed in the United States of America

1 2 3 4 5 6 7 8 9 10

First edition

First printing: May 2017

Illustration © 2017 Tom Edwards

TomEdwardsDesign.com

Faolan's Pen Publishing logo is a trademark of Faolan's Pen Publishing Inc.

Read more books from Glynn Stewart at faolanspen.com

1

Antioch System

14:00 September 10, 2736 Earth Standard Meridian Date/Time

BC-305 Poseidon

THE CRUISER WAS DOOMED.

The Antioch Space Navy's only battlecruiser was more modern than Commodore James Tecumseh of the Terran Commonwealth Navy had expected, but it didn't appear that either the ship's capability nor her crew's clear competence was going to change anything.

The convoy she was supposed to protect was in no better shape. Tecumseh's own *Poseidon* and *Chariot* had opened the dance with a salvo of capital ship missiles that had wiped away the ASN's old starfighters in a beautiful and terrible choreographed dance of anti-matter explosions.

Now the two TCN ships hung back out of sensor range of their enemies, watching as the pirates they'd armed and enabled swooped in at the older cruiser. Twelve ships, each barely a tenth of the battlecruiser size, burned toward her at two hundred and fifty gravities—and missiles led the way.

Those were modern missiles, too. Commonwealth-built Stormwind capital ship missiles, delivered into the pirates' hands by one Commodore James Tecumseh.

James stood on *Poseidon*'s flag deck and tried not to feel a black stain sink across his soul. He was four hundred light-years from home, on the far side of the Rimward Marches his commander was charged to annex for the Commonwealth, attacking civilian shipping as a distraction.

"Lieutenant Amoto," he summoned his communications officer. "Inform Colonel Barbados that he is to deploy his assault shuttles to board any ship that appears to be escaping Coati's raiders."

"Yes, Commodore," the young man, a dark-skinned native of Earth's Japanese islands, replied. He paused. "What about *Crusader*?"

James shook his head, the black braid hanging down the back of his neck swinging heavily.

"Coati's ships are unconventional, but with our missiles and those Federation fighters they've somehow acquired, *Crusader* has no chance," the Amerindian Commodore told the junior officer. "Pass the orders."

He turned his attention back to the main holotank, using his neural implant to layer in more detail than the tank could display. "Commodore Coati" had twelve ships, a strange hybrid of sublight gunship and Alcubierre-drive warship that needed at least four of them to merge together and go FTL.

The missiles kept the cruiser occupied, her defensive lasers and positron lances lashing out into space as she tried to thread the fine line between trying to protect her charges and protecting herself, but with twelve different ships, all faster than she was, it was only a matter of time.

The only saving grace James could see was that his orders strongly opposed revealing his task group to any ship with an active q-com—so he didn't need to participate in the murder of a crew defending their citizens himself.

———

THE DOZEN pirate ships spread wide as they closed with *Crusader*, starfighters filling the gaps as they formed a wall of ships that covered any escape route for both the cruiser and her freighter charges. The raiders didn't carry many missiles launchers, however, and the cruiser managed to shoot down every missile they threw at her as they closed.

The raiders and *Crusader* carried much the same class of positron lance...and the raiders were smaller and had more modern electro-magnetic deflectors to shunt aside the beams of charged antimatter. They had almost a hundred-thousand-kilometer range advantage.

James mentally saluted *Crusader*'s crew as they managed to *survive* the first salvo of beams, half-megaton-a-second lances cutting through space to miss the old ship as she danced in the fire. The cruiser lashed out with her own beams—and *not* at the raider ships.

The pirate starfighters had "known" they were out of range of *Crusader*'s anti-fighter beams and had only been following cursory evasion patterns. They were *not* out of range of the battlecruiser's main lances, however, and the ASN crew had dialed the fighters in perfectly.

Thirty-six pirate starfighters died in a perfectly timed set of fire-balls...but *Crusader* didn't get a second shot. Three quarters of the heavy beams from the raiders slammed home after a moment of adjustments, streams of antimatter converting the battlecruiser's armor and hull into pure energy.

Nothing humanity had ever built could withstand a positron lance for long, let alone multiple capital-ship-grade positron lances. *Crusader* gutted the pirate's fighter strength before she died, but she died none-theless...and it wasn't starfighters Coati would be using to capture the freighters.

There were four of those ships, the convoy representing easily ten percent of Antioch's gross system product. Three of Coati's raider ships went after each of them, but James and his people were running the vectors, and it seemed that *Crusader*'s sacrifice had served a purpose after all.

James felt as much as heard a new presence on his neural net as *Poseidon*'s commander reached out to him. Commodore Daryush Sherazi was James's subordinate by virtue of seniority and Marshal Walkingstick's orders, but he'd caused less trouble than James had expected for all that.

"Daryush," he mentally greeted the presence in the net.

"Commodore Tecumseh," the junior man replied. "Target Four is going to evade Coati's people. Should we move to intercept?"

James studied the display.

"Colonel Barbados has four shuttles in position," he noted calmly. "They'll intercept without problems."

He felt Sherazi shake his head.

"I suspect they'll be happier to be boarded by Barbados than Coati," *Poseidon*'s CO said softly. "The only intercept we can pull on any of them is with missiles, and by God, sir, I'm tempted."

"I don't like Coati either, Daryush," James pointed out, "but there's no reason to think he's going to be worse than our people. And either way, Barbados will have at least a platoon on each of those ships."

That platoon wouldn't be *recognizably* Terran Marines, but they would at least be more professional than Coati's pirates.

"I've cleaned up after too many pirates for this to sit comfortably," Sherazi admitted.

"Belay that, Commodore," James said firmly. "Even between us, that needs to stay in our own heads, clear? The crews dislike this op enough without *us* undermining their morale."

"Yes, sir," the other man said crisply. "Still got a bad feeling about this."

"Me too," James admitted. "But we have our orders."

———

JAMES WATCHED in silence as the convoy tried to run for Antakya, Antioch's inhabited planet. There were enough starfighters, missile platforms and gunships in orbit of Antakya that Coati's raiders wouldn't risk approaching too close, though the Terran task group could have smashed their way in with ease.

If any of the freighters made it to Antakya, they'd be safe. None of them were going to.

4

The same attachments and grappling gear that allowed Coati's raiders to latch onto each other to generate an Alcubierre-Stetson drive field worked perfectly for latching onto and boarding their natural prey. With a hundred-and-fifty-gravity advantage in acceleration, matching velocities was straightforward and the raiders latched onto the fleeing freighters three at a time.

The other freighter *would* have made it; her vector and the raiders' were sufficiently far apart that she should have been able to loop into Antakya orbit before the raiders could do more than launch a missile at her—except that Colonel Barbados's shuttles had been quietly moving out to block any escape. An even dozen of those shuttles intercepted the last freighter, slamming into her hull with bone-crushing force to disgorge their payloads of armored Marines.

Other shuttles joined the raiders, a carefully allocated balance putting at least sixty power-armored soldiers in the middle of each boarding action, and James Tecumseh waited to see how the consequences of Coati's victory played out.

The boarding actions had been underway for less than a minute when Barbados commed him.

"Target Four is secure," the Colonel told him, his voice tense. "We demanded their surrender in exchange for their lives, and they were most cooperative."

"The others?" James asked.

"We arrived after Coati's people," the Marine said shortly. "There is active fighting on all three ships, though my people haven't engaged yet. Everyone *we've* run into has surrendered."

That wasn't a good sign. There were q-coms—quantum entanglement communicators linked back to switchboards in Commonwealth space—aboard the Marine assault shuttles, though the Marines had to communicate with the shuttles themselves via radio. The pirates had no such luxuries, which meant that Barbados almost certainly had a better idea of what was going on than Coati did.

If everyone the Marines, notably more professional if hopefully not overtly soldiers, ran into surrendered...then Coati's people weren't even *asking* for surrenders.

5

"Move your people in deeper and take prisoners as you can," James ordered. "This could go very wrong very fast."

"I'm afraid it's already going wrong," his Marine CO replied. "How far do we go, sir?"

He winced as he processed Barbados's question.

"You don't have enough people aboard those ships to start a fight with our allies," he told the other man gently. "Do what you can...but your people's safety has to be the priority."

The channel was silent for a long time.

"That was an order, Colonel," he finally added.

"Yes, Commodore," Barbados said flatly. "I understand."

2

Castle System
08:00 September 11, 2736 Earth Standard Meridian Date/Time
New Cardiff

VISITING OFFICERS' Quarters at the Castle Federation Joint Command Center on Castle weren't exactly designed as the epitome of luxury. For all of that, Captain Kyle Roberts was quite certain that the weight of two O-7 capital ship commanders had claimed the best suite in the building for his girlfriend and him.

That meant that instead of both of them dressing at once being an impossibility, he and Captain Mira Solace each had their own roughly four square feet to put their uniforms on in at the end of their single precious week back home.

"Unless something's come up that neither my XO nor the shipyard have told me about, we're heading back to the front tonight," the tall and elegant black woman whose affection he'd somehow lucked into told him. "My last communique from Alstairs was *very* clear that I was to enjoy my leave thoroughly—but also that she wanted her flagship back as soon as possible *afterward*."

Kyle chuckled as he sealed his gold-piped black shipsuit. The one-piece garment, capable of protecting its wearer from vacuum, did its best to resemble slacks and a turtleneck. Given his own towering height and muscular build, the illusion worked better with the uniform jacket that went over it. The suit itself outlined the figure rather frankly —a side effect he greatly enjoyed while he watched Mira braid her shoulder-length black hair with practiced skill.

"I'm fairly certain the good Admiral knew exactly what your leave entailed," he said wickedly.

"Oh, yes," Mira replied, her own rare smile equally amused. "She had a list of recommended stores for me to check out in New Cardiff," she continued. "I'll admit to checking out the lingerie store she sent me, and I don't recall any complaints!"

"None whatsoever," Kyle agreed with a self-satisfied smirk. "They completed the upgrade without issues?"

Camerone had been in for repairs, and the Castle Federation Space Navy had decided to bring the battlecruiser's electromagnetic deflectors up to the next-generation standard while they had her.

"Everything I've heard says the new deflectors are purring like kittens," she replied. "They'll be a lovely shock for the next wave of starfighters the Terrans send at my girl."

"Good," he said approvingly. "My attachment to *Camerone* is minimal, but I'd very much like certain members of her crew to come back alive."

She shook her head at him, but she was smiling.

"What about you?" she asked. "Your leave's up too. Can you tell me where they're sending you this time?"

A Captain in the Castle Federation Space Navy was a junior flag officer in many ways, commanding both the shipborne weaponry of her starship and the starfighter squadrons almost every military starship carried now. Mira understood need-to-know, but she wasn't entirely comfortable that Kyle's entire last command was considered outside of hers.

"I don't know," he admitted. "Last time, that got me dragged into a black op, but this time…I think Vice Admiral Kane just didn't want to spoil his surprise."

She pointed a long finger at him.

"Check the daily download," she told him. "Flag list promotions came out this morning and Kane made full Admiral. *Don't* call him Vice Admiral in your meeting."

Kyle blinked, checking the information in his neural implant and nodding as he saw Admiral Mohammed Kane, the head of the Castle Federation military's Joint Department of Personnel, on the list of flag promotions.

It was a short list. Alcubierre-Stetson drive warships were mind-bogglingly expensive and the Federation barely fielded a hundred of them, which left a limited number of slots for Admirals. Another name popped up.

"I see Alstairs made Vice," he noted approvingly. "And I see Kane," he admitted, shaking his head. "Still not used to having to actively look up implant data, so thank you."

He'd been a starfighter pilot once, and the level of neural implant capability he'd needed for that job had made implant data literally part of his own knowledge base with no split. Anything downloaded to his implant, he'd simply *known*. The same injury that had forced him to transfer to the Navy had robbed him of that ability, though, and he stumped by with the same type of access everyone else used.

"I'm meeting him at noon," he continued. "I can't talk about my last mission, but I think we made a real difference—enough of one that I'm confident I'm getting a new ship."

Her hair braided, Mira pulled on her jacket and rounded the bed to give him a kiss.

"So am I," she told him. "You're not the best we have—that's *me*—but you're pretty good, Captain Roberts."

"I appreciate the vote of confidence, Captain Solace," he replied. "Let's hope the Joint Chiefs share it."

With a smile, Mira pulled the hand-drawn picture off the mirror where he'd stuck it. It was a drawing of the carrier *Avalon*, Kyle's command *before* he'd been dragged into black ops—and extremely well done for having come from the big man's twelve-year-old son.

"Don't forget Jacob's drawing," she told him. "He'd be heartbroken if you did, and I promise I would betray your secret instantly."

He took the paper and carefully folded it, placing it in the inside pocket of his jacket as he shook his head at Mira, a moment of seriousness lowering the levity.

"I never would," he said softly. He'd missed the first ten years of his son's life, having fled town and joined the Navy when he got his high school girlfriend pregnant, but he was learning how to be a father.

If the war ever let him.

"Come on, big guy," Mira said after a couple of seconds' hesitation. "There's an aircar on the way for me. Let's get going."

———

His possessions, including his son's drawing, stored in a Navy locker, Captain Kyle Roberts made his way through the busy halls of the Castle Federation Joint Command Center. While three hundred-story skyscrapers adorned the surface of the Center, tucked away in the mountains ten kilometers outside one of Castle's largest cities, the vast majority of the facility was underground.

From these underground caverns, the Joint Chiefs ran a military of over a hundred FTL starships, twenty thousand starfighters and almost forty million people. Kyle's implant was informing him of the presence of no less than *ten* wireless networks it could link into, each with different levels of security and authorizations.

Around him, the senior noncoms and junior officers who worked in the back offices that kept the Federation's military machine running moved at a carefully fast but not hurried pace. Kyle's size and the barely smaller Marine looming at his right shoulder bought him a degree of space, but the hallways and transit pods that delivered him to Admiral Mohammed Kane's office were packed.

Once into the main offices of the Joint Department of Personnel, however, the crowd eased. A pair of Marines stood just inside the door and one of them waved him to a halt.

"Implant ID, please," she ordered him.

He opened a channel from his implant, allowing her to access the specific vault in his mental databanks that contained his Navy identification.

The Marine nodded and smiled but also produced a small device that she ran over his arm. It flashed a green light as it verified his DNA against his Navy file, and she stepped back and saluted.

"Thank you for your patience, Captain Roberts," she told him. "Admiral Kane has a visitor, but I was instructed to send you directly to his office."

"Thank you, Corporal."

"My pleasure, sir," she told him. "It's an honor."

He returned her salute and followed the route she'd transferred to his implant. He knew the way to Kane's office, but leaving the assigned path in the secure sections of the Command Center was unwise.

The path led him and his bodyguard through to a second set of security, but these Marines had known he was coming and waved him through. Their job was to make sure that only people who were supposed to be in "the bubble" made it in, where the front door guards' job was to make sure that people were who they said they were.

A blonde Senior Lieutenant who was probably gorgeous when she wasn't actively projecting grimness to maintain the authority of her role as the Admiral's secretary waved Kyle forward.

"The Admiral is meeting with a guest right now," she told him. "My understanding is that Mister Kellers will be participating in your meeting as well, but the Admiral asked me to wait until your appointment to send you in."

"Understood, Lieutenant," Kyle replied, recognizing the name of his local Member of the Federation Assembly and wondering what the politician was doing here. "Five minutes, as I understand?"

"Yes, sir. Would you like a coffee or water?"

———

EXACTLY ON TIME for his eleven hundred Earth Standard Meridian Date/Time appointment, the Lieutenant started doing the odd rapid blink any citizen of the implant generation recognized as a sign of someone having a conversation via neural implant.

"Admiral Kane is ready for you, Captain Roberts," she told him. "Go right on in."

There was nothing distinguishing Admiral Mohammed Kane's plain office door from the hundreds of other metal-reinforced wooden doors in the Command Center except for a small name plate.

The plate, Kyle noted, hadn't been updated for Kane's new rank—but the associated data tag that his implant picked up had been. The software was always faster to pick up new data than the hardware.

"Come in, Captain Roberts. Have a seat," Kane instructed. The Admiral responsible for the fragile edifice of the Federation's manning and personnel requirements was a tall man, his face visibly aged from the last time Kyle had seen him. He'd lost weight, growing even more gaunt with time, and his black turban didn't fully conceal his rapidly graying hair.

"I believe you know Mr. Daniel Kellers?" the Admiral continued, gesturing toward the other man in the room. Kellers was a heavyset man of Kyle's own age with a ruddy face already marked with laugh lines, and-pitch black hair.

He was also the boyfriend of the mother of Kyle's son, a status that had made most of Kyle's meetings with the man awkward, though much less so than he suspected they both had feared.

It helped that Jacob absolutely adored both older men, and that Kellers hadn't entered the boy's life until after Kyle had reentered it.

"Daniel and I are acquainted," Kyle allowed with a cheerful smile. "Though I'll confess I'm not certain why he's here."

"That's fair," Kellers allowed. "Normally, the role I'm playing today would be filled by one of the Senators, but…" He shrugged. "With the war and the Alliance, some items have been dropped to the bottom of the priority list, and some Assembly Committees that should be headed by Senators…aren't."

Kyle nodded his understanding, though it didn't fully answer his question.

"I apologize for not filling you in on our plans for you earlier, Captain," Kane told him gruffly, "but to be perfectly honest, we weren't entirely certain what role you would be playing until yesterday."

The Member of the Federation Assembly coughed gently and shook his head at Kane.

"You may as well tell him, Admiral," Kellers replied. "Lisa and I were planning a damned *party* until the rug got yanked out. I don't *think* Jacob picked up on it, but if he did, let's not expect a twelve-year-old to keep the secret for us."

The Admiral sighed.

"Captain, you are aware that the list for flag promotions came out this morning?" he asked.

"Yes, sir. Congratulations are in order, I have to add."

"Thank you," Kane said, a fleeting but real smile crossing his face. "It's not news, I imagine, to a capital ship commander of the Navy that there are more politics involved in flag promotions than there should be.

"Every flag officer promotion is approved by both the Assembly and the Senate, though as often as not, both bodies simply sign off on the list the Joint Chiefs send them," he continued. "In this case, the Assembly approved it, but the Senate stripped several names out at the last minute."

Kyle leaned back in his chair, studying the two other men. They couldn't possibly be suggesting…

"It was an out-of-the-zone promotion," Kellers told him, "so the Chiefs highlighted it in the list, but the Assembly gladly signed off on your promotion to Rear Admiral. Technically, that list is confidential and I shouldn't even have shared it with Lisa, but I knew what your schedule was like."

Doctor Lisa Kerensky was Keller's girlfriend and Kyle's ex. Until quite recently, she and their son had still lived with Kyle's mother, but she'd bought her own house now that she was actually working—as a junior neurosurgeon at one of the planet's most prestigious hospitals.

Kyle realized he was focusing on that to distract himself. They'd *promoted him to Rear Admiral*? But…

"Senator Randall killed it," Kane said flatly, and Kyle finally nodded in understanding.

Technically, the thirteen-person executive that ran the Castle Federation rotated its members among the Federation's fourteen full member systems, and those members were all equal members. In practice, the Castle System was never rotated off the Council, and the Senator for Castle was more equal than others.

And one Kyle Roberts had been responsible for Senator Joseph Randall's son going to jail for treason.

Kane shook his head.

"There aren't many people fully briefed on Blue Sunbeam who don't think you earned the damned star," he told Kyle. "But the Senate debated for *two days,* and it was eventually decided for us to pull your name from the list to get the rest of the promotions through without further acrimony."

"I..." Kyle swallowed, then nodded firmly. "I appreciate the vote of confidence putting my name forward represents on the part of the Joint Chiefs," he told Kane. "Had the vote gone in our favor, I would have done my best to live up to the responsibilities. But I am very junior to be looking at an Admiral's star, and I'm not bothered by the delay."

Kane chuckled.

"You were our youngest Captain ever, but you won't be our youngest Admiral," he pointed out. "There are no less than three cases on record where officers were Captains for less than three months before receiving their stars. At least one was political bullshit," he admitted, "but the other two earned it the hard way."

"I am content to serve as the Federation requires, sir," Kyle replied. "I'm guessing you have a ship for me, then?"

"We do," Kane said with a nod. "And a mission. I want to warn you from the beginning, however: we're leaving you in charge of the mission and you were expected to have a flag captain, not command a ship yourself."

"We do as we must, sir."

"We're giving you command of *Kodiak,*" the Admiral told him, and Kyle understood the warning as he nodded slowly. *Kodiak* was an

Ursine-class ship out of the Reserve, an older carrier half the size of his last non-black-ops command.

That big a step down could easily be seen as an insult, though given that politics had taken Kyle's last official command away, he would have accepted it with a smile either way.

"Your XO is one of our best," Kane continued. "Senior Fleet Commander Cearbhall Taggart is only a few months at most away from his own command. You will also be accompanied by the *Conqueror*-class battlecruiser *Alexander*, under Captain Sarka."

A *Conqueror*-class battlecruiser was one of the most modern warships the Castle Federation possessed, only barely edged out in mass and overall effectiveness by the *Sanctuary*-class supercarriers like Kyle's old *Avalon*. Seventy-two starfighters, twenty-four megaton-and-a-half-a-second positron lances... Their fighter wing could take on many older warships on their own, and nothing would survive entering the range of *Alexander*'s massive beams.

"That is quite a bit of firepower," Kyle concluded.

"Yes," the Admiral agreed. "Sarka is junior to you by almost a year; she was only promoted two months ago—after *Alexander*'s original Captain was killed during Fourth Fleet's offensive. Like you, she commanded well in action after her CO was killed and the decision was made to leave her in command once *Alexander* had completed her repairs.

"Nonetheless, both she and her crew need a less strenuous work-up than sending them right into the crucible of the main front, which brings us to your mission and Mr. Kellers' presence here."

The Member of the Federation Assembly smiled thinly, an uncomfortable-looking expression on his cheerful face.

"I head the Committee for Rimward Foreign Affairs," he told Kyle. "Like I said earlier, the Committee *should* be headed by a Senator...but they're all focused on the war, so I got the job as my own focus is on business and merchant shipping.

"Depending on which map and whose estimates you're looking at, there are somewhere between fifty and one hundred and twenty inhabited systems Rimward from the Alliance of Free Stars," Kellers continued. "Since we're between those stars and the Commonwealth, they look to us as the center of technology and civilization the same way we look to the Commonwealth when they're not trying to conquer us."

"We're hardly the only major power here, though," Kyle noted, and the MFA nodded.

"Exactly. Before the last war with the Commonwealth, we, the Renaissance Trade Factor, and the Coraline Imperium were all competing for influence and trade deals among the systems that now make up the Alliance...and the systems to the Rim of us.

"Those nations in the immediate path of the Commonwealth's advance joined the Alliance and we stopped competing for influence in those systems. Those to Rimward, though..."

Kellers shrugged.

"They were too poor and too far away to be of value to the Alliance or under immediate threat from the Commonwealth," he concluded. "So, they didn't join the Alliance, and we continued our delicate dance of protection and trade treaties—in the area of immediate concern, in competition with the Coraline Imperium."

The Imperium was the second-most powerful state in the Alliance, a constitutional monarchy whose Imperator wielded real and direct power. They were valued allies now, but the fleet the Castle Federation had stopped the Commonwealth with in the previous war had been built to stand off *Coraline*, not Terra.

"Our trade with those systems helps maintain the economy and industry that build and arm the Navy," Kellers told Kyle. "We *need* those trade routes, but we got a lot of them by promising to protect these systems if they came under attack."

"And I'm guessing they're under attack," Kyle replied. "The Commonwealth?"

"We wish," Admiral Kane said bluntly. "If it was the Common-wealth, we could send an Alliance task group to fight them. So far as we can tell, however, what they're facing is 'simply' a severe outbreak of homegrown piracy."

"There are three systems in the region we're sending you to that are utterly critical," Kellers noted. "Antioch, Serengeti, and Istanbul were the organizers of a major trade pact in the region that was helping leverage the best part of twenty systems out of poverty.

"Now, Antioch, Serengeti and Istanbul were getting the *most* benefit, but their neighbors weren't hurting for their involvement in the free trade zone. Those three, however, owned almost all of the ships and were the only ones wealthy enough to buy warships from us and Coraline."

"And several of those warships have now been destroyed," the Admiral explained. "They are desperately calling for help—calling on us to honor our promises and send a fleet to defend them."

"We don't have a fleet to spare," Kyle said quietly. His last mission had been a do-or-die strike at the heart of the Commonwealth to try and trigger another front in the war, for the simple reason that the Alliance didn't have the hulls to keep fighting the Commonwealth head-on.

"But we can spare two ships—two ships, and a mission commander whose name carries as heavy a weight as another carrier," Kane told him. "They'll see the Stellar Fox as the aid they were promised, and we're sending every ship we can spare."

All two of them. Kyle might hate the nickname the media had hung on him, but he could see the value in this case, and he nodded confidently.

"I'll need a full intel briefing and time to sit down with both Sarka and Taggart," he concluded. "But unless these pirates have managed to acquire modern warships, I think we can handle the situation."

"We're also giving you the first fruits of Project Vulture," Kane told him. "You'll have three squadrons of Vulture-A-type prototype bombers, half a flight group, aboard *Kodiak*, the first ones built. The name is appropriate, as the first-generation prototypes are basically the Terran design you stole with our control systems bolted on."

"I saw the Terran bombers in action at Tau Ceti," Kyle replied. "I won't turn down whatever we've got."

"We want battlefield testing," the Admiral said. "The intent is that the final Vulture design we put into mass production will be an upgrade over the Terran platform, but simulations will only get us so far. These pirates represent an opportunity for a lower-threat-environment test of the weapons."

"I understand, sir."

"Realize, Captain, that you will be passing beyond Alliance space and speaking for the Federation as a representative of our government," Kellers told him. "We will be assigning a diplomat to your staff and I strongly recommend you listen to him, but...*you* will speak for the Federation, not him."

"I understand," Kyle repeated. "I will not fail the Federation, sirs."

3

Castle System
16:00 September 11, 2736 Earth Standard Meridian Date/Time
Gawain Orbital Yard Complex

"THOSE KATANAS ARE on an intercept vector; their missiles will hit us before we can launch."

The report echoed both inside Flight Commander Michelle Williams's head and audibly in the cramped cockpit of the Vulture-A bomber she was flying. The dark-haired pilot shook her head to clear the implant echo, studying the battlespace as her bombers lunged toward the Commonwealth carrier waiting ahead of them.

"The Katanas are Rodriguez's problem," she told her junior squadron commander. "Set your ECM for full defensive and prep a Starfire salvo to keep them occupied, but focus your attention on your Gemblades.

"That carrier is our objective," she told her people firmly. At two percent of lightspeed, her torpedoes had a range of almost twenty light-seconds, but the new generation of starfighter missiles on both sides in this encounter were carrying could still reach a fifth of that—and the fighters were *much* closer to her bombers.

Seconds ticked by, the range dropping down as the fighters closed.

"Starfires away," her gunner reported, the bomber trembling slightly as four of her lighter fighter missiles launched into space. "Arming Gemblade torpedoes. Launch range in one hundred sixty seconds."

"Katanas have fired, I read one sixty, repeat one six zero, Javelin missiles inbound at one zero five zero gravities."

"Understood," Michelle snapped back. Where the *hell* was Rodriguez? "Flight Commander Rodriguez, report! We need our cover!"

"Launch delay," the other senior officer for the test flight responded grimly. "We are one hundred seconds out of range, launching Starfires in intercept mode, but..."

He didn't need to finish the sentence. Starfires were fighter missiles, designed to kill starfighters in small groups or capital ships in massed salvos. They sucked at shooting down other missiles. She'd missed the launch delay on her backup when they'd booted the sim, and it was going to *hurt*.

"All bombers," she said, her voice surprisingly calm. "Break formation, go full evasive. We've lost our cover but *someone* has to get close enough to launch torpedoes."

She paused.

"And if someone actually kills that carrier, I'm buying the drinks tonight!"

———

FOR A STARFIGHTER SQUADRON COMMANDER, any broad focus tended to be lost once the battle was joined. Squadron leaders were also their own pilots, and while the AI and neural interface systems they used allowed for an amazing amount of multitasking, just surviving in the maelstrom demanded all of their attention.

Michelle had found it wasn't *as* bad with bomber command, but with her bombers uncovered by their fighter escorts—a situation she *should* have noticed and kicked herself for now—the only way they were going to survive to launch was by their own skill.

And she might have been flying a bomber for two months at this point, but Michelle Williams knew she was one of the better pilots the Alliance had. The Vulture bomber was just as maneuverable as the Falcons charging to her rescue; it just normally engaged from far enough away that they weren't used to needing that capability.

With over half a dozen missiles targeted on each of her bombers, they were going to need every advantage they could get.

"Jamming fields up," her engineer reported calmly. "Spinning up defensive lasers."

"Vasil, stay on target," she told her gunner. "I want those torps launched the moment we have a full solution."

"Yes, ma'am."

Michelle smiled as the timers began to tick down and the sensor jamming began to threaten the integrity of her tactical displays. Three squadrons of bombers, twenty-four ships, blazed through space. Their locations were relayed to her by the q-com blocks aboard each spacecraft. Everything *else* in Gawain orbital space, however, she was starting to lose track of.

In real life, this would have just become a suicide mission. Since it was a sim, she could deal with that. All she had to do to win, after all, was kill the Terran carrier that had launched the Katanas at her.

"Torpedo launch in twenty seconds," Vasil reported. "Enemy missiles at ten seconds and closing."

Rodriguez's missiles had done *some* good, she noted. There were still far too many missiles closing in for all of her bombers to survive, but some of them might survive long *enough*.

She sank into the neural link, focusing her entire attention on the age-old dance of the fighter pilot. She threw her bomber all over the sky while her engineer filled the space around them with jamming and anti-missile lasers.

Linked into the neural network, she *felt* her crews begin to die. Each sparkling fireball would have been three dead in the real world, though today they just represented another spacecraft dropped out of the sim.

Every loss was a spasm of self-flagellation, though, one that undermined her ability to fly and dodge. Somehow, though, she managed to twist the bomber through the first wave of missiles, their momentum carrying them off safely into deep space.

"Range!" Vasil snapped. "Torpedoes away."

Four of her ships had survived and sixteen torpedoes jumped into space, lunging toward the distant carrier—and then the second wave of missiles from the closing Terran starfighters struck home.

———

BLINKING at the sudden cessation of the full neural link, Michelle rose from the chair in the cockpit of her bomber—still sitting safely in its docking cradle aboard the Weapons Development Station in orbit of the Castle System's largest gas giant.

"Well, that sucked," Ivan Vasil said flatly, her swarthy gunner looking disgruntled as he stretched without leaving his own chair. "What was Rodriguez playing at?"

"The sim threw us a wrinkle," Michelle replied. "Wasn't his fault."

She skimmed the observer feed on the simulation from her neural feed as she spoke, and smiled.

"That said, we got the carrier," she pointed out. Three torps had made it through and the computer had ruled the Terran ship was crippled, allowing Rodriguez's wing of forty-eight Falcons to easily finish the job.

"I guess we're holding you to that beer," Vasil replied. "But we lost the entire bomber wing doing it."

Michelle nodded wordlessly, not even needing to say the words that came to mind. Twenty-four bombers and a dozen or so of Rodriguez's fighters lost would have barely totalled over a hundred casualties—to destroy a ship that had a crew of seven thousand and took fourteen months to build.

"If I survive the debrief with the Vice, I'll buy those beers," she concluded as her implant pinged her with an alert. "But it looks like I'm first on the carpet, so we'll see how much of me he leaves."

Vice Commodore Terry Mixon was a graying officer of middling height, and the man in charge of the Starfighter Projects Section of the Joint Department of Technology's Weapons Development Station.

He was sitting behind his desk when Michelle entered his office and returned her salute crisply, gesturing her to a seat while the screen on the wall ran through the simulated exercise at ten-to-one time compression.

"A *Volcano*-class carrier destroyed with its entire complement of fighters in exchange for twenty-four Vultures and sixteen Falcons," he said calmly. "That's inarguably an exchange in our favor, except..."

"It should have been cleaner," Michelle agreed instantly. "I screwed up, sir. Got over-focused on my own section of the mission and didn't think to check on Rodriguez's wing."

"Interesting," Mixon replied, studying her with unreadable eyes. "Many would point out that Flight Commander Rodriguez didn't inform you of the delay until you asked him. Especially given your history with the Flight Commander..."

"I have written Santiago Rodriguez up for harassing female members of my squadron three times," Michelle said flatly. "He's a sexist pig I wouldn't trust to watch my parents' dog, but he's also a damned fine soldier.

"I suspect he was thrown for as much of a loop as I was by the unexpected delay but assumed that I was paying attention," she continued. "If I had been paying attention to what was going on, it wouldn't have been necessary for him to *tell* me his squadrons were delayed—I should have known already.

"We hadn't had that kind of wrinkle thrown into an exercise yet, and in a real action, I'd have been notified by Flight Control of the delay," she noted. "Nonetheless, the responsibility to realize that I had taken my Wing forward without support was mine. I made a mistake, and in the real world, my people would have died for it."

The Vice Commodore nodded gravely—and approvingly?!

"Good," he said aloud, his eyes brightening in a smile that didn't reach his mouth. "I wondered if you'd recognize that—and I suspect that is not a mistake you'll be repeating."

"No, sir," she told him instantly. "I would like to live to see my girl-friend again, sir."

Which would require her surviving a damned long time, given that her girlfriend, Navy Nurse-Commander Angela Alvarez, was currently running half the hospital aboard a naval support ship with Fourth Fleet.

"Right now, Commander Williams, you are the only fully qualified bomber force commander in the Federation," Mixon pointed out. "The Federation would strongly prefer you live long enough to train others."

"We're working it all out as we go at this point, sir," she pointed out. "Most of my people know as much as I do. They're a good team."

"They are," he agreed. "And Command, in their wisdom, has decided that they want to see the bombers and your people in action before they finalize the mass-manufacture design for the Vulture."

He slid a small velvet case, the kind used for jewelry, across the desk to her.

"I'm glad you took the right lesson away from the exercise," he noted, "because it would have been damned awkward for me to take these back."

The case contained two gold circles, the insignia of a Federation O-5—a Space Force Wing Commander.

"Sir, I..." She stared at the insignia. She hadn't even been a *Flight* Commander for a year.

"We're deploying your bomber wing," Mixon said calmly. "The Space Force doesn't want any questions of authority or command, which would arise if the wing only had three Flight Commanders. You've earned it."

"Yes, sir," she said slowly. "Thank you, sir."

"Don't thank me yet," he said brightly. "We're transferring you and your bombers to *Kodiak*, one of the old *Ursine*-class carriers, which is being dispatched Rimward on an anti-piracy mission under Captain Roberts.

"I believe you served under the Stellar Fox before?"

"I was at Tranquility with him, sir," Michelle admitted, shivering as she remembered the sight of her carrier *ramming* a Commonwealth battleship after a close-in FTL emergence. "It was…memorable."

"It doesn't sound like his career has been quieter since," Mixon replied. "I understand this should be a straightforward operation, one that will give us an opportunity to test the Vultures in real combat well away from the front."

"From my understanding, we can use the live data," she said.

"I agree. Your people and your ships are to report aboard *Kodiak* by twelve hundred hours tomorrow," he concluded. "Any questions, Wing Commander?"

Swallowing, Michelle pinned the new insignia to her collar and considered.

"Is Rodriguez coming with us?" she finally asked.

"Rodriguez will be remaining here and continuing to work on bomber-protection tactics," Mixon told her, his eyes sparkling with that half-hidden smile again. "A detailed file of his notes and tactics so far will be forwarded to Vice Commodore Song. You won't be working with him there."

She smiled thinly but said nothing. There wasn't anything she *could* say that wouldn't be a violation of decorum.

"I should inform my people," she told him. "I owe them beer as well—I really didn't expect us to take out the carrier."

"I've told the Joint Chiefs that the bombers appear to be a game-changer, Commander," Mixon told her. "Prove me right."

4

Castle System
10:00 September 12, 2736 Earth Standard Meridian Date/Time
Gawain Orbit, DSC-052 Kodiak

KYLE ROBERTS STUDIED both ships of his new command with a practiced eye as the shuttle carried him toward *Kodiak*. The two ships had been built twenty years apart, and the evolution of technology in the intervening years was clear just looking at them.

Kodiak was just over a kilometer long, an abbreviated arrowhead one hundred and seventy-five meters wide at the front and three hundred meters wide at the back. She was bigger than his first command, the original deep space carrier *Avalon*, but less than half the size of his last official command, the new *Avalon*.

She was also less than half the size of the battlecruiser *Alexander*, a sixteen-hundred-meter-long spike in space that orbited Gawain just above and behind the carrier. Over double the carrier's volume and twice its mass, the battlecruiser was a modern ship barely a year old.

By now, though, Kyle was well practiced at picking out the scars of combat. Fourth Fleet had met and shattered a major Commonwealth offensive earlier in the year, but the price had been high. He could pick out the sections of slightly lighter-colored hull where new ferro-ceramic plating had been installed to replace armor vaporized by near-misses and direct hits.

Carefully studying the battlecruiser, he could see where a positron lance hit from a starfighter had torn clean through the warship, turning armor and hull plating into mind-bogglingly powerful explosives and vaporizing *Alexander*'s bridge.

He looked forward to meeting Captain Sarka. It seemed they had a great deal in common.

"Loop us around *Kodiak* again," he ordered the pilot, turning his attention to his own ship. The *Ursine*-class might be older and smaller than he'd like, but she still carried sixteen squadrons of starfighters—made up of modern Falcons and experimental Vultures this time around.

The carrier might not be much to look at, but her armament would help stand off any immediate threat while her fighters and bombers annihilated the enemy.

The older ship had none of the scars and discoloration that marked *Alexander*. She'd served ten years in active duty and then gone into the Reserve, only to be one of the last ships reactivated. *Kodiak* had never fired a weapon or launched a starfighter in anger in her entire career.

That, Kyle was grimly certain, was going to change.

"Anything in particular you want me to fly over, sir?" the pilot asked.

"No," he admitted after a moment. "Take us in."

———

A FULL FORMAL greeting party was waiting for Kyle when he left his shuttle, double files of Marines forming a clear path across the carrier's flight deck to the two officers, one male, one female, with the doubled gold circles on their collars of Federation O-6s—one Space Force Vice Commodore and one Space Navy Senior Fleet Commander.

Kyle took the time to study his two most senior subordinates as he approached, amused by the contrast between the pair. Melania Song was a tall, dark-skinned woman with notably slanted black eyes and short-cropped black hair, where Cearbhall Taggart was a squat, broad man with shoulder-length blond hair, bright green eyes and extremely pale skin.

"Vice Commodore, Senior Fleet Commander," he greeted them once he was within a few meters, returning their crisp salutes.

"Welcome aboard *Kodiak*, Captain Roberts," Taggart told him, offering a handshake. "I've arranged for the rest of our officers to meet with us at twelve hundred hours, but I presumed you would want to read yourself in and tour the ship first? I can move the officers' meeting up if you wish."

"No, that's fine," Kyle told his new XO with a smile. Taggart was actually older than he was and presumably knew he was on the short list for his own command, but there was no resentment in the man's gaze or handshake. A positive starting point.

"Is there anything with regards to *Kodiak* or the Flight Group I need to be aware of?" he asked as he shook Song's hand as well.

"We off-loaded three squadrons of Falcons this morning in preparation for the arrival of a new strike wing of Vulture bombers," Song told him in a soft contralto voice. "I believe we should have all twenty-four Vultures aboard by noon, though I don't know if their commander will be able to join us for the officers' meeting."

"I've worked with Wing Commander Williams before," Kyle replied. "It won't be a problem if she misses the meeting."

Williams had also almost *killed* him once, but it had been an accident and he didn't hold it against her.

"And *Kodiak*?" he asked Taggart.

The squat executive officer shrugged.

"We are fully stocked on munitions and expendables," he reported. "We're waiting on one last delivery: the torpedoes to go with the bombers, but we should have the torps and the design for our fabricators before the Vultures themselves are aboard."

"Good," Kyle told them. "I was on the receiving end of the Terran version of those ships and weapons, people. I look forward to seeing our pirate soon-to-be-friends dealing with them.

"For now, if you both could escort me to the bridge, Senior Fleet Commander Taggart is correct: I do need to read myself in."

———

"*Kodiak* Flight Control, this is Flight...apologies, *Wing* Commander Michelle Williams, inbound with twenty-four V-types assigned to SFG-122. Requesting docking permissions and vectors; ident authentication attached to transmission."

Michelle stretched in the pilot's seat of her bomber, studying the approach paths of her three squadrons. There were a dozen small ways that she could tell the Vulture wasn't a Federation design, though no one had *admitted* to her that the base design was a stolen Terran pattern. The layout of the cockpit was different, for one, and significantly more open than the Federation usually built.

Unless she was mistaken, the Vulture had been designed to have the flight engineer up front with the rest of the crew instead of at the damage control station the Federation included near the engines. Given that nanites and drones did all of the actual repair work, she could see the logic both ways. When the Federation had built the current generation of Vultures, however, they'd added the separate DC station but hadn't reduced the size of the cockpit to account for one fewer person.

No starfighter pilot was a claustrophobe, but she didn't mind the space to stretch.

"Commander Williams, this is *Kodiak* Flight Control," the carrier crew responded. "Identification codes verified for all personnel. Note that your designation is now Echo Wing, *Kodiak*."

"Understood, *Kodiak*," she replied.

"Echo Leader," Flight Control continued after a moment, "we are currently clearing the flight deck from the Captain's side party. Estimate ten minutes before you're cleared for landing. Any vector concerns?"

She quickly checked her people's speed and angles.

"Negative," she told them. "We'll establish a holding pattern at one thousand kilometers and wait for landing vectors."

"We'll have you aboard shortly, Echo Leader. *Kodiak* Actual sends his regards, ma'am. Welcome to *Kodiak*."

"Thanks, *Kodiak* Control," she replied. Through her neural implant, she was already flagging her companion ships and advising them of the holding pattern. "Will stand by for landing clearance."

———

KODIAK'S BRIDGE was silent as Kyle strode onto it, his CAG and XO trailing behind him. With the advent of neural link networks, the rumor mill aboard a starship had become literally as fast as a thought. No one was going to be in mid-conversation when the new Captain entered the bridge; they'd all had far too much warning.

The bridge itself, like that of most modern warships, was extremely plain. While there were displays at every station, they were a backup tool more than anything else. The ship was run in the network maintained between the computers and the brain implants of every crew member.

Technically, Kyle could run his ship from anywhere in the galaxy within ten thousand kilometers of a quantum entanglement array. In practice, putting everyone in the same room *always* worked better.

He walked up to his command chair and stood next to it as he removed a sheet of parchment from inside his jacket. Under it was a chip that he slotted into its place on the command chair, but tradition required the parchment.

"Bosun, please report."

That worthy could have been Taggart's older brother, a stocky man with white hair instead of blond, and appeared at Kyle's shoulder instantly.

"Sir."

"Please record for the log," he instructed. The computer *should* do so automatically—and broadcast his words shipwide, for that matter— but human verification of this step was both traditional and important.

"To Captain Kyle Roberts from Admiral Mohammed Kane, Joint Department of Space Personnel, September eleventh, year two thousand seven hundred thirty six Earth Standard.

"Upon receipt of these orders, you are hereby directed and required to proceed to the Castle System and report aboard the Deep Space Carrier *Kodiak*, hull number DSC Zero Five Two, there to take upon yourself the duties and responsibilities of commanding officer of said vessel in the service of the Castle Federation.

"Fail not in this charge at your peril."

A soft bleeping noise from the command chair informed everyone that the ship's computers had scanned his order chip and confirmed the transfer of command. A wave of not-quite relaxation swept through the bridge as Kyle took formal responsibility for their lives and mission.

"I assume command, Senior Fleet Commander," he told Taggart.

"I stand relieved, Captain Roberts," the older man replied. "May I say, sir, that it is a privilege to serve under an officer of your reputation?"

"It is an equal privilege to command officers of your and Vice Commodore Song's reputations," Kyle told him. "We've got quite a bit of work still to do and not a lot of time. Shall we get to that tour?"

5

Castle System
12:00 September 12, 2736 Earth Standard Meridian Date/Time
Gawain Orbit, DSC-052 Kodiak

KYLE FOUND himself surprisingly grateful that Wing Commander Williams had managed to get her wing aboard in time to attend the officers' meeting Taggart had called to introduce the new Captain. Without the presence of the dark-haired pilot, he'd have been facing a room full of strangers.

Not that one familiar face made that much difference. The long table was full of new ones, starting with his two senior officers Taggart and Song next to him, followed by Song's other four Wing Commanders and Taggart's senior subordinates: the ship's chief engineer tactical officer, navigator and operations officer

Nine O-5s, two O-6s, and him. The twelve men and women in the room were responsible for enough firepower to sear a world clean of life—but the final authority was his.

"All right, people," he said once they'd all settled. "I'm not going to pretend that any of you except Commander Williams are more to me than a face and an implant file yet, but we'll have a lot of time to correct that as we proceed on our mission."

"Do we know what that mission is going to be?" Commander Archie Sterling asked. *Kodiak*'s tactical officer was probably the oldest person in the room, a portly bald reservist recalled to the colors after war had been declared. Both of his eyes were artificial, a consequence of the action that had seen him retire to the Reserve, but his mind was still sharp and his record was glowing.

"We're heading Rimward on a purely Federation op," Kyle told them. "Several systems out there have activated the protection clauses of our trade agreements with them. *Kodiak* and *Alexander* are being sent to respond to that request."

"That seems...well, a low-priority assignment," Commander Maral Houshian, the carrier's navigator. Houshian was a frail-looking woman with night-black skin and a shaved head, a native of the Federation's Ankara Protectorate.

"Frankly, it is," Kyle agreed calmly. "But nonetheless, we promised these systems protection—and as the media happily likes to quote me from before Tranquility, there may yet come a day when the Federation must break its word from the necessity of war—but that day has not yet come.

"And it will not on my watch," he told them. The words felt more pretentious today than they had when he'd been taking a half-crippled carrier on a suicide mission, but if the media was going to keep quoting his damned speech, he'd use it to his advantage.

"The downside, of course, is that we will be operating well outside our normal bases and supply lines," he continued after a moment. "Commander Trent, do you have any concerns about *Kodiak*'s ability to function on her own resources?"

Commander Ivy Trent was his Chief Engineer, and her long pause before responding did not fill him with faith. The nature of their mission was news, but that wasn't a question the redheaded engineer should have had to think about.

"Naw," she finally drawled slowly. "The fabricators have all checked out. So long as we have the parts, we can build anything you want, skipper. We *do* have the parts, don't we, Commander Tsien?"

Kyle kept his gaze on Trent for several seconds after she'd tossed the verbal hot potato over to *Kodiak*'s Operations Officer. Logistics and inventory fell under Lieutenant Commander Tsien Tao-ling's purview, but he would have expected the engineer to be able to answer questions about his ship's long-term sustainability.

He already suspected he and Trent were going to have some long conversations.

"JD-Logistics gave me a heads-up that we were heading on a long tour three days ago," Tsien told the rest of the senior staff in a soft rumble. He was a massive man, easily equal to his Captain in size, with faded brown skin and close-cropped bronze hair. "Lieutenant Commander Mathieson aboard *Alexander* and I have managed to arrange most of the supplies and parts we'll need.

"Our biggest issue is Wing Commander Williams' bombers," he continued. "I was only advised they were coming aboard this morning. While I'm advised we're getting torpedoes for them, spare and replacement parts for the bombers or their torpedoes appears to have slipped everyone's mind."

Given certain parts—the exotic-matter cores necessary to build the mass manipulators that a modern starship used for everything from artificial gravity to compensating for acceleration to out-speeding light, primarily—the fabricators Trent had mentioned could build anything the carrier needed, including new bombers and fighters.

Without the right parts and designs, however, it became much more difficult.

"Do you need me to drop a bag of hammers on anyone?" Kyle asked cheerfully. "We have a forty-eight-hour deadline to ship out, and I do *not* want to be explaining to the Senate why we're late."

Tsien shook his head.

"We've already arranged a shipment," he confirmed. "It'll be later than I'd like, but we'll have enough parts, food and everything else for a six-month journey."

"I appreciate your foresight," Vice Commodore Song told the big man. "I should have thought of that, but I'm not used to having more than one type of starfighter aboard."

"We'll have to get used to it," Kyle pointed out. "I've seen the bombers in action, people. If the Terrans had sprung them on us without warning, the surprise and their effectiveness could have carried Marshal Walkingstick all the way to Castle and Coraline.

"I'd rather any unexpected changes in the balance of power go in our favor," he concluded. "Wing Commander Williams's people are our first field test of the concept, but we're hopefully going up against a lower tier of opposition on this operation.

"That said, if you have any clever ideas on how best to integrate *Kodiak*, *Alexander*, the Falcons and the Vultures, don't hesitate to run them up the flagpole," he told them. "A lot of very clever people have been writing the rulebook on the new bombers, but we've only had the idea for a few months. Every set of eyes on the things is a bonus right now."

He'd known about the bombers for longer than anyone else, but exactly how was classified. So far as he was aware, even Williams didn't know where the Alliance had acquired the bomber schematics.

———

ENTERING HIS NEW OFFICE, Kyle glanced around, mentally measuring for the beer fridge he'd need to install. It had come with him on his shuttle, along with a pallet full of Castle microbrewery beers that would go into general cold storage.

He didn't like the beer the Navy served, and he'd found beer was a fantastic icebreaker.

"Have a seat," he told Song and Taggart, shedding his uniform jacket onto the back of his own chair as he ran through the implant menus necessary to authorize himself on the office's electronic systems.

"I presume both of you have updated readiness reports on the computers?" he asked as he took his own seat. The chairs across the desk from him had been pushed next to each other for cleaning and he half-expected his two senior officers to move them apart.

They didn't, which suggested either a high level of comfort with each other or a high level of *discomfort* with him. If it was the latter, he definitely needed that beer fridge.

"We do," Taggart answered for both of them. "We didn't know who was taking command, but we knew *someone* would be, after all."

"We didn't expect the Stellar Fox himself," Song added, and Kyle grimaced.

"For the record, while I will *use* that name and the reputation that goes with it, I don't particularly like being *called* that," he pointed out. "Someone once said that heroes happen when other people fuck up. A *lot* of people fucked up for the situation at Tranquility to end up how it did, and we had a lot of bad luck.

"I'd rather not have assumed command of *Avalon* because the entire bridge crew was killed, after all. A feeling I understand that Captain Sarka likely shares," he said with a chuckle.

"I'll review your reports to make sure I'm familiar with *Kodiak*'s status, but I wanted to be clear from the beginning where we all stood. I am *Kodiak*'s Captain, but I'm also going to be commanding the task group we're taking out to Antioch and its surrounding systems.

"I have no staff for that purpose and will be handling much of it myself, as well as diplomatic responsibilities once we reach our area of operations," he told them. "I expect to need to lean on both of you even more than usual to help me keep *Kodiak* fully functional.

"Do either of you have any major concerns that may get in the way of our operations that couldn't be raised in front of the other officers?"

The two exchanged an unreadable glance, then shrugged in almost-perfect unison.

"I'm not entirely enthused with being saddled with the bombers," Song admitted. "Williams's record is mixed, but I'd be pleased to have her as a squadron commander, and while she's junior for Wing Commander, I've no concerns with her there either.

"The *Vultures*, however… They're an untested concept that has never seen action. I'm not even entirely sure what to *do* with them."

"We'll learn," Kyle told her. "I've seen the Terran version in action; when and why is classified, but I can tell you that much. They're not unstoppable and I'm sure we're going to discover their vulnerabilities, but they are a *very* powerful addition to our arsenal. Williams has been working with the concept for several months now; use her knowledge, but don't hesitate to wring her and her people dry in simulations, either.

"The Terrans have the same tech. We need our doctrine to be better."

"We'll make it work, sir," Song said with a nod, then glanced at Taggart, wordlessly passing the torch of the conversation. The two seemed to work together *very* well, and Kyle made a mental note to check how long they'd served together. That smooth a machine in his senior staff would be useful.

"My only concern with *Kodiak* is that, frankly, she's an old ship," the XO said. "Our deflectors have been upgraded and we're flying modern fighters, but her beams are weak and our mass manipulators and engines are below grade.

"We're less maneuverable and less deadly than a modern ship," he pointed out. "A *Sanctuary*-class carrier can handle herself if something gets in close, but we're in serious danger if even a pirate ship gets into lance range."

"We'll outgun and out-accelerate any ship the pirates are likely to have," Kyle replied. "And in the worst-case scenarios, we'll have *Alexander* to deal with anyone who gets impertinent.

"But you're right," he allowed. "We'll be relying on SFG-122 for our main striking force, so I'll need you and Vice Commodore Song to cooperate extremely closely.

"I haven't seen anything yet to suggest that will be a problem."

———

"WING COMMANDER, PLEASE HAVE A SEAT," Vice Commodore Song instructed as Michelle stepped into her office. "Are your people settled?"

"The space set aside for us will work well," she replied. "*Kodiak* isn't set up to split into five wings, but the Chiefs have done a good job of making it work."

"If you haven't learned yet that the Chiefs run the Space Force as thoroughly as they do the Navy, let that be a lesson to you," Song said with a gentle smile. "You're right, an *Ursine*-class traditionally only carries four Wings, but I agree that keeping the bombers in their own unit makes the most sense.

"Not, of course, that my opinion was asked."

"The doctrine we were drafting called for the bombers to be deployed in full wings of six squadrons apiece, the same as the starfighters," Michelle pointed out. "Every carrier will have one once the Vulture goes to mass production."

"But we're the lucky ones to play guinea pig," Song replied. "They don't even look like Federation fighters."

Michelle considered for a moment, then shrugged.

"They aren't Federation fighters, ma'am," she admitted. "The new Vultures JD-Tech is working on will be, incorporating our designs and combat experience, but these ones...the Vulture-A prototypes..." She shook her head.

"They're Terran to the bone, ma'am," Michelle told her new boss. "I don't know where the schematics came from or how we acquired them, but the Vulture-A is a Terran design with a Castle Federation Space Force logo painted on the side."

"Huh." Song paused, seeming to process the new data. "That makes a surprising amount of sense, Wing Commander, though it leaves more questions open. Do you know where the skipper would have run into Terran bombers?"

"No, ma'am," Michelle admitted. "The combat data we were given to review was sanitized; I don't know which ship of ours was there or even where the battle was. We only have data on one engagement, though, so I suppose Roberts was there."

"You served with him before, correct?"

"On the first *Avalon*," the junior officer confirmed. "I was at Tranquility with him as well."

"Did he actually ram a battleship?" Song asked.

"It wasn't planned," Michelle told her. "We rode the needle and emerged in combat range of the Commonwealth fleet...except we came out even closer than we intended. It was a fluke, they dodged the same way *Avalon* did, but she was one of the first carriers, built with the neutronium armor to stand off mass driver rounds."

"So she punched clean through," Song concluded. "I'd wondered; even with his reputation, that seemed like a damn-fool stunt."

"Don't misestimate him, ma'am. He played chicken with the Commonwealth follow-up force entirely intentionally," Michelle pointed out.

"It's hard to read a man with his reputation," the Vice Commodore said slowly. "Officers called things like 'the Stellar Fox' tend to be glory hounds, but he doesn't feel like the type."

"He isn't, ma'am. I'm not quite sure what he *is*," Michelle admitted, "but he isn't a glory hound or a rules-stickler. He's a fighter first, I think."

"And that's what we need," Song concluded. "Thank you, Wing Commander, you've given me food for thought."

"My job is to back you up, ma'am."

"So it is," the older woman said with a smile. "Which means, Commander, that you and I are going to go over some exercises to set up some worst-case scenarios for your pilots. We'll test them hard—because the harder we test them, the easier they'll find the enemy!"

6

Castle System
16:00 September 12, 2736 Earth Standard Meridian Date/Time
Gawain Orbit, DSC-052 Kodiak

THE INSTALLATION of his beer fridge interrupted Kyle's review of the readiness reports his senior officers had prepared, a trio of ratings under the command of a grouchy-looking Chief carting the multipurpose appliance in.

"In the back corner," Kyle told them. "It needs to be hooked up to the water line as well; it makes coffee and tea, too."

"Quite a piece of tech," one of the ratings said before the Chief's glare silenced them.

"Was my entire first paycheck back when I left the Academy," the big Captain said with a cheerful grin. "Stores beer and liquor, makes coffee, heats water for tea. I've never regretted it."

The installation was a quick job, and a fourth rating arrived as they were finishing up with the case of beer that Kyle had labeled as the first delivery.

"Thank you, spacers," he told them, pulling five beers out of the fridge and passing them around. "Drink these when you're *off* shift," he admonished, meeting the Chief's eyes levelly.

The man nodded firmly, both accepting that the ratings would be allowed the beer...and that they *wouldn't* be drinking it until they were off duty, and chivvied his charges out of the office.

Kyle was certain the ratings weren't as young as they felt to him— even in war, the Federation wouldn't be putting anyone in uniform without at least two years of intensive training, which meant they were all at least twenty standard years old.

They just *looked* younger to his eyes now. He was getting old himself, a reflective thought that had him drawing a coffee from the machine instead of a beer.

A decision he was grateful for a few minutes later when his implant chimed.

"Captain, we have incoming q-com request for you from Admiral Kane," the communications officer of the watch, a chipper and far-too-young-seeming Junior Lieutenant, informed him.

"Thank you, Lieutenant. Please put him through," Kyle ordered.

He transferred the channel to his office's wallscreen and waited for a moment while the Seal of the Castle Federation, a stylized castle surrounded by fourteen stars, orbited on the screen.

Then the image of the Admiral, looking just as tired as the day before, appeared on the screen.

"Captain Roberts," Kane greeted him. "How is *Kodiak* treating you so far?"

"Welcoming so far," Kyle replied. "I'll need to speak with Captain Sarka aboard *Alexander* before the day is over, but I expect to be able to ship out on schedule."

"Good," the Admiral said. "I've confirmed with our friends at Foreign Affairs about your diplomatic representative. He'll be coming aboard shortly, with your shipment of parts for the bombers."

"I'm looking forward to meeting him," Kyle said. "I wasn't looking forward to trying to deal with planetary governments entirely on my own."

"You've done all right in the past, Captain; I have faith," Kane told him. "But I'll admit we're hoping for better than *all right* this time. A proven ability in diplomacy alongside your tactical record will go a long way to forcing that promotion through."

Kyle nodded wordlessly. He was trying not to think about the operation in those terms—if the Joint Chiefs wanted to make him an Admiral, he'd take the job and the star, but he wasn't going to do his job any differently to get there.

"Your diplomat will be useful, but I have to warn you about him," the Admiral continued grimly. "Voyager picked him, Roberts. I wouldn't have."

Vice Admiral Nicholas Voyager was a senior member of the Castle Federation's Joint Department of Intelligence—and had been in charge of the operation that had taken Kyle to the heart of the Commonwealth.

He'd become something of a partisan of Kyle's, but a diplomat the spy had selected...

"What am I getting into, sir?" he asked flatly.

"Karl Nebula is a Foreign Affairs diplomat, yes," Kane replied. "Officially, that's all he is. Unofficially, I am certain he is also a JDI operative and I have reason to believe he's one of Voyager's pet *assassins*."

"Are we expecting me to need an assassin?" Kyle asked.

"No. Nebula is a snake, Captain. He's *our* snake, but that doesn't make him any less poisonous. Be careful."

"So long as he doesn't try to assassinate *me*."

Kyle's last experience with a Joint Department of Intelligence assassin, after all, had been...more personal than he'd have liked.

———

HESITATIONS ASIDE, Kyle was on hand to meet Nebula when the diplomat arrived several hours later. The fast transport that had been dispatched from Castle was too large to fit into *Kodiak*'s flight deck herself, so a series of heavy transport shuttles were looping across the gap between the ships, each leaving a cargo container on the deck that the Space Force tractors latched on to and cleared away.

One of those shuttles stayed on the deck for a few minutes longer than the others, a ramp sliding down to disgorge two dozen people. Most were in uniform, a final group of recruits and personnel to fill out a few gaps in *Kodiak's* roster.

Four, however, were dressed in neat civilian suits. Two men and two women, all of much the same perfectly turned-out early-thirties mold. The one in front had close-cropped hair and an ageless look to his face that warned of complex and *expensive* surgery and enhancement.

"Captain Roberts?" he asked, approaching Kyle and giving a reasonably civilian approximation of a salute that Kyle did not return. "I'm Karl Nebula, Federation Foreign Affairs."

"Welcome aboard *Kodiak*, Mr. Nebula," Kyle told him. "I look forward to working with you; we appear to have a rather large undertaking ahead of us."

"Indeed," Nebula confirmed. He waved airily back toward his three companions. "Miller, Tsovaritch, Saqqaf," he introduced each of the three in turn. "My staff. All three are experts on the Antioch-Serengeti Free Trade Zone and the systems involved. We'll keep you informed on everything going on, above and below board."

"I appreciate the assistance," Kyle replied. "If you have a briefing you can provide myself and my senior officer on the Trade Zone?"

"Of course," Nebula replied. "We'll put something together while we're on our way. Do your people have quarters prepared for us?"

"Chief Ryder"—Kyle gestured the NCO standing with him forward —"can you get Mr. Nebula and his people settled?"

"Of course."

"I'd like to meet with you in private at your earliest convenience, Captain," the diplomat continued. "I have verbal and written instructions to pass on to you from the Joint Chiefs."

That was...unusual, to put it mildly, but Kyle nodded.

"Of course, Mr. Nebula. Please have Chief Ryder put you in touch with my Operations Officer," he replied. "Lieutenant Commander Tsien will find you a slot in my schedule."

Nebula smiled and inclined his head, clearly recognizing when he was being put in his place.

"Hopefully soon, Captain," he murmured. "Your navigator will need new instructions before we leave, if nothing else."

Kyle concealed a sigh. He'd been hoping that leaving his Q-ship command behind would get him *away* from the cloak-and-dagger, but it seemed JD-Intel wasn't done with him yet.

THE BIGGEST CLAIM on Kyle's time that made him unwilling to meet with Nebula immediately, regardless of his willingness to be at the diplomat's beck and call, was his need to actually make contact with his junior Captain.

There was enough for a new Captain to do that he'd let Sarka schedule the meeting and spent most of the day running around taking care of *Kodiak*'s minutiae, like meeting Nebula on his arrival aboard the ship.

Tsien had kept him informed of the junior Captain's availability, however, so he managed to return to his office with roughly thirty seconds to spare before initiating the conference, just enough time to grab another coffee.

Captain Kristyna Sarka was a hook-nosed, swarthy woman. An ugly scar ran from just above her mouth, up through her left eye and around to where her left ear should have been. The eye was a cybernetic replacement, though a high-quality one that would have passed for normal without the rest of the scar.

She hadn't been an attractive woman to start with, and the impact of the scar gave her an intimidating shock factor. It was also missing from her file photo, and Kyle had to swallow his surprise at the sight of it.

"Captain Sarka," he greeted her. "I appreciate you making the time to talk to me."

"I know who's in command, Roberts," she said bluntly. "Not exactly doing you a favor to obey orders, am I?"

He smiled.

"I would have given you at *least* until tomorrow to make contact before I started giving you *orders* to talk to me, Captain," he told her.

"There is a certain respect due the Captain of a starship, regardless of the chain of command and seniority."

Sarka seemed to pause, as if processing that, then swallowed and nodded a wordless apology. Kyle suspected at least one other Captain had taken her lack of seniority as an excuse to try and walk over her.

"This is your meeting," she said, her voice calmer, at least. "I'm at your disposal, Captain Roberts."

"This is mostly a meet-and-greet, Captain," Kyle told her. "We're going to be working together over the next few weeks and likely months as we head out Rimward and bring things out there under control. I need to know which way you're going to jump and you need to know which way I'm going to."

"Toward the sound of the guns, from your reputation, sir," she replied.

"Fair," he admitted with a chuckle. "That said, Captain, I know where you're coming from with being a junior Captain promoted to command of a powerful unit due to the death of your predecessor," he continued seriously. "While I doubt you need my backup with your own crew"—if she did, she wasn't going to get to *keep* her golden planet insignia—"if you start getting any flak from our fellow Captains, let me know. So long as you're part of our little task group, shit they give *you* is shit they're giving *me*, and I will back you. Understood?"

She looked taken aback but nodded her acceptance.

"Yes, sir."

"I have to ask," he said after a moment. "Your scar and cybernetics aren't in the file. What happened?"

Her face twisted uncomfortably, exacerbating the scar dramatically.

"What the reports of *Alexander's* damage and Captain Tongue's death miss is that the positron lance struck *deep* in our hull," Sarka said quietly. "It took out the bridge...and it barely missed Aux Con. Debris took out a third of our backup bridge crew and, well..." She touched the scar. "...a third or so of my face."

"You took command," Kyle observed.

"Had the medic slap a bandage on my face and give me a local," she confirmed. "We were in the front line and going toe to toe with a Commonwealth battleship assault. *Alexander* had to stay in the fight."

And the fact that the wounds hadn't been treated quickly explained the severity of the scars, too. The bandage, the local anesthetic, and her internal nanite suite would have kept her alive and functioning, but there would have been a lot of damage. Damage that even modern medicine couldn't fully repair.

"I understand," he said quietly, then smiled. "I'm even impressed, Captain. You'll do just fine."

"I don't need your approval or your babysitting, sir," she said.

"No," he agreed. "But there are two people in this task group you can talk to about the nightmares, Captain—your ship's doctor and me. My door is open."

She jerked as if struck, then noticed his smile and seemed to relax.

"We all have them, Captain Sarka," he continued. "Rank hath its privileges…and its prices."

"Yes, sir," she replied. "Thank you, sir."

7

Castle System
22:00 September 12, 2736 Earth Standard Meridian Date/Time
Gawain Orbit, DSC-052 Kodiak

IT WAS LATE—BY the clock of a faraway line on a far-away world that was used as a standard for all humanity—by the time Kyle actually managed to free up time to meet with Karl Nebula, though the diplomat seemed unbothered when he ushered himself into the Captain's office with a brown paper bag in one hand.

"Voyager figured my odds of not pissing you off were somewhere between 'none' and 'a snowball's chance in hell'," Nebula said cheerfully as he dropped the bag on Kyle's desk. "So, consider this a preemptive peace offering—we're on the same side, but I can guarantee we won't always see the same solution to a problem."

The bag revealed itself to contain a six-pack of a microbrewery ale that Kyle had failed to find any of on this shore leave. As if he needed *more* evidence of how closely JD-Intel was watching him these days, though right now, it was for his protection.

"I was expecting you to actually pretend you *were* a diplomat," Kyle pointed out, pulling two of the beers out and sliding one across the desk to Nebula. Even Castle's tiny breweries went in for packaging that kept the drinks at the perfect temperature, and he took an appreciative sip.

"I *am* a diplomat," Nebula told him. "I also work quite closely with Voyager and the rest of his department. My staff are purely diplomats; they don't have my experience in extracurricular activities."

"Which are?"

"Varied," the diplomat replied. "I have been a spy and a liar and a thief and a cheat, Captain Roberts, but I serve the Castle Federation above all else—and I owe Nicholas Voyager my life four times over.

"So, understand this." The cheer suddenly faded and Nebula focused a cold black gaze on Kyle. "Kane will have warned you about me. I don't know the words; he might have been poetic, he might have called me a psychopath.

"He is entirely correct. I am a high-functioning sociopath with a fundamentally broken sense of morality. Men like me are useful to any government, especially when we imprint on that government as a replacement morality.

"Do you understand, Captain?"

Kyle blinked, and the sudden frozen darkness of Nebula's face was gone.

"No," he admitted. "But as you said, we're on the same side."

"I will do whatever is necessary to preserve the Federation's interests," Nebula told him, his voice less frozen. "Normally, that would potentially include actions that would sacrifice you or your crew, though they would be my last choice, as you have value to the Federation.

"However, my…skills and mindset aren't truly needed on this mission. I am on this mission, Captain Roberts, to protect you."

"Me?"

"Voyager likes and trusts you," the diplomat told him. "I can count on the fingers of one hand the number of people Nicholas Voyager trusts, Captain Roberts, and even I am not on that list.

"He has charged me to keep you alive, in the face of both your personal enemies and whatever threats face the Federation out in the Rimward stars. I won't tell you that you can trust me, Captain." He smiled. It was an extraordinarily predatory expression.

"I will tell you that my primary mission is to keep you alive and see *your* mission succeed."

"I see," Kyle said slowly. Voyager's idea of a favor was apparently to send him a pet assassin.

"You said you have messages for me from the Joint Chiefs?" he finally asked.

"Written and verbal," Nebula confirmed, pulling a chip from inside his pristine black suit jacket. "The written orders are basically 'the Department of Foreign Affairs needs a favor; give it to them,'" he added. "You can check if you like."

"Why don't you summarize the headache you're about to drop on my lap?" Kyle asked, shaking his head with a weary smile and taking another mouthful of beer.

It was *good* beer, but Voyager might have underestimated how much Nebula was going to get on his nerves.

"The Coraline Imperator has formally requested the presence of Captain Kyle Adrian Roberts, the victor of Huī Xing and the rescuer of over twenty thousand Imperial POWs from the Commonwealth in said system, on Coral for a formal presentation."

"Of…what?" Kyle asked.

"To be honest, his Imperial High-Handedness didn't bother to tell us," the diplomat replied. "It was polite, for all that, though that might have been in comparison to some of the other crap I've read recently. I don't suppose you saw Dictator Periklos's official response to our offer of membership in the Alliance?"

Periklos ran the Stellar League, a nation whom Kyle's own efforts had recently embroiled in war with the Commonwealth. That war was opening a second front that the Alliance of Free Stars desperately needed, and coordinating with the Dictator would have made it even more effective.

Since that war had started because the Alliance had managed to get Periklos blamed for their own covert operation…

"No," he admitted. "I don't think it was made publicly available."

"Probably not," Nebula agreed. "I think it was the first time I've ever actually seen the words 'Go fuck yourselves' included in a formal diplomatic communique."

"I'm...not surprised," Kyle admitted.

"You did set up the Commonwealth to bend him over for a reaming," the diplomat agreed cheerfully. "Not that their punitive expedition is enjoying their visit to the New Edmonton system. *Someone* may have leaked their plans to the League before they got there."

Kyle shook his head. He felt a bit guilty over that, and yet...the Federation and her allies had needed to drag the League into the war. And the Commonwealth would have tried to bring the League into their embrace sooner or later.

The Terrans were convinced that all of humanity would be unified under their banner in the end, after all.

"But we have no idea what the Imperator wants?" he asks.

"He's going to stick a shiny piece of metal on your chest as a PR move to impress both our citizenries with your bravery and with how well our two nations are working together," Nebula told him. "And you, my dear Captain, are going to smile and take it, because anything else would risk the alliance that's the only thing keeping the Federation, the Imperium, and three dozen other star systems free."

"That is inarguable logic," Kyle agreed, chuckling and shaking his head again before drinking more beer. "It will delay our deployment out to Antioch, though," he pointed out.

"The Foreign Affairs analysts think that if there's a Commonwealth component to the raids, their plan is to drive a wedge between us and Coraline," the diplomat told him. "Which means that adding some glue to that relationship is worth a delay in deployment. The Joint Chiefs agree, which is what those orders"—he gestured at the chip—"say."

"Orders are orders," *Kodiak*'s new Captain concluded. "We'll make it happen, Mr. Nebula."

———

"THIS CHIP CONTAINS your formal orders for what has now been designated Operation Glorious Elephant."

The image of a gray-haired woman in the Navy's blue-piped black uniform with three gold stars on her collar filled the wallscreen in Kyle's office as he finished his beer and played the message on the chip. The woman was Fleet Admiral Meredith Blake, the current Chairwoman of the Castle Federation Joint Chiefs of Staff and the uniformed commander of the Federation military.

"Your first task is unrelated to the existing issues," she noted with a twist of her lips. "Foreign Affairs has requested your presence in response to an invitation from the Imperator for you to attend a formal presentation on Coral itself.

"The courier this chip was sent with has more details, but yes, Captain Roberts, you are expected to go to the Coraline system and meet with the Coraline Imperator on his planet. He needs us as badly as we need him, but we all have to work together to survive this war.

"You will take *Alexander* with you to the Coraline System. A single ship, even as powerful as *Alexander*, will not fill the requirements of the systems that have called for our help.

"She might meet their *needs*," Blake admitted, "but we must show that we take their call for aid seriously.

"Once you have finished at Coraline, you are to proceed to Antioch and meet with their civilian and military leaders to establish a full understanding of the situation. They've provided a lot of information via q-com, but there is no substitute for direct conversation with the people involved.

"All of the information they have given us has been forwarded to your ships, and we will update as the situation evolves.

"From Antioch, how you progress will be up to your discretion. We would strongly prefer that Antioch, Serengeti and Istanbul survive unharmed with as much of their merchant fleet intact as possible. While we would certainly be pleased if the surrounding systems are unharmed, those three must be your priority.

"Your mission is the destruction of the pirates that have been raiding those systems," Blake concluded. "Protection of their infrastructure and ships is a higher priority than dead pirates, but we both know dead pirates are the best guarantee of the long-term safety of the region.

"We have limited real intelligence about the area and no resources to provide you once you are in the AO," she warned. "Both of your ships have extensive self-repair and resupply capabilities if Antioch and the others prove uncooperative, but if you are in major need of supply or aid, report via q-com and we will try and make something happen.

"If Antioch and the others prove severely uncooperative, you may be recalled," Blake continued, "but that would represent a failure of the mission. We don't need these systems in the Alliance, but we do need our trade with them to fund the fleet.

"Keep them safe, Captain Roberts."

8

Castle System
09:00 September 14, 2736 Earth Standard Meridian Date/Time
Gawain Orbit, DSC-052 Kodiak

SOME DAY, Kyle would take command of a ship that wasn't in a hurry to be deployed somewhere. It would probably be after the war was over, however, so he had no expectation that "some day" would be anytime soon.

Forty-seven hours after his arrival aboard *Kodiak* and three hours ahead of deadline, he sat in the command chair on the carrier's bridge and watched as both of the ships under his command got underway.

There was a faint tremble through *Kodiak*'s bones as her massive antimatter engines opened up, a momentary adjustment as her mass manipulators swung into play, creating a gravity field that exactly offset the crushing acceleration.

Alexander loped ahead for a few moments, Sarka taking advantage of the battlecruiser's higher acceleration to slide into a forward escort position and then adjusting her engines to match *Kodiak*'s course.

"We will be clear for Alcubierre-Stetson drive in an hour and forty minutes," Houshian reported.

"Do you have a course laid for the Coraline system?" Kyle asked.

"Yes, sir," she reported crisply. "Eleven days, peak velocity five point five light-years per day. We will arrive in-system in the early morning on September twenty-fifth."

"Carry on, Commander Houshian," Kyle told her. "You have the call on the drive."

"Yes, sir," she replied, a flash of cheer and confidence flickering across the neural network as Kyle leaned back to watch his crew get to work.

Thirty light-years away and the Imperial capital system was less than two weeks' travel—and instantly reachable by q-com for virtual discussions. The scale of operations that the Alliance worked with was mind-boggling, but the A-S drive made it possible.

Of course, the same shield projectors and mass manipulators that made faster-than-light travel possible were incredibly expensive. The five Class One mass manipulators *Kodiak* carried to produce her Alcubierre drive field were easily a third of her cost...and a full percentage point of a moderately wealthy system's GSP all on their own.

Linked in to the ship's systems, Kyle quietly reviewed Commander Trent's status report on the Class Ones. The status itself appeared fine, though the status report itself was...lacking. There were items he had to dig for that should have been front and center, and unless he was mistaken, one of the Class One's statuses was entirely missing.

Kodiak only needed four Class Ones to create her bubble of warped space, but all Federation warships carried the fifth as a safety precaution and to help with her normal maneuvers. A few mental commands linked Kyle into the engineering net and allowed him to pull the status directly from the manipulator's own computers.

Eighty percent readiness. That was...not good. Not when they were *leaving* their refit slip. The other four were at ninety-nine or above, but the fifth, redundant mass manipulator wasn't.

That was a problem. Not a big one, but a problem.

A bigger problem was that the information hadn't been included in the official status report and that Trent had tried to conceal that by making the report nearly incoherent.

He apparently needed to have that conversation with his chief engineer sooner rather than later.

———

ALEXANDER AND KODIAK cleared the zone around Gawain where the gas giant's gravity made it impossible to enter Alcubierre drive exactly on schedule, the two immense ships accelerating out of the planet's gravity well at over two hundred gravities.

"Captain Roberts? All identified gravity sources are beyond effect range," Commander Houshian told him from her seat. "Current gravitational force is beneath one picometer per second squared. We are prepared to warp space on your command."

"You have the call, Commander Houshian," Kyle told her, settling back in his chair to watch.

"Aye, aye, Navigation has the call," she confirmed. She opened an audio channel to Engineering, unnecessary but traditional as part of this process outside of a combat situation.

"Engineering, this is the navigator. Please confirm status of Class One mass manipulators."

"All Class Ones are functioning within parameters," Trent replied over the channel. "*Kodiak* is ready to warp space."

A tiny window inside Kyle's implant feeds watched Sarka's bridge crew going through the same motions, though the junior Captain was still making the call herself. She'd learn when that was and wasn't required—there were no transitions better charted by the Castle Federation Space Navy than the ones in the Castle System itself. It was a good one to leave to a junior.

Houshian glanced back at him, clearly uncertain that he was truly leaving the whole process in her hands. He smiled and nodded to her to continue.

Swallowing, the tiny navigator opened a shipwide channel.

"All hands, prepare for Alcubierre drive," she declared over the channel.

A countdown appeared on Kyle's implant displays, counting down the requisite sixty seconds between the warning and the actual transition.

"Initiating interior Stetson fields."

Hundreds of small projectors across *Kodiak*'s hull powered up, and faint haze descended across all of the carrier's views of the outside world. The interior Stetson stabilization field would protect *Kodiak* from the radiation of her own warp bubble and the gravitic affects of the drive's singularities.

"Interior Stetson field active," the navigator reported. "Exterior field on standby, mass manipulators on standby."

Houshian made one last look back at Kyle, and then the ship shivered as she lit up the Class One mass manipulators.

Space outside the ship seemed to warp as four micro-singularities took form—and the exterior Stetson field wrapped around them to protect the Castle system from their presence.

"We have singularity formation. Exterior Stetson field is active; containment is one hundred percent and holding.

"Initiating warp bubble now."

The massive arrays of zero-point cells that fueled *Kodiak* flared to life, and the Class One mass manipulators expanded their singularities, the distortion of the space around the carrier growing and moving until a bright flash of blue light encapsulated the ship.

There was a moment of disorientation as the starbow compressed to a strange purple haze, and then *Kodiak*'s computers replaced the visual pickups with a simulated view of their position in the universe.

"Captain Roberts, we are under way," Houshian reported with a sigh of relief.

"Thank you, Commander," Kyle told her. Looking around the bridge, he rose from his chair with a smile. "Thank you, everyone; that was well done. Commander Houshian, you have the watch."

"Yes, Captain!"

———

THE CENTRAL ENGINEERING core of a modern warship was an awe-inspiring place, a large open void near the heart of the vessel, containing the largest of the zero-point cells that provided the incredible amounts of power that fueled a starship.

While *Kodiak* had over a hundred zero-point cells scattered through her hull, even ignoring the positron lances which were basically the same technology, the eight that filled her engineering core provided the power that allowed her to outspeed light.

Offices and drone control centers surrounded those core cells, as did the primary routing nexuses for power, heat, air and water throughout the massive starship. The primary engineering control center was easily a rival to the bridge or auxiliary control in terms of processing power.

Kyle dodged a trio of welding robots as he approached the control center, the drones moving in sync with a distracted-looking engineering Specialist who didn't even notice he'd almost run over the Captain.

He stared after the robots and the engineer for a long moment as they continued on their way, half-waiting for the man to stop and apologize and half in pure shock that they'd come so close to an accident and not *noticed*.

Finally, he added the incident to his mental list and stepped into the primary control center. Just post-transition, it was still a buzzing hive of activity, though there were already signs of consoles and screens being shut down as engineering switched over to the somewhat slower tempo of FTL watches.

To his surprise, however, Commander Ivy Trent wasn't in the central command chair of the control center. An unfamiliar Lieutenant Commander, with the shaved head and visible circuitry common to the Federation's transhumanist minority, occupied the chair, overseeing the stand-down from transition.

They spotted him and leapt to their feet with a crisp salute.

"Captain Roberts, sir! Lieutenant Commander Innes Harvey," they introduced themselves. "How can I assist you?"

"I was looking for Commander Trent," Kyle said in a dangerously mild tone. Even with the transition over, if there were any problems with the Alcubierre-Stetson systems, now was when they were most likely to show up. The engineer should have been there.

"The Commander is in her office, sir," Harvey replied. "I took over the stand-down from transition. Everything is going smoothly."

"Good," the Captain agreed. "Is this the ordinary procedure aboard *Kodiak*, Lieutenant Commander Harvey?"

"Yes, sir!" Harvey answered brightly. "Either myself or one of the other seconds sees to the stand-down."

"I see. In her office, you said?"

"Yes, sir."

"Thank you, Lieutenant Commander."

———

TRENT'S OFFICE WAS LOCKED, set up to require anyone entering to intercom in and request entry. Unfortunately for the Commander, *Kodiak*'s security was quite hierarchical in its setup, and the engineer couldn't actually lock her office against the Captain.

He overrode the security in mid-step, forcing the door to slide open and charging into the Commander's office. He was half-expecting to find her asleep or watching porn or something similarly unacceptable, but instead she was working at her console, looking up in surprise at his entrance.

"What the hell, Captain?" she demanded.

"That was my question, Commander Trent," he told her. "That was my question when I realized that one of our mass manipulators was in worse shape than I expected. That was also my question when I realized you'd omitted that from your report—and it was *certainly* my question when I arrived in your control center fifteen minutes after transition to discover you'd left the stand-down and initial safety checks to a subordinate."

"How I run my department is my business, Captain."

"No, Commander Trent, it is not," Kyle said flatly. "Especially not when standards and policies that exist for a reason are being ignored by a senior officer, and the rot appears to be spreading into her subordinates."

"My seconds are all competent officers; I will not stand—"

"I don't mean your officers," Kyle interrupted. "One of your technicians almost crushed me on my way down here, Commander. That shouldn't have happened—and it should have been caught by a superior and dealt with.

"It wasn't, because *you*, Commander, are hiding in your office and your subordinates are taking their cues from you and sticking their heads in the sand. So, Commander Trent, do you understand why I am somewhat irritated with you?"

Trent looked about ready to yell back at him, but then swallowed, seeming to realize that she wasn't going to win a yelling match with her commanding officer.

"That...shouldn't have happened," she agreed. "I'm not certain I agree with your assessment of the cause, but I agree that the incident shouldn't have happened. I will look into it."

"Why aren't you at your post, Commander?" Kyle demanded. "You should be in the middle of everything, making sure your people know you are there—both to back them up and to stop them short."

"My officers are more than competent to handle the day-to-day affairs of Engineering," Trent told him. "They don't need me to babysit them through the boring parts."

"The boring parts," Kyle echoed. "Commander, the 'boring parts' are the parts that keep this ship safe—and are your damned job!"

"I trained my subordinates to handle them so I wouldn't have to," she said flatly. "They get better experience and I get to focus on the more interesting parts of the job. It was a win for everyone."

"And a violation of Navy Policy," he pointed out.

"Which is more important, the Policy or a functioning ship?"

"The latter," Kyle admitted, "except that hasn't been what you've delivered to me, Commander. Your department appears to be fraying, and *you*, Commander Trent, failed to inform me that one of our Class One mass manipulators was only at eighty percent readiness."

As he spoke, he took control of her wallscreen and threw the status display up for the five Class Ones up on it. Studying it now, he saw that *none* of them were where he'd have expected them to be just after leaving port. One through Four, at least, were all over ninety-five percent—but they should have been at almost one hundred percent... and Trent's report had showed them at ninety-nine.

"All are within safe parameters."

"For normal operations," Kyle replied. "Barely, in the case of Five. And what happens, Commander Trent, if I order you to take the ship to Tier Three acceleration?"

The "tiers" were plateaus of fuel efficiency in the interaction of anti-matter engines and mass manipulators. Tier One was used by civilian ships, supremely fuel-efficient but only about one hundred gravities. Tier Two was now around two hundred and fifty gravities, enough for capital ships. Tier Three was usually reserved for starfighters, at five hundred gravities, and Tier Four came with dangerous radiation and inertia leakages, and was reserved for missiles.

The carrier was theoretically capable of Tier Three acceleration, but would be burning through days' worth of fuel for minutes of flight.

"That would be crazy," Trent pointed out.

"Why? It's something we've done in the past, and something this ship is capable of—but not with Manipulator Five barely sufficient for regular operation," he pointed out. "I'd also like to note, informally before it goes into your permanent record, that the status report you gave me lacked any information on Five and overstated the readiness of One through Four.

"If you have a good explanation, Commander, I'd start talking. Now."

"Anything above ninety percent readiness is perfectly acceptable, Captain," Trent replied. "Manipulator Five has a problem, one I was trying to find a solution for before I brought it to your attention."

"Above ninety percent readiness would be acceptable if we'd been in the field for a month," Kyle snapped. "On leaving the refit yard? We should be within point one percent of a hundred, or *someone*"—he looked at her pointedly—"hasn't done their damn job."

"That's a matter of opinion."

"Perhaps," Kyle agreed. "But it's a matter of the *Captain's* opinion, Commander Trent. Which means you have forty-eight hours to get all five Class Ones up to at least ninety-nine percent of maximum readiness, understand?"

She opened her mouth and he raised a hand.

"That's an *order*, Commander," he pointed out. "If you need assistance from Commander Tsien or to majorly adjust the fabrication schedules, we'll make that happen, but I want this ship capable of doing *anything* I ask her to—and it's your job to make that happen.

"Preferably while keeping your department from running anyone over!"

She sighed and nodded, reaching across the table to rotate the smaller screen she'd been working on to show it to him.

"We can probably get One through Four up in that time frame," Trent admitted. "It's often a waste of parts and labor, but it is your call."

"It won't happen with Five," she drawled, lighting up the diagram of the Class One mass manipulator on her screen. "The exotic matter coil is misaligned. They broke something, putting her into reserve. It's subtle, basic tests didn't pick it up and we've still got eighty percent power on Five, but…we're never getting more than that."

"How bad?" he asked, pleased to have actually found some *thought* on the part of the overly clever engineer.

"It's in the coil itself, Captain," Trent said. "We can't fix it; I've been trying to find a way for weeks. We'd need to replace the coil and it's just not worth it."

The exotic matter coil was the most expensive part of any mass manipulator—and the Class One mass manipulators were the most expensive machines of any kind aboard *Kodiak*. The carrier's five exotic matter coils were the single most expensive and irreplaceable part aboard.

"I should have been informed of this," he told her. "I doubt the decision would have been different, but it wasn't your decision to make, Commander. JD-Ships should have known and *I* should have known, without my having to drag it out of you."

The Joint Department of Ships had handled the refit. Someone in the yard should have noticed what Trent had seen even if she hadn't told them…but that, at least, was not currently Kyle's problem.

"I thought I had an answer," she admitted. "But I kept running the numbers, and no matter how I tried, it didn't work."

"It's an exotic matter coil, Commander," Kyle pointed out. "We don't even have the gear to open the damn thing up safely, let alone try and work with the exotics themselves."

He shook his head.

"All right, I guess I won't expect a hundred percent from Five," he conceded, "but I expect the other four in top shape, and I expect you to keep an eye on Five. From your command center, because I think your department needs to know that you're actually doing your job and not sleeping in your damned office."

"I was never sleeping!" Trent objected.

"I believe you," Kyle agreed. "But I also guarantee you that that's what your subordinates thought you were doing."

9

KDX-6657 System
10:00 September 14, 2736 Earth Standard Meridian Date/Time
BC-305 Poseidon

"How bad?"

Rank had its privileges in the Terran Commonwealth Navy, and one of those privileges was the private "media room" attached to a flag officer's office. It was a smallish room, still half the size of the Commodore's immense office, lined with the best holoprojectors the Navy had. It was, in theory, intended for tactical planning and visualization.

James Tecumseh was quite certain that most flag officers used it more for porn. He'd certainly used it for that himself, though he wouldn't *admit* it, but his main use of it was actually for meditation. The holo-projectors made it possible to create the illusion that one was simply floating in space, with no starship around the viewer.

Right now, he was "floating in space" above a dead world four light-years from Antioch used as an anchor point by Commodore Coati's pirate fleet, looking down at a planet that glowed with active fields of lava.

There was *nothing* in the KDX-6657 System to make it remotely appealing—which was exactly why Coati operated from there and why Commodore James Tecumseh was here.

And why Colonel Alric Barbados, a man so pale-skinned he'd glow under a black light, was with him in that quiet chamber...

"However bad you think it was, it was worse," the Marine said flatly. "The ship we boarded ourselves surrendered with barely a fight, no casualties on either side.

"The ones Coati's people boarded..."

Barbados was behind James but the Admiral could almost feel the shiver in the other man's voice.

"We took three hundred and forty prisoners," the Marine said after several moment's silence. "But that's *including* Target Four, sir."

James winced.

"Those ships weren't a standard design I recognized," he admitted. There was an unspoken question in the admission.

"Locally built except for one from the Renaissance Trade Factor," the Colonel told him. "Average crew three hundred."

Twelve hundred people. There had been twelve hundred people across those four ships, and almost nine hundred of them were dead—and they hadn't died quickly or easily. Coati's people had tortured and murdered their way through the ships James's intervention had allowed them to capture.

"We'll arrange to have our prisoners ransomed," James said with a forced calm. "We have some ties out here that aren't linked to Coati, they'll go home. And without creating any suspicion, either. That kind of thing is more normal than Coati's...butchery."

"Sir..."

"We have our orders, Colonel Barbados," the Admiral snapped into the silence. "I don't like our pirate friend any better than you do, but..."

"His people have shit gear and worse training," the Marine pointed out. "You give the word, we could take all of his build-a-block corsairs in twenty minutes. Use his ships to run the raids ourselves—mission only says there has to be pirates, not that it has to be *Coati*'s pirates."

James chuckled, grateful for the interruption of his dark mood.

"While I suppose that would be within the letter of our orders, it would be pushing the spirit, Colonel," he warned. "We're supposed to be able to pull out and leave our pirate friends to the tender mercies of the Alliance once they start sending ships this way." He shook his head. "And I'll admit, I'm looking forward to it. Give me a clean battle any day, not this backstabbing bullshit."

"Sir, my troops are Marines," Barbados said slowly. "They're disciplined. They're loyal. They're obedient. To a point.

"I *know* at least one of Coati's people took an 'accidental' friendly bullet, and that was with my Sergeants well aware of our orders. Next time…" The Marine sighed.

"Sir, next time, I don't think I'll be able to stop my people shooting the sons of bitches. They didn't torture anybody in front of us, but now we know it happened, and I don't know if my Marines will stand for it."

"They probably won't," James agreed. "And if they did, they wouldn't be worth their damned uniforms. I'll talk to Coati, Colonel, try and make him understand."

"He's a pirate, sir. What exactly is he going to understand?"

"That next time, I won't be ordering your Marines not to interfere."

———

JAMES TOOK an entire platoon of Marines with him to the pirate station. He didn't inform Coati that he was coming until the assault shuttle was blasting clear of *Poseidon*'s hull, and he didn't give the pirate warlord any choice about the visit.

If he'd needed to, he was prepared to have the Marine piloting the shuttle blow open the transfer station's armored dock and make an assault landing. He figured he wouldn't have to go much past that, but forty Terran Commonwealth Marines in powered battle armor would go through Coati's scum like a hot knife through butter if needed.

The controller for the dock clearly decided better of playing chicken with an assault shuttle and opened the doors in time to allow James's shuttle to sweep in to a perfect landing in the middle of the collection of aging junk that passed for Coati's shuttle fleet.

Standing out like a sore thumb among the shuttlecraft were the gleaming forms of sixteen Castle Federation Cobra-type starfighters. They were older ships, sixth-generation starfighters phased out just before the current war had started, but still among the deadlier starfighters in space.

Coati's people might not keep the place *clean* and their shuttles were almost as old as the Amerindian flag officer, but they understood what parts of their hardware *needed* to be kept in shape. The transfer station might have been a mess, but the air was clean and the automatic fueling system fully operational.

The robots were the only ones waiting for James, though, and he was about to collect his armored escort and head deeper into the station when the doors slid open and a quartet of power-armored figures swept out.

The armor was fifty-year-old Coraline Imperium manufacture, according to James's implant. Any two of his escorting Marines could have taken all four of the pirates, but that wasn't the point. The four guards took position around the door, attempting to loom at the impassive Terran Marines, and then the door opened again to disgorge Commodore Coati.

It was hard to tell with Coati how much of his oddities were by choice and how much were the result of pre-birth genetic engineering. James was *relatively* sure the iridescent scales that the man had for skin had been genetically engineered before the man's birth, but Coati's gem-like eyes and multicolored hair could be implants or modifications, too.

Certainly, the strange little pirate had made the most of them, wearing a tight-fitting black leather uniform that made the glittering colors of his scales stand out even more than they would have otherwise, and his hair was drawn up into a gloriously rainbow-colored mohawk—that James knew readily folded down over the side of the man's head to fit under a helmet.

"Tecumseh!" the pirate warlord greeted him loudly and cheerfully, as if the Terran Commodore *hadn't* just forced his way on to the base. "Welcome to *l'Estación de Muerte*."

Death Station. Fitting for a broken-down shithole in orbit of a world that would never know life. James hadn't even known the place had a name; it was just the "KDX-6657 Station" to his people.

"I appreciate your alacrity in meeting with me, Commodore," James told the other man. "We have matters to discuss." He glanced around the hangar, almost entirely empty of humans, and smiled thinly. "In private, of course."

"*De nada*, Commodore. Of course!" Coati agreed. "We pulled some *maravilloso* brandy off one of the ships in Antioch; I'll have my people send us a bottle!"

James concealed a sigh. He was very close to hating Coati's guts, but the man insisted on drinking through all of their business meetings. On the positive side, at least, Coati had an amazing taste in liquor.

THE AIR aboard *l'Estación de Muerte* might have been clean, but the station itself was not. Without cleaning bots or anything similar, the pirates living in the base simply kicked garbage to the side when it got in the way. You could traverse the station, but the edges of the corridors were visible mounds of food wrappers and other debris.

Coati and his guards seemed unbothered by the mess, stepping around it or kicking it to the side as needed to lead the way through the station. James and his own men were less cavalier, but they made their way forward regardless.

The Commodore had been here before, even if no one had bothered to tell him the place had a name. He'd warned his guards just what they were going to see, and if the Marines were bothered, nothing made it through the ceramic masks of their powered armor.

"The troops can wait out here," Coati suggested as they reached a door. "Canaste, get them food, beer!"

"We're fine," the platoon Sergeant rumbled. "We'll wait."

"Suit yourself," the pirate warlord told them, then led James through the door into an observation deck looking out over the dead world below.

The observation deck was the first completely clean room James had seen aboard the station, probably because it was part of Coati's personal space. A table next to the window held two glasses and a bottle of brandy, lit up a brilliant purple in the light of the burning world behind it.

Coati crossed to the table and poured brandy into the two glasses, but his affable cheer was gone as he offered one of the glasses to James.

"Do you think this is a fucking game, Tecumseh?" he snapped. "You fuck with me, you make me look weak. I look weak, I need to do something drastic to stay in control. Do you get me, *Commodore*?"

"What I 'get', *Commodore*, is that your people killed nine hundred civilians we were planning to capture and ransom," James snapped back. "Regardless of the issues my personnel—who you know *damned* well are real soldiers—have with that, that's a lot of damned money your people butchered."

"And next time we call on some idiot fucking merchant to haul over, they'll obey without us having to goddamn board them," Coati replied. "'Cause they'll know what'll happen if they don't roll over and show their bellies—we'll rip 'em out!"

"I'll warn you, Coati, my people won't stand by and watch another atrocity like that," James told him. "Next time your scum start raping and murdering their way through a ship, they're going to have my people up their asses with battle rifles."

"Goddamn tight-assed Marines," the pirate snapped. "I don't need your fucking armored paladins, Tecumseh. If you can't control 'em, don't let 'em in the boardings—it's that simple. I didn't sign on with your Marshal's plan to have a bunch of useless twats get their panties in a twist!"

Coati swallowed the brandy, glaring at the Terran Commodore.

"I op my way, and *you* need to be seen showing *respect*," he continued. "You disrespect me, and I have to be seen taking it out of your hide, you get me, Commodore?"

"Try it," James murmured, holding his own brandy but not touching it. "I am here because I have my orders, Coati. And my people will follow my orders—but *you* need to play cleaner or this will cease being a 'fucking game' and become a fucking nightmare.

"*Your* fucking nightmare. Do *you* get *me*, 'Commodore'?"

10

IN REALITY, Wing Commander Michelle Williams's bomber nestled in its cradle on *Kodiak*'s flight deck, the zero-point cells that skimmed both electrons and positrons from the quantum foam of reality stood down while it drew its power from the surrounding carrier.

In this state, the deadly bomber was quiescent and harmless, software and hardware interlocks keeping the seven-thousand-ton spacecraft from activating anything except its computers.

The screens and neural feeds supplying Michelle and her flight crew with information showed a very different scene. The bomber floated in deep space, surrounded by the other hundred and twenty-seven starfighters of *Kodiak*'s flight group. Immediately to hand were the other twenty-three bombers of Michelle's Echo Wing, their neat parade-ground formation a reassuring sight around her.

Thirteen squadrons of Falcons, still the deadliest starfighter in space despite the deployment of seventh-generation fighters by every power in the war now, and three squadrons of the new Vulture bombers.

It was a lot of firepower, enough to send a shiver of contemplation down Michelle's spine. *Kodiak* was an older ship, but her fighter wing was completely modern. They could have won the last war on their own.

Today, those fighters were taking on their own compatriots, *Kodiak*'s flight group zipping through virtual space toward *Alexander* and the battlecruiser's own nine squadrons. In theory, this wasn't even a fair fight, *Alexander*'s own firepower more than making up the seven-squadron difference.

"So, Commander Williams," Vice Commodore Song said in Michelle's mental ear. "The skipper says your bombers should make this actually doable, but I know neither Vice Commodore Altena nor Captain Sarka think that we can take *Alexander* without *Kodiak* providing fire support. Or even with that fire support, to be honest," she said crisply.

"Ideas?" the senior asked.

"*Alexander* can't stand off a full salvo of torpedoes from the bomber wing," Michelle replied. "That's almost a hundred missiles with capital-ship-grade electronic warfare suites. Our *range* is more limited than a cap-ship missile, but the brains and projectors on our birds are just as capable."

"But as much as Altena and Sarka underestimate your ships, they're still not going to let you get them into range without trying to kill you or having Altena's birds in position for missile defense," Song pointed out. "They know the Fox thinks you can make the difference, so they're going to focus on you."

"Wouldn't be smart in a normal fight, but it'll work here," Michelle agreed. "But..."

She studied her ship's systems for a few seconds, then grinned wickedly.

"We may not have a Falcon's ECM systems, but the Vulture's are nothing to sneer at," she told her boss. "But since Altena *knows* the Falcons' systems are better... I have an idea."

———

KODIAK'S STARFIGHTER group swirled in a pattern that caused even Michelle to lose track of individual fighters for a moment, and then split in two. Alpha, Delta and Echo "dove", adding a fifteen-degree vector away from their straight-line approach to *Alexander*, while Bravo and Charlie went up, adding a fifteen-degree vector in the opposite direction.

At five hundred gravities, that thirty-degree difference meant that their velocities were suddenly adding a component away from each other at over six kilometers per second squared. Across the multi-million-kilometer distance between them and *Alexander*, they were going to add enough distance that Altena couldn't engage both forces simultaneously.

There were eight squadrons in each sub-group, and *Alexander*'s flight group outnumbered either one. For at least a minute, however, Vice Commodore Altena and her fighters continued down the center, and Michelle smiled grimly.

Her Wing's three squadrons of bombers were currently pretending to be Falcons, and three squadrons of Bravo Wing were pretending to be Vultures…that were pretending to be Falcons and failing.

Michelle caught herself holding her breath. If Altena took the bait, she'd run seventy-two Falcons into sixty-four, better odds than *Alexander*'s group had faced before—but the bombers would be clear all the way to launch range, which left the battlecruiser doomed.

"There they go, ma'am," Ivan Vasil reported, the younger man flexing his tattooed muscles unconsciously as he highlighted the data for her. "They're breaking for Group Two. Poor bastards."

Vasil was right. The entirety of *Alexander*'s flight group was breaking "up", heading to intercept Bravo and Charlie Wings. They'd all have to vector toward the battlecruiser in the end, so Altena was likely expecting to kill the bombers and then sweep back to clean up the rest of *Kodiak*'s fighters before they reached *Alexander*.

It wasn't going to work out that way. The whole plan was a sacrifice gambit, one Michelle wouldn't have been comfortable suggesting in a real fight unless desperate, but it also gave them a real chance at taking out *Alexander*...which also meant that Group Two didn't need to save any of their missiles *for* the battlecruiser.

The game was up the moment the two closing fighter groups reached missile range of each other. Bravo Wing dropped their ECM, and seventy-two Falcons went to rapid fire on all of their missile launchers, dumping over a thousand virtual missiles into space in under fifteen seconds. Michelle's Vultures would have launched half again as many missiles as the Falcons that were pretending to be them, so the deception was no longer necessary.

Altena's people had to keep *some* missiles back if they were to have a chance at Group One, but *Kodiak*'s fighters were leaving the cruiser to the bombers. They threw *everything* at the closing starfighters, then broke off, their engines blazing a new vector that would keep them out of the cruiser's positron lance range.

It wasn't enough to save them all, but over half of them managed to break free—and their missile salvo took out over forty of Altena's Falcons. A better exchange than they had any right to expect...and one that was entirely irrelevant to the outcome of the battle.

"Torpedo range in ten seconds," Vasil reported calmly. "Birds one through four report green; I have the target loaded in."

"Flight Commanders, reports," Michelle ordered.

"Echo One Actual: all ships are go, all torps are green."

"Echo Two Actual: we have one torp on yellow but should be go for full launch."

"Echo Three Actual: all green. Good to launch."

A mental clock ticked downward and the Wing Commander smiled grimly.

"Fire."

The torpedo Echo Two-Six's systems had warned as yellow—a random chance on any missile in the sim, higher for the not-quite-prototype torpedoes than most missiles—blew itself apart barely a light-second away from its mothership.

The other ninety-five torpedoes flashed across the eight-million-kilometer range to *Alexander*, Altena's fighters desperately trying to get into position to intercept for the entire ten-minute journey...but failing.

The battlecruiser's defenses were designed to stand off about thirty capital ship missiles or three hundred starfighter missiles, a number easily tripled or quadrupled by appropriate use of her starfighters to protect her.

The torpedoes came in with the same penetration aids and electronic warfare as capital ship missiles, and Vice Commodore Altena and her people were too far out. Fifty simulated missiles struck home, and the simulation calmly concluded as the virtual presentation of the Federation battlecruiser *Alexander* vanished in a ball of thankfully simulated flame.

———

MICHELLE STEPPED out of her bomber to discover that Song had beaten her out onto the flight deck, the Vice Commodore applauding gently as the junior woman dropped to the metal flooring.

"Well done, Wing Commander," Song told her. "That was *very* clever, and now Vice Commodore Altena owes me a drink."

"We all did our part, ma'am," Michelle replied, glancing around at the flight crews exiting their craft around her. "I was impressed by Bravo and Charlie," she continued. "I thought we were going to lose them all; I'm not sure I could have made the suggestion without it being a sim."

"It was your plan," her superior replied. "And it was a good one. It would have been the right call in a real fight, even if we *had* lost Bravo and Charlie," Song noted grimly. "Two wings for a battlecruiser? It hurts for us, but that's a trade I can't argue with."

"We exist to be expended so the capital ships live," Michael agreed in a murmur. It wasn't a sentiment Castle Federation Space Force officers *liked*, but it was certainly one they understood.

Song glanced past Michelle's shoulder, and the younger woman could have sworn she saw a ghost of a soft smile drift over the Vice Commodore's face.

"That said, we will have a full debrief and see if it's a tactic we'll want to repeat," she told Michelle. "Twenty hundred hours, make sure you and your squadron heads are there."

"Yes, ma'am," Michelle replied, saluting as her superior swept past her. She turned to follow Song's path almost unconsciously, watching as *Kodiak*'s CAG crossed the flight deck to where Commander Taggart was waiting for her.

The two spoke for a moment, then stepped out of the flight deck and out of sight.

Strange that the XO hadn't waited for them to finish the cool-down from the exercise before stealing the CAG away, though Michelle's implant pinged with the information on the debrief as the thought ran through her head.

"I see you've been paying too much attention to me," a familiar voice interrupted her contemplation of her superior's not-*quite*-inappropriate disappearing act, and she glanced up to see Captain Roberts leaning on the torpedo pylon of her bomber, the big red-haired man grinning at her.

"That stunt looked like something I'd try," he continued. "In fact, I've added it to my mental file of 'crazy enough to work'. Well done."

"You were watching, sir?" she asked.

"This ship's main weapon is its fighter wing, Wing Commander," Roberts reminded her. "I need to know the temper of my sword."

He glanced around. "*Kodiak* tells me your official debrief is in two hours. If you don't mind, I'd like to pick your brain on the bombers before then. I've seen them from the wrong side," he told her, "and I'd like to know what they look like from yours."

"You're the Captain, sir."

———

A RELATIVELY QUICK debrief of her own squadrons later, which Michelle only barely managed to keep from devolving into a pure backslapping session, she arrived at the Captain's office with an hour to spare before she had to meet with the rest of the flight group.

"Enter," Roberts ordered, the door instantly obeying the command and allowing her into the office.

It was still strange to Michelle to see Roberts working on paperwork on a screen. Space Force officers were selected for having an exceptionally high level of neural interface compatibility, allowing them to handle far more data through their implants than most people.

Space Force officers did almost all of their work via their implants, and Roberts had been unusually capable even in those ranks, able to process the contents of entire reports before most people could even access them.

That had been then. Before an errant shot by one Michelle Williams had detonated an antimatter missile less than a kilometer from his starfighter and the radiation had burnt out his original implant. The replacement was just as capable, but the scarring in the Captain's mind had left him with a barely above-average interface capacity.

And invalided him out of the Space Force, a fate that had saved at least two star systems and a hundred thousand prisoners of war by Michelle's count.

That didn't stop the flash of guilt she felt as she saw Roberts working on a set of datapads and a wallscreen to get through his daily paperwork. He looked far older now, more than the year since they'd last served together should have aged him.

The massive grin on his face, though, was familiar. The big Captain rose and pulled a pair of beers from the minifridge underneath *Kodiak*'s commissioning seal of a rifle-armed bear in a gold circle.

"Have a drink, Wing Commander," he told her, using the base of his beer to push a datapad out of the way so he could slide the second over to her.

"I am on duty, sir," she pointed out carefully.

"My ship, my rules," he replied, the grin growing even larger. "And my rules say you can have a beer in the Captain's cabin, *especially* when you just turned every member of our little task group into believers in the bomber concept."

"I don't know if I was that successful, sir," Michelle said, but she took the beer and sipped it. She was unsurprised that it was good—she doubted the Captain would have anything less in a fridge in his office.

"Without *Kodiak*, that simulation should have been an open-and-shut case," the Captain told her. "Splitting the fighter group to draw Altena's people out of position was a good plan in any case, but it wouldn't have been enough if you'd been taking Falcons in."

She nodded.

"It's almost back to the original pylon-based fighters," she said quietly. "We could easily see the bomber replacing the starfighter entirely."

"Different roles, I think," Roberts pointed out. "Sometimes you need a positron lance, after all. And a bomber is a one-shot weapon—once your torpedoes are in space, you're a reduced threat. You're also inferior anti-missile platforms, where a starfighter is a key part of our defensive doctrine."

"It sounds like a Commonwealth system, sir," Michelle pointed out carefully. "Starfighter as a purely defensive platform mated with a new offensive weapon."

The Captain paused, the grin fading for a moment, then he chuckled.

"You're too clever for your own good," he pointed out. "I'll neither confirm nor deny your suggestion, Wing Commander. But yes, the Commonwealth does have the same system."

"You said you saw them from the other side," Michelle reminded him. There was no way he'd done that in exercises; she knew exactly who everyone she'd flown against as an opposing force had been. "There's no other way unless they were Terran."

"My big mouth," Roberts admitted. "Yes, I've commanded against Terran bombers. I can't tell you where or why, but I can tell you they almost killed us. If the Commonwealth had deployed bombers without us knowing they were coming…" He shook his head. "It would have been a massacre."

Michelle considered it herself and the image that came to mind was terrifying: *Alexander* blowing up because Altena had misjudged where her bombers were…except without the Alliance crews even knowing the bombers existed. Fourth Fleet probably would have taken the brunt of it…

"It would have been bad," she agreed. "We'd have lost the forward fleets at least."

She and Roberts shivered simultaneously and she considered him for a moment.

"You have someone with them?" she asked after a moment, wondering if she was getting too personal.

"Yes," he confirmed. "Captain Solace aboard *Camerone*, with Seventh Fleet. You? Alvarez?"

Michelle was a little surprised that the Captain even remembered her girlfriend from the old *Avalon*, but she'd do the same for any of her ex-subordinates, so…

"Yeah," she agreed. "She got bumped to Nurse-Commander and is serving aboard *Blacksmith*. She's one of the Reserve ships. Half of her main lances weren't working when they reactivated her, so she's being used as a hospital ship.

"Alvarez runs the nursing team for one of their main clinics," Michelle told her boss with no small amount of pride. "We don't get to see each other much anymore, but…she's doing well."

"We take what we can get during the war, Wing Commander," Roberts agreed. "We'd all rather spend time with our families and loved ones, but…our job is to make sure everyone else gets to as well."

"Agreed."

11

Coraline System
06:00 September 25, 2736 Earth Standard Meridian Date/Time
DSC-052 Kodiak

"STETSON STABILIZATION FIELDS SHUT DOWN," Houshian reported. "Welcome to the Coraline System, everyone. We are exactly on schedule."

It was early in the morning by the ship's schedule, and the daily shift change wasn't for another two hours, but every one of Kyle's senior officers and department heads had "somehow" ended up on the night watch when they would enter the home system of the Federation's largest ally.

"Our q-com was just pinged by Coraline Traffic Control before we exited FTL," Lieutenant Commander Teresa Jamison, the communications officer, reported. She was a dumpy woman with a perpetual smile, though Kyle was reasonably certain she was smarter than the befuddled expression made her look.

She was a junior department head on a capital ship, after all.

"We've confirmed our arrival and authentications," she continued.

"Hold one moment." Jamison's eyes took on the slightly glazed tone of someone communing with their implant. "Coraline Traffic Control confirms our orders and has asked us to hold position while they chart us a course. Traffic is apparently busy."

"You can say that again," Sterling noted. The balding tactical officer was embedded in the carrier's sensor arrays. "Take a look, everyone."

The tactical plot feeding into everyone's implants and showing on the main screen began to fill in as Sterling's people analyzed the data they were received from sensors. A first layer of rough detail appeared, then updated as the Commander linked into the network of Alliance q-probes—sensor platforms with quantum entanglement communicators —laid throughout the system.

Coraline was a dense system wrapped around a weak K-class orange dwarf star. In the same distance where Sol had three worlds, Coraline had six. Only one, Coral, was habitable, but the others provided easily accessible resources. Two massive gas giants orbited farther out, along with another half-dozen chunks of rock and ice.

Human industry had touched every single one of Coraline's four-teen worlds, from cloudscoops on the gas giants to massive mining operations on the uninhabitable inner worlds to observation posts and fighter bases on the outermost rocks.

Sublight ships, lacking the immense Class One mass manipulators needed for Alcubierre-Stetson drives, swarmed the space between those worlds. Hundreds of ships cut long, arcing courses through space, fueling and maintaining the heavy industry of the Imperium.

Kyle's trained eye, though, picked out the differences from his home system. The cloudscoops were physically bigger, their immense heat signatures warning of inefficiencies in their design made up for with size. There were more ships than there were in Castle, but the ships were smaller, slower.

For all of the energy and swarming activity in the star system, the informed observer could *see* why Coraline had a gross system product easily ten percent lower than Castle's. Different approaches to a thou-sand things added up to massive differences in freedom and economic prosperity.

"Captain, CTC is back in contact," Jamison told him. "They have a course for Houshian, and then they requested that I link you in directly to the Palace."

Coraline, of course, was also an *Imperium*—a constitutional monarchy with a caste-divided multicameral legislature. The Imperator was limited in many ways, but he wielded a direct power to make the Senators who ruled the Castle Federation green with envy.

"Of course," Kyle agreed. "Link me in."

He activated a privacy system on his implant, taking the call entirely in his head, where the rest of his crew couldn't see or hear. The image on the channel was of an older woman, with tightly braided white hair and a pristine old-fashioned black and gold uniform.

"Greetings, Captain Roberts," she said calmly. "I am Vera Strobel, Seneschal to His Excellency, Imperator John Erasmus von Coral."

Kyle's memory warned him that Strobel was dropping at least three of the Imperator's names. This was an informal call, it seemed.

"We appreciate your government and yourself taking the time to visit Coral and meet with His Excellency. The debt owed for the rescue of our people in Huī Xing cannot easily be paid, but His Excellency wishes to acknowledge the existence of the debt, if nothing more."

"I understand," Kyle told her. "I did my duty, my lady Seneschal."

"If only our own officers and Elector caste did their duty as bravely and as completely, Captain," Strobel told him with a smile. "I have made arrangements for you to meet with His Excellency tomorrow evening local time in Coral City. That will be ten hundred hours ESMDT," she concluded, making sure of the distinction.

"We will be there," he confirmed. There was no way he *wasn't* going to be exactly where the Imperator asked him to be.

"I've also been asked to request that you reach out to Elector Reuter," she continued. "He remembers your efforts on his behalf in the Huī Xing system and, I believe, will be inviting you to a private dinner tonight. He is in Lombard, which is more closely aligned with ESMDT than Coral City," she concluded with a smile.

"Welcome to the Coraline System, Captain Roberts. If there is anything you or your ships require, I am forwarding a q-com code for my staff office here at the Palace. We will make certain any need of yourself or your task group is met in full."

———

PURE IMPLANT CONVERSATIONS gave Kyle a headache now, an unwelcome souvenir of the injuries that had grounded him from being a fighter pilot. Shaking his head against it, he checked the status of his ship.

"Houshian, do we have the course from CTC laid in?" he asked.

"We do," she replied instantly. "It's a bit of a zigzag, but it'll get us to orbit in about six hours. We're being directed to the Coral-Reef Lagrange Three Point. It's their main fleet anchorage; we'll be sharing it with two carriers, three cruisers and a battleship."

Six capital ships was a *lot* of mobile firepower, but Kyle couldn't begrudge the Imperium the defense of their homeworld. Castle had just as many starships, and both systems had literally thousands of starfighters positioned throughout their space.

If the Commonwealth wanted to tangle with the core worlds of the Alliance, the Terrans would pay for the privilege—and if they truly wanted to bring the Alliance into their Unity, sooner or later, they'd have to.

The thought wasn't as reassuring as it could have been.

"Forward the course to *Alexander*," he ordered. "I'll be in my office if needed. Commander Sterling has the watch."

"Yes, sir," Sterling replied with a crisp salute.

Kyle returned the salute and exited the bridge. His office was literally steps down the corridor, positioned so he could easily return to the bridge in an emergency. With the carrier's systems, he could command the ship from anywhere aboard, but his crew needed to see him.

Closing the door behind him, he stopped at the minifridge slash automated bar and served himself a cup of coffee. He might have already been up for several hours, but it sounded like he was going to need to be up well into his own "evening" as well.

Settling into his chair, he brought the communication system up on his wallscreen and plugged into the number for Elector Wilhelm Reuter, a member of the Imperium's caste of military nobility who he'd met as Vice Admiral Wilhelm Reuter, a Commonwealth prisoner of war.

The screen chirped and loaded a spinning "waiting" screen of *Kodiak*'s ursine-soldier commissioning seal for a minute or so, then the image of the old officer they'd pulled out of a Terran prison camp greeted him.

Time had been better to Reuter than it had to many. He remained a slim old man with pure white hair and an obvious cybernetic eye, but he was no longer gaunt with stress and hunger, and his eyes were brighter than they had been before.

He wore a prim civilian suit despite the early hour in his city and smiled brightly as he saw Kyle.

"Captain Roberts!" Reuter exclaimed, then paused. "It is Captain now, correct? Not Force Commander?"

"Force Commander is always a temporary title, Vice Admiral," Kyle explained. "It is simply Captain now."

"There is nothing simple about you, my dear Captain," the old man said with a chuckle. Age still undermined his voice, but the quaver he'd spoken with in Huī Xing was gone. "You are in Coraline, yes?"

"I am," Kyle confirmed. "Your Imperator summoned me here."

"Good boy," Reuter replied with another chuckle, clearly recognizing the incongruity of describing the ruler of twelve systems as a "boy." "I've spoken to our good Seneschal as well; she told she'd pass my request on to you."

"She said there was a dinner invitation?" Kyle asked carefully.

"Yes! The least of the tiniest of beginnings of repayments of the debt I owe you, for my life and the lives of my crew," the Imperial noble told him. "Once I knew you were coming, I arranged a small private dinner at my estates. I would be honored if you and your senior officers would be able to join me."

"How small are we talking, Elector?" *Kodiak*'s Captain asked. "My senior officers are easily half a dozen strong."

"I will have a few guests of my own," Reuter told him, his eyes dancing gleefully. "Individuals of some importance you should likely meet. Feel free to bring as many of your officers as you wish. Believe me, my estate has the space and my chef will enjoy the challenge."

"As you wish, Elector," Kyle replied, recognizing the sparkle in the old man's eyes. "Transmit the coordinates and the time to my ship? I will make sure I and my staff are there on time."

"Of course, Captain. Dress uniforms, if you please, though don't feel obliged to wear your decorations. I certainly won't be wearing mine, after all!"

"Thank you, Elector."

―――

KYLE HAD BARELY FINISHED PASSING the invitation on to his CAG and XO; as well as Captain Sarka and her own senior officer; when the door to his office—technically secured, even during working hours—slid open without any warning and Karl Nebula entered.

"You know, advertising the fact that you can override the Captain's locks is probably not the best idea in the galaxy," Kyle said mildly, keeping his glare at slightly below lethal levels. "We are sensitive about the illusion that we are gods aboard our ships."

"I recommend losing all illusions about gods, stars, voids or whatever spiritual nonsense you adhere to," Nebula replied calmly. "I've been clinically dead twice. No light, no god, just…nothing."

"You've lived an interesting life for a diplomat," the Captain told him. "Why exactly are you barging into my office, Mr. Nebula?"

"This dinner tonight. You didn't think it worth mentioning to the *diplomat*?" Nebula asked.

"Apparently, I didn't need to," Kyle pointed out. "I'll confess, Mr. Nebula, you're not top of my mind when someone asks me to bring my senior officers along to a private dinner."

"Vice Admiral, retired, the Elector Marquis von Terrace Secundus Wilhelm Reuter is not just 'someone,' Captain Roberts," Nebula replied, and Kyle suspected there was a great deal of effort involved in the diplomat not visibly rolling his eyes.

"Reuter is, more than any other person alive, responsible for the current Imperator getting his job," the diplomat continued. "There were *twenty-five* men and women with sufficient connection to the Imperial Line to stand as candidates after Caleb von Coral died. Five did, including his son.

"Reuter was the one who begged, borrowed, bullied and bribed the rest of the Electors to vote for Caleb's son instead of the other, uniformly older and more experienced, candidates. The triumph of hope and romanticism over practicality—though I suspect much of it was that Reuter simply *knew* John Erasmus von Coral and understood just what that young man was capable of."

"He seems to have done all right," Kyle noted. He didn't study Imperial politics except where they impacted Alliance operations.

"'All right,' he says," Nebula laughed. "The Imperium has done more to close the economic, industrial, and technological gap between them and the Federation in the ten years John has been Imperator than in his father's entire rule. He's a dangerous man, valuable on our side but a risk for the future."

"And your point?"

"My point, my dear naïve Captain Roberts, is that it is unlikely that Wilhelm Reuter is hosting a private party of people he feels are important without including the Imperator. If he is there, however, it is because the *Imperator himself* wishes to speak with you informally.

"Now, Captain, do we at least agree that is not a conversation you want to walk into unarmed and without your best ally at your side?"

Kyle sighed. He didn't know enough about Imperial politics to argue Nebula's conclusions, which gave a certain weight to the man's point.

"This isn't supposed to be political, Nebula," he pointed out.

"When you're Wilhelm Reuter, everything is political," the diplomat replied. "And when you're the Stellar fucking Fox, everything is political. I'd suggest getting used to it."

"Fine. You're invited," Kyle snapped. "Now, can I have my office back? Shocking as it may seem, I actually *do* have work to do."

12

Coraline System
18:00 September 25, 2736 Earth Standard Meridian Date/Time
Coral, Private Estate near Lombard City

As Kyle's shuttle settled down onto the landing pad, it began to finally sink in just what kind of "somebody" Elector Wilhelm Reuter actually was.

There were, according to the latest files he'd seen, just over two million members of the Elector caste in the Imperium. Spread across twelve worlds, their main distinguishing privilege was the right to vote for the next Imperator. In exchange, they were expected to serve the Imperium in public service of some kind, usually government or military, despite generally being of well-above-average means.

Very few of them, he suspected, owned massive estates wrapped around a home that was as much built into a mountain as on it. Terrace Secundus was a sprawling complex wrapped around three mountains, with mining operations carefully concealed beneath sweeping valleys of farms and vineyards, all curving back up to the immense gothic monstrosity of the central manor itself.

Decorative as the artificially aged stone towers that flanked the landing pad were, however, his implant warned him that the shuttle was being painted by targeting scanners from them, presumably linked to either short-range railguns or even surface-to-space missile batteries higher up the mountain.

"Look there and there," Nebula told him over his implant, dropping icons onto Kyle's vision that highlighted soldiers manning carefully concealed weapons positions covering the entrance to the manor. "Those aren't Reuter's guards. Those are Praetorians.

"Von Coral is here."

Kyle nodded, burying his trepidation under his trademark bright grin.

"Well, then," he said aloud. "Let's go meet our hosts."

———

REUTER WAS WAITING for them alone on the landing pad as the collection of Federation officers disembarked. He strode over and shook Kyle's hand firmly, bestowing a warm smile on the rest of them.

"Welcome to Coral, officers," he told them. "My estate air control informs me that the shuttle from *Alexander* with Captain Sarka and her officers is only a few minutes behind you. We should make our way to the safety zone."

"Agreed."

The aged aristocrat led them back behind a safety barrier, with a solid twenty seconds to spare before even the first warmth of the shuttle's engines began to wash over the landing pad. For several minutes after that, even the safety barrier wouldn't permit conversation as the shuttle dropped to the surface, switching to chemical thrusters for safety at the last moment.

Sarka's pilot dropped the craft neatly beside the shuttle from *Kodiak*, the pair of Federation craft holding pride of place in the center of the landing pad. They were, in fact, the only craft on the landing pad at all.

"I take it your other guests didn't arrive by shuttle?" Kyle asked.

"No," Reuter confirmed. "We have a landing strip around the other side of the mountain for aircraft of all types; only the surface-to-orbit shuttles require the true ceramacrete pad. Come, I have transportation waiting to get us to the main house."

Once Sarka and Altena, a bulkily built, attractive woman of Kyle's own towering height, had exited the shuttle, along with a slim man of average height and faded black skin Kyle presumed to be Sarka's XO, Reuter gestured for everyone to follow him.

A quartet of high-based electric utility vehicles waited at the edge of the pad, with drivers in plain black uniforms out and standing by the doors. Kyle didn't need Nebula's warning icons to identify them as bodyguards more than chauffeurs. Just the way the men stood told him that; the spy highlighting the concealed holsters wasn't necessary.

"If you, Captain Sarka, and Mr. Nebula would like to join me?" Reuter said Kyle, gesturing toward the lead vehicle while calmly revealing he knew who the diplomat was.

"Of course," Kyle agreed cheerfully, following the old ex-officer into the vehicle. Once the four of them were seated, the driver stepped back into the gray-painted SUV and immediately put it in gear.

"It's only a few minutes to the house," Reuter told them. "We'll be scanned along the way for any unexpected surprises, weapons or explosives, for example." His smile turned pained. "I wish I could pretend our concern was for Commonwealth infiltrators, but I won't deny that our system has created certain…disadvantaged groups that would see value in damaging our alliance with Castle."

"It would take a lot to damage that alliance," Kyle pointed out. "We are, after all, at the point where we will hang separately if we don't hang together."

"Well said, Captain," the Imperial replied. "The Commonwealth is determined to conquer us. We are determined to remain free. But…" He sighed. "There are those inside the Imperium who do not regard themselves as free.

"How right they are is a matter of debate," he conceded, clearly realizing that none of the Federation officers could politely comment on the Imperium's system of castes and classes of citizens. "What matters right now is that their grievances lead them to threaten the war effort, which we cannot afford."

As he spoke, the vehicle came to a halt and a trio of soldiers in black power armor stepped out to surround them, arm-mounted sensor packs sweeping the vehicles.

"Those are Praetorians," Nebula murmured, echoing his earlier comment to Kyle. "Is the Imperator *here*?"

Reuter chuckled.

"That answer is complicated and a matter of politics," he explained. "For the Imperator to attend a dinner, it is a state affair, a matter of diplomats and courtiers—especially when officers of even an allied foreign military are involved.

"I did not wish that rigmarole, so I did not invite the Imperator. I did, however, invite my late best friend's son, John von Coral."

"Who comes with Praetorian Guards and might, *perhaps*, be the same person as the Imperator?" Kyle asked.

"Indeed," Reuter confirmed. "But I did not invite the Imperator. Do you understand?"

"Nope," Kyle replied cheerfully, "but I suspect the niceties are more relevant to the Imperium than to a gruff, straightforward Federation soldier like myself."

Reuter coughed a chuckle.

"This is true, Captain," he confessed. "But you must allow us our games. What kind of Byzantine imperial court would we be without them?!"

————

THE OUTSIDE of Reuter's home might have looked like an old Earth castle transplanted onto a new world, but the interior was as modern as it could be. Hidden lights suffused the entire space, lighting both the immense foyer that the aristocrat led them through and the smaller but still intimidating dining room just off from it.

The walls had been cut from the native stone of the mountain, a pale gray granite, and done so well enough that it was impossible to tell where the part of the house built on the side of the mountain ended and the part dug into the mountain began.

There weren't many people waiting around the large dark-red wooden table Reuter led them to. Two were clear bodyguards, Praetorians in black suits instead of combat armor, but twitching with a contained energy that allowed Kyle to identify them as combat cyborgs.

Three others, two women and a man, were strangers to him, though Nebula threw IDs on them. The youngest of them was Lord Captain Meredith Reuter, their host's granddaughter and the commander of one of the supercarriers orbiting above them. She shared her father's height and slim build, but her golden blond hair had so far avoided the white that marked the old Admiral.

The other strangers were Xi van Coral, the enigmatically unreadable dark-skinned woman married to the Imperator, and Melech Herschel, the Imperium's Chancellor of the Treasury, a hook-nosed man with jet-black hair.

The last two Kyle recognized. He'd only met them once, in a video conference where the fate of a world he'd liberated from the Commonwealth had been decided. Standing next to Captain Reuter was the solid and shaven-bald form of Sky Marshal Octavian von Stenger, the supreme uniformed commander of the Imperium's military.

The only person sitting in the room occupied the head of the table, one leg lazily hooked over the arm of the chair in a relaxed pose that would have horrified two star nations' worth of protocol experts. The dark-haired man was younger than Kyle, but the plain platinum circlet he wore around his head told the truth.

John Erasmus Michael Albrecht von Coral, Imperator of the Coraline Imperium, was not a man to be taken lightly, regardless of his age.

He sprang to his feet at the arrival of the Federation officers, however, approaching with a smile and extending his hand directly to Kyle.

"Captain Roberts, it is a pleasure to meet you in person," he told Kyle. "Could you introduce me to your officers? The smell of William's chef's preparations is starting to drift in here and I just heard Octavian's stomach growl, but we can make time to know our allies, can we not?"

Something in the mildly pained expression of one of the six men and women who ran the Alliance's war effort told Kyle that John von Coral was a *very* different person in private than Kyle had expected.

13

IT SEEMED THAT SOMEONE, probably von Coral himself, had given the Imperial contingent strict orders not to discuss business over dinner. Kyle found it extremely unlikely that this collection of three of the senior members of the Imperium's government, an aristocratic ex–flag officer and a current capital ship commander normally went two hours without any business coming up.

Dinner was, unsurprisingly, one of the best meals Kyle had eaten in a very long time, and not just because he spent most of his time eating meals aboard a warship. Reuter clearly employed an extremely skilled chef, one who knew not only how to work with the finest ingredients but also when the best option was simplicity.

Once the meal was finished, the servers brought out small glasses of brandy, and von Coral rose to his feet.

"If I could have everyone's attention," he said calmly, his carefully trained voice cutting through the conversation. "We are here today for a more informal version of what I will be doing in the morning: thanking Captain Roberts for the rescue of twenty-one thousand, four hundred and eight civilians and military personnel of the Coraline Imperium.

"Tomorrow, Captain, I will hang a fancy piece of jewelry around your neck for the galaxy to see," von Coral told them. "But for tonight, a toast: to the Stellar Fox! Long may he confound our enemies!"

"The Stellar Fox!" everyone except Kyle cheered back, and he raised his own glass in silent salute to the Imperator.

"Now, I need to steal you for a few minutes, Captain Roberts," von Coral continued, his voice now pitched to carry to Kyle alone. "Mr. Nebula may come with you if you like; Octavian and Melech will accompany us. Xi and William will take good care of your officers, I promise."

"Karl," Kyle murmured to the diplomat with an accompanying implant note. "With us, please."

He rose, sent Taggart and Song an implant message letting them know what was going on, and followed the Imperator as the young man slipped through a not-quite-concealed door in the side of the dining room.

The other side of the door was an elegant drawing room, with carefully upholstered wood furniture in a style that came and went out of fashion on every world...and hadn't been in fashion on Coral since Reuter had been Kyle's age.

The ruler of twelve systems stepped over to a sideboard and calmly poured out five glasses of brandy, waiting for his subordinates to file in and close the door behind them.

"I meant every word I said, Captain," he told Kyle. "I only know three of the people you pulled out of Huī Xing personally, but the other twenty-some thousand of my subjects were no less my responsibility and no less deserving of my attention for that.

"I owe you. Tomorrow's stately formalities are an acknowledgement of that, not a payment of it. Though," he added with a wicked smile, "I suspect that the Imperial Starburst will be a useful stick for your friends on the Senate to use when beating Randall over the head to get you your promotion."

Kyle swallowed hard and said nothing. The Imperial Starburst was the Coraline Imperium's highest award for valor. That would put him at…three. The highest awards for valor from *three* of the Alliance's members, not including his own home system, where he'd only received the *second*-highest award. Twice.

"You're going to need a separate wall just for awards that are normally given out once in a lifetime," the Sky Marshal observed dryly. "You might just set a new record before you're done, Captain."

"I am not the first to be awarded by multiple Alliance powers," Kyle replied. "I believe there were four officers and two enlisted personnel awarded both the Senatorial Medal of Honor and the Imperial Starburst in the last war."

"You'll be at three tomorrow, and politics is the only reason you don't have an SMH and an Admiral's star," von Coral said flatly. "Both may yet still come your way, though the Starburst will admittedly only help with the rank, not the medal.

"The record, if you're curious, is five," he continued. "William's older brother held the highest awards for valor from Coraline, Castle, Phoenix, the Trade Factor, and Hessian."

"Unfortunately, the one from Hessian was posthumous," von Stenger said quietly.

"Your time here is limited, my liege," Herschel pointed out, the Chancellor taking a sip of his brandy. "We should get to the point."

"This is part of the point, my dear Chancellor," the Imperator replied. "But you're right; we need to be back on a suborbital in forty minutes.

"Captain Roberts," he turned back to Kyle. "We are, of course, aware of your mission, even if it isn't taking place under the auspices of the Alliance. Antioch and their allies also reached out to us. They were desperate, and I don't think they realized just how much stress that action could potentially place on the relationship between our nations."

"They bloody well did," Herschel replied. "Don't be fooled, my liege. Antioch might not have realized…but the request for *our* aid came from the Istanbul government. Since Antioch had already called for Federation aid and been promised it, the only reason Istanbul would ask for *our* help is if someone put them up to it."

"They are also desperate," von Coral said calmly. "But yes, it seems likely there are hands working in the shadows here, Captain Roberts. Even if these pirate attacks are entirely homegrown, *someone* is working to use them as a weapon against our Alliance.

"And I am quite certain that someone is Terran. I will not permit the Alliance of Free Stars to fail," he stated flatly. "My father and I have poured too much treasure and precious blood into turning back the tide of Commonwealth expansion. I will not allow our conflict for influence over irrelevant worlds to weaken the bulwark we have constructed.

"Do you understand me, Captain Roberts?"

"I believe so, my lord," Kyle confirmed. "I have no desire or intent to cause difficulties with whoever you have sent to the region."

"We haven't sent anyone yet, but Istanbul does have the right to ask for our help," the Sky Marshal interjected. "Just as Antioch did to ask the Federations. We cannot not send help without risking the trade agreements."

"And those agreements are as valuable to us as they are to Castle or the Renaissance systems," Herschel told him. "The Rimward Stars are...poor and scattered and barely industrialized by modern standards, but they are a massive market mostly lacking in internal FTL transport capacity. Trade into that region fuels much of the war effort of the Alliance's key powers."

"Like Castle, we cannot spare much," the Imperator told Kyle. "I both want to avoid conflict with Castle and achieve the maximum effect out of what we can send. While this won't be an Alliance operation, I think it is wise for us to coordinate our efforts, agreed?"

Nebula's stiff motionlessness next to Kyle warned him that he was in dangerous waters, but he had a good idea of what the Imperium wanted now...and it was what Castle wanted too. To solve the pirate problem *without* triggering an economic power struggle between the Alliance's two main powers.

"We are dispatching a single ship, the *Rameses*-class strike cruiser

Thoth," von Stenger told Kyle. "Commanding officer, Captain Elector Yann von Lambert. He's junior to you by a full grade; *Thoth* is an older ship. The entire *Rameses* class only avoided decommissioning due to the onset of the war."

"Von Lambert is also at Coral-Reef LaGrange Three," von Coral noted. "He has been informed he is under your command. His ship has been fully loaded with the Arrow-B type fighters, and her deflectors have been retrofitted to a modern standard."

"This is far more help than we had hoped for," Kyle told them. "I and the Federation are grateful."

"We fight a common enemy, Captain Roberts, and I see Terra's hand in this mess," the Imperator replied. "Find them, Captain. Find them and bring them to ground. We cannot afford knives in our back!"

"That is my mission, my lord. I do not intend to fail."

14

Coraline System
16:00 September 26, 2736 Earth Standard Meridian Date/Time
DSC-052 Kodiak

KYLE HAD to admit that the Imperial Starburst was an utterly *gorgeous* piece of jewelry, managing to be elegant and understated while still being made of platinum and living coral. It was the first medal he'd been given to require *feeding*, but they'd included a carefully designed and sized box that would handle that for him.

The Imperium knew how to keep pieces of coral from their homeworld's ocean alive indefinitely, though Kyle's understanding was that only the Imperator himself was allowed to give it to anyone.

Any chunk of Coraline coral meant the bearer was in the Imperator's favor—and this particular one also told anyone who saw it that the wearer was regarded as a hero by the Coraline Imperium and, like most nation's highest medals of honor, entitled him to take a salute from Imperial officers of any rank.

He spent a good two minutes studying the medal and the box,

thankful that the ceremony had been simple—if broadcast live across the entire Alliance. There was, after all, simple…and *simple*.

His allocated time for ego-wallowing over, however, he placed the Starburst in its box and slid it into the drawer that also contained the highest awards for valor from the Tranquility and Alizon system governments.

"Commander Jamison, can you get me a q-com link to the strike cruiser *Thoth*?" he asked. "I need to speak to Captain von Lambert at his earliest convenience."

"Yes, sir," his communications officer responded instantly. "Give me a few moments; I'll coordinate with von Lambert's people and see if he's available."

"Carry on, Lieutenant Commander," Kyle told her. He stretched and grabbed a beer while he waited for the crews of the two warships to sort out their Captains' schedules. He suspected that von Lambert would give him flag officer priority, which wouldn't leave him much time.

He managed to at least make it back to his chair and open his beer, which was *slightly* longer than he'd expected, before Jamison pinged his implant.

"Sir, I have Captain von Lambert on the q-com for you. Shall I connect him?"

"Please, Commander," he ordered, linking the channel to his wall screen and leaning back to survey the face of his new not-quite-subordinate.

"Captain Roberts," Yann von Lambert greeted him. The Imperial Captain was older than Kyle had expected, with multiple visible scars crisscrossing his face. His skin was naturally quite dark, but the injuries laced it with white lines.

"Captain von Lambert. Thank you for taking my call," Kyle told the scarred man.

"We're heading the same way, as I understand," the Imperial replied. "And I presume the Sky Marshal has informed you of my orders?"

"We're both headed to the Antioch-Serengeti Free Trade Zone to deal with pirates. The Sky Marshal suggested we should work together."

Von Lambert chuckled.

"I *know* that's not how the old man phrased it, Captain Roberts. I and *Thoth* are under your command for the duration. I appreciate your attempt to spare my ship's fragile ego," von Lambert continued with a grin, "but let's avoid games that would put us at risk of a critical miscommunication in the middle of a firefight. This may not be an Alliance operation, but I think operating under those established protocols will avoid potential issues. Do you agree, Captain Roberts?"

"That makes perfect sense to me, Captain von Lambert," Kyle agreed with a smile. He should have expected that the Sky Marshal would have picked the officer they put under his command very, very carefully.

"Before we get tied up in protocols and formalities, Captain, I need to say thank you," von Lambert continued quietly. "We have never met, but you have changed my life twice. My brother was in the Huī Xing prison platforms…and my daughter was on *Ansem Gulf*."

Kyle winced. *Ansem Gulf* had been a passenger liner with fifteen thousand passengers seized by pirates before the war started. His ship, the battlecruiser *Alamo,* had gone to rescue the civilians. When the dust had settled, Flight Commander Kyle Roberts had been in command of the survivors of *Alamo*'s fighter wing…and the ship had been retaken.

"Twice you have saved the lives of those close to me, Captain Roberts. Serving under your command is a privilege."

"I hope you feel the same once we're done," Kyle told him, more than a bit touched by the man's words. Meeting the families of those he'd spent the blood of his people to pull out of the fire reminded him why he did what he did.

"I'd like to invite you, your XO, and your CAG aboard *Kodiak* for a final planning dinner before we set off for the Free Trade Zone," he continued. "Captain Sarka and her senior officers will join us as well. We have a lot of work in front of us, and the sooner we get to it—"

"The fewer people die," von Lambert finished. It might not have been exactly what Kyle was planning to say, but it carried the meaning better.

"Exactly, Captain. May I have my staff expect you aboard at twenty hundred hours?"

"We will be there," von Lambert confirmed.

———

WITH THE SENIOR officers from three ships aboard, the small dining room attached to Kyle's quarters felt almost cramped. The room was intended to host all of his department heads with room to spare, but nine officers required squeezing in extra chairs.

If he'd wanted to include anyone else, Kyle would have needed to open up *Kodiak*'s currently sealed and unused flag officer quarters. That felt presumptuous enough he'd avoid if possible, though, and the Captain's dining room fit everyone in.

Captain Kristyna Sarka, Vice Commodore Elsie Altena and Senior Fleet Commander Hanif Kanaan represented *Alexander*, occupying one side of the table.

Captain von Lambert, who was only senior to Altena and Kanaan by virtue of time in grade given the difference between where the Federation and the Imperium ranked a Captain, sat at Kyle's right hand. Kyle or Sarka's equal in Imperial service would have been a Lord Captain, but the Federation declined to give starship command to anyone below O-7, whereas the Imperium had some of the older ships under O-6s like von Lambert.

Von Lambert's XO was a shaven-headed older man named Hanne Knef with an almost silvery tinge to his skin. It appeared to be a cosmetic mod, not a transhuman's circuitry, which was odd to see in a naval officer—especially an *Imperial* naval officer. If a man with visible cosmetic mods had risen to full Commander in the Imperial Navy, he was probably *very* good at his job.

Thoth's CAG was possibly the oldest person in the room, a small woman with wispy white hair and multiple obvious cybernetic replacements. Lieutenant Colonel Radomíra Horaček was a veteran of the last war who'd sacrificed an eye, an arm and a leg against the Commonwealth—and then returned to the colors when the war began anew.

Vice Commodore Song and Senior Fleet Commander Taggart sat directly opposite Kyle, the pair neatly tag-teaming the Imperial officers over the course of the meal to pull them into the conversation.

Once the meal was over and the stewards had cleared away the plates, Kyle picked up his glass and rose to face the table.

"Ladies, gentlemen," he said calmly as he held up his glass in a toast. "Spacers of the Free Stars, I give you liberty and the Alliance!"

"The Alliance!" the others chorused back.

"This isn't exactly an Alliance op," he continued after a moment, "but the toast seems appropriate nonetheless. One of the reasons our governments have put so much emphasis on this mission is to avoid any risk of this crisis triggering conflict between us—the Alliance of Free Stars is the only bulwark either of our nations has against the Commonwealth's expansion."

He let that sink in.

"Of course, the truth is that the economies of the Alliance run on trade as much as industry," he reminded them. "And trading with each other only takes us so far. Without the peacetime trade routes into Commonwealth space, the systems to Rimward of our nations become far more economically vital.

"Even if we had not signed agreements binding us to protect these star systems, it is critical to our interests that freighters be able to move through this area safely. Until recently, this was enabled by us selling warships to the richer powers at bargain prices."

Everyone in the room had been briefed. He didn't need to tell them what had been happening to those warships.

"So far, the pirates don't appear to have grown bold enough to attack even minor systems directly, but..." Kyle shook his head. "Given how rare any pirate with interstellar ships is, that can only be a matter of time," he warned them. "The possible haul from raiding even a poor system will become tempting, especially as Alcubierre-Stetson ships become rarer on the ground."

"We can't let that happen," von Lambert pointed out. "Putting aside any economic consideration, that would be an atrocity of a scale not seen in those stars...ever."

"Easiest way to stop it is to find and kill the pirates," Sarka replied. "Do we have a plan?"

"Our first priority has to be the protection of shipping between the star systems," Kyle told them. He sent an implant command and a holoprojector descended from the ceiling, lighting up the space above the table with a three-dimensional map of the area of operations.

"We are sixty light-years, roughly sixteen days' travel, from Antioch," he continued. That system flashed in gold on the map. "Serengeti and Istanbul represent the other key systems of the Free Trade Zone." All three systems now flashed gold.

"Around those three are sixteen other systems of various economic weight that don't have their own interstellar shipping or warships and are dependent on the FTZ shipping lines." Those systems flashed silver.

"Traditionally, the FTZ has run about thirty ships, funded by a mix of investment by their governments, private investment, and investment by Castle, Coraline, and the Renaissance Trade Factor," he noted. "Right now, over half of those ships are missing or confirmed lost. That's a *lot* of money and a lot of lives, people.

"The Antioch government started convoying shipments a month ago. They lost *Crusader* in that effort, leaving Antioch without any interstellar warships. They've been holding ships inside their sublight defense perimeter since. The original intent was to wait for Serengeti's carrier to arrive, but the timeline on that is... Well, we'll be there first," he finished.

Kyle watched his officers' faces as the numbers sank home. An Alcubierre-Stetson drive interstellar freighter was, roughly, two percent of the GSP of a prosperous system to build. The only reason the three systems at the core of the Antioch-Serengeti Free Trade Zone had managed to assemble thirty was because the Alliance powers had subsidized their purchases.

Losing fifteen of those ships could easily be a crippling blow to the Free Trade Zone. Losing more would destroy it and likely undermine the economic and technological advance of the sector by a century.

"Since the largest concentration of remaining shipping is in Antioch, we are heading there first," Kyle continued. "From there, *Kodiak* will proceed to Istanbul, *Alexander* will proceed to Serengeti, and *Thoth* will either escort a convoy through the secondary systems or accompany one of the other ships, depending on where people are headed from Antioch.

"While our first task is the protection of the local ships and systems from the pirates, information gathering is extremely high-priority. We *need* to know more. We need to know who these pirates are, where they're based, and whether or not the Commonwealth is supporting them or simply stirring the pot."

"Imperial Intelligence is over ninety percent certain the Commonwealth is involved," von Lambert told them. "But…"

"But that could simply be them pulling strings in the local governments," Kyle replied. "I put the odds at no better than fifty percent that there are actually Commonwealth warships out here…but if they're here, our job will be to put them down.

"Along with the pirates."

15

Salvatore System
09:00 October 4, 2736 Earth Standard Meridian Date/Time
BC-305 Poseidon

WHOEVER HAD NAMED the habitable planet in the Salvatore system "Neverwinter" had clearly already completed the climate survey, James Tecumseh concluded. The planet sat in the inner portion of its yellow star's Goldilocks zone and had zero axial tilt.

The equatorial zone was barely habitable by human standards, but the massive archipelagos farther north and south were basically tropical paradises. The weather was calm, the soil had taken readily to human-compatible crops and there was enough sunshine to allow solar power to be a main source of energy.

The planet was a paradise by any standard. Now…it was a tourist destination for the rich and wealthy of a dozen star systems. The local economy was surprisingly weak, Neverwinter having acquired a culture of doing just enough to get by—"getting by" in paradise, after all, being better than many people in the galaxy worked for.

GLYNN STEWART

Interstellar tourism was a game for the wealthy from the tourists' side and a game for scale on the transport companies' side. A single ticket on an interstellar vacation ship could cost as much as six months' salary for an average worker—but an Alcubierre-Stetson drive liner carried between fifteen and twenty thousand people.

Which meant that there were no possible circumstances under which Commodore James Tecumseh of the Terran Commonwealth Navy was going to let "Commodore" Coati anywhere near a tourist liner.

So, *Poseidon* and *Chariot* found themselves in the Salvatore system, cutting a fast ballistic orbit toward the scheduled emergence point of the cruise liner *Ocean Dreams*.

"What's the status of the jamming platforms?" he asked Commodore Sherazi over their implant link.

"We have eighty-five in space accompanying us on our orbit," the other man told him. "As soon as they go live, no one in Salvatore is going to see anything but static and IR flares for at least an hour."

"It better work," James murmured. His orders were to avoid detection.

"It will work," Sherazi told him. "It will definitely work better than letting those psychopaths loose on a ship full of twenty thousand rich idiots."

Planetary populations were large. Finding twenty thousand people rich enough to pay for an interstellar ticket wasn't easy, exactly, but it was definitely doable...but it made those people a target.

"Starfighters?" he asked his flag deck staff aloud.

"Colonel Duke and Colonel Costanzo have their wings ready to deploy," Lieutenant Amoto told him. "They report all launch tubes are loaded and they can have all their birds in the air in under sixty seconds."

James grunted his acceptance, watching the screen.

He didn't *like* commerce raiding, but he saw the value—especially of capturing thousands of rich(and hence *visible*)tourists. Plus, if his intelligence was correct, Serengeti's government saw the value as well and...

"Alcubierre emergence! We have two ships—confirm ID on *Ocean Dreams* and a second ship."

"I need ID on that other ship," James snapped.

"Warship, Renaissance Factor design," Sherazi told him. "Looks like a carrier, I'm going to guess *Livingston*-class, which would make her *Maasai*."

"There's only one RTF-built warship out here," James agreed. "Trigger the jamming platforms and launch the starfighters. We have our customer."

———

JAMES mentally saluted *Maasai*'s commander. A bubble of space two million kilometers across dissolved into static and random heat flares, rendering their sensors almost completely useless at any extended range…and they had starfighters and q-probes in space in seconds.

"Inform Colonel Duke she has the call," he instructed Amoto. "*Poseidon* and *Chariot* are clear to engage with missiles but are not to approach within one million kilometers of *Maasai*. Even with this jamming, we cannot risk approaching closer with the capital ships until *Maasai* is captured or destroyed."

And *captured* was unlikely.

"What are we looking at for starfighters?" he asked, watching the tactical feed through his neural implant as the ninety starfighters aboard his two cruisers blasted into space. *Maasai* was an old-enough carrier that she only had ten squadrons aboard, which meant his people outnumbered the Serengeti ships…but if the Serengeti crews had modern ships, they could take a lot more losses than he wanted.

"Warbook is calling them Typhoons," the analyst running his data feed told him. "Castle Federation fifth-generation fighter, a pretty standard export product for the Federation. Slower, more lightly armed and more lightly shielded than our Katanas."

"And the Serengeti military knows it," James murmured. "Duke, you getting this?" he asked his senior starfighter officer.

"Aye, sir," she replied over the link. Even with the communication taking place at the speed of thought, the starfighter pilot managed to sound distracted. "They're holding position around *Maasai* while their probes try and nail us down. They're not sure what to do with this jamming."

"I'd hope not," James said dryly. For each jamming platform they'd fabricated, they'd used up components intended to manufacture *four* missiles, and he wasn't expecting to get them back. The cost of the scheme vastly outweighed its effectiveness...except that it allowed him to go after a ship full of civilians without bringing Coati.

"They know how old the Typhoon is," he continued. "Don't assume they match the warbook."

"Agreed," Duke replied in a tone that suggested that the flag officer shouldn't be telling her how to do her job. "Most likely modernized the deflectors and upgraded the engines. Q-probes aren't showing a sufficiently overcharged zero-point cell to feed a more powerful lance, though, which means I have them outranged."

She paused.

"We'll deal with them, sir. What about the carrier?"

James closed his eyes, sighing internally and making sure it didn't carry over the neural link. He didn't like it, but...they couldn't demand that the carrier surrender.

"Take her out," he ordered flatly. "Leave *Ocean Dreams* for Barbados. We'll have missiles leading the way, but I can't afford to spend many of them."

"I wasn't planning on using any of mine," Duke told him with a chuckle.

"Good hunting, Colonel."

The pilot dropped the communication channel and James leant back in his command chair, studying the battlespace.

Sherazi's engineers had done them proud. The jammers were an extravagant overkill to a complex problem, but they *worked*. Even *Poseidon*'s computers, which were running the jamming platforms, were having problems making sense of the hash of radiation and heat signatures the platforms were turning everything into.

Scattered through the chaos were islands of greater accuracy where the Commonwealth battle group's q-probes moved. The battlecruiser's computers were crunching all of the data from the probes and the starfighters, resolving over a hundred separate datapoints into a *relatively* clear picture.

The Serengeti crews clearly didn't have as many q-probes out and didn't have the advantage of being linked into the jamming platforms themselves. James's people couldn't localize the enemy probes, but he could guess at their maximum reach simply because their starfighters remained stubbornly wrapped around *Maasai*.

"Starfighters are ten minutes from contact. Fighter missile range in two."

"Watch for the Serengetis to launch missiles," James ordered. "Are our birds in the air?"

"First salvo firing now," Sherazi interrupted. "Three salvos from each ship, just under a hundred missiles total. If they haven't upgraded her..."

"They've upgraded her," James concluded into the silence his flag captain left. "It's a question of how much."

"We'll see in sixty seconds," *Poseidon*'s CO told him. "They'll pick them out of the jamming in time for the starfighters to intercept as well. Even this mess won't hide missiles for long."

The missiles were clearly the first thing the defenders picked up. They were still almost a full light-second out when the starfighters finally sortied, sixteen remaining in a tight defensive net around *Maasai* while the other sixty-four charged out at the missiles.

They were presumably guessing that the starfighters were coming on the same vector as the missiles.

"When will they pick out Duke's people?" James asked.

"They should have already," his analyst replied. "Hell, if they don't pick them up before they hit the missiles, Duke may well get a free shot right at them."

They'd see the Terrans before then, James was certain. There was no way his people outclassed the locals that badly. He was certain of that.

He still found himself watching carefully and feeling like he'd just shoved something helpless into a piranha pond. *Maasai*'s starfighters were swinging out in a pure anti-missile formation, and they were well inside missile range of Duke's ships.

Then their formation finally scrambled, their vectors and patterns dissolving into garbage as they clearly finally spotted Colonel and her ninety starfighters.

"Too late," James murmured. "Make a choice."

They could take out enough of the missiles to make sure *Maasai* was safe…but only by flying straight enough that Duke would rip them apart.

The Serengeti commander saw the same dichotomy and James mentally saluted them as the formation straightened out—and then every Typhoon launched missiles. They emptied their magazines at Duke while they laid their own beams on the incoming capital ship missiles.

Explosions tore through space, Duke's people opening up on the fighter missiles and the defender's tearing into the capital ship missiles simultaneously. Dozens of gigaton-range fireballs lit up the void, each adding to the chaos the jamming platforms were throwing across the battlespace.

Poseidon's computers did their best to resolve the chaos, drawing in positron lance beams as sterile white lines on the tactical display. Where those sterile white lines intercepted the icons of enemy fighters, more explosions lit up the void as the beams of pure antimatter ripped through the spacecraft.

"First salvo neutralized. Enemy missiles closing on our starfighters."

"Duke's in range," a second analyst reported. "Targets are minimally evasive, starfighters engaging."

More sterile white lines on the display, the computer showing James the dance of death Aimee Duke led her people through with a calm dispassion.

"Duke reports targets neutralized," Amoto told James, the comms officer looking up from his console. "If any of them survived, she can't pick them out of the jamming, but they still have missiles inbound."

"She's clear to do whatever she thinks is necessary to preserve the fighter wing," James ordered. "*Maasai* isn't going anywhere now."

Duke, quite sensibly, hadn't waited for James's permission. Her formation split apart, each of her starfighters adding new and complex layers of vector as a tight, if random-seeming, formation opened up into a mobile cloud of starfighters.

It cost her delta-v toward *Maasai*—a lot of it—but combined with the jamming field it dramatically increased the survivability of the starfighters and opened up dozens of new lines of fire on the incoming missiles.

"Duke has a clean sweep on the starfighter missiles; our remaining missiles are closing on *Maasai*."

James had to double-check the analyst's comments to confirm for himself, but they were right. The Terrans had taken ninety starfighters against sixty-four and hadn't lost a single ship. They'd known they would *win*, but a clean sweep was better than he'd hoped.

"Second salvo is fully neutralized but we took out two of their fighters. Last salvo now closing."

There were two capital ship missiles in the salvo for every starfighter the Serengeti carrier had left, and the warship went all out to try and save herself. Lasers and positron beams lanced out through the jamming, trying to track the incoming missiles.

"Damn! They just took out one of their own starfighters!"

A starfighter had zigged instead of zagged, and a seventy-kiloton-a-second secondary positron lance had taken the Typhoon dead center and incinerated it, creating a momentary gap in the defenses—a gap that lasted too long.

Three more fighters collided with missiles as they rushed to cover the gap, and two missiles made it past everything the defenders could throw at them. Two bright explosions lit up deep space, and James breathed a sigh of not-quite-relief.

"Colonel Duke, is *Maasai* disabled?" he asked aloud.

"She's spinning and has ejected at least one major zero-point cell," the starfighter pilot reported after a moment. "Your orders?"

Maasai was mission-killed, but…

"Get at least one squadron into position on her," James ordered. "If she tries to engage, blow her to hell. If she's *smart*, leave her. That carrier is dead whether we vaporize her or not."

"Yes, sir."

"Get me Barbados," James told Amoto. "Time for his people to earn their keep."

———

EIGHT HOURS LATER, *Ocean Dreams*, escorted by the two Commonwealth warships, jumped back to FTL, leaving *Maasai* drifting crippled in a long ballistic orbit of Salvatore. Neverwinter had enough sublight ships to carry out search and rescue for the warship, though they quite sensibly hadn't even budged from orbit while the jamming platforms were in place.

"All ships are under Alcubierre-Stetson," Sherazi reported. "Your orders, Commodore?"

"Blow the jamming platforms and q-probes we left behind," James ordered. "No evidence we were there can be allowed."

"Done," the junior Commodore replied instantly. "Holding q-probes to confirm jamming platform destruction..."

Sherazi paused for a moment, then James got the clear impression of a nod over the neural link.

"All jamming platforms destroyed, detonating the q-probes. We no longer have live data from the Salvatore system." He paused. "Do we have a destination?"

"Drop us one light-year from KDX-6657," James ordered. "We'll retrieve the Marines and redirect *Ocean Dreams* there."

"Understood."

James breathed a sigh of relief. It appeared they'd made it in and out of Salvatore without being identified. There was a chance that *Maasai* had acquired clear-enough data to be able to identify the fighters...but it was a small chance, and one he was prepared to accept to not have to murder the survivors of her crew.

He'd been sent to raid commerce, not commit atrocities, and he had a *damn* good idea of where the line was drawn. It was the same reason why he had no intention of taking *Ocean Dreams* into a system Coati controlled.

"Get Barbados on the line," he ordered Amoto. He trusted the Marine to tell him if he was still too busy to talk to the Commodore, though since they had control of the ship's bridge and engineering, the Marine CO *shouldn't* be.

It still took several minutes to get the Colonel on a channel, but the q-com link was to the liner's extremely luxurious bridge. The Marine sat on the very edge of the captain's chair, as if concerned the overstuffed, automatically adjusting leather seat would try and eat him.

"Commodore Tecumseh," he greeted James. "We are in control of *Ocean Dreams* but the situation here remains…irritating."

"*Irritating* isn't a tactical assessment I'm familiar with," the flag officer replied. "What's going on?"

Barbados sighed.

"The crew understand the reality of the situation and are cooperating," he explained. "I've removed them all from the bridge and we're running with a prize crew here, but Engineering is still mostly their people.

"The *passengers*, however, are the worst collection of rich *idiots* I've ever had the displeasure of interacting with, and don't seem to understand that they are prisoners and we're not going to wait on them hand and foot the way *Dreams'* crew did."

"It is an interstellar tourist liner," James pointed out. "Are we going to have a problem?"

"Well, let's just say it's a good thing *Dreams* has a good doctor," Barbados said grimly. "My people didn't board with electron lasers, sir. At least a dozen civilians had close and personal introductions to rifle butts, but there don't appear to be any permanent injuries."

"Good. Are you getting the stunners issued?" The pulsed electron laser was the twenty-eighth-century version of a taser, a ranged weapon that used a focused beam of electricity to achieve the same disabling shock effect.

It wasn't a perfect nonlethal weapon. It was just better than everything *else* humanity had tried.

"Pulling my people back to the shuttles to swap out squad by squad," Barbados confirmed. "There's a few bodyguards scattered through this mess I don't trust not to try something stupid if not watched, so we're keeping our eyes very open."

The Marine paused, seeming to marshal his thoughts, then asked quietly.

"What are we doing with these people, sir? They may be pricks and rich idiots, but there's twenty thousand civilians on this ship and they don't deserve what Coati's people would do to them…"

"We're not bringing them anywhere *near* Coati," James said firmly. "Intelligence gave us a contact for ransoming captives back to their families and selling ships; we're going to hand *Dreams* and her passengers over to him with instructions to take any offer from their families.

"We have to ransom them, because anything else makes it obvious just who we are, but we can make sure they get home while making ourselves look desperate for money," he concluded. "We'll pull most your people back aboard *Poseidon* and send *Chariot* with *Dreams* to make sure everything goes according to plan.

"Coati will get his share of the money, but his pet psychopaths aren't getting anywhere near these people."

Barbados nodded slowly as he considered James's words.

"Good."

16

Antioch System
11:00 October 12, 2736 Earth Standard Meridian Date/Time
DSC-052 Kodiak

FOR A TASK GROUP that had never even drilled together, they impressed Kyle with their emergence into the Antioch system. All three capital ships emerged simultaneously, in the exact same formation they'd entered FTL sixteen days beforehand.

Alexander led the way, the battlecruiser's massive lances and missile batteries the first shield against ambush, followed by *Kodiak,* and then *Thoth* bringing up the rear. Old as two of the three ships were, it was still likely more firepower than the Antioch system had ever seen.

"We are deploying Combat Space Patrol," Song reported calmly over the neural network. "One squadron of Falcons from *Kodiak*. Echo Three is standing by if we need bombers."

"Thank you, Vice Commodore," Kyle told her. "Sterling, what's the system status?"

"Feeding to the tactical display now," his aging tactical officer replied. "I'm only picking up three…maybe four FTL-capable ships, all in low orbit of Orontes. Even the in-system shipping appears to be flying under starfighter escort, though the gunships, again, are in orbit of Orontes."

Antioch was a surprisingly sparse system. No asteroid belts, only a few comet formations, and a mere six worlds. The second world, Orontes, was a dry but habitable rock with no real oceans but a network of lakes and rivers across the planet's surface.

Most of the in-system shipping moved from Orontes to Seleucus, the system's outermost planet and single gas giant. Antioch was a wealthy system by Rimward standards, and there should have been an almost-steady stream of sublight clippers making the run between the fusion plants that fueled Orontes' orbital industries and the Seleucus cloudscoops that fed those fusion plants.

Instead, clusters of fifteen to twenty ships dotted the route, each guarded by an equal number of starfighters—Federation Cobras, a last-generation design sold to Antioch under a special deal.

The system's ten gunships, half-million-ton sublight warships built around fighter-tier acceleration and capital-ship-tier weaponry, were in high orbit of Orontes, positioned to intercept anyone going after the industrial plant or the tiny handful of A-S drive ships left.

"They're terrified," Sterling concluded. "How badly have they been threatened that they're convoying shipping in their own system?"

"Six months ago, the Antioch Space Navy had two battlecruisers," Kyle reminded his bridge crew. "Now they have none. Nebula." He turned to the diplomat. "Anyone in particular we should be reaching out to? My brief says Admiral Belisarius."

"I would agree," the diplomat concurred. "I'll reach out to some of the civilians myself, and you'll probably be meeting with the Premier before the end of the day, but Belisarius should be our first point of contact."

"Jamison?" Kyle asked his coms officer.

"Already on it, sir. There's a block of Federation q-bits on their switchboard; we've got codes to reach them FTL." She paused, her eyes glazing over as she communicated with her counterparts on the planet.

"I have Admiral Belisarius for you, sir," she concluded after a moment. "He was waiting for you."

That was...not a good sign.

"Put him through."

Belisarius was significantly younger than Kyle had expected, appearing in his early forties at most. Unusually young to be the supreme commander of an entire star nation's military. He was a plain-faced man, average enough to blend into any crowd, and he met Kyle's gaze with a visible degree of relief that was almost terrifying.

"Captain Roberts, welcome to the Antioch system," he greeted the Federation officer. "You have no idea how glad we are to see you. The last few months have been...troubling."

"We know. We are here to help," Kyle replied. "I have three ships under my command, one of them an Imperial ship. We will need to coordinate with you and the other Free Trade Zone ships to make certain we are covering space most efficiently."

Belisarius closed his eyes and slumped forward.

"There won't be much coordinating, I'm afraid," he confessed. "We just confirmed this morning that *Maasai* is unsalvageable and the Istanbul Self-Defense Force lost contact with *Sultan* two days ago.

"We have no choice but to assume *Sultan* is lost, along with her convoy," Belisarius said quietly. "There are no warships left to us for you to coordinate with, Captain Roberts, which leaves us entirely dependent on your good graces for the safety of our ships."

Kyle inhaled sharply and exhaled slowly, nodding his understanding as he did so.

"We do what we must," he said finally. "I'll need every scrap of intelligence you and your allies can provide, and as up-to-date information as you have on the location of every A-S freighter in the area.

"We will keep everyone safe," he reassured the Admiral. "And when we find these bastards, we will end them."

"Everything my people have is at your disposal and will be forwarded to your ships," the ASN Admiral told him. "Are you in need of resupply?"

"We'll need food and consumables if nothing else," Kyle replied.

"We'll enter orbit of Orontes and plan from there, Admiral. I'll speak to you again once we've arrived."

————

FOUR HOURS LATER, the trio of warships settled into an Orontes orbit just behind the gunship squadron and protectively above the freighters. Kyle spent most of that time in his office, reviewing the intelligence packet Belisarius had provided.

It was even worse than the Admiral or his briefing had suggested. Antioch, Istanbul and Serengeti had, between them, fielded five FTL-capable warships and thirty-four FTL-capable freighters.

All of the warships were gone. Three confirmed destroyed. *Sultan* missing, presumed lost. *Maasai* crippled when the pirates had stolen an entire passenger liner in Salvatore.

The last sent familiar shivers down Kyle's spine. Memories of the human wreckage aboard *Ansem Gulf* were going to haunt his nightmares again, but there was nothing he could do for *Ocean Dreams*.

His door chimed, an implant code advising him that Nebula was actually being polite this time.

"Enter," he ordered and the diplomat slipped in.

"I hate to impose," Nebula told him, "but do you have any of that beer?"

"I tend to keep it for rewards," Kyle told him. "But sure. Grab me one."

"It's that kind of day," the diplomat slash spy agreed, pulling two beers from the fridge. "I have now spoken to our ambassador, the Imperial ambassador, our chief spy on the planet and head of the Imperial economic analysis team. Their chief spy," he concluded, in case Kyle hadn't guessed.

"Have you spoken to anyone from Antioch?" Kyle asked, taking the beer.

"The Premier's secretary, the First Chancellor, the Minister for Foreign Affairs, the Minister for the Navy, the Minister for the Free Trade Zone, *all* of their aides, and the Premier's ex-mistress," Nebula reeled off.

"Busy day."

"I like this part of my job better than others," the diplomat replied with a smile. "But...this place is a mess, Roberts."

"Anything I haven't learned already?"

"It's not just the military and economic situation, Captain," Nebula warned. "The Free Trade Zone was always...controversial. To a certain extent, it was imposed on a number of the minor systems involved by a combination of economic and military force.

"Not everyone in those systems or in Antioch was okay with that. So long as everybody benefited, even if the core three benefited more, most people got in line.

"Now..."

"Now no one's benefiting," Kyle said grimly.

"Exactly. Antioch's parliament elects one fifth of its seats each year, and the elections are in a month. Premier Yilmaz can hold his majority together if he loses basically every seat up for election, barely, but *he's* up for re-election next year, and his majority won't survive two bad years.

"Istanbul's worse in many ways. They're *not* a democracy in the strictest sense, so their replacement process is considerably more...*lethal* to the incumbent Sultan."

"And Serengeti?" Kyle asked.

"Serengeti's hard to get a handle on," Nebula admitted. "Tricameral legislature, one elected, one appointed by the corporations, one appointed by the leaders of the original families. The corporations and the families all made a *lot* of money from the Zone, but... if their profits and their lives are at risk, they may pull out as well."

"So, the entire Free Trade Zone is at risk of collapsing."

"Exactly," the diplomat confirmed. "And if it does, the amount of economic value the Alliance members working out here get out of the region goes down *fast*. We can't let that happen, Captain."

"Not to mention the collapse of the entire region's economies and the attendant loss of quality of life and actual *lives*," Kyle pointed out.

"Yes, that too," Nebula agreed dismissively. "They need us, Captain. But we need them, too.

"We have a meeting with the Premier and Admiral Belisarius in an hour," he concluded. "Dress uniform, Captain. Dig up at least *some* medals, if you please. I know you have them."

"'We'?" Kyle asked.

"You, me, the other Captains if you want them. The invitation was pretty limited."

Kyle shook his head. Nebula *probably* should have checked his availability, but on the other hand, even capital ship commanders usually bent to the whims of heads of state.

"All right, Nebula."

17

Antioch System
17:00 October 12, 2736 Earth Standard Meridian Date/Time
Orontes, City of Antakya

ANTAKYA HAD BEEN BUILT on the plain between where two of Orontes's largest rivers converged into the planet's single largest river. The city didn't have beaches in the traditional sense, but there were expanses of stunningly violet sand stretching along the interior of both rivers to provide entertainment for Antakya's citizenry.

The same purplish stone that the rivers had ground down into the sand had been incorporated into the construction of the city itself. Orontes's citizens had kept most of their heavy industry in orbit, and whatever was left was far away from their capital, building Antakya from the beginning as a center of display and pride.

The Antioch system might be desperately poor by Castle Federation standards, but they were still wealthy by Rimward standards... and poverty on a planetary scale could still allow for pockets of wealth and grandeur.

And Kyle had to admit that Antakya was grand. Broad boulevards lined with imported Earth palms cut through the city toward a central square and immense purple marble fountain in front of the planetary parliament building. Every business, apartment building and home fronting on those boulevards had clearly been built to a very specific esthetic, and well maintained since.

Experience told him that even Antakya likely had more run-down areas, but the road from the spaceport to the center of government ran down what he suspected was the most carefully maintained boulevard in the city.

The Antioch System government had sent open-topped cars to pick him and his captains up, a surprisingly vulnerable form of transportation, given the paranoia visible off-world.

The drivers were clearly linked in to security channels, though, and he caught at least one glimpse of low-flying aircraft hovering above them. He suspected they weren't nearly as unprotected as they looked —and the open-topped cars allowed the slowly gathering crowd to look at the occupants of the three vehicles.

Kyle was aware of his reputation and certainly unafraid to use it as a tool, but it was still a shock to realize that literally *thousands* of people were coming out to watch, to get a chance of seeing the Stellar Fox.

To get a chance to see the man they thought would save their world.

———

PREMIER SUKIL YILMAZ was a squat man, almost overflowing out of his saffron suit, with a shaven head and hands heavy with jewels and rings. Standing next to Admiral Belisarius, however, Kyle could see a clear familial resemblance—cousins, he guessed, which potentially explained the Admiral's surprising youth for his role.

"Come in, Captains, come in," Yilmaz greeted them in an oily voice. "I'll have Jess pull together some refreshments. Any preferences?"

"Water, please," Kyle said instantly, setting a hard limit for his people. He could have a beer and still work, but he suspected they needed to be on the top of their game…and that Yilmaz would happily get them very drunk.

"Of course, of course," Yilmaz allowed with a wave of a bejeweled hand. "Jess, water and baklava for our guests."

The woman in question turned out to be an almost disturbingly young attractive woman in a tight-fitting green dress and headscarf. She emerged through a swinging door with a platter of glasses and small plates of pastries moments after the premier gave the order.

"I know Recep has already told you this," he said to Kyle, waving at Admiral Belisarius, "but we are unimaginably grateful that you are here. These attacks have grown beyond anything we can deal with. We've never seen anything like this."

"Few have," Kyle replied. "Interstellar piracy is rare. We see in-system piracy far more often, but that's readily suppressed outside the poorest of star systems."

"This group—we believe it is a single group," Yilmaz admitted, "has been growing for some time. We think their first raid was almost a decade ago, but…ships are lost to many causes."

"We think they used the Class One manipulators from their first prizes to build their corsair ships," Belisarius noted. "We have… minimal information on them, but none of the vessels we've confirmed appeared to be A-S capable in their own right."

"But they're definitely moving between systems?" Kyle asked.

"Indeed. The ships are too big to be carried but too small to make FTL on their own," the Admiral confirmed. "We believe they may be using manipulators on multiple ships to create a single A-S bubble."

Kyle sat back and sipped his water, surprised.

"I'll have to check with my engineers," he said slowly. "I didn't think that was possible."

"Neither did our Captains, Captain Roberts, neither did our Captains," Yilmaz said bitterly. "And now many of those Captains, both civilian and military, are gone. These pirates have shed much blood and stolen much treasure, and we find ourselves at the limits of the stability of the alliance my predecessors put together and I have sustained."

He spread his hands wide, rings clinking against each other.

"We have truly, truly reached the ends of our own resources, so we have called to your nations for aid," he concluded. "The trade between our systems and the Federation and Imperium has benefited us both, but it cannot continue if our starways are plagued by pirates!"

"Of course, Premier Yilmaz," Nebula interjected. "That is why Captain Roberts and his people are here. The Castle Federation does not make promises we cannot keep."

"You've made enough bloody money from us," Belisarius grumped. "Those starfighters—"

"Are the only thing permitting our people to sleep at night," Yilmaz snapped. "Without the Cobras that, as the Admiral says, cost us so dearly, we would be defenseless now. Tell me, Captain, what is your plan?"

"The situation is worse than we expected when I left Castle," Kyle admitted. "We planned around being able to use Free Trade Zone ships to support our operations, but that clearly will no longer be an option.

"The best option I see is for my ships to take over the convoy system you've already set up. We will escort the convoys to Istanbul and Serengeti from here, then set up a schedule with the shippers to make certain that no vessel travels unescorted."

"Our own ships were doing that, and it solved *nothing*," Yilmaz told him. "I'd hoped for better."

"It's a starting point," Kyle replied. "And, no offense to Admiral Belisarius and his people, my ships are more modern, my sensors are more powerful and my fighters are more advanced. There is no crew in my task group that aren't veterans of the war against the Commonwealth. We've fought Terrans, Premier. Pirates are nothing."

"That still doesn't solve the problem," the Premier whined, and Kyle smiled grimly at the man.

"It's a starting point," he replied. "We fight them when they come to us. We destroy their ships, capture their survivors, and we find out where they're coming from.

"Then we find their base and we blow it to hell. Then, Premier Yilmaz, your pirate problem will be very much solved."

The Premier clasped his hands together with an audible clank of rings hitting each other and smiled, his mood shifting instantly. "Good, good, Captain. Any assistance we can provide, let us know. For now, may I invite you and your Captains to join me for dinner?"

18

Antioch System
19:00 October 12, 2736 Earth Standard Meridian Date/Time
DSC-052 Kodiak

"I CAN'T SAY MUCH, LOVE," Angela Alvarez warned Michelle, the gorgeous blonde nurse leaning against her desk with visible bags under her eyes. "There was a battle. We won, but it's been a long few days."

Michelle reached out to run her fingers along her lover's face on the screen.

"Are you all right?" she asked. Angela was still with Fourth Fleet, though *Kodiak* was now out of the loop for anything so classified as the movements of one of the Alliance's main combat formations. Certainly, even a Wing Commander couldn't say if the battle her girlfriend had just been through had been a defensive or an offensive one.

"Yeah, we stay out of the fight and wait for the casualties," Angela said quietly. "A lot of fighter pilots, love. And they're the lucky ones."

"It's the job," Michelle reminded her. "Better a few flight crew than an entire ship's crew."

"I know the logic," the nurse replied. "It's hard to swallow when every pilot I look at, I think it could be you."

"I'm sorry."

"No, don't be." Angela made a throwaway gesture. "I'm just maudlin after a twenty-hour shift, but I didn't want to miss our time slot. Do you know when you'll be back home and available for leave?"

"No idea," Michelle admitted. "The people out here...they're terrified, Angela. They need us. They need to know *somebody* cares. A lot of wives and husbands aren't coming home who should have."

"And there you go right into the heart of it at the Fox's heels again," her lover said with a smile. "At least you're only fighting pirates; the odds seem better there."

"I'm just glad you have a battleship wrapped around you."

"*Blacksmith* is an experiment," Angela replied. "I don't have enough data to know what Command thinks of her success, but at least this way, the wounded are out of the line of fire and behind some kind of defense."

"And my favorite nurse is too," Michelle told her with a smile. "I miss you."

"And I miss you. I worry, though."

"I know," the pilot acknowledged. "I don't have a safe job, but... someone's got to do it."

"I worry about the future," Angela admitted. "Not if we'll still want to be together." She smiled. "I won't pretend I don't occasionally think you only love me because I helped you put yourself back together, but I'm pretty sure we'll at least give it a shot."

"If we both live that long."

Michelle touched the screen again, and this time, Angela put her own fingers out to hold them against each other.

"We will," she promised fiercely. "We're going to live through this, we're going to go back home, and our parents are going to harass us about grandchildren. Do you hear me, Commander Alvarez?"

"Aye, aye, ma'am," Angela said with a laugh. "Be careful. I know pirates aren't up to the Commonwealth's standard, but they're still dangerous."

"I will be," Michelle promised.

———

AT LEAST ON *KODIAK*, Kyle wasn't surrounded by people looking to him to solve the most existential problem their society and political power base had ever faced. The crew of his carrier merely relied on him to keep them alive in the face of whatever enemy they fought today, and *that* was a pressure he was well used to handling now.

Song and Taggart were waiting on the flight deck when he and Nebula disembarked from their shuttle, and he gestured for them to fall in with him and the diplomat.

"My office," he instructed. "This is a conversation we all need a damned beer for."

"Do you have anything *other* than beer?" Song asked delicately.

"Honestly? It's a full service auto-bar," Kyle replied. "It can do coffee, tea, or four different liquors. I won't speak to the quality of what my steward has stuck in it, but there is whisky, vodka, rum and tequila in the bar."

The delicately featured Vice Commodore made a face. "I'll stick with the beer."

"I'll take that whisky," Nebula replied. "I'm not sure beer is enough for this."

Walking through the door, Kyle waved the diplomat to the bar.

"Help yourself, Nebula. You've worked out how it works by now. Then, once you've got that whisky, brief them."

The diplomat was, unsurprisingly, more diplomatic in his expression of distaste than Song had been, but he pulled three beers from the mini-fridge, then poured himself a glass of whisky. He didn't bother with ice.

"The long and short of it is that the Free Trade Zone is completely, utterly and unquestionably fucked," Nebula concluded after a large swallow of hard liquor. "They've lost every interstellar warship any of them had in commission and over half of the Alcubierre-capable shipping in twenty star systems.

"Even with convoying and our protection, the economy here will take years to recover from the impact of the last six months—but the pirates are running out of prey, too. If they have the firepower to take down *Crusader* or the other ships, they have the weight to take any of the secondary systems easily."

"And if they're willing to take a risk, they could be a serious threat to even Antioch or the other core systems of the Zone," Kyle concluded as he popped his beer. "Escorting the remaining shipping will push off the inevitable, but these systems are going to need a major investment of new ships, civilian and military, from somewhere to claw themselves back up."

"The Alliance has neither to spare," Taggart said after exchanging a glance with Song. "None of us do."

"We can send more civilian shipping this way, but we can't spare warships to sell them," Kyle agreed. "Which means that we can't just protect the existing ships—wiping out the pirates has gone from 'best-case scenario' to 'absolute necessity'."

"That's...a tall order, sir," Song replied. "Three ships? Twenty systems? Stars alone know how many uninhabited systems a pirate could be based in."

"Federation Intelligence has been working on one end of the problem," Nebula told them over his half-empty whisky glass. "At least *some* of the crews from these ships have been ransomed back to their families, usually through the auspices of Amadeus's Great Houses. The Houses are scum, but they're usually honest scum."

Amadeus was one of the member systems of the Free Trade Zone... in theory. In practice, Amadeus didn't have a functioning government, with between six and fifteen Great Houses, depending on how you classified them, vying for control at any given point in time.

Since the planet was barely above poverty level, that meant the Houses didn't exactly bother with things like legalities or moral codes. But, by and large, if you paid a ransom through one of them, the kidnap victim made it home.

"Our Intelligence team, working with the locals, is trying to follow the money trail back," Nebula told them. "If we're lucky, we might trace them all the way back to a base. If not…well, we might at least find a rendezvous or somewhere we can ambush."

"From our side, we run protection as planned," Kyle continued. "We kill anything that crosses our path…but we keep the Marines ready to go and we at least *try* to cripple pirates. We need prisoners, and making that possible is going to mostly fall on you, Song."

"That's a lot of risk to ask of our pilots," Taggart objected with a coded glance at the CAG, and Kyle was struck with a moment of suspicious realization. The two were sitting together again. They were *always* sitting together, and often communicating with a glance and not even neural implants…

"It is," Kyle agreed, putting that thought aside for the moment. "But unfortunately, it's a risk I need to ask of them."

"Against Terrans, it would be unwise," Song said slowly. "Possibly suicidal against remotely even odds, but against pirates…" She nodded firmly. "We'll need to be careful, keep Williams's bombers in reserve for if something goes wrong or we run into actual Terran ships. I won't guarantee prisoners from every ship, but if we short-circuit two or three raids…we'll get someone with answers."

"I don't even care about answers," Kyle admitted. "I want coordinates. I don't care if we're tearing them from someone's flash-frozen implant, so long as I can *end* these bastards."

Sadly, that particular bit of imagery wasn't helpful as anything but hyperbole. You could back up an implant's contents, but the files inside were intimately linked to the brain that had stored them. They could only be restored or read in the mind that had created them.

Starship data cores and living prisoners, that was what they needed.

"We'll do what we can," Song told him. "I'll touch base with the other CAGs, though I assume they're getting much the same briefing?"

"Probably without the beer or whisky, and lacking in Mr. Nebula's eminent presence, but yes," Kyle agreed.

"We also have to remember the joker in the deck, people," he told his officers. "If Terra is involved out here, all of our careful plans go out the window—and much as I'd like them, we're not going to try for Commonwealth prisoners.

"If we see TCN ships, Echo Wing drops and we blow them to hell with everything we've got," Kyle said grimly. "Just knowing they're out here would change the game, people. That confirmation would be almost as valuable as finding the pirate base."

———

ONCE EVERYONE ELSE HAD LEFT, Kyle sat in his office with a beer and the holodisplay of the region for a long time, searching for some easy solution that could end the crisis. He wasn't particularly surprised not to find one—without data on where the pirates were striking from, he couldn't launch an offensive. Couldn't do anything except stick his ships on top of the most likely targets and wait for the bastards to come to him.

And, Gods knew, *he* wasn't the best defensive tactician in the galaxy.

"Expanding my horizons, right," he muttered, checking his system. To his surprise, he had a message from Mira—he hadn't heard from her in a few days, but that wasn't unusual, and they usually went for live conversations.

"Hi, Kyle." The image of the insanely beautiful woman who'd decided to keep him appeared on his screen. "*Camerone* and Seventh Fleet are going dark, so I'm not sure when you'll get this."

He nodded in understanding. Q-coms might be totally secure, but the computers they ran through weren't necessarily. So, any Alliance formation about to go on the offensive would go dark except for critical communications, sending the last set of messages from its crews at random intervals over several days to confuse anyone who *was* listening.

"I presume you'll be briefed once things are moving, but I can't say anything," she continued. "I'm glad you're on the far side of the Alliance, though. Walkingstick is playing the attrition game again, seeing what he can cut off our formations for minimal losses of his own.

"I'm not planning on letting *Camerone* fall victim to that, but the problem with war is that the enemy gets a say." Mira sighed, her dark eyes focused somewhere past the camera.

"This isn't likely to be my last message, but it's always possible," she told him. "So, you take care of yourself until you hear from me again, Kyle Roberts. Don't let that reputation of yours drag you into something you can't win."

She smiled.

"But since this definitely is *not* my final message, I suggest you start planning something fun for when we next both have leave back home. I expect to be impressed, Captain Roberts." She waved a finger at him. "Rumor has this latest gig of yours as an audition for a flag, after all."

Her smile tightened.

"But be careful," she reiterated. "I'd rather have *Captain* Kyle Roberts home than posthumously promoted *Admiral* Roberts's flag and medals in a box.

"I'll see you on the other side. Fly safe."

Her image froze and he reached out to touch it gently. War was hell on relationships, though that thought brought back his realization about Taggart and Song.

As *Kodiak*'s Captain, he was going to have to call them out on it, he realized with a sigh. They weren't in violation of regs, as the XO wasn't in the CAG's chain of command…but there was enough of a potential conflict there that they should have *told* him.

That, at least, was a problem he could deal with easily.

Well, it was going to be easy for *him*.

19

Antioch System
08:00 October 13, 2736 Earth Standard Meridian Date/Time
DSC-052 Kodiak

"Sɪʀ, we're receiving a q-com transmission for you from Antioch," Jamison's bubbly subordinate told Kyle over the intercom. "The Premier's office relayed them to us."

"Well, if the Premier thinks we should talk to them, we probably should," Kyle allowed. "Link them through."

Morning hadn't brought solutions to any of his problems, though it *had* at least brought confirmation that all three of his ships were now fully stocked on consumables. With the zero-point cells and modern recycling, a warship could go for years without resupply...but nobody wanted to eat recycled ration bars.

Everyone was all too aware of just what they were recycled *from*.

The transmission came to his implant first, but he flipped it to his wallscreen immediately. The woman who appeared on the screen was something of a surprise. He was, vaguely, aware of the *existence* of the traditional Islamic burqa, but he'd never seen someone wearing it.

"Is this Captain Kyle Roberts?" she asked.

"That would be me, yes, miss…"

"I am Trade Coordinator Yassifa Aksoy," the woman told him calmly, and his brain got past the surprise of her outfit to catch up to the quality of it. It might have been an all-encompassing full-body veil, but it was made of silk with actual gemstones woven into it to form the pattern of a galaxy across her torso.

"I serve as the head of the board of directors of the Free Trade Zone Shipping Commission," she continued. "I am also CEO and primary shareholder of Alshrq Aljadid Shipping. Two of the ships currently in Antioch orbit are mine. One of the vessels waiting in Istanbul orbit is mine. Four of the ships lost to pirates in the last few months were mine," she finished harshly.

"I appreciate you reaching out to me, Coordinator," Kyle replied. "It seems we'll be taking over convoy security from the local militaries, which I presume will require close coordination with the Commission. Is there someone I should specifically be speaking to?"

"Me," Aksoy said simply. "I cannot overstate the importance of our situation to the Commission and the Free Trade Zone. I have lost friends and family to these murderers. What can we do to assist you, Captain Roberts?"

"For the moment, I'm afraid all we can do is assist you," he admitted. "I understand that the ships in Antioch orbit were originally for at least two convoys. Has that changed, given how long they've been sitting here?"

"No," she told him. "Two, including one of mine, are heading to Istanbul. The other two are heading to Serengeti, via Lodestone and Salvatore. The ships in Istanbul and Serengeti will have to wait for an escort, and there is a vessel in Lodestone belonging to another shipping line."

"That works with my own plans," Kyle replied. "My Imperial compatriot needs to travel to Istanbul, and I intend to accompany them there while sending *Alexander* to escort the other convoy. When will the ships in orbit be ready to leave?"

"Captain, they've been ready to leave for weeks," Aksoy told him with a chuckle. "Every day they sit in orbit, both their owners and their captains are pissing money down the drain. I will forward your communications people the contact information for all four ships. They will be ready to move when you are."

She paused.

"Are you certain you can keep our people safe, Captain?" she asked. "We have lost too many already, and our own militaries have failed to keep us safe."

"My ships are more modern, my starfighters more advanced," Kyle assured her. "I cannot guarantee anything, Miss Aksoy. We don't know enough about these pirates to be certain, but I promise you that my people will do everything within their power to protect your ships and your crews."

"That's all we can ask, I suppose," she allowed. "Thank you, Captain. It has been a dark time, and your arrival is a ray of light and hope."

"We do what we can," he replied. "And we will keep doing what we can. We'll find these bastards."

———

AFTER A FEW MORE PLEASANTRIES, they cut the channel and Kyle ordered Taggart and Song into his office. While they were entering, he raised Jamison on his implant.

"Lieutenant Commander, we'll be receiving contact information for our escortees from the FTZ Shipping Commission," he told her. "I'll need you and your people to reach out to them all and get them set up for a coordinated ship-out time. I want both convoys moving by eighteen hundred hours tonight.

"Make it happen."

"Yes, sir!" she replied. "I'll let you know immediately if there are any problems we can't handle."

"Good. Roberts out."

He turned to his two subordinates, gesturing for them to sit. He didn't offer drinks and wondered if they even noticed.

From the way they shifted slightly closer together, they did…and their reaction confirmed his suspicion.

"You heard my conversation with Jamison," he told them. "Are there any problems with *Kodiak* that would prevent us shipping out on that schedule?"

If there were, he should already know about them, but the possibility of something having come up always existed.

"No, sir," Taggart replied. "We're shipshape and ready to take on the galaxy."

"We won't be going that far," Kyle said, "but the odds are good we'll be taking *Kodiak* and her wings into action against pirates that have demonstrated both ingenuity and firepower. We won't be able to afford unpleasant surprises, so I need you two to turn over every rock, check every flaw. Double-check that Trent has actually *done* her job instead of getting distracted.

"Is there anything going on I need to be aware of?" he asked in conclusion, giving the pair one last chance to come clean.

"There's a gambling ring going on in Engineering," Taggart volunteered. "I think Trent has missed it, but there haven't been any problems yet, so I'm just keeping an eye on it, with a stack of bricks ready to fall on them if it *becomes* a problem."

That was the kind of minor problem Kyle would normally hope to hear about in this kind of session, things not normally brought to the Captain's attention but that could be issues later on. Today, however, he was after something else.

"The Flight Deck is running cleanly," Song said slowly, "but I get the feeling you're poking for something specific, sir."

"Perceptive of you, CAG," he told her. "Would you care to make a guess, Vice Commodore, or do I need to call the two of you on the carpet like a pair of ill-behaved teenagers?"

The room went very silent and very still.

"I thought we were being discreet," Taggart finally admitted. "We never let it impact our jobs, sir."

"Discretion is all well and good, Commander Taggart," Kyle ground out, "but keeping it from getting in the way of your jobs is the *minimum standard* in this kind of mess; do you understand me?"

"Sir."

"What you did *not* do," Kyle continued, "is make sure it didn't get in the way of *my* job. Do you understand?"

Both swallowed hard.

"I'm not sure I follow, sir," Song admitted.

"You aren't in violation of regulations, *quite*," he told them. "It's generally considered a bloody stupid idea, but the XO is out of the CAG's chain of command unless the Captain dies. Regardless of however professional or competent you are, however, a relationship leaves you both emotionally compromised."

"We've been avoiding that!" Taggart objected.

"But he's right," Song told her lover. "That we have to be consciously aware of not letting our relationship impact our work and keeping it secret *does* compromise us."

"Exactly. Which is why you're supposed to *tell* me about shit like this," Kyle snapped. "Because that way, if nothing else, at least one damned person can tell you if you *are* letting it get in the way."

"Sir," Taggart clipped out.

"So, how about we start from the beginning?" the Captain replied. "'Mister new Captain sir, I'm in an inappropriate but not technically regs-violating relationship with the CAG. We're trying to be good about it, but life just happens.' Sound like something that *should* be familiar?"

"Yes, sir. Apologies, sir," the XO ground out, glancing helplessly at Song.

"Our previous Captain…didn't want to know," the CAG admitted. "We got in the habit of hiding it from everyone."

Kyle sighed.

"Which, I'll point out, you don't actually need to do. *Discretion* is required, yes, but there is no need for this to be a deep, dark secret. We have to trust each other, people, and right now, the evidence says that I can't necessarily trust you. Do you see why that's a problem?"

"Yes, sir," Taggart admitted. "Like Melania said, Captain Cindre didn't want to know about relationships amongst the crew, so we kept it under wraps. We were in the habit once you came aboard, awkward as the habit is. We didn't mean…" He sighed.

"We fucked up," he said flatly. "You're right; you should be able to trust us. I can tell you that you can, but that doesn't change whether or not you do. If you want my resignation, you can have it."

"And mine," Song agreed quietly.

Kyle looked each of them in the eyes in turn, holding their gazes for several moments as he gauged their sincerity.

"That won't be necessary," he finally told them. "Even if we were somewhere I could reasonably replace you, it wouldn't be necessary. You make a damned fine team, one I'm learning to lean on. This might be a big stupid mistake, but it's only one mistake."

He held up a finger.

"Don't make more."

20

KDX-6657 System
10:00 October 14, 2736 Earth Standard Meridian Date/Time
BC-305 Poseidon

"SOMEBODY HAD A WORSE week than we did, I see. My heart simply *bleeds.*"

Pure implant communication carried as much emotion, if not more, as a conversation in person. Sherazi's commentary on the tactical feed *Poseidon*'s Captain was sending James dripped sarcasm and gloating satisfaction.

"We do need to work with them," James told Sherazi mildly, focusing the feed in on the collection of Coati's ships.

The Terrans weren't entirely sure how many of the strange combinable corsairs the pirate warlord had, but six currently orbited *l'Estación de Muerte*—and two of them, as Sherazi had pointed out, had been handled quite roughly.

"Positron-lance hits?" James queried aloud.

"Looks like. Charlie took at least three hits from what CIC is calling forty-kiloton-a-second beams, fighter guns, and Epsilon took a clean hit from a three-quarter-megaton beam just front of Engineering. I'm guessing she only made it back because the rest carried her."

The pirate ships *had* names. James's people even knew them, but his officers and crew continued to refer to them by the letter designations CIC had assigned them when they'd first arrived.

"Intel says *Sultan* went missing while we were gone," James reminded his subordinate. "Unless I misremember, she had seven-fifty beams, didn't she?"

"That's what my implant database has," Sherazi confirmed. "She was an old cruiser, but damn. That's..."

"That's a clean sweep of the local warships, and Coati probably grabbed the entire four-ship convoy," James concluded. "If the Alliance hadn't finally shown up, the entire sector would be open for him to take."

"The Alliance is here, though. Mission accomplished, I guess," *Poseidon*'s Captain said slowly. "What happens now?"

An icon flickered in the corner of James Tecumseh's mental "screen."

"Well, first, it appears I'm going to talk to our pirate friend," he told Sherazi. "But then...then I need to talk to the Marshal."

"Good luck," the junior Commodore replied. "On both of those."

"Thanks. We'll talk later, Daryush."

Sighing, James activated a full-privacy implant communication channel and transferred the com request from Coati into it. They didn't have q-com links with the pirate, but they were close enough to *l'Estación de Muerte* to avoid significant time delay.

"Commodore Coati, a pleasure as always."

"Commodore Tecumseh, you seem to be missing a ship," the brightly colored pirate told him with a massive smile. "I'm guessing that means your mission either went very well or very poorly."

"Well, Coati. *Ocean Dreams* is on her way to Amadeus under *Chariot*'s watchful eye. It's a roundabout route; she'll be a while."

His own route back to KDX-6657 had taken almost half again as long as a direct flight from Salvatore. It was a pain in the ass, but... the vector of a ship entering A-S drive could be tracked, and any given line in space would only have a handful of stars along it at most.

Stopping a light-year outside the system had added over a day to the trip, too. The A-S drive accelerated at roughly a light-year per day squared, but you had to decelerate to zero as well to avoid incinerating both your ship and a significant portion of your destination with radiation release.

"We had our own successes while you were gone," Coati told him. "Your captains must have been happier without my 'psychopaths'… and mine were happier without nursemaids with sticks up their asses."

"Are you *trying* to aggravate me, 'Commodore'?" James asked sweetly. "Thinking you might not need us anymore?"

"Every warship in this sector is gone, Commodore Tecumseh," the pirate replied. "It's almost time for me to begin planning my triumphant return to Serengeti as their new king. Want a planet, Commodore? I may not need you anymore, but I could use you…and I can be generous."

The thought of working *for* Coati instead of *with* Coati turned James's stomach, but practice kept his face and emotions level. He had a filter on his implant channel to minimize emotional transfer, but it worked best if he kept his emotions under control.

"I wouldn't plan your coronation just yet," he told the pirate. "A Federation task group arrived in Antioch two days ago, under the command of the Stellar Fox himself. It appears we've drawn some powerful attention."

"Huh," Coati said, then grinned. "Then I guess it's a good thing you're almost unaggravatable, isn't it, Commodore? It seems I may still need you after all. Now that your enemies are here, what *is* your plan?"

"I'll let you know," James promised. "I need to call home."

"Like a good dog." The pirate sighed. "All right, Commodore. You lick your master's heels, then tell me what he says."

"We'll talk," James said sharply, then cut the channel and rubbed his temples.

Coati gave him a headache on a *good* day.

JAMES RETREATED to the quiet meditation chamber off his office to call his superior, taking a few moments of blessed silence to compose himself.

Fleet Admiral James Calvin Walkingstick, Marshal of the Rimward Marches, was one of the most powerful military officers in the Commonwealth. He and James Tecumseh both hailed from the Amerindian tribes of Earth's North America—indeed, both came from families that still preserved many of their people's ancient traditions. They had that and a first name in common, which had occasionally seemed to trigger a mentorly attitude in the older man.

Then the Stellar Fox had happened. Kyle Roberts had pursued a Commonwealth warship guilty of a horrendous atrocity into James Tecumseh's area of responsibility, and faced with a choice between an enemy in pursuit of justice and a theoretical colleague guilty of mass murder...James had stood aside and let Roberts blow a Commonwealth battleship to hell.

It had cost him his own ship and left him working on logistics for the offensives against the Alliance instead of commanding a starship, but James couldn't bring himself to regret it. Captain Richardson had been a blot not merely on the honor of the Terran Commonwealth Navy but of the human race.

This mission was both a chance to rehabilitate himself...and a rather pointed reminder that wars could not always be fought with perfect honor.

James Tecumseh was no longer quite as impressed with Marshal Walkingstick as he had once been, but the Marshal remained his commanding officer.

With a sigh, he linked into *Poseidon*'s q-com systems and pinged the battleship *Saint Michael*. The systems promptly proceeded to demand a series of authentication and security codes to confirm who he was, and then the wallscreen of his meditation chamber began to show a slowly spinning version of the multi-starred seal of the Terran Commonwealth.

It took a surprisingly short five minutes for the man in charge of a massive interstellar campaign of conquest to become available and appear on the screen. Walkingstick was a tall man, with darker skin and heavier features than James himself, with a long single braid of black hair hanging down his back, and unreadably dark eyes.

"Commodore Tecumseh," he greeted James. "It appears congratulations are in order for a well-executed first phase. Your actions have caused great confusion in the capitals of the Alliance at a most convenient time."

"Thank you, sir," James replied. "We have confirmed that three capital ships have arrived in the Antioch system under the command of Captain Kyle Roberts. We're not sure of the classes, but that is a significant commitment."

"Indeed," Walkingstick agreed thoughtfully. "Successful indeed, Commodore, though not as much as we'd hoped. It appears the Alliance is still hesitant to commit too much force to that region."

"I suspect they sent the Stellar Fox instead of more ships," the junior man replied.

"Fair enough if they did," the Marshal replied with a chuckle. "That man seems worth another wing of starfighters all on his own; I'm perfectly happy if they want him on the far side of nowhere and not taking a supercarrier into the middle of my plans again."

"If we want more forces diverted, I may need to become further involved," James warned. "Tempting as feeding our local allies into the wood chipper of an Alliance task group is, it wouldn't draw more forces out here."

"Believe me, Commodore, I don't expect or desire this situation to end very well for our pirate friend," Walkingstick told him. "But yes, I need the Alliance to commit more than three old ships and one first-class tactician to hunting him down.

"You're going to need to engage the Fox's ships directly," he continued. "Isolate and destroy one of his ships, preferably the most modern one. If you can take out Roberts himself, I certainly won't object.

"They sent a task group to the Free Trade Zone, Commodore. I want them thinking they need a *fleet*. Do you follow?"

"I understand completely, sir," James confirmed. He'd *rather* have been told 'mission complete, come home,' but Walkingstick's logic made sense. "I'll speak with Coati and prepare an operation. We'll keep the Alliance looking over their shoulders, sir."

"Good. Keep it up, Tecumseh, and there'll be Admiral's stars and a task group waiting for you when you come home.

"Good luck, Commodore."

───────

EVEN THOUGH JAMES hadn't warned Coati he was coming, he was completely unsurprised to find the scaled and multi-colored pirate waiting for him when he disembarked from his shuttle, power-armored Marines in tow.

"Sooner or later, Commodore, you and I are going to have a reckoning," Coati said cheerfully, his smile bright but strained. "You can brazen your way around my authority in front of my men only so long."

"That, Commodore, is your problem," James replied, his voice equally cheerful. "We need to talk. There are plans to be made, and I don't think this decrepit hangar is the place for them."

Coati grunted and gestured for James to follow, leading the way to the now-familiar office in the structure and pouring a strange, almost fire colored, liqueur for them.

"Red opalfruit liqueur," he explained as he passed the Terran officer a glass. "The rare bottles that make their way all the way to Earth go for tens of thousands...and it was originally a waste product on Serengeti. They grow the trees to harvest *blue* opalfruit, but about half of the crop is always red."

Blue opalfruit was a staple of Serengeti's exports, a naturally evolved fruit that filled about a quarter of a human's daily dietary needs in a single fist-sized lump *and* was a mild stimulant.

"I thought red opalfruit was toxic?" James asked, eyeing the beverage. He didn't *think* Coati was going to poison him, but...

"Ha!" The pirate downed half of his tumbler in a single swallow. "*Unprocessed* red opalfruit is toxic. Mix it with Terran yeast, however, and leave it for two months, and you get this. The yeast eats all of the poisonous crap and spits out alcohol. Win all around."

James took a single, very careful sip and inhaled sharply in delight. It was definitely alcoholic, but it danced across his tongue like a dozen flavors rolled into one, stimulating his taste buds in a cascade of tastes.

"Wow. And blue opalfruit gets harvested in preference to this?" he asked.

"Can't feed a family on alcohol," Coati pointed out. "Where blue opalfruit gets you high *and* feeds you well. But there's a reason no one has engineered trees that only produce one type of opalfruit," he finished with a mocking toast.

"I'm impressed with your intelligence network," the pirate told him, the sudden change in topic almost enough to catch James flat-footed. "We're a long way out of the Commonwealth's area of concern, and you knew about the Fox's arrival before I did. I have confirmed it now, of course."

"Of course," James murmured. They might work together, but Coati didn't trust the Terrans further than they did him.

"I'll note that these worlds are occupied by humanity," he told the pirate. "That means that they are part of our area of concern. All of humanity will unify eventually. It's inevitable."

The price might be higher than, say, one James Tecumseh was entirely comfortable with...but he'd seen the worlds in the Common-wealth and the worlds in places like the Antioch-Serengeti Free Trade Zone. Quality of life, life expectancy, general health...the Common-wealth might not be far ahead of places like the Castle Federation, but worlds like these *needed* the Commonwealth.

And many of the members of the so-called Alliance were closer to worlds like these than to worlds like Castle.

"And you people think I'm the scary one," Coati replied. "You know what you're going to get with a pirate: I'll steal your shit, kill you if you're inconvenient, rape you if I'm bored. A fanatic, though? One of you lot might do any of those things if you think it's justified... but you'll convince yourself it's all for a higher cause."

"Most of us have our honor," James objected. "There are lines the Commonwealth will not cross."

"Right. So, we were talking about a plan to deal with your enemy's warships that are out here to stop me raping and pillaging my way across twenty star systems, weren't we?" the pirate warlord said dryly.

"We were," the Commodore grated out. Coati had an absolute *gift* for finding sore spots. "Have you learned anything of value?"

"As a matter of fact, I have. Your intel is good on Alliance fleet movements. Mine? Mine tells me what the *Shipping Commission* is doing," Coati told him. "They had four ships at Antioch. Two have left for Istanbul; two have left for Lodestone on their way to Serengeti."

"We can intercept the Serengeti convoy more easily," James pointed out. "Do you know which warships went where?"

"They're even stopping at Salvatore, which will give us more time to get into position," the pirate concluded. "I don't know which ships went where, Commodore, but I know only one ship went with the convoy to Lodestone."

"Convenient," the Terran said softly. "Don't underestimate these people, Coati. I'll take *Poseidon* to Serengeti; I expect you to bring your corsairs to meet me there."

"How many would you like?" Coati asked.

"As many as can make it," James told him. "If they sent two ships with one convoy and one with the other, the single ship is the more modern, more powerful one.

"You've never fought a real modern warship, Commodore Coati. Do not expect this to be easy."

21

Deep space en route to Istanbul System
00:05 October 15, 2736 Earth Standard Meridian Date/Time
DSC-052 Kodiak

MIDNIGHT. The middle of an FTL dark watch.

There was no quieter time aboard any Alcubierre warship, especially on the flight deck. Flight operations were impossible. Attack was impossible. Engineering issues were possible—one had made the Old Man skipper of the old *Avalon*—but that didn't make it onto the flight deck.

Michelle sat on the nose of her bomber, looking down the rows of stacked spacecraft. For all that the ships only had a crew of three apiece, they were massive things. A Falcon was a thirty-meter-wide triangle, a Vulture a forty-meter-long egg-like pod with wing-like torpedo mounts.

They dwarfed the tiny humans who flew them, but were dwarfed in turn by the scale of the vessels that carried them between the stars...

and by the energies those tiny humans could unleash to destroy any of the spacecraft they had built.

The Vulture she sat on was unarmed at the moment, the twenty-meter length of her torpedoes missing and rendering the craft strangely skeletal in their absence.

Which was about how Michelle felt without Angela. She didn't need the other woman to *complete* her, she was pretty comfortable on her own two feet now, but without Angela around, she felt like she was missing a few extra pieces.

"Penny for your thoughts, Wing Commander," a voice cut through the dimly lit gleam, and she looked away from the machines to see Vice Commodore Song also pacing the deck, her face almost invisible in the interplay of shadows.

"About a step and a half away from bad romantic poetry," Michelle admitted. "Missing my girlfriend."

"She's with Fourth Fleet, right?" Song asked. "They saw some heated action, but it sounds like most of them came through all right."

"Angela's on the new hospital ship they're testing the concept for," the junior woman said. "She isn't in danger unless the whole damned fleet has come apart. I'm afraid she spends more time worrying about me than herself."

"That's war," Song agreed. "Tears apart lovers, families. The lucky ones get put back together in the end, but it's almost never the same."

"You have someone, ma'am?"

"What, the rumor mill hasn't betrayed all of my secrets already?" the Vice Commodore asked with a sad smile. "I'm widowed, Williams. My husband died in the opening salvoes of the war."

"I'm sorry, ma'am."

"I'm not alone," Song told her. "Richard died a long time ago now, and I found some comfort with a dear friend who became more. I'll keep some of my own secrets still, though."

"Do you ever wonder what'll happen when the war's over and we go home?" Michelle asked.

"Not really," the CAG replied. "I have today. It's easier for me, I suspect. My lover isn't on the front lines."

Michelle was pretty sure she knew who the CAG's lover was, but if the older woman didn't want to share, she wasn't going to prod.

"I just wonder..." She sighed. "...if maybe the best idea isn't to wait until it's all over before making long-term plans."

"I don't know," Song admitted. "I...survived Richard's death, but I won't pretend I'm all put back together. Maybe once the war's over, I'll consider the future. But for today, I can't see past the next sortie, making sure all of my people come home."

"Fair, ma'am. I'm not sure I can be that...focused."

"Don't need to be," the CAG replied. "Up to you what path you want to take. A lot of people got married before going off to war. A lot of others waited till they came home. Do what works for you."

"Useful advice," Michelle half-complained.

"Oh, I know," Song agreed. "But I'm a bitter widow with a comfortable bedwarmer. Don't let my cynicism warp you!"

The way Song spoke of her lover made it very clear that he was more than "a comfortable bedwarmer," but the essence was true, and Michelle shook her head.

"War wounds us all," she finally said. "One way or another."

———

THE STRATEGIC BRIEFING made for rough reading. If Kyle had been able to sleep, he'd have left it for morning, but his dreams were full of exploding battleships and dying friends tonight. The office attached to his quarters didn't have all of the amenities of his main workspace by the bridge, but it did have a fridge and a coffee machine.

He'd talked the latter device into producing hot chocolate while he sat in his office chair and went over the details that the Alliance Joint Chiefs felt all capital ship commanders had needed to know.

A Commonwealth offensive, apparently under the command of Marshal Walkingstick himself, had slammed into Midori, site of one of the biggest early battles of the war. They'd wrecked most of the resupply infrastructure in the system, along with battering three Federation carriers into impotent wrecks before Fourth Fleet had arrived.

Walkingstick had declined a fleet engagement, leading Fourth Fleet in a long-range missile and starfighter duel across the system before withdrawing. Fourth Fleet's analysts suggested they'd permanently crippled at least two ships, but the fighter losses had been roughly even, and the loss of the station and its defending carriers put Second Midori cleanly in the Commonwealth's win list.

The details on the Alliance response were sparse, but if it was Seventh Fleet at the core of it, there were only a few options. He trusted Admiral Alstairs, Seventh Fleet's commander, but their best option was to hit a fleet base they'd been driven off from before.

The only *good* news, such as it was, was the intelligence reports that the vicious knife fight in the New Edmonton system of the Stellar League seemed to have finally drawn to a close. The estimated casualty reports from that battle left Kyle feeling guilty, but he couldn't argue the cold logic.

He'd been involved in the black op that had provoked the Commonwealth punitive expedition into New Edmonton, an expedition that had now been sent packing after Dictator Periklos had finally concentrated a real fleet instead of sending mercenary formations in piecemeal.

Kyle was grimly certain that the massacre of many of the more egotistical League mercenary units had been no accident. The League might be short a dozen carriers and their battle-hardened crews and starfighters, but the rest had fallen in line behind their new Dictator.

A Dictator who knew *perfectly* well why this war had come to his systems. There were going to be consequences for that, but right now both the Alliance and the League were struggling for their lives against the nine-hundred-kilo gorilla of the Terran Commonwealth.

And right now, his girlfriend was in the middle of an Alliance attempt to poke the gorilla in the eye.

His command was as far from the main action as he could get, dealing with minor powers on the opposite side of the Alliance from the Commonwealth. There was nothing he could do to turn the tide of the main war except resolve the pirate situation as quickly as possible.

Hopefully, Istanbul would have some more answers.

22

Istanbul System

16:00 October 22, 2736 Earth Standard Meridian Date/Time

DSC-052 Kodiak

"WELL, CAPTAIN? HOW WAS LODESTONE?" Kyle asked the image on his wallscreen.

Sarka ran her fingers along the scar on her face thoughtfully. The two Captains were each in their own offices, steps from their bridges but private for now.

"Smooth," she finally said. "Well, for us." She chuckled. "Lodestone seems to be more than a bit grumpy with the Free Trade Zone and are taking advantage of the current problems to levy import fees that are forbidden under the Zone's rules.

"I don't know how well that's going to end for anyone, but they didn't harass *us* for money! The ships in the convoy, however, had to pay or they wouldn't be allowed to land cargo."

"Not our problem," Kyle confirmed. "No issues otherwise?"

"None. Our merchant skippers swallowed their pride after I told them I wasn't here to enforce the Trade Zone's rules. They paid the bill, delivered their cargos and picked up new ones. We also picked up a lost stray that was here waiting for an escort."

"What's your ETA to Salvatore?" Kyle asked.

"Nine more days," she told him. "We know Serengeti lost a carrier there, so I'm planning on being very careful in Salvatore. The freighter captains, fortunately, agree with me."

Given the intimidation value of Captain Sarka's scar and glower, Kyle suspected they wouldn't have said anything if they *didn't* agree.

"I'm guessing Lodestone's government didn't have any intel we didn't already know?" he asked.

"Not a peep," she confirmed. "We should get some clearer sensor data on the jamming mess at Salvatore when we get there. That whole stunt stinks to me."

"Agreed. If you can spare the time, I'd love the old light on that," Kyle told her. That kind of precision FTL jumping was hard but doable. "I'm not sure we'll be able to resolve a lot more with our sensors on month-old data than we can get out of their sensors, but...it might be worth a shot."

"It'll add a couple of days, but I can't see anyone complaining. These skippers *need* these pirates gone so they can get back to their lives.

"Any news out of Istanbul?"

"We're still about an hour from going sublight," Kyle told her. "We'll see what the Sultan's court holds for us. Most of their communication has been with the Imperium so far, though they do have a treaty with the Federation as well."

"That's not a great sign, sir."

"And making sure we deal with the warning sign before it becomes a problem is part of why we're here," he agreed. "And is definitely why Nebula is here."

"Can we just point him at the politicians and hide?" Sarka asked.

"You could, if you were here," Kyle said cheerfully. "*I*, on the other hand, am in command of this situation, which means I have to talk to them regardless. I'll survive.

"After all, no one is going to try to kill me."

Which made Istanbul safer than his own home system recently.

EVEN WITH EVERY ship linked together by instantaneous communications that didn't care if they were in warped space or real space, coordinated emergences were a nerve-wracking endeavor. A ship under Alcubierre-Stetson drive couldn't see the universe outside its bubble of warped space.

Interstellar navigation involved far more dead reckoning than any navigator wanted to admit or any spacer was comfortable thinking about. Modern technology made getting to a specific system straightforward; even getting to a specific spot in a system was easy enough.

Making sure four ships made it to another system in roughly the same spot without hitting each other somewhere along the way was why a civilian navigator was one of the most highly paid officers aboard a freighter.

Kodiak and *Thoth* executed it perfectly, emerging still in step with each other and exactly fifty thousand kilometers apart. Their two civilian charges weren't quite as perfectly in line, but they still emerged between the two warships, guarded from any potential attacker.

"Patrol launching," Song reported crisply. "Echo Two on standby for bomber support, Charlie for first-strike scramble."

That was all her call to make, which left Kyle metaphorically comfortably sitting on his hands, watching his team swing into action while he studied the Istanbul System.

Istanbul had eleven planets, five of them midsized gas giants whose gasses fueled the system economy, named Cyrus, Darius, Alexander, Demetrius and Khosrau. The fourth planet, the only habitable one, was named Constantinople.

And the capital city, according to his files, was named Byzantium.

Whoever had been naming the planets here had been having too much fun, he concluded.

Unlike in Antioch, a steady stream of sublight ships continued to make their way between Constantinople and the five gas giants, though the ships were smaller and cruder than those in Antioch.

According to his sweeps, most weren't even using antimatter engines. Most were instead using cheap-as-dirt high-impulse, low-thrust ion engines.

An ion engine ship wouldn't get places very quickly, but combined with mass-manipulator tech, it could get there very, *very* cheaply.

"Well, that's an interesting solution," Sterling murmured over the tactical net. "I've got six semi-mobile platforms in long transfer orbits between Constantinople and the gas giants. I'm guessing they're fighter bases, sublight ships to protect the in-system traffic."

"Most systems just have the starfighters deploy to patrol themselves," Kyle noted. "Why would they bother with those? They do have reasonably modern fighters."

"It would allow them to keep their fighter crews in a higher level of comfort," Taggart pointed out. "And save fuel: those bases are in a fixed orbit that would have at least one of them within ten million kilometers of every part of the route at all times. It's efficient, though we wouldn't have bothered…"

"And you're assuming that their entire fighter force is modern, too," Song pointed out. "They bought Typhoons from us, Slingshots from the Imperium. All of those are fifth-generation fighters, still effective ships, but"—she paused, accessing records—"they only bought a hundred and fifty Typhoons from us and didn't buy the design or manufacturing licenses. I imagine they got about the same from Coraline, so many of their fighters may be home-built and short-legged."

"I think we might be about to find out," Sterling cut in. "I have three ships heading at two hundred gees. Sublight units, but big ones. Ten million cubic meters, four million tons or so. If they were bigger, I'd say they were A-S carriers, but…"

"But they're half the size of even an old carrier," Kyle agreed. "Has anyone from Istanbul actually bothered to contact us?"

"No, sir," Jamison reported. "I'll check in with *Thoth*."

"Good call," he told her. Istanbul had called for Imperial help, after all. They might have reached out to the Coraline ship first.

"They haven't heard anything either," his communications officer said a moment later. "They wouldn't have ignored us and reached out to the freighters, would they?"

"Unlikely," Kyle said grimly, studying the three ships heading his way. They were still almost fifteen million kilometers away, but they were making him nervous. "We have a q-com code for Istanbul space traffic control, correct?"

"Yes, sir."

"Get me a channel."

It took a moment, but Jamison flashed him a thumbs-up a moment later.

"Istanbul Control, this is Captain Kyle Roberts of the Castle Federation carrier *Kodiak*, accompanied by the Coraline Imperium cruiser *Thoth* and the Antioch merchant ships *Dreamer* and *First Sale*. We notified Istanbul of our expected arrival upon leaving Antioch.

"Please confirm our approach vectors and orbital slots."

He paused.

"We are also detecting what *may* be Istanbul Self Defense Force units approaching the convoy," he noted. "Please be advised that if those vessels do not identify themselves shortly, I may be forced to regard them as hostile and act appropriately to defend the convoy."

Kyle waited for a response, then glanced over at Jamison.

"We got a link," she replied. "They got the message, but…"

"I have fighter launch!" Sterling exclaimed. "Each of those ships just spat out eighty of the smallest starfighters I've ever seen. I'm reading them at a thousand tons each, but they're headed our way at five hundred gravities."

A thousand tons. The Falcons *Kodiak* carried massed just over six thousand tons and carried a dozen missiles and a fifty-kiloton positron lance. Likely, these ships didn't carry a lance at all and only had a handful of missiles…but two hundred and forty of them could put a lot of missiles in space.

"Song," he said slowly. "Get the rest of the group ready to launch, but stand by for my order."

"Sir?"

"If Istanbul wants to play chicken, let them. I'm not blinking first."

"Yes, sir."

"Get me a direct radio channel to these people, Jamison," he ordered calmly.

A flickering icon told him he was live.

"Unidentified vessels, this is Captain Kyle Roberts aboard the Castle Federation carrier *Kodiak*, escorting Free Trade Zone convoy ZGK-512. Under the terms of our treaties with both Antioch and Istanbul, I am authorized to use lethal force in the protection of this convoy.

"Identify yourselves and stand down, or I will engage you to defend my charges."

His implant played the short message back to him to confirm, and then he sent it out, winging its way across the light-seconds at lightspeed.

"Sir!" Jamison reported about ten seconds after the message would have reached the ships. "I have Istanbul Control."

"Control, this is Captain Roberts," Kyle greeted them.

"Stand your people down, Roberts; the incoming ships are an ISDF security patrol," a harsh male voice ordered. "You are not authorized to deploy fighters in this star system; withdraw them aboard immediately."

"To whom am I speaking?" Kyle demanded.

"I am Commodore Nurullah Aytaç Mataraci," the speaker told him flatly. "I am in command of orbital defense of Constantinople. You will stand down your fighters or I will be forced to destroy them."

"That, Commodore Mataraci, would be an act of war against the Castle Federation, the Coraline Imperium *and* the Antioch Republic," Kyle replied. "How many wars would you like to start today? Per the treaties of trade and protection signed between the Kingdom of Istanbul and the Castle Federation, I am permitted to maintain a four-ship combat space patrol at all times in this system. So, I'll note, is Captain von Lambert of *Thoth*, which means our single patrol is already understrength.

"Given the tense circumstances, I am prepared to overlook your unexpected aggression, Commodore, but I am prepared to defend this convoy with all necessary force." He paused. "As per my original message to Istanbul Control, I need approach vectors and orbital slots for my warships and the convoy.

"We're not here to cause trouble, Commodore, but this is turning into a farce."

There was no visual attached to Mataraci's transmission, but Kyle could almost hear the tension ratchet up in the man's voice.

"I am not used to being dictated to in my own system," he spat. "Stand. Down."

Kyle smiled.

"Vice Commodore Song?" he said calmly. He didn't cut the channel with Mataraci, letting the Commodore stew.

"Sir?"

"Full-deck launch, if you please. Jamison, get me von Lambert."

"Roberts," the Imperial Captain answered instantly. "What the hell is going on?"

"We're being threatened by the ISDF," Kyle said cheerfully. "I'm launching my starfighters to protect the convoy; I request you do the same."

Von Lambert was silent for several seconds, though the emotional side channel Kyle was getting suggested he was swinging between amusement and irritation.

"Of course, Captain Roberts. We'll have our birds in the air momentarily."

"What are you *doing*?" Mataraci demanded.

"Fulfilling my treaty duty to Antioch to secure the safety of this convoy," Kyle told him, checking his tactical feed. Even without deploying Williams's bombers, he had almost as many fighters as the ISDF task group did...and his were all six- or seven-thousand-ton seventh-generation ships.

If it actually came to a fight, it would be a *massacre*.

"Do you want to continue escalating this dick-waving contest, Commodore, or shall we both pull our fighters back and proceed like reasonable adults?"

There was a long silence.

"Very well, Captain Roberts. My Sultan *will* hear of this," Mataraci snapped. "Control will have your vectors shortly."

"Thank you, Commodore," Kyle replied. "And you are correct. Your Sultan will hear about this."

23

Istanbul System
02:00 October 23, 2736 Earth Standard Meridian Date/Time
Constantinople, City of Byzantium

"OH, MY," Kyle whispered as the shuttles came close enough to Byzantium for him to make out the mountain that rose out of the middle of the city. Nature had provided a flat-topped plateau a half-kilometer on a side in the middle of a flat plain.

Man had turned it into something incredible. Pathways had been carved into the side of the mountain, some large enough for heavy transport but most footpaths. Even from the air, he could see that they were full of people traveling up to the top.

A wall studded with minarets surrounded the outside of the plateau, and two distinct complexes filled it. One had the base of a more modern structure melded with the rounded roofs and reaching minarets of old Middle Eastern architecture, where the other was a sprawling complex of traditional domes and towers.

"The New Grand Mosque," Nebula told Kyle, the diplomat sitting next to him patiently. "The original settlers brought five pillars, each of five stones from Mecca itself, to Constantinople with them." He chuckled. "Only a third of the colonists were Muslim, and the ratio is lower now, but they left their stamp on the system.

"All Muslims bow to Mecca when they pray," he continued, "so they bowed to the stones at the New Grand Mosque. So, of course, the Sultan built his palace right next to the Mosque."

"Which left people bowing to him as well as God," Kyle concluded. "That must have gone over well."

"It's been a century and a half. People mostly ignore it now," Nebula noted. "Though I imagine it has something to do with their tradition of assassinating Sultans who get too egotistical."

"Wonderful. What do I need to watch for? Poison? Knives?" Kyle was relatively sure Constantinople was safe, but...

"They won't try and kill you," the diplomat replied. "Tradition says only the Sultan can be assassinated. The reality is...bloodier, but they certainly won't touch a guest."

"That doesn't mean they're going to be particularly pleasant to us," he warned.

"Karl, our shuttles are currently being escorted by atmospheric interceptors that could shoot us down," Kyle pointed out, gesturing toward the sensor screen.

Both *Kodiak* and *Thoth* had sent down a single shuttle, though Kyle had made certain they'd left both XOs and CAGs in space in case something went wrong. Each of the two shuttles arcing toward the Sultan's palace was being escorted by four ugly-looking interceptors.

The assault shuttles outmassed the interceptors twenty or thirty to one. This might be the aircraft's native environment, but they'd lose a straight-up fight. A surprise attack, however...

"We're being directed to a landing pad on the north side of the palace complex," the pilot reported. "Right under a lovely set of anti-aircraft cannon. Such kind, welcoming souls."

"Welcome to Constantinople," Nebula said dryly. "Some of the nastiest backstabbing practitioners of *realpolitik* in the galaxy."

"And someone here actively tried to get us into a conflict with the

Imperium," Kyle pointed out. "I have to wonder if they did that on their own, or if Terra put them up to it."

"Finding out is my job," Nebula replied. "So's dealing with it either way. *You* worry about the pirates."

———

KYLE AND NEBULA exited the shuttle onto the landing pad, escorted by a quartet of Federation Marines. Despite being in the middle of the night by the standard clock of Earth used across the galaxy, it was a late-spring afternoon in Byzantium and some of the day's warmth lingered.

The minareted wall had shaded the landing pad from the sun, however, leaving Kyle glad for the temperature-management systems of his shipsuit-based uniform. Standing in the shade, just behind a safety barrier, were an even dozen men, all of similar height with shaved heads, in tightly fitted black-and-gold uniforms.

Standing in front of them was a tall athletic man in a white-and-gold uniform with a pitch-black turban and grandiose waxed mustachios. Unlike his men's perfectly functional rifles, he wore a scimitar on his left hip and a modern-looking pistol on the left.

Stepping forward, he bowed deeply to Kyle and Nebula.

"I am Colonel Simon Abdullah Osman, commander of the Second Household Guards," he greeted them. "We are waiting on one more, I am given to understand?"

"Yes, Captain von Lambert's shuttle is directly behind us," Kyle replied.

"Good, good," Osman agreed cheerfully. "I suggest we step behind the safety barrier."

As Kyle followed, Nebula pinged him with an implant message: "Watch the Scimitar. It means our Colonel is in the succession."

Kyle sent back his wordless acknowledgement and understanding. No one who stood in the succession on Constantinople was going to be entirely safe. The Colonel was a member of a group that was explicitly expected to assassinate and replace the current ruler if he was failing the planet.

As a military officer from a functioning democracy, Kyle couldn't even begin to imagine what impact that would have on your mindset.

"Unfortunately, His Eminence has ordered that your guards must wait here," Osman told Kyle.

"I am the commander of a capital ship in the Castle Federation Navy," he replied. "I'm not actually permitted to travel off-ship on a foreign world without escort."

"I understand," the Istanbul officer agreed genially. "However, my orders forbid me to bring armed soldiers into the presence of my Sultan. If you insist, I can arrange a virtual conference."

"That won't be acceptable," Nebula replied. "We have serious concerns; we must meet with the Sultan and his senior officers."

"Then you must leave your guards here," Osman told them. "I swear to you, upon my own honor, that you will be seen safely to the Sultan and back to your ship."

Kyle shared an uncomfortable glance with Nebula, but nodded as Sarka and her own Marines approached.

"Very well, Colonel," he agreed. "We place ourselves in your hands." He smiled.

He didn't need to mention that he had warships in orbit or what would happen if they were injured or kidnapped. From the glint in Colonel Osman's eyes, the man was *very* aware of the situation.

―――――

THE INTERIOR of the Sultan's palace was a study in contrasts in both people and architecture. The lower levels of the building were built to relatively standard designs, office blocks that would have been at home on any planet Kyle had visited. Their roofs were old Arabic architecture, but the main body was modern.

Their interior walls, however, owed more to the colonists' desert lineage than anything else. The designers had carefully sliced slabs of sandstone and marble to line the walls, and then painted murals of the journey from Earth and colonization of Constantinople across the stone.

The staff varied from soldiers in the tight-fitting black-and-gold uniforms, to officers in the same white, black and gold as Colonel Osman, to bureaucrats in suits that would have looked as at home on most worlds as the basic buildings around them.

Everyone, though, was male. It took Kyle several minutes to even realize what was making him uncomfortable, but once he'd realized it, he couldn't ignore it. He wasn't sure he'd *ever* been in a workspace that only had one gender present, and situation sent a sinking uncomfortable feeling through his stomach.

"Here we are," Osman announced as they passed down another gorgeously decorated corridor to a pair of ten-foot-tall doors, each carved from a single slab of marble. "The stone for the doors was brought all the way from Earth," he noted helpfully as he reached out to rap his knuckles on the stone. "Welcome to the Hall of Scimitars."

In response to the knock, the two massive doors swung gently inward, clearly powered to prevent any mere human from having to move their multi-hundred-kilo weight.

Osman led the two Captains and the diplomat through a three-story-high hall lined with sandstone pillars on each side, spaced two meters apart to form a massive court leading to a raised dais with an immense marble throne.

Despite the scale of the room, it was nearly empty. There were benches tucked between the pillars to allow an audience to watch public affairs there, but today there was only a relative handful of people in the room.

A single man occupied the throne. Sultan David James Seleucus was a massive man, equal to Kyle in bulk, and if there was a single spare gram of fat on his muscular frame, it was hiding well. Seleucus wore his black hair in a short, military-style crop and sat with a golden scimitar across his lap.

The first woman Kyle had seen since landing on Constantinople sat one step down from him on the dais, clad in the same black-and-gold uniform as the Household Guards. A dozen men in the same uniform stood around the dais, clearly looking to the woman as their commander.

Finally, four older men in black, shipsuit-based uniforms stood rigidly on the bottom step of the dais. All four of them had the three gold stars of an Istanbul Admiral at their collar, but none wore the scimitar of standing in the succession.

"Honored allies!" the woman greeted them loudly. "Approach the throne of His Eminence, Sultan David James Seleucus, and be welcome!"

The three men approached, stopping at the base of the dais, facing the four Istanbul officers.

"So," Seleucus said flatly. "Our so-called allies and protectors finally arrive. Our ships burn, and you do nothing. Our people bleed, and you do nothing. Only when We summon you and *demand* you honor your treaties do you answer our call!"

"We are at war, Your Eminence," Nebula responded, a quick ping on Kyle's implant warning him to let the diplomat handle this. "Our treaties do not call on us to pre-emptively defend, only to come when you call.

"Both the Federation and the Imperium are locked in a struggle for our very lives against the expansion of the Terran Commonwealth, but still we have sent ships to answer your summons. What more would you have of us, Sultan Seleucus? We are your allies, not your overlords, after all."

Seleucus glared down at them.

"We expect you to *help*," he snapped. "Our own brother died aboard *Sultan*. You have arrived too late to honor your obligations; you have *already* failed."

"That is unfortunate, Your Eminence, and you have our deepest sympathies," Nebula replied, "but I repeat: *we are at war*. At war with the most powerful nation in human history, a state whose economy and fleets match nearly the rest of humanity combined.

"We came when you called, but we can do no more. If you would have us leave, we will leave, but I and these Captains would rather defend your people than abandon them."

Nebula was *good*. Even the Admirals on the dais looked uncomfortable in the face of his impassioned screed. Kyle could also see Osman out of the corner of his eye, and the Colonel looked...thoughtful.

"Perhaps then Our Kingdom should look to Terra for protection!" the Sultan boomed.

"You may try," the diplomat replied. "But we offer protection and trade—Terra offers only unity."

Seleucus chuckled, but there was no humor in the noise.

"Perhaps. Your companions, so silent. Let them approach and be known."

Nebula gestured them forward.

"May I present Captain Elector Yann von Lambert of the Coraline Imperial Navy, commander of *Thoth*, and Captain Kyle Roberts of the Castle Federation Space Navy, commander of *Kodiak* and designated commander of the task group sent to the Free Trade Zone."

"The Stellar Fox himself," one of the Admirals said before he stopped himself, glancing back at his Sultan.

The muscular ruler leaned back in his throne and gestured for his officer to continue.

"We have heard of Captain Roberts, of course," the Admiral said. "His victories at Tranquility, Alizon and Huī Xing are told across the sphere of human space. We welcome your skill and knowledge, Captain."

Kyle might not be a politician, but he could recognize carefully arranged theater when he saw it. The Admiral was apparently the designated good cop, flattering the commander of the Alliance ships while his monarch hammered them over their delays.

"I was one of many at all of those battles," he told the flag officer. "The plans may have been mine, but there were many soldiers and spacers involved in the execution."

"And do you have a plan, Captain Roberts, for dealing with these pirates?" the Admiral asked.

"Yes," Kyle confirmed. "It is not complicated, gentlemen. We escort the convoys. We wait for them to come to us, and we interrogate the survivors.

"Once we have learned the location of their home bases, we smash their defenses and board them with Marines to learn the locations of any bases we missed. We burn them out root and branch."

"And you can succeed where all of our fleets have failed?" the Admiral asked.

"I am the Stellar Fox," Kyle reminded them. "You *have* heard of me, haven't you?"

The Sultan laughed, his booming voice echoing from the pillars and walls of the Hall of Scimitars.

"Bring food and drink for Our guests," he ordered the woman at his right hand. "Let us sit and eat together, and plan how we shall bring about the end of the enemies of Our Kingdom."

Kyle managed to swallow a sigh of relief. If the Sultan was feeding them, they appeared to have navigated the minefield of a conversation with a near-absolute monarch.

He hoped.

———

WHEN THEY FINALLY LEFT THE Hall of Scimitars after a good but extremely mentally draining meal, Nebula immediately pinged Kyle with a simple warning:

"Everything is being recorded. Say nothing until you're back aboard *Kodiak*."

"Understood," Kyle signaled back, following Colonel Osman—who had been silent through the entire dinner—back toward the shuttle pad.

"Colonel, I will need to meet with the Federation's Ambassador before I return to orbit," Nebula told Osman. "Would it be possible for you to escort me?"

The Istanbul officer turned to look at Nebula, then glanced at Kyle. There was a question in his gaze, Kyle was relatively certain, but the Captain wasn't sure what it was.

"My people should be able to see you safely to the pad, Captains, if that's acceptable?" he finally asked.

"I don't see why not," Kyle allowed. He wasn't sure what Nebula was up to, though it was likely that the man did need to speak to the Ambassador. It was just unlikely that was *all* the spy was up to.

"Thank you," Osman said with a small bow. "Sergeant, please see Captain von Lambert and Captain Roberts to the shuttle pad. I will escort Mr. Nebula to the Federation Embassy."

"My thanks, Colonel."

"What's going on?" Kyle demanded over the implant link.

"Diplomatic matters," the spy responded calmly. "Even this link may not be secure, Captain. We will talk again aboard *Kodiak*."

The two starship captains went one way, and the spy and the local officer went another. Kyle mentally sighed.

He wasn't sure he trusted Nebula to tell him everything, but he did, at least, trust the man not to be acting against the Federation's interests at least.

"Would you be able to give me a lift back to *Kodiak*?" he asked von Lambert. "I'd prefer to leave my shuttle here for Nebula, along with some Marines."

"Of course, sir," the Imperial officer agreed with a sidelong glance at their escorts. "We'd be delighted to give you a ride."

24

Istanbul System
09:00 October 23, 2736 Earth Standard Meridian Date/Time
DSC-052 Kodiak, in Constantinople orbit

"I'M NOT sure why they even bothered with those starfighters," one of the other Wing Commanders snipped at the morning briefing. "Our Falcons would go through them like a knife through butter."

Michelle and *Kodiak*'s other Wing Commanders were gathered in the briefing room next to the main flight deck. With only six of them in the room, including the CAG, they were gathered around the table at the front of the room, with an image of the Istanbul "Needle" starfighter hovering on the holodisplay.

"If you made it to lance range, yes," Michelle pointed out.

"We'd make it to lance range," John Redwood, Bravo Wing Commander, replied. "They've got no ECM, bugger all for anti-missile defense...sheep to the slaughter."

Song chuckled and her subordinates looked at her. "Finish the explanation, Michelle. I'm not surprised you picked it up."

"What?" Redwood demanded.

"Listen, Commander," Song ordered, then gestured to Michelle to continue.

"They're not intended to mix it up at lance range," she told them. "They don't have a lance at all. They're a pure missile platform, closer to the Vultures in design than the Falcon. Though, honestly, they're more a development from the original Ferret type we deployed at the beginning of the last war."

The Ferret had been the first starfighter ever deployed. A pathetic lance by modern standards, four crude starfighter missiles—and deployed in the face of the Commonwealth offensives, the Ferret had killed Terran battleships by the dozen.

"In the Federation, we focused on building a better starfighter. A bigger platform, a more powerful positron lance, more missiles. Istanbul clearly targeted building a *cheaper* starfighter. Smaller platform, shorter range, no positron lance...but the same four-missile salvo as a Falcon opens with.

"We'd have follow-up salvos. The lance. But they're not designed for that," Michelle concluded. "They're solely designed to extend the missile range and capacity of their mothership. If they've got point one cee of delta-v, I'd be stunned, but they're carrying thousand-gravity missiles.

"And four hundred modern missiles are going to ruin your day, Commander Redwood, ECM or not. And the Needle is a one-man starfighter that costs maybe a twentieth of what a Falcon does." She shivered. "I don't think the ISDF *cares* if they're destroyed after they've launched."

Redwood was silent and she was pretty sure she caught him shivering as well.

"We're expendable," he said, his voice much quieter than before. "But we *try* to come home."

"I'm sure the ISDF officers do care," Song pointed out. "And the pilots are definitely trying to come home! But the ship is designed to be a one-shot, short-range weapon. From a strategic perspective, any of them you get back after launching are a bonus."

"They're not intended to be used on an offensive platform," Michelle concluded. "They're designed for exactly the purpose we saw them in: overwhelming expendable force for home defense."

"There's probably four or five hundred of them scattered around the system," Redwood said slowly. "We could take them, but you're right." He shook his head. "That would hurt."

"Fortunately, while they may be assholes, Istanbul's an ally," Song reminded them. "Keeping it that way, however, is why no one's getting shore leave."

————

KYLE WAS on both his second coffee and his second donut when Nebula finally entered his office, the diplomat looking completely exhausted. He wordlessly gestured the man to a seat while finishing his swallow.

"Do you have more of those?" Nebula asked after dropping into the chair.

For a moment, Kyle considered pointing the other man to the coffee machine, but the sheer exhaustion Nebula was carrying bought a few scraps of consideration. He slid the half-empty plate of donuts across the table and rose to refresh his own coffee and grab a new one.

"Busy night, I take it?"

Nebula took a massive swallow of still-steaming coffee, blinking against the temperature as he swallowed, then nodded.

"Colonel Osman and I had a very productive discussion on the way to the embassy," he said. "Then I met with our ambassador, then our intelligence section." He shook his head. "We have some damned competent people here; I was impressed."

"Learn anything useful?" Kyle asked.

"Nothing good," Nebula admitted. "But plenty useful. Did you know there's a Commonwealth embassy on Istanbul? I sure as hell didn't, because it's brand new. Been in place six months."

"That sounds unusual for out here."

"It is," the diplomat said flatly. "Sultan Seleucus specifically invited them. Laying groundwork for if we lose the war, is our ambassador's opinion."

"Which is reasonable," Kyle pointed out. "We can't expect systems like Istanbul to rely on us proving victorious against the most powerful nation in existence."

"Fair enough," Nebula allowed. "What we *can* do is expect them to not stab us in the back, Captain Roberts. The decision to ask the Imperium to send assistance was *after* Antioch informed Istanbul they'd asked us for assistance...and came directly from the Sultan himself.

"Seleucus isn't stupid. He knew exactly what kind of tension that was likely to create, and to follow up on that by leaving his commanders with the kind of orders you've been running into since we arrived? No fighter patrols? No bodyguards?

"The treaty specifically allows us to have our Captains and diplomats escorted by Marines, even into the Sultan's presence," Nebula noted. "I'm not certain what Seleucus's game is, but what I *know* is that he met with the Commonwealth ambassador between being informed of Antioch's request to the Federation for help and his request to the Imperium for help."

"And even in the most positive light, he knew that was going to mean more ships out here," Kyle admitted. "There's not much we can do about that, though, beyond watching our backs here."

"The ambassador has his hand on the pulse of what's going on in Istanbul," Nebula agreed. "It's under control now, I think. We'll see.

"Where do we go from here?"

"I'm not sure yet," Kyle told him. "I have a conference with the freighter captains in an hour or so. We'll be on our way by morning Earth Standard; the only question is where and whether I send *Thoth* off on her own."

"Keep me informed, Captain, if you would," Nebula asked. "For now, I'm going to go pass out. It's been a long day."

———

KYLE WAITED PATIENTLY while the freighter captains argued over the conference channel, doing his best to process what each of them wanted while they tried to beat each other into submission.

"All right," he finally said, cutting off the captain of *Midsummer Night's Dream* pointing out that her cargo was the latest of all of the cargos in question. "*All* of your cargos are late. If your recipients aren't understanding of the situation, they're going to be almost as angry over a few days as a few weeks.

"My priority is getting all of you to your destinations alive. I presume we can all agree that is at least *somewhat* important?"

The captains mostly quieted, waiting to hear what he had to say. There had been three freighters waiting in Istanbul. Combined with the four he'd brought, there were now seven ships he needed to deliver safely—fully half of the remaining shipping in the Free Trade Zone.

"I am hesitant to split you up," Kyle told them. "I have two ships here to protect you with, but the pirates have demonstrated their ability to take on a single warship."

An older warship, yes, but Kyle wasn't prepared to rank *Thoth* that much higher than *Crusader*. The Antioch warship had actually been of equivalent age, and while her fighters had been older, *enough* extra pirates could make up that difference.

"The seven of you have three different destinations, as I understand," he continued. "Two of you want to go to Antioch. Three of you want to go to Serengeti, and two of you want to go to Reinhardt."

Kyle had needed to check his implant to confirm where Reinhardt was. He'd been surprised to have two ships headed there, until he realized that the planet was primarily a mining colony...and had been having a minor famine.

"I need to get to Serengeti myself," he told them, "but...bluntly, people, I'm going to prioritize people in need of food over just about everything else. Reinhardt isn't particularly far off the route to Serengeti"—though the need to decelerate to stop at Reinhardt would more than double the travel time to that system—"so we're going there first.

"From Serengeti, we will rendezvous with my third ship and make new plans to get everyone to where they need to go, with sufficient escort."

Most of the merchant skippers were nodding, though one or two looked mutinous.

"I'd ask if that worked for you all, but, well, I'm the one with the warships and that's the route we're taking," he told them with a grin. "You're welcome to take a different route if you wish, but you won't have an escort."

25

Salvatore System
19:00 October 29, 2736 Earth Standard Meridian Date/Time
BC-305 Poseidon

THE SALVATORE SYSTEM had a single massive gas giant named Waterdeep. Emerging on the far side of it from the planet of Neverwinter was a useful way to hide the distinctive massive energy flare of an Alcubierre-Stetson drive emergence from the locals.

The locals, of course, weren't blind to this fact, and poverty on a star-system scale was relative. They'd long maintained a network of sensor platforms above Waterdeep to make certain that no one sneaked up on them.

Even before James and the Commonwealth battle group had arrived, Coati had made a habit of showing up every so often and blowing those platforms to pieces. That recurrent destruction had enabled the destruction of *Maasai* and now had allowed the assembly of the strike force they would take up against *Alexander*.

James was impressed by the force that Coati had managed to

assemble for the plan. The corsair ships the pirate used had arrived in sets of four, linked together to project a bubble of warped space.

Now sixteen of the ships, each barely a tenth of *Poseidon*'s size and firepower but terrifying in combination, had gathered around the big Terran ship.

Hopefully, it would be enough.

"*Alexander* and her convoy are due in approximately two hours," Sherazi reported. "You realize there's no way we can leave this to Coati's people, right, sir? The *Conqueror*-class ships are easily *Poseidon*'s superior in every sense. She's almost a third bigger than we are. We've only recently cracked the Federation's latest generation of stabilizers."

Which was the problem, of course. The latest generation of Castle Federation warships had *no* equals. They were eighty million cubic meters to the sixty-four million of *Poseidon* and her sisters. The Commonwealth was currently constructing a new generation of ships that clocked in at seventy-five million, but until they deployed, the Federation's top-line ships were unbeatable one on one.

James was surprised they'd sent one of their limited number of *Conquerors* out this way, though it gave him the opportunity to deal a serious blow to the Alliance.

But Sherazi was right. If *Poseidon* couldn't take *Alexander* on her own, even all sixteen of the ships Coati had brought combined were out of their league.

"I know," James confirmed. "Our orders were clear: we were to take one of Roberts's ships, and powerful as *Alexander* is, she's an easier target than both of the other ships." He shook his head.

"Our orders have changed at this point," he told Sherazi. "We'll engage directly once *Alexander* arrives. Katanas, missiles, and try to close to lance range. We'll make a fight of it."

"Then they'll know we were out here."

"The goal is to divert Alliance forces," James reminded his subordinate. "Any attempt to sow friction between the Imperium and Federation was entirely secondary. At this point, we almost want them to know we're out here.

"Let *Alexander* call for help. It will only help our mission in the end."

And the sooner the Alliance sent major forces out this way, the sooner one Commodore James Tecumseh could go home and leave "poor" Commodore Coati to face an Alliance fleet on his own.

———

"So, how many of our friends out there are actually new?" James asked his analyst as the clock continued to tick down. They'd been tracking Coati's ships all along, and he was pretty sure the pirate was playing games with just how many they'd actually seen.

The pirates obviously had at least the sixteen ships they'd brought today, but...

"We had drive signatures and other IDs on thirteen ships before," Leila Kosta, the dark-haired and diminutive Lieutenant Commander who headed the Flag Deck Analysis Team, replied. "Current analysis says nine of those ships are out here."

James whistled silently.

"Only nine? What's the certainty on that?" he asked.

"Over ninety percent," Kosta replied. "That put Coati's total strength at at least twenty ships."

"That doesn't make any sense," James pointed out. "I'll give you that he's captured more than enough freighters to give him the twenty Class One manipulators, but those corsairs are custom built. They're unique. Who the hell builds *twenty* purpose-designed pirate ships for someone like Coati?"

"I don't think anyone built them for him," Kosta told him. "The only way he has that many ships is if he's building them himself—it wouldn't need to be much of a shipyard to build twenty ships over the ten years he's been operating."

"That's a lot more resources than we thought he had," the Commodore said. "If he has a shipyard..." James shook his head. "I figured l'*Estación de Muerte* was a secondary base, but that suggests his core base is..."

"Huge," the analyst replied. "Would explain where he get the Federation starfighters from, too: he got his hands on the design at some point and has been building them himself."

James looked back to the display with its sixteen pirate ships. Each of those ships carried a single ten-ship squadron of Cobra starfighters, totaling more starfighters than many carriers. It was definitely more second-line Federation starfighters than he suspected Castle had ever lost track of, and Coati had replaced the three dozen fighters he'd lost in the Antioch raid far too quickly.

"We may have underestimated our ally," he said softly. "But it's too late now. Commodore Sherazi," he reached out to *Poseidon*'s Captain. "What's our status?"

"Starfighters ready to launch, missile tubes primed. We are fifteen million kilometers from the estimated emergence point, and *Alexander* is due in under five minutes. Any change to our orders?"

"No," James told him. Kosta's analysis suggested all sorts of consequences for the long run, but it wasn't going to change *Alexander*'s fate.

"Engage as per the plan."

———

"WE HAVE EMERGENCE."

"It's always nice when people are punctual," James observed, watching the multiple jump flares as the convoy entered the Salvatore system. "It's a shame we don't have the jammers this time."

They hadn't had the time or the resources to duplicate the network of modified missiles that had allowed them to take on *Maasai* without being identified. This time, they would be seen and *Poseidon* would be identified.

And this time, it wouldn't matter.

"Launch all starfighters," James ordered. "Move up and keep pace with Coati's ships. *Poseidon* at the core, Commodore Sherazi. *Alexander* is going to target us first; keep us intact."

The Commonwealth and pirate formation unfolded, spreading out to envelop the incoming ships now they had a firm location for them. Thirty Katanas flashed free from *Poseidon*'s launch tubes, joining with the hundred and sixty Cobras Coati's ships launched.

Alexander reacted far faster than any crew had any business moving, and James inhaled sharply as the Federation ship's starfighters flashed into space, three squadrons at a time. One launch. Two. *Three.*

Seventy-two starfighters formed up around the battlecruiser and *Alexander* flipped in space, pointing the massive spike of her bulk right at *Poseidon.*

"She's coming right for us," Kosta told James briskly. "The freighters are going in the opposite direction; they're all pushing to Tier Two acceleration and running for safe gravity zones."

"Damn," the Commodore replied. He was actually impressed. Emergence had given the convoy a significant velocity in-system that the freighters were going to need to dump to escape, but the freighters were spending fuel freely to get up to almost two hundred gravities and boost away from the pirate fleet.

"We have Coati on the channel," Amoto reported.

"Put him through."

"We need to engage faster," the pirate snapped at James as soon as the link was established. "Our prey is getting away!"

"Our prey, Commodore Coati, is *Alexander,*" James replied. "And our Federation friend is heading straight for us. If we can't handle her, it's not going to matter how far the freighters got. I suggest you prepare for a fight. *Alexander* is one of the most powerful warships in existence, after all."

The pirate glared at him silently for a few seconds, then cut the channel.

"Sherazi is launching missiles," Kosta told James. "Fighters are moving forward. We've got them outnumbered almost three to one."

"Which is about the only odds I'd be comfortable sending Cobras against Falcons with," James agreed. "Our Katanas are a match for them, but Coati's ships are utterly outclassed."

"I'm not sure I *care,*" the analyst admitted, and James chuckled.

"Right now, I care," he told her. "Because right now, I need those Cobras to help kill one of the Federation's most powerful battlecruisers."

The missile salvo passing through the fighter formation was impressive. Each of Coati's modular ships only carried four missile launchers, but sixteen of them put a *lot* of missiles into space.

Combined with *Poseidon*'s launch, eighty-four modern capital ship missiles blazed toward *Alexander* at a thousand and fifty gravities.

Alexander launched a twenty-missile salvo in return, and James hid a sigh of relief. She carried twice as many starfighters as his ship, so he'd worried just how many missile launchers the Federation ship carried.

Then *Alexander* fired again after an eighteen-second delay, and his sigh of relief disappeared. *Poseidon*'s launchers had a thirty-two-second reload, and they needed to wait for Coati's people with even older launchers to fire full salvos.

The attackers would have an eighty-four missile salvo every forty-six seconds. *Alexander* would be launching five salvos to their two... and the intelligence James had seen suggested the battlecruiser had the magazines to keep that up for far longer than this battle was going to last.

"Sir..." Kosta studied the screen, her voice quiet. "Are we sure we brought enough ships?"

"*Chariot* wasn't back yet," James pointed out. "While we know Coati has more in hiding, I think this will be enough. Commodore Sherazi, hold our Katanas back for missile defense.

"We're going to do this by the book."

"Use starfighters to shield us while we close to lance range?"

"Exactly. Our deflectors are as strong as hers and so are our lances. We'll both range at one point five million klicks, and I have faith in your gunners."

"All right," *Poseidon*'s Captain said grimly. "Let's hope Coati's people can keep up."

The Falcons had moved out in front of *Alexander* to form a shield, then reduced their acceleration to match their mothership's two-hundred-and-fifty-gravity acceleration. ECM, lances and lasers reached out from them as the first missile salvos closed.

The Commonwealth's Stormwind capital ship missiles were smart, capable weapon systems, but so were Falcons. Most of the first salvo died when they ran into the starfighters, and the handful that survived were no match for the battlecruiser's own defenses.

"What the?!" Kosta exclaimed. "Sir, three of Coati's corsairs just went to five hundred gees!"

"What are they doing?" James demanded. "Get me Coati!"

The link to the Commodore resumed a few moments later, the pirate leader watching his own holodisplay.

"What?" Coati asked grumpily.

"What are your people doing?"

"Going after the freighters," the pirate replied. "Those are *our* objective, even if they're not yours. Half of my starfighters are going with them."

James saw that as the pirate said it, their fighter formation splitting into three now. The Katanas, holding position a fixed distance in front of the fleet to shield them against the incoming Federation missiles. Eighty Cobras slowing to join them but not quite aligned with the Katanas.

And eighty more Cobras, cutting away from the group with the three pirate ships to try to catch the fleeing freighters.

"You realize you're sending them to their deaths, right?" James asked softly. "They're not going to clear *Alexander*'s lance range on their way by."

The first Federation missiles salvos slammed into the starfighter screen as they spoke. Even as he argued with Coati, part of the Terran Commodore's mind was watching that clash. The missiles were wiped out, but three of the pirate Cobras died with them.

The pirate flight crews were sloppy. Half-trained. Coati didn't seem to value them or their fighters much, which was telling in and of itself. Neither starfighters nor starfighter flight crew were easy to replace, but the pirate warlord treated them as not merely expendable but disposable.

"They'll pass over two million kilometers from *Alexander*," Coati objected. "They'll be fine."

"With the deflectors your ships have? She's going to gut them like fish," James told him. "She's a modern battlecruiser, Coati. Do *not* underestimate her!"

"One of us has to make a profit here, Commodore Tecumseh," the pirate snapped. "You focus on *Alexander*, I'll focus on my part."

The channel cut out and James shook his head.

"Time till *Alexander* ranges on those idiots?" he asked.

"Assuming she has the same beams we do, she'll range on the ships in less than five minutes," Kosta told him. "The starfighters might make it past her, depending on what she does."

James studied the tactical feed. Coati was going to lose a sixth of his ships no matter what, but the starfighters…

"The fighters will overhaul the freighters before they can go FTL?" he asked.

"Two of them, at least."

"What are you prepared to sacrifice, Captain?" James murmured as he looked at *Alexander*'s icon on the feed. If they diverted their starfighters, the missile salvos heading for the battlecruiser could be deadly…but if they *didn't* intercept Coati's starfighters, they could disable or destroy the ships *Alexander*'s whole charge had been intended to protect.

The second salvo from the pirate fleet hit the Federation fighter screen while he was watching. Missiles blew apart in their dozens, and this time, several of the Falcons were caught in the blast zones.

The surviving missiles were too few to punch through *Alexander*'s defenses, but the starfighters didn't even seem to be paying attention. As soon as the missiles cleared their intercept zone, the Falcons were swinging about and going to full acceleration.

"There they go," Kosta concluded. "Their course will intercept Coati's Cobras at less than ten thousand kilometers, and then put them in Neverwinter orbit before anyone else can intercept them."

All sixty-plus surviving fighters were moving, James noted. That was going to leave *Alexander* without fighter cover against the missile salvos already closing in.

He'd barely finished the thought before the Federation ships demonstrated exactly how they were going to handle that. Their leading salvo reached the next salvo from James's ships in space, then swerved in space on intercept courses as their jammers went to full strength.

Explosions pockmarked the tactical feed and twenty missiles wiped out over thirty…and then the salvo ran into the *next* set of Federation missiles.

Less than a dozen missiles survived that intercept, and those ran headlong into *Alexander*'s defenses.

"Kosta, check my analysis here," James said slowly. "Their missiles perform better in defensive mode, don't they?"

The analyst was silent for a moment as she checked her data.

"Yes, sir," she confirmed. "It's not just that we weren't allowing for the possibility; they're at least thirty percent more effective at the close-range maneuvering necessary for the role."

"Interesting," the Commodore noted. "Make sure that gets in our report to the Marshal, will you? It's important to know."

Capital ship missiles were rarely wasted in a defensive role, and it was rare to get solid data on the interactions when they were. Any detailed information on the use of Alliance missiles in that role was valuable.

"I'm not sure we could do what *Alexander* is doing," Kosta admitted, watching as the Federation ship maneuvered her missiles into the course of the incoming salvos again and again. "Damn, they're good."

"We'd better hope Sherazi's gunners are better, or this is going to be a rough day," James told her. "There go Coati's ships."

The pirate ships were smaller than a true capital ship, but they were still big targets and their deflectors were significantly more out of date than their weapons. *Alexander* opened up with her positron lances as the modular ships crossed the two-and-a-half-million-kilometer line.

A positron lance was a lightspeed weapon. With an eight-second travel time, hitting the target wasn't easy, and they missed with the first salvo. Over twenty beams of pure antimatter, each powerful enough to shatter a planet, flared into existence, and James swallowed a moment of fear.

Commonwealth Intelligence had badly underestimated the *Conquerors*' lance armament—not least because nothing had ever survived entering range of one of the battlecruisers' beams. *Alexander* had a third again as many of the megaton-and-a-half-per-second weapons as *Poseidon* did.

And her gunners were good. The first beams cut into space for about three seconds, sweeping around for their targets and failing to make contact before they cut out. There was a two-second pause, allowing the pirate ships to sweep closer—and to begin to panic, flipping in space to desperately try to escape *Alexander*'s wrath.

They didn't make it. They *couldn't* make it. The second salvo of twenty-four beams lashed out, and while three quarters of them missed, six didn't.

All three ships disappeared in balls of blue-white fire, their own mass turning into explosives and tearing them apart.

"Federation starfighters are launching missiles at Coati's ships," Kosta announced. "Our missiles are getting closer, but I don't know if we're going to get any through. Their missiles aren't getting past our screen, but Coati's lost another half-dozen ships."

She shook her head.

"I swear some of his pilots have never even been aboard a real starfighter before," she told James. "They're not qualified to fly in combat."

"Coati seems to be extremely cavalier about them," he agreed. "Crews and starfighters alike."

Even as they were speaking, the group of pirate fighters chasing the freighters ran headlong into the two-hundred-odd missiles the intercepting Federation fighters had launched. Eighty Cobras should have been able to handle less than four missiles apiece.

Should.

Explosions lit up the display and less than a quarter of the pirate starfighters survived long enough to meet the *second* Federation salvo.

Then *Alexander*'s starfighters shot through the debris field and continued on their way toward Neverwinter. To be able to intercept the pirates, they'd had to accept a vector that took them out of the fight, but by continuing on that course, they were safe.

Now it was down to the remaining pirate ships and *Poseidon* versus *Alexander*, a duel that James Tecumseh was grimly certain was going to cost him and Coati dearly—but a duel *Alexander* couldn't win.

"Wait, she's breaking off!" Kosta announced. "Oh, Starless Void."

The acceleration data attached to *Alexander* on James's tactical feed explained the exclamation. The battlecruiser had been heading toward *Poseidon* and her pirate companions at two hundred and fifty gravities.

Now she was burning at ninety degrees to that course, increasing the range at which she'd pass her enemies...at over *five hundred* gravities.

"That's going to cost her," James murmured. The difference between fuel consumption at Tier Two and Tier Three acceleration was orders of magnitude. Several of them. Every second that *Alexander* maintained Tier Three acceleration took enough fuel to accelerate for about eight hours at Tier Two.

"But it's working. Her closest approach is going to be one point eight million kilometers," Kosta calculated aloud. "That's outside beam range, if intel is even close on her deflector strength."

"Keep up the missile pounding," James ordered Sherazi. "That's our best chance—we can still kill her, or at least slow her down."

He was not looking forward to his conversation with the Marshal if *Alexander* escaped unharmed.

"Sir, Coati's on the channel again."

"Put him on."

The pirate was standing on the bridge of his ship now, pacing back and forth before stepping up to the camera with his fists clenched.

"You were right," he ground out. "We're not getting any loot out of this shitshow, and now my people are telling me that fucking battle-cruiser is going to get away? Why aren't you sending your damn fighters in?!"

"Because thirty Katanas can't take down a modern battlecruiser, and your starfighters apparently aren't worth the duct tape holding them together," James snapped. "Unless something changes, that bitch is going to get away and there is nothing we can do except keep pounding her with missiles."

Coati growled and cut the channel again, to James's amusement.

If *Alexander* wanted to run, he was willing to let her. With Coati's ships in support, he was reasonably sure *Poseidon* could take her...but he wasn't *certain*.

"Stars Eternal!" Kosta exclaimed. *"We got her!"*

James returned his attention to the display, where *Alexander* was spinning in space and spewing atmosphere.

"Sherazi's people got a missile through, somehow," the analyst told him. "Her acceleration just went to nothing; she's gone fully ballistic."

"How long till lance range?" James demanded.

"If she doesn't get her engines back, two minutes."

And maybe, just maybe, the cruiser had lost enough beams to make it an even fight.

"Commodore Sherazi?" he asked smoothly.

"We see," *Poseidon*'s commander replied. "Warming up the lances now; let's see if she makes a fight of it... Wait, what the—"

The icon on the feed dissolved into a swarm of static that it took James a solid several seconds to identify.

"Stetson fields!" Kosta said aloud just as he recognized them. "She's going FTL."

Space tore...and *Alexander* was gone.

Mostly.

"Is that what I think it is?" James said slowly.

"If you think it's about a hundred-meter-wide chunk of *Alexander*'s outer hull... yeah, yeah it is."

26

Deep Space en route to Reinhardt System
22:45 October 29, 2736 Earth Standard Meridian Date/Time
DSC-052 Kodiak

"WE'RE STILL PICKING through the damage," the recorded message from Senior Fleet Commander Hanif Kanaan noted from the main holoprojector on *Kodiak*'s bridge, "but we've lost our backup Class One Mass manipulator, our primary antimatter containment units, and at least five of the eight main engines.

"Worse, our fighter bays are wrecked, as is the entirety of Broadside Charlie," *Alexander*'s executive officer continued grimly. "All told, we're down eight of the main positron lances and seven missile launchers, and I'm not sure we can trust the ship's power network sufficiently to energize the remaining main beams or more than a dozen secondary beams."

Kanaan shook his head, his eyes almost as dark as his skin.

"Captain Sarka remains in surgery as I record this. The prognosis is positive but it looks like she'll lose her right arm and the one organic eye she had left. Our casualties were...heavy. We're still sorting out the exact details, but we're at almost two thousand KIA and MIA, plus a thousand wounded."

Kyle winced. *Alexander* was a big, modern ship, but her crew was still barely over five thousand people. Sixty percent of the crew of one of his ships was wounded or dead, and they'd lost over half their firepower.

"Fortunately, we have enough Stetson stabilizer emitters to maintain both inner and outer fields, so we are capable of FTL." Kanaan shook his head. "Some of the worst damage was when we went FTL, but there was no way we could fight without engines.

"I think Captain Sarka made the right call. I'll be in touch again once I have a more complete damage report and an update on the Captain's condition, sir.

"*Alexander* out."

Kyle was glad he'd kept the actual partial damage report that had accompanied Kanaan's message to his own console. The rest of the crew on the bridge for the late-night FTL dark watch was looking shaky enough when he turned his gaze on them.

"*Alexander* just got jumped by almost half again her mass and cubage in warships," he pointed out to them. "And she's still with us."

Barely. From the sounds of Kanaan's description, Captain Sarka's ship was a wreck. Fortunately, however, she was an *FTL-capable* wreck, which had saved the lives of everyone left aboard. Humanity's ability to deliver energy to target had far outstripped their ability to protect those targets—a ship would usually survive a single one-gigaton antimatter warhead, but it wasn't something you could rely on. She would almost never survive two.

"Both *Alexander* and her convoy are headed to Serengeti," he continued. "So are we after Reinhardt. We'll meet them there and we'll make sure everyone's okay, but there's nothing we can do until everyone gets there.

"There's definitely no point in panicking, understand?"

"Do you want us to keep this quiet?" one of the Chiefs asked, glancing at the tiny dark watch crew.

"No," Kyle replied after a moment's thought. "I'll include it in the morning all-hands update. Just don't go spreading panic, all right, people?"

"We're the Castle Federation Space Navy, sir," the same Chief replied. "We don't panic."

"Good." Kyle shook his head. "Ping Commander Taggart and Vice Commodore Song for me, plus Mr. Nebula," he ordered. "Have them meet me in my office in thirty minutes. Then get ahold of Captain von Lambert, let him know I'll want him, his XO, and his CAG on video conference at the same time."

That would give them time to shower and put clothes on. This was important, but with *Alexander* and her charges clear of Salvatore, it wasn't truly *urgent*.

He still wasn't going to wait until morning to check in with the Alliance Joint Chiefs.

THE DIPLOMAT and his two senior officers stumbled into his office exactly on schedule, slumping into seats and gratefully accepting the cups of hot coffee Kyle's steward pressed on them. From the looks of it, all three had been sleeping. His wallscreen showed Captain von Lambert's office aboard *Thoth*, where the three senior officers of the Imperial ship were in a similar situation. From von Lambert's posture, Kyle guessed he'd heard…but his officers hadn't.

"Our entire situation just changed, people," he told them calmly once everyone had taken at least a few swallows of caffeine. "I received preliminary reports from *Alexander*'s arrival in Salvatore half an hour ago, and things just went to shit."

"I take it that it wasn't a quiet stopover," Nebula said.

"No. *Alexander* was jumped by a fleet of pirate ships, sixteen of the modular corsairs we know were involved in *Crusader*'s destruction… and a *Hercules*-class Terran Commonwealth Navy battlecruiser."

His office was suddenly very, very quiet.

"Captain Sarka successfully protected the convoy she was guarding and escaped into FTL," Kyle continued. "Unfortunately, while I haven't received final damage assessments, it appears that *Alexander* was badly damaged in the fight. We're looking at somewhere in the region of three thousand casualties, fatal and otherwise, and a fifty-percent reduction in firepower along with significant hull damage.

"I'm going to wait until the final survey by her engineers, but I suspect we're sending *Alexander* home—and being happy we're still sending her home in one piece."

"Damn. That's...a lot more than a third of our firepower," von Lambert pointed out. "*Alexander* was our most powerful ship."

"Which I suspect is why they went after her," Kyle replied. "They were making a point. I doubt the ass-kicking that Sarka handed them was the point they were after, but we got the message loud and clear: the Terrans are out here, and they're working with the local pirates."

"That makes sense," Nebula said. "A lot of my contacts have said that the main pirate group out here has been growing bolder lately, and *Crusader* was taken down by modern munitions. It would make sense if a Commonwealth task group had moved in and made an alliance with the bastards."

"Then why reveal themselves now?" Song asked. "If they've gone this long without even being identified..."

"They're making a point," Kyle repeated. "They *want* us to know they're here now. We sent a task group to deal with pirates, and they're trying to show us it won't be enough. They want a major force deployment out here—which will weaken us back home."

"So, we can't even ask for help?" Taggart demanded.

"I wasn't planning on it," Kyle told them. "We have a carrier, a strike cruiser and a bomber wing. Even assuming the Terrans have two *Hercules*es out here, which I'm afraid is reasonable, we can take them."

"That's...that's daring, sir," Taggart replied. "Do we really think the bombers will make that much difference?"

"Yes," Song cut in. "Having watched Williams's people in training? They can make up the difference in weight, especially if the Terrans don't see them coming."

"We'll need to make sure we do this carefully and we do this right," Kyle warned his officers. "*Alexander* is five and a half days out of Serengeti. Cutting our stop in Reinhardt to the bare minimum, we're seven days out ourselves.

"Put your brains to work, people. By the time we're all in Serengeti, I want a plan for getting the Terrans to fight us—on *our* terms."

———

AT THIS POINT, Kyle would have had to consult his implant and consciously analyze data to be certain how many times he'd spoken with Fleet Admiral Meredith Blake, the commanding officer of the Castle Federation Space Navy. He'd never met her in person, but the q-com-enabled video conference he found himself in at midnight ESMDT wasn't the first long-distance conversation they'd had.

He had actually met Sky Marshal Octavian von Stenger in person now, though that didn't make being in a conference with two of the senior members of the Alliance Joint Chiefs any less intimidating.

"Thank you for finding the time to speak with me," he told them.

"We were the members of the Joint Chiefs awake, Captain Roberts," Blake replied. "Conveniently, we were also the ones with ships out there. From the priority of your message, I'm assuming our worst-case scenario has been confirmed?"

"Yes, ma'am," Kyle said instantly. "*Alexander* was engaged by a TCN *Hercules*-class battlecruiser. The Terran had the support of a local pirate fleet of significantly greater strength than we expected as well, and *Alexander* was badly damaged.

"While final judgment will wait until we're all at Serengeti and can review her status in detail, I suspect we're sending *Alexander* home," he warned them. "My current estimate is that we are facing a *Hercules*, likely an additional equivalent Terran warship, and a pirate fleet of roughly equal combat capability to another *Hercules*."

The two Admirals on his screen exchanged a tired glance.

"I'm not sure we're in a position to reinforce you," von Stenger finally said.

"Most of our free units have been deployed forward in Operation Third Catacomb," Blake added. "We've drawn the defenders at Via Somnia out of position, and Seventh Fleet is about to bring the hammer down on a Commonwealth Fleet Base for the first time since the last war."

"But between Fourth Fleet, Seventh Fleet, and the task forces supporting Seventh Fleet, the cupboard is bare, Captain," the Imperial said. He exhaled, considering. "I can probably convince the Imperator to…"

"No," Kyle cut him off. "I have two capital ships, one of them equipped with a bomber wing, and I know my enemy now. I wouldn't turn down reinforcements, sirs, but we can't strip the home systems of any of the core Alliance powers—that's what Walkingstick wants. If he can punch out Castle or Coraline, the war is over."

"Captain, this is not the time for ego or pride to get in the way," Blake pointed out. "We owe the systems of the Antioch-Serengeti Free Trade Zone our protection, and if it's a Commonwealth fleet out there, then it is now an *Alliance* problem."

"Ma'am, I'm not sure we'd get any ships out here in time to make a difference," he admitted. "This situation needs to be resolved fast or the Zone may well collapse under the damage already done.

"Since that's the case, I can't justify asking for reinforcements that have to come from the Home Fleets."

"Is there anything we can do, Captain Roberts?" Blake asked.

"Distance is the biggest factor, ma'am," he admitted. "I'm grateful to the Sky Marshal for making sure that *Thoth* was with us. Without her, we'd be facing a serious fight I'm not sure even cleverness and aggression could carry."

"Cleverness and aggression are useful weapons, Captain Roberts, but they are not miracles."

"No, ma'am," he agreed. "My people perform the miracles. We'll make it happen."

Somehow.

Blake shook her head.

"Pull this off, Roberts, and both the Federation and the Alliance will be in your debt."

"Again," von Stenger added. "Good luck, son. You're going to need it."

27

Deep Space en route to Reinhardt System
10:00 October 30, 2736 Earth Standard Meridian Date/Time
DSC-052 Kodiak

"It's good to see you, Captain Sarka. After I heard the extent of your injuries, I was more than a little worried," Kyle told his subordinate over the q-com link. "As it is, I think he must have been exaggerating. You look as good as I've ever seen you."

"God, Roberts, I didn't think I was *that* ugly," Sarka replied with a chuckle that rapidly turned into a wince. Her right arm and eye had been replaced with blocky metal emergency prostheses. "I can barely see or use the damn arm, but it's better than nothing. The docs tell me both will learn, and either I can keep these—which work just fine once they've learned—or transfer the software to a proper cybernetic like my other eye."

"So far, I've managed to avoid needing those," he admitted, "though at least you missed needing a neural implant regrown."

"I'm currently just mentally complaining about every single person

I know who's had limbs regenerated," Sarka told him. "Bitching at them in my head helps distract from the fact that my face hurts."

"I read your doctor's report," Kyle replied, the humor fading. "You need to be transferred to a top-line hospital, preferably groundside back home. You might not regen, but you're still due a new limb and a month of physical therapy."

"I'm not even the worst hurt on my crew," she admitted. "Modern medicine is wonderful, but..." She shrugged eloquently. "I lost a lot of people, and some of those who lived won't even walk for a while. At least being allergic to standard regen means they *do* stick these chunks of circuitry on me straight away."

The emergency cybernetics were perfectly functional, but the process of installing *any* cybernetic rendered regen almost impossible. Doctors preferred not to install them, giving up immediate functionality for the ability to fully restore the patient later.

"You saved the entire convoy, Captain Sarka," Kyle told her. "I've reviewed *Alexander*'s automatic after-action report, though I look forward to both your and Kanaan's commentary on it, and I can't see anything you could have done differently. They brought overwhelming force and you kicked it back in their teeth.

"Gods, Captain, you did well," he insisted. "And my own report on the affair will reflect that."

"Thank you, sir. What happens now?"

"Well, since someone sensibly set her scatter point at Serengeti and that's where I'm heading, we all rendezvous there. From there, I think *Alexander* will likely be heading home with the wounded—most definitely including *you*, Captain Sarka—and the rest of us are going hunting."

"I'm almost more bothered by the pirates than the Commonwealth," she admitted. "They had Cobras, sir. A lot of Cobras—and those modular ships of theirs are no slouches, either. Shitty deflectors, but four missile launchers and God only knows what for lances, plus able to combine multiple ships to make a single A-S bubble?"

"My chief engineer is, for once, not bored and causing trouble because of that," Kyle replied with a soft chuckle. "She's says it shouldn't *be* possible, but if it is, she's damn well going to work out how… and perhaps more importantly, if the ships built to do it are vulnerable somehow."

"So, you're going to take them on?" Sarka asked.

"Yes," he confirmed. "I've got a few plans I'm mulling through, and I'm looking forward to hearing from the rest of the team. We'll get these bastards, Kristyna. Commonwealth and pirate alike."

She sighed, shaking her head.

"I've talked to the merchant skippers out here," she said. "These pirates…they're as bad as a bad lot comes. They don't do ransoms. They just kill their victims, make sure there's no witnesses. That kind of atrocity…"

"It's out of character for the Terrans," he agreed. "Even when their fanatics fall into atrocity, it's a grander level of grotesque than that. Worlds burned, not crews raped."

"Believe me, if the Commonwealth has hitched their wagon to these scum, my sympathy for any of them is limited. I'm going to see all of the bastards burn, Terran and local pirate alike."

"Damn it, sir, now you've got me wishing I could stay and hand you the matches."

"You need two good arms to hand me enough matches," he said with a chuckle. "I need you to go home and heal. We need every *Conqueror* we can get, and I'm not losing one because I was stupid enough to send a crippled ship into a fight.

"Understand, Captain Sarka?"

———

AFTER *ALEXANDER*'S encounter in the Salvatore system, Kyle made certain that his entire crew was awake and on duty when *Kodiak* arrived in Reinhardt. For himself, the distraction was welcome. Being on duty meant he wasn't thinking about the fact that Mira was apparently commanding the flagship of one of the biggest offensives the Alliance had launched to date.

"Emergence complete," Houshian reported. "All ships on target and on vector for Schwarzwald."

"Sterling? Any unexpected visitors?" Kyle asked his tactical officer.

"I'm reading a small number of sublight ships in orbit of Schwarzwald and two squadrons of Typhoons on a high-orbit patrol," the older officer replied. "Nothing outside the immediate vicinity of the Schwarzwald planetary system, nothing big enough to be A-S-capable and nothing I'd call hostile."

"Good," Kyle acknowledged. Reinhardt's main economic drivers were the massive open pit mines on Schwarzwald's "moon" Rhine, an airless planet seventy percent of the habitable world's size but completely lacking in atmosphere. Orbiting foundries above Schwarzwald and Rhine churned the products of those strip mines into raw metals and simple products that had been sold across the region even before the Free Trade Zone.

Schwarzwald itself, while habitable, was a harsh world for humanity to live on. Much of the profits and production of the heavy industrialization of Rhine went to simply keeping the two hundred million people in the system alive and comfortable despite their cold and tectonically active planet.

The history in his implants suggested that this was hardly the first time Schwarzwald had needed emergency food shipments, though the scale was new—and the delay was more than anyone would have anticipated.

"Let them know we're here," he told Jamison. "They should be glad to see our two grocery carts."

"I may phrase that more politely when I speak to them, sir," she said repressively, and he grinned at her. It was a forced thing, but he was *reasonably* sure his crew couldn't tell.

He had a lot of practice appearing more cheerful than he might feel.

"*Anteater* and *Golden Aurochs* are beginning their acceleration toward Schwarzwald," Sterling reported.

"Take us after them, Houshian," Kyle ordered. "Nice and slow."

"Sir, I have *Anteater's* Captain on a q-com channel for you," Jamison reported.

"Put her on," he told her.

A *very* pale-skinned woman with a burgundy hijab appeared on his screen, an easy smile marking Captain Al-Assani's face.

"Captain Roberts, I've been speaking with Captain Berenstein aboard *Golden Aurochs*," she told him. "We heard about *Alexander* and, well, this system looks pretty clear to us. Are you seeing anything we've missed?"

"Our sensors aren't seeing much either," he agreed, wondering where she was going.

"If you can get the Reinhardt Space Force to, say, send one of those starfighter squadrons out to meet us, I think we can get ourselves the rest of the way if you want to head on to Serengeti."

That would cut as much as a day off his trip, but it would also put a significant risk on the two ships he was leaving behind.

"You'd be stuck here until we had another escort come through," he warned.

"We can deal with that," Al-Assani told him. "It'll take us days to offload this food, Captain. Longer to load a new cargo of metals. We can wait until the next ship comes by, and a day may make all the difference for you—and if you succeed in your mission, Captain, we won't need an escort anymore."

"I'll talk to the RSF," he promised. "Thank you, Captain Al-Assani. You're right. Timing might be everything right now."

"Inshallah, all will go well and I won't see you again, Captain Roberts," she said. "Fly safe and fight hard. The whole sector is looking to you."

The channel dropped and Kyle sighed.

"Have we contacted Schwarzwald Control?" he asked Jamison.

"We have," she confirmed. "They're pleased to see us and have assigned vectors. We have q-com codes for them now, relaying through the Castle and Antioch Switchboard Stations."

"All right. Get me RSF command," he ordered."

———

QUANTUM ENTANGLEMENT WAS AN INHERENTLY point-to-point system. One particle changed, its entangled partner changed—no matter how far apart, no matter what was between. But since only that one other particle changed, it didn't allow for omnidirectional transmission.

To solve the problem, humanity's engineers had resurrected the concept of a switchboard. The blocks of entangled particles in *Kodiak*'s q-com array linked to a number of space stations across human space, mostly the one in Castle orbit, that contained millions of similar blocks. Those stations were linked to other ships and to other switchboard stations.

The routing code that Schwarzwald Control had given Jamison had their transmission going to the Castle Switchboard Station, where it was relayed to a set of particle blocks entangled with particles aboard the Antioch Switchboard Station, which then relayed the message to the RSF command station in orbit of Schwarzwald.

Time delay was almost nonexistent, but it still took several minutes to actually get someone on the other end of the channel. Finally, a blue-haired man in a simple white uniform with a single star on his collar appeared on Kyle's neural feed.

"I am Rear Admiral Vincent Merkel," he greeted Kyle. "I apologize for the delay; how can I be of assistance?"

"Admiral Merkel," Kyle returned his greeting. "I am Captain Kyle Roberts of the Castle Federation Space Navy. We're escorting a convoy of ships, two of which I believe you were expecting."

"*Anteater* and *Golden Aurochs*," Merkel confirmed. "We're glad to finally see them, Captain Roberts. Things have not become truly dangerous down here, but some of our towns and cities were starting to run perilously close to the wire where even rationing wasn't going to get everyone fed."

"With the pirate situation, it was dangerous for them to move alone," Kyle replied. "That said, the situation with the pirates has escalated and I need to move on to the Serengeti System as soon as possible. Would you be able to deploy starfighters to escort the two food freighters in to a safe orbit?"

"This is a safe system, Captain Roberts," Merkel objected. "They will be fine regardless."

"Admiral, Antioch lost a battlecruiser in their *own* system," Kyle pointed out. "I'm not certain any system here is safe."

The Reinhardt man winced.

"I hadn't considered that aspect of *Crusader*'s fate," he said slowly. "I'll have our fourth squadron move out to rendezvous with the ships," he promised. "Will you be able to meet with my senior officers and the President before you leave?"

"No," Kyle told him. "If you can escort *Anteater* and *Aurochs* in, we're going to be leaving immediately. I have a damaged warship to take care of."

"Ah." Merkel nodded slowly. "Very well, Captain. Our fighters will be on their way momentarily. Safe travels, and good luck with your mission."

"Thank you, Admiral."

He cut the channel and turned to his staff.

"Houshian, set up the course to get us to Serengeti and transfer it to everyone else. Sterling, let me know as soon as those fighters are moving. We'll let them get to about thirty minutes' flight from the freighter, and then we're going to be on our way, though they should make orbit before we're clear to go FTL.

"We have a date with some pirates and I don't want to be late."

28

Deep Space en route to Serengeti System
20:00 November 3, 2736 Earth Standard Meridian Date/Time
DSC-052 Kodiak

"ENTER!"

The door to Captain Roberts's office slid open at the barked command, and Michelle Williams stepped through. She wasn't entirely sure why she'd been called up to the Captain, and she was feeling more than a little nervous at the summons.

That lasted about ten seconds after she came through the door, long enough for Roberts to gesture her to a seat with the beer in his hand and raise a questioning eyebrow at her.

"Beer, Wing Commander?" he asked. "Or coffee, tea? I even think the machine can handle most vodka-based cocktails."

"Beer is fine, sir," she said slowly. "I'm technically off duty, but..."

"Once you're past a certain point, we're never off duty," he agreed. He popped the lid off a dark bottle and slid it across the table. "This is the last of my supply of microbrews from the Corona breweries," he admitted. "Anston Brewery is one of my favorites, but they don't keep enough stock on hand for my taste. I'd leave orbit with a pallet of their stuff every time if I could."

Michelle was actually familiar with Anston Brewery, though her salary certainly didn't extend to picking up entire pallets of their product! Or, at least, her Flight Commander salary hadn't—she hadn't exactly looked at her bank balance since they'd shipped out.

"Thank you, sir. What's this about?"

"This, Commander, is about the joys of being in charge of our entire inventory of bombers and currently being the most experienced bomber pilot and commander in the Alliance," Roberts told her. "We're all wracking our brains trying to think of clever ways to take out these pirates, but I realize that we're neglecting one of our most effective weapons.

"None of us, including me, really know everything your bombers can do, Williams," he continued. "We're up against the odds enough that we need to use every advantage at our disposal, so I wanted to pick your brains on just what we could do."

Michelle took a thoughtful sip of the beer, considering.

"Our biggest advantage is that I don't think anyone out here even knows they exist," she pointed out. "We launch, people are going to think we're just starfighters until our torps launch. Even then, they'll probably underestimate what our torps can do until they're in terminal approach."

"I'm already leaning toward bait and trojan horses," Roberts admitted. "Both of our warships are the same size as more modern freighters. It's not a deception we can maintain for long, but we can lure them in."

"They would expect the freighters to have an escort, though," Michelle pointed out. "We can't send out ships without an apparent escort or they'll know we're trying to fool them."

"Taking people by surprise in space usually involves making them look one way while you're winding up your fist in the other direction," the Captain agreed.

Michelle smiled as a thought struck her.

"So, we make them look at the warships," she suggested. "And have my bombers somewhere else. While they're not designed overly well for it, I suspect we can rig up an interface to dock the Vultures with the freighters' service airlocks."

"Which would keep your people from going stir-crazy trapped on their starfighters, while having the bombers be somewhere the pirates aren't expecting at all," Roberts agreed, his grin turning evil. "I like it, Commander. It's not an answer all on its own, but it's a good trick— one they won't see coming."

"Have the freighters run away, rig our vectors so it looks like we made a mistake?" she said.

"They'll bring the *Hercules* at us but send the corsairs after the freighters," he pointed out. "Which…works, to be honest. Your bombers will annihilate those pirates, and I'll take *Thoth* and *Kodiak* against an unsupported *Hercules*. We'll have to run some scenarios, but I like it. I didn't even think of using the bombers on their own."

"Thank you, sir," she replied. "Though, if possible, I'd prefer we had at least some starfighters with us. My Vultures aren't defenseless against starfighters, but we only have so many fighter missiles, and those pirate ships do have fighters aboard."

"We still have a few days to sort out details; I don't expect to be leaving Serengeti immediately," the Captain told her. He took a long pull of his beer, studying her.

"How are you liking your new command, Michelle?" he suddenly asked, his body language and tone shifting dramatically. Suddenly, he was no longer the task group commander, the master-after-god of two starships and ten thousand souls, but her old commanding officer, checking in.

"The bombers are something different," she said slowly. "I see a lot of ways we can improve on them with our own technology and design paradigms—it's pretty obvious that they're a prototype design and not even ours, after all.

"The crews took being thrown into a combat formation under my command better than I expected, too. We were test pilots, but I think we all knew we were going back to war. Made it easier."

"Easier than any of us had it at the start of the war," Kyle admitted.

"And yourself? You were put back together even by Tranquility, but you seem to be even better now."

She hesitated. That was more personal than she'd actually expected Roberts to get, even though they had served together before. She'd nearly accidentally killed him once, after all.

He'd also been the man who'd discovered that she'd been raped and made absolutely certain that James Randall was brought to justice. Rumor said that the consequences of that had been extreme, but that didn't show in the Captain's eyes.

"I am," she agreed. "Modern medicine is a wonderful thing, and time is a powerful tool. I don't think *any* of us are going to be okay until the war's over, now, but I'm at least as okay as everyone else aboard *Kodiak*."

"That's true on both counts," Roberts admitted with a shake of his head. "War rips apart our families, our partnerships. We lose too many friends along the way."

"Like Stanford," Michelle said softly, and the Captain nodded with a wince.

"Michael's death hurt," he admitted. "He'd been my strong right hand since I first came aboard *Avalon*, and he was a friend. But war... war has no respect."

She nodded her understanding, pausing in silent hesitation for a moment before speaking again.

"Sir, rumor has it you have a girlfriend with Seventh Fleet?" she asked hesitantly.

He eyed her questioningly but nodded.

"I do. Why?" he asked simply.

Michelle swallowed, recognizing that she was going further across the line between personal and professional than he had. She was *reasonably* sure this conversation still fell under "counseling an officer", but it was also heading in the direction of awkward.

"How do you handle it, sir?" she asked softly. "Angela is with Fourth Fleet, on the hospital ship, and I still can't not worry about her."

Captain Roberts chuckled, glancing at her bottle to check her remaining beer, then rose to check the fridge again.

"Here," he told her, sliding another beer across the table. "From the Imperator's personal micro-brewery. Most of Coral's beer *sucks*, but this one is decent. And this is not a conversation to have without a beer in hand, you get me?"

"Sir?"

"We're off the record now," he told her. "Call it a counseling session, call it crying on the boss's shoulder, whatever. Drink your beer."

She obeyed, finishing off the excellent Anston Brewery ale while waiting for her Captain to organize his thoughts.

"Having a lover on the front lines sucks," he finally told her. "It's not any better for them, but you knew that. Probably worse for Angela than for myself, Mira or you. The rest of us are on capital ships, but you're flying a starfighter—and no one in the Navy is unaware of the loss ratio for fighter strikes."

"I've made it this far," Michelle replied, "but I know. I'm not sure how to reassure her."

"You can't," Roberts said bluntly. "Any more than she can reassure you. Gods, Williams—my girlfriend is commanding the flagship of the biggest offensive we've launched to date. *Reassurance* isn't on anyone's damned agenda there."

"Damn," Michelle breathed. "I didn't know, sir."

"If you had known, someone would be having a lovely discussion about OPSEC," he pointed out. "And I won't give you more details than that. But...yeah. We deal, Commander. With various degrees of difficulty, I'm afraid."

"Enjoy what we have, then?"

"Basically. We don't know when it will end," Roberts admitted. "We could find out tomorrow they're gone. They could find out tomorrow we're gone. We take what time we have."

"No plans for the future?" Michelle asked, and the Captain sighed.

"I don't even know," he admitted. "I've always told people not to ask me for relationship advice; my track record is unimpressive. I've always been better at planning a military operation than my own personal future, so I have no idea."

GLYNN STEWART

"No getting engaged in wartime?" Michelle said, and Roberts laughed.

"That serious, huh?" he asked.

Michelle blinked in shock. She'd meant it as a joke, but...

"Maybe?"

"Go with what feels right," the Captain told her. "We don't know if we'll have tomorrow—but we don't know we won't, either!"

That...was more helpful than it might have been, and she nodded slowly, taking another swallow of beer.

"Thank you, sir. I appreciate it."

"You're welcome," Roberts replied. "Making me think myself, Commander. Sometimes, you just have to take a step back and try and decide just what you're after—and what you're prepared to risk for it."

29

THE REPORTS, simulations and data feeds hadn't truly prepared Kyle for the sight of *Alexander*. He understood, better than many, exactly what an antimatter missile strike did to a ship, but he'd never seen a ship this badly damaged that had managed to fly away.

Alexander was a rough arrowhead with the tip missing to make space for the fighter bay. Now…now, she was missing a hundred-meter chunk of her starboard "wing", ripped off when the battlecruiser had gone FTL. A massive blackened crater marked her upper flank on the same side, where an explosion fit to shatter planets had smashed into her massive armor.

Kodiak approached from behind, a screen of starfighters sweeping out to cover the wounded battlecruiser. More starfighters helped *Thoth* escort the convoy of freighters into Serengeti orbit, but none of the merchant captains had even blinked when *Kodiak* had taken off to rendezvous with *Alexander*.

"She's in rough shape," Sterling said aloud. "Going FTL like that… it was risky. The right move, but damn."

"I've seen worse," Kyle admitted. His first command, the Federation's first carrier, had been old and obsolete when he'd taken command…and a shattered wreck when he gave it up. His second command, the newest *Avalon*, had been in only slightly better shape than *Alexander* when he'd sent her in for repairs.

His last command, the black ops ship *Chameleon*, well… No one was going to admit to ever having seen her, regardless of how many pieces he'd brought her home in.

"Yeah, but was that still flying?" his tactical officer asked.

"Flying home. No more," Kyle agreed. "Which is all that Captain Sarka is going to be doing. Jamison—have you confirmed the Captain's arrival time?"

"Yes, sir. Her shuttle will be leaving in about five minutes; she'll be aboard at eleven hundred forty."

"Thank you, Lieutenant Commander. I'll be on the deck to meet her. Commander Taggart has the con."

"I have the con," his XO confirmed, stepping up next to his chair. Like everyone else on the bridge, Taggart was distracted by the feed of *Alexander*'s state.

"She looks awful," he murmured.

"She made it back," Kyle replied, equally softly. "And any fight you walk away from, Commander, is a fight you didn't completely lose."

———

THE FLIGHT DECK'S gravity fields grabbed the shuttle as it flew through the rapidly cycling airlock doors, and gently settled it to the floor. An honor guard of Marines snapped to attention as the doors opened and Captain Sarka limped out, a brace on her leg and the blocky metal replacement for her arm hanging heavily from her shoulder.

While eyes and other complex organs were usually replaced with cybernetics, most humans could have limbs regenerated. Sarka, it turned out, could not. The advantage for her was that she had prosthetics immediately, crude as the emergency devices were.

The disadvantage was that prosthetics were all she would ever have. The Federation made high-quality cybernetics, ones no one else would ever be able to tell from her original limb, but they would never feel quite right to the possessor.

Sarka saluted with her left hand, leaving the metal block of her right arm hanging, as she passed through the honor guard of Marines and reached Kyle.

"Captain Sarka, welcome aboard *Kodiak*," he greeted her as he returned the salute. "Don't push yourself," he warned. "Between your doctor and my doctor, I'm not sure I'd survive letting you overexert yourself."

She chuckled. "Believe me, sir, that was made *very* clear to me."

"Shall we, Captain?" Kyle suggested, gesturing out of the deck. "After the week you've had, I don't think I should keep you standing!"

———

SHE'D PUT on a good face, but Kyle heard Sarka's sigh of relief as she dropped into the chair in his office. He'd even turned on the smart-adjust feature of the piece of furniture he normally ignored, allowing it to adjust to properly support her injured leg and replacement arm.

He had a coffee on the desk in front of her before she even asked, and slid into his own chair to wait while she sipped.

"Thank you, sir," Sarka told him. "It's been… a hell of a couple of weeks."

"You got yourselves and your convoy out of a very well-set-up trap," he pointed out. "That was well done."

"Not much of a shield against the letters to the families," she said softly. "Too damn many of my people aren't coming home."

"One is too damn many, Captain," Kyle replied. "But it's our job to make sure they don't die in vain, and you did that with flair."

She shook her head.

"I ran, Captain Roberts," she admitted. "We had that *Hercules* outgunned and outclassed, but I ran."

"*Alexander* versus one *Hercules* is an uneven but not entirely unfair fight," Kyle pointed out. "Throw in *sixteen* of those damn pirate ships, whose abilities we're still not entirely certain of, and the odds weren't nearly as in your favor…and that was before you took a missile hit.

"You made the right call, Captain, and my own report reflects that," he concluded. "If you'd lost your ship, there'd be a Board. But you didn't, and even a damaged *Alexander* is still your ship.

"You're still here, Captain Sarka, and so is your ship. Your mission wasn't to kill Terrans or even pirates; it was to get those freighters out safely."

"Yes, sir. I know, sir," she admitted.

"Good. It's not going to make the rest of this conversation any more pleasant," he warned her, "but you did well."

"You're sending us home, aren't you?"

"I don't have a choice, Captain Sarka," Kyle told her. "*Alexander* may still have functioning weapons, but she doesn't have fully functioning deflectors, intact armor, or even all of her damn engines. You're not combat-capable, and you need a shipyard to fix that."

He slid a chip across the table.

"Those are your formal orders, already countersigned by the Joint Chiefs," he continued. "You're to take *Alexander* back to the Castle system and report to the Merlin Yards. Depending on the repair estimate, you may be held to resume command, or transferred to another ship."

"Or a desk job," she replied.

"Or a desk job," he agreed unflinchingly. That was what had happened to him when *Avalon* had gone in for repairs. He'd taken a black ops command instead, but that was unlikely to be an option for Sarka.

"But I doubt it," he continued. "You didn't screw up and you have a surprising shortage of political enemies. If they send you to an Academy stint, it will be to hold you in place to resume command of *Alexander* once she's repaired."

"I can hope."

"You can," he confirmed. "Now. This Terran ship. How good were your scans of her?"

"You got everything we got," she told him. "We couldn't ID her, though there are only twenty-six *Hercules*es left in existence."

The Commonwealth, Kyle noted with a smile, had built forty. He was responsible for a significant chunk of that reduction in numbers himself.

"Was there any evidence of a second Terran ship?" he asked. "I'm assuming there's something backing up the battlecruiser; they're unlikely to have sent only one ship this far out."

"No direct evidence, though…" Sarka trailed off thoughtfully. "The pirates were firing top-line Stormwinds, the Fives with their extra fifty gravities of acceleration. A *Hercules* doesn't have heavy-enough magazines or parts storage for them to have stripped her supplies to arm pirates. There's got to be a logistics ship somewhere."

"You're right," Kyle said. "Two warships and a logistics support vessel. I can't see them sending anything less this far out into functionally hostile territory."

"Though if they have local support…from, say, Istanbul," she pointed out.

"*That's* an ugly thought," he said grimly. "And my problem now, not yours.

"I'll need you to offload your spare fighter parts and missiles before you go," he continued. "We'll coordinate with the Serengetis, but I'm thinking we'll use your supplies to set up a temporary logistics facility here."

"Someone is going to have to go pick up my starfighters," Sarka pointed out. "They should have made Reinhardt safely, and while they don't have any FTL warships, I wouldn't want to tangle with their system defenses."

"We'll get them," Kyle promised. "No one gets left behind, Captain Sarka."

"Thank you, sir."

"Thank me by getting your ship home and fixed up," he ordered. "We'll deal with the Terrans here, Captain. They do not know what hornets' nest they've poked."

———

"Sir, we have Serengeti Fleet Command hailing. They're looking for you," Jamison told Kyle over his implant. He'd only barely seen Sarka back to her shuttle and had been heading for lunch, but...

"Understood," he told her. "I'll take it in my office."

Fortunately, while he didn't generally make use of the privilege, he did have a steward who could bring him lunch. The man was more efficient than Kyle gave him credit for as well, which meant that a steaming grilled sandwich was waiting on his desk as he sat down to take the call.

"This is Captain Kyle Roberts aboard *Kodiak*," he greeted the image that appeared on his wall. "How can I assist you?"

"Captain Roberts, I was more hoping I would be able to assist *you*," the albino-pale but green-eyed woman wearing a navy blue uniform on his screen told him. "I am Admiral Jale Szwarc, the commanding officer of the Serengeti Fleet. I am also, with the destruction of *Maasai* with Admiral Tesarik aboard, our only remaining Admiral.

"Your mission is my mission," she concluded, "but I now lack the capacity to project power beyond my own star system. Our First Minister has ordered me to provide any and all assistance that I can to your task group."

"We appreciate the willingness to assist, Admiral," Kyle told her. "Your welcome of *Alexander* was a desperately needed helping hand. We have discovered our true enemy, but that...well, that's not exactly reassuring."

"Indeed," Szwarc agreed. "The presence of actual Terran warships in this sector is an aggression we cannot afford—but also, unfortunately, one we cannot prevent. The core trio of the Free Trade Zone once possessed five Alcubierre warships.

"Now we have none," she said grimly. "I was confident in the ability of my local forces to defend the Serengeti system, but the presence of a modern Terran warship working with the pirates... I am no longer so certain."

"We came here to deal with pirates, Admiral," Kyle said. "But we half-expected to find Terrans here, so we are prepared. There are a few arrows in my quiver they're not expecting, though I'm working through the best options for deploying them."

"I doubt our supplies of munitions are necessarily of use to you, but if you need fuel or food or any replacement parts we *can* provide, they are yours for the asking," she offered. "My analysts have prepared a summary of our intelligence on these pirates that I will forward to you. I doubt we know much that you don't, but I can at least put a name to your enemy."

"Not, I am presuming, the Terran commander?" Kyle asked.

"No. But I know who commands the pirates they've allied themselves with," Szwarc replied. "Commodore Antonio Coati was once one of mine, commander of a deployed detachment in one of the Free Trade Zone systems."

Her tone was leaden, but she carried on with grim determination.

"He apparently used the gunships he'd been assigned to pirate ships in that system, doing exactly the *opposite* of what he was there for, and then... Well, to be honest, I don't know how he went from a squadron of sublight gunships and a stolen Alcubierre freighter to a fleet of unique warships with Terran allies, but he's been building to this for fifteen years."

"You knew him." It wasn't a question.

"He was my first squadron commander," Szwarc confirmed. "Knew him? Hell, I almost *married* him. Though, to be honest, he was a prick then. He was just an exotically pretty asshole."

"And now he's an exotically pretty pirate warlord," Kyle concluded. "With a unique type of ship I've never seen before that is sadly *perfect* for piracy."

"And I have no idea where he got them from," the Serengeti officer replied. "Everything we know will be forwarded. Is there any other way we can assist?"

"Several, actually," Kyle realized aloud. "First, we'll be offloading a quantity of supplies—munitions, starfighter parts and so forth—from *Alexander* before she ships home. If you have a secure storage facility we could put them in, that would be *very* useful."

"We have several orbital facilities inside the planetary fortifications that could serve," she told him. "We'd be delighted to put them at your disposal. Anything else?"

"Your intelligence network has to be more capable out here than ours," he said. "The pirates seem to know too much about the convoys. There's a leak, probably several."

"I agree. We've identified several possibilities, but not with enough certainty to act yet."

"I don't need them removed," Kyle told her with a wide grin. "I need them leaked to."

———

"I GOT IT!"

Kyle looked up, blinking in surprise at the unexpected opening of his office door, to see his chief engineer standing in the middle of the room with a datapad in her hand, her hair a tangled, unkempt mess, her uniform jacket askew, and an expression of pure triumph on her face.

"Got what, Commander?" he asked Trent carefully. Taggart hadn't reported any further issues in Engineering, so he'd presumed that Trent had taken their earlier conversation to heart. Her current state, however...

"How the bastards built the modular ships," she replied, dropping the datapad on his desk. "It's not supposed to be possible, but once you know it is, it's just a question of math and engineering."

"I don't follow," Kyle admitted.

"The position of the Class One mass manipulators and Stetson stabilizers on a ship is a matter of detailed calculation, down the micrometer," she insisted. "You can lose some stabilizer emitters, or spread the power over more Class Ones, but the positioning of every-thing has to be *perfect*.

"You can't *do* that with modular ships, not unless you're always having the *exact* same ships linking together in the exact same ways. Except..."

"Except?" he prompted.

"Except if you set up just *enough* extra stabilizers, at the right frequencies and positions, you can use them as a reinforcing network and cancel out the inherent instability of the warp bubble you create by not having exact positions for everything. It's *genius*, sir."

"I...am not going to pretend I followed that entirely," Kyle admitted. "But...that's a complete change in how A-S drives work, isn't it?"

"It's revolutionary, Captain," she told him. "If I've run my calculations correctly, by increasing the materials cost by three percent, we could cut assembly time of an A-S drive by over *sixteen* percent. That's a major difference in construction time and costs."

"Package it up and send it back to Joint Command," he ordered. "That's valuable, Ivy, I agree, but it doesn't help us today—unless you've worked out some way to magically make any ship built like that disappear."

The engineer paused with her mouth half-open, whatever she was about to say forgotten in a flash of inspiration.

"It would be even more vulnerable to interior shear interference," she said slowly.

Kyle sighed. He was a long way from stupid, but Trent was losing him again.

"Explain for the people with only one university degree?" he asked gently.

"They couldn't have planar gravitic or electromagnetic fields inside the bubble," she told him. "Like deflectors. They couldn't even have zero-point cells outside a certain distance from the sections of hull with the stabilizers."

He stared at her.

"You're saying there's an entire side of their ship that can't have weapons or defenses?" he asked carefully.

"Exactly. The shear interference risk for the combined FTL would be too high. They'd risk losing all of the ships."

"Damn," Kyle murmured. "Now, that, Commander Trent, is useful. Anything else I should know?"

"They have to have one Class One per ship, no more, no less," she reeled off. "They can't generate a warp space bubble with less than four or more than six ships. Significant hull damage will render a ship incapable of helping generate the bubble; the only way a damaged ship could travel would be to completely shut it down and wrap four of its friends around it."

"That's one hell of an operational vulnerability," Kyle pointed out.

"I don't know if we'll be seeing these ships in Alliance service on that grounds alone."

"It's brilliantly done," Trent repeated, "but the principle is better applied to making the construction of proper A-S drives faster."

"Make sure your notes make it home," Kyle reiterated. "And...Commander?"

"Yes, sir?"

"You have about five days to work out how to detect the unprotected side of one of these bastards from missile range.

"Good luck."

30

KDX-6657 System
19:00 November 8, 2736 Earth Standard Meridian Date/Time
BC-305 Poseidon

"MY DEAR COMMODORE, so pleased you can make time for me!" Coati grinned through James's screen. "Where is your dear *Chariot*, though? I expected to see them by now."

James smiled thinly. "They'll be around," he told the pirate. "A lot of people were asking questions on Amadeus; Captain Modesitt chose to keep her ship well out of sight and send in the prisoners by shuttle. Last I heard, we had a near-complete set of ransoms and the last of the shuttles were heading back out. Carefully."

"I am aware of the concept, but damn, it takes so much time," the pirate replied. "And you seem to have turned a whole new leaf on keeping yourselves hidden!"

"Captain Modesitt went out on our older orders," James reminded him. "And there's no reason to show more of my hand that I have to.

Chariot is an older ship; if our dear Fox hasn't seen her, he will likely assume my consort is more powerful."

"Why would he even think you have a second ship at all?" Coati asked.

"Because Kyle Roberts is not stupid, and likely has figured out that I have three ships, one of them a support vessel," the Navy officer replied. "It's the logical force to have sent out this far into hostile territory. He can rely on the locals for resupply. That was not so certain for me."

Coati spread his hands wide with a disingenuous grin.

"Have we not been supportive?" he asked. "Food, weapons, fuel... all that you have asked, we have given. Have we not been proper allies?"

"You have," James allowed. He didn't *trust* the pirate warlord, but the man had certainly met their resupply needs. "We could not be certain you would be so willing or so able. We were prepared for the worst."

"And instead, you got me!" Coati replied, his grin widening. "We have been lucky, my dear Commodore. My sources in Serengeti have learned where Roberts plans on taking his growing collection of stray merchantmen next: he is heading to Salvatore to enable the deliveries we short-stopped before, and to pick up the fighters they abandoned.

"You'd think he'd have learned that system was unsafe for his people."

"My sources have established his full ship strength," James pointed out. "Neither a *Rameses* nor an *Ursine* are new ships, but both carry significant fighter wings that I am certain have been fully updated. A hundred and ninety seventh-generation starfighters, even assuming that we manage to keep the seventy they left behind out of the fight, is more than I'd want to take on in a straight fight, even with your corsairs."

"My intelligence has their emergence loci, their course, everything," Coati replied. "They're expecting an ambush, sending in the Imperial strike cruiser first to try and lure us out of position. But, since we know what they're doing, we can arrange our vector to completely miss the *Rameses* and just hit the *Ursine* and the convoy."

James sighed. "Show me," he told the pirate.

Coati grinned, lighting up part of the screen with the information that he'd acquired. Times, vectors; the pirate really did have everything he'd said he did. The convoy would be leaving Serengeti in a few hours, heading back to Salvatore with two warships and seven freighters now.

The data even had the arrival sequence. The Imperial cruiser—apparently *Thoth*—would arrive first, roughly fifteen minutes before everyone else. She would presumably deploy q-probes and starfighters to sweep the area to make certain no one was lurking there, but knowing their arrival vector would let the pirates evade that with a reasonable degree of certainty.

Then the *Ursine* carrier—*Kodiak*, Roberts's ship—would arrive, followed almost immediately by the rest of the convoy. Location estimates wouldn't be perfect, but there was more than enough data to execute a perfect ambush, separating the freighters from the warships and sneaking the corsairs into range of at least *Kodiak*.

The data was complete, comprehensive, and dangerous.

"It's a trap," he told Coati. "Data this complete? There's no way it leaked by accident. Roberts isn't an intelligence officer, but he has them to hand and we *know* the Federation and Imperium have solid networks out here."

"Doesn't matter if he's expecting us if he follows this pattern," Coati pointed out. "Physics says he can only have drones and fighters in so many places from those vectors, so we won't be in those places. If they break the arrival pattern, we can abort. Be careful, as you're so determined to be!"

James shook his head.

"You need to leave in less than three hours to get there in time," he pointed out. "You don't have time to prepare, time to make sure your numbers are right. You're going after him on his own terms, in a place where he knows you'll be coming."

"With *Poseidon* along, how clever do we need to be?" the pirate demanded. "You outgun either of his ships now."

"I'm not taking *Poseidon* into a trap," James told him. "Once *Chariot* is back and we've had a chance to analyze the pattern of Roberts's convoys, I'll go after him. We'll hit him when he isn't expecting us, with overwhelming force, and we will crush him.

"Anything less *careful* is risking everything for very little gain. We're in no hurry here, Coati," he pointed out. "If you want to build your little kingdom out here, you'll need patience."

The truth, James knew, was that Coati was already doomed. Once the Alliance actually moved to remove the Commonwealth task group he'd brought, he would return to Terran space—and leave the pirate to face a fleet.

A fleet that would not care if Coati had made himself king of any of these worlds—but more important from the Commonwealth's perspective, a fleet that wouldn't be available to defend the Rimward Marches.

"Roberts isn't a god, isn't some magical tactician," Coati snapped. "He's just a soldier, same as you. Even if he's got a trick up his sleeve, the laws of physics are the same for him as us. We can do this."

"Then you don't need *Poseidon*," James told him mildly. "If everything works perfectly, you can blow *Kodiak* apart at close range, then steal most of the freighters before *Thoth* can reverse course to meet you.

"If your data is accurate and there's no trap, Commodore, you don't need me at all."

"Really, Commodore?" Coati snarled. "You want me to think you're unnecessary? I'm not sure you want to convince me of that!"

"No, I don't," James agreed. "But I'm not going back to Salvatore and walking into a trap."

"I don't think our Federation friend understands just what his 'trap' is going to catch," the pirate told him. "You're right, Commodore Tecumseh. I don't need you for this. But trust me...if this goes wrong because you aren't there, there will be a price to be paid."

"If you walk into the lion's den after being warned, that's your own damn problem."

———

JAMES WATCHED as the twelve corsair ships in KDX-6657 accelerated toward the edge of the gravity well, slowly and carefully matching

228

vectors and combing into three much larger, Alcubierre-capable constructs that eventually vanished into FTL.

Two of the corsairs remained, orbiting above *l'Estación de Muerte* to keep an eye on the two Terran ships. The precaution was almost funny, to a degree. *l'Estación* was armed as well, but *Poseidon* could wipe out both ships and the station in a single volley. They were close enough, in fact, that they could do it with positron lances, lightspeed weapons the pirates would never see coming.

Not that Commodore James Tecumseh was considering an unprovoked massacre of his allies.

Well. Not *very* seriously.

"You asked to see me, sir?" Colonel Barbados said softly behind him.

"I did," James confirmed without turning around, his gaze still on the screen where *l'Estación de Muerte* orbited. "Have a seat."

"Sir."

The shuffling sound behind him told him the Marine had obeyed, and the Navy Commodore sighed and turned around.

"What can I do for you, Commodore?" the pale-skinned Marine asked as he met James's gaze. "I see that we are suddenly short of pirate friends."

"I'm sure all of our hearts ache for their absence," James told him. "They're off to try and ambush a Federation-defended convoy based on data Serengeti leaked them."

Barbados winced.

"Coati isn't that stupid, is he?"

"No, he knows it's a trap," the Commodore confirmed. "He's just convinced he can turn the trap on the Federation, steal half a dozen freighters in one strike, and punch out a carrier for good measure."

"I've fought the Federation, sir," Barbados said slowly. "I'm not under the impression that their capital ship commanders are more incompetent than their Marines, and their Marines are a match for our best."

"Exactly."

"He's going to get reamed."

"I agree. And he has already implied he will take out his displeasure on us," James told the Marine. "I want you to go over all of our security plans for *Poseidon*, *Chariot*, and *Stormcloud*. Consult with Commodore Sherazi, Captain Colton, and Major Petrovsky—and Captain Modesitt when she gets back. I want to know our ships are secure."

The oddities of Commonwealth ranking structure meant that, depending on how you looked at it, there were either two Commodores or two Captains aboard *Poseidon*. Commodore Sherazi was the battlecruiser's captain, while Captain Petrovsky was his XO. To avoid confusion, an O-6 Captain who wasn't a ship's commander was often given the courtesy title of Major.

James figured that given, oh, another hundred years of grinding down tradition, the title of Captain would just be dropped from the Navy table in favor of Major to avoid the confusion.

"*Stormcloud* has two thousand Marines aboard, sir," Barbados pointed out. "I think Captain Colton would laugh in my face if I raised security concerns."

"Then let her get it out of her system, and then go over the security plans," James said flatly. "I don't trust Coati, and since he's taken the opportunity to make threats, let's make sure he doesn't have the capacity to follow through."

Barbados nodded thoughtfully.

"Sir, does it count as failing our mission if *we* kill the pirate warlord we're trying to get the Alliance to chase?"

"At the point he turns on us, he is fair prey," James replied. "And at that point, I will burn this hive of scum to the goddamn ground."

31

Deep Space en route to Salvatore System
22:00 November 9, 2736 Earth Standard Meridian Date/Time
Antioch-Registry Freighter Satie Dun

THE CREW of the freighter *Satie Dun*—*Golden Dawn*, if Michelle's translation was correct—had been more than willing to accommodate the crew of the half-squadron of bombers they'd bolted onto the freighter's airlocks.

There was only so much they could do to make them comfortable, sadly, as *Dun* was built for exactly the number of crew she carried and had no passenger facilities. The cots and couches they'd set up for Michelle and her people in their secondary mess were still infinitely more comfortable than sleeping on the bombers would be though.

That was something the Federation redesign was going to fix, Michelle was certain. A Falcon was reasonably comfortable for the crew to live aboard, designed for independent in-system deployments of up to two weeks.

The prototype Vultures were not. There was a set of folding-down bunks, but the closest thing it had to a kitchen was a coffeemaker. Ration bars would keep Michelle's people alive regardless of whether or not they could cook, but it wouldn't keep them happy.

The one thing the freighter's crew couldn't provide the bomber crews was any significant degree of privacy for secure coms, which left Michele back on her bomber tonight, caressing the image of Angela Alvarez's face her implant projected onto her optic nerve.

It would have looked silly to anyone there, but Angela's smile confirmed that the thought was appreciated.

"And what daring adventure is my dashing pilot up to tonight?" the nurse asked.

"Ha! You know I can't tell you anything," Michelle pointed out. "I can tell you, though, that it almost involved living out of a starfighter for a few weeks. We came up with a better plan, but that was a near-run thing."

"I've been inside a starfighter," her lover replied. "Is that even *possible*?"

"Oh, it's possible," Michelle confirmed. "It's just not any fun. Though"—she grinned at Angela—"I can certainly think of people I wouldn't mind being trapped in a confined space with for a week."

"I like this plan," Angela said with a giggle, "but can we pick somewhere more comfortable than a starfighter? A hotel room, an apartment, something like that?"

"Does either of us even *have* an apartment?" the fighter pilot asked hesitantly, and Angela shook her head.

"No, I'm never home long enough," she admitted. "And you don't either, do you?"

"No," Michelle confirmed, hesitating again and letting a silence drag out for several seconds. "Do you…want to get one together when we're next both home?"

"My dear, are you asking me to move in with you?" Angela asked, her voice suddenly pitching higher and leaning in to the camera.

"Um. Yes? Maybe? Sort of…"

"I think that's a great idea! I…wasn't sure if you wanted to move much forward, with us both in the fleet," Angela told her. "Things could happen..."

"But they also may not," Michelle said, echoing the Captain's words to her. "And while we have to accept that the worst-case scenario is a thing, we can't *plan* for it. There's a lot of steps ahead of us, love, but I think we should start on some of them."

"Be careful, Commander Williams," the other woman said with a smile. "If you don't slow down, I might make you meet my parents!"

Michelle laughed.

"I'd like that," she admitted. "My folks would want to meet you too."

"Well, then, it looks like we're going to have a busy leave when you get back from your mission to the boonies," Angela told her. "I look forward to it."

"Me too."

DSC-052 Kodiak

"ARE YOU SURE THIS WILL WORK?" Song asked as she took a sip of her beer in Kyle's office. "This is risky."

"It is," Kyle agreed. "But not as much as it looks on the surface. It's a standard deployment pattern for running into an ambush, with just one tiny vulnerability added."

"One vulnerability," Taggart said slowly, "that might allow the Terrans to get a *battlecruiser* into range of us with the freighters for a backdrop. That could hurt, sir."

"But to get there, they'll pass well inside Williams's range before ranging on us," Kyle pointed out calmly. "Even a *Hercules* is going to feel it when she sends a hundred torpedoes at them from only a million klicks."

"We're putting a lot of risk on the freighters, too," Taggart pointed out. "At the point they see the bombers, they may open fire on them."

"That's the part I really don't like," Kyle admitted. "I'm honestly trusting to the fact that the pirates want those ships intact and, well, most Commonwealth officers are at least *familiar* with the rules of war."

"Their past record suggests otherwise," Song grumbled.

"Their past record says they've got a bunch of fanatic idiots amongst their ranks whose political reliability gets them promoted," the Captain said grimly. "Most Commonwealth officers realize that those fanatics are a problem."

He sighed.

"But how do you tell the difference between someone thoroughly committed to unifying the rest of the human race and someone who's going to snap and bomb a world?" he asked rhetorically. "We try to avoid having fanatics in charge of warships, but the Commonwealth finds it convenient."

"And every so often, one of their fanatics blows up and a world goes with them," Song said bitterly. "I had friends on Kematian. I know that bastard burned, but that doesn't bring back the half a planet he wrecked."

"I know." Kyle sipped from his beer without saying more, unpleasant memories flashing before his mental eye. Song might have had friends on Kematian, but Kyle had been there when a Terran officer bombed the planet.

Kyle had also been the one to pursue that officer halfway across the Alliance and blow him to hell.

"To be fair, though, there were Commonwealth ships there when we caught up with that bastard, and they stood aside," he pointed out. "I wouldn't have expected that of our own officers in the same place. Somebody has a stick of iron up his ass."

"If I was picking for this mission, I'd take the biggest fanatic true believer I could find," Taggart replied. "Commerce raiding is an ugly, ugly business."

"I'll hope for one with some honor," Kyle told them. "But you're right, I'm not expecting one with much. Fortunately, it doesn't take much not to blow away a bunch of freighters."

"If this all goes wrong…" Taggart trailed off.

"It's on my head. The Free Trade Zone probably wouldn't survive losing this convoy, either," the Captain said quietly. "We'll keep them safe, people. One way or another."

32

"THOTH HAS MADE emergence and is deploying q-probes," Sterling announced. "Captain von Lambert reports nothing is showing up so far, but they've got probes sweeping toward Waterdeep."

"Let's drop some of those in a permanent orbit," Kyle ordered, studying the tactical feed coming to his implant and overlaid on the bridge's main screens. "Then give Neverwinter the q-com codes. That gas giant gives them far too much of a blind spot."

"According to the brief, they've replaced their Waterdeep surveillance net four times in the last ten years," Taggart pointed out from Secondary Control. "They're aware of the problem—but so is this Coati bastard."

"And for him, it's an opportunity," Kyle agreed. "Well, let's give them half a dozen q-probes and hope that helps tide them over until we kill Coati."

"I'm looking forward to it," the XO growled. "I reviewed the Serengeti intelligence file on him. He doesn't just give the Serengeti Fleet a bad name; he gives every Naval officer in the galaxy a bad name."

Kyle nodded his agreement as he checked the timers. Serengeti Intelligence estimated that Coati was responsible for the loss of at least a dozen interstellar freighters, plus the destruction of five warships now and raids on dozens of outer-system platforms... They had very little information on the capabilities of his corsairs or even how many of the modular ships he had, but they had a disturbingly good idea of how many people he'd killed.

"So, do we think they actually decided not to play or just hiding really well?" he said aloud.

"We gave them enough data to make sure *Thoth* couldn't see them," Sterling pointed out. "There's no way we can know."

"Fair enough. Houshian; I see no reason to change the plan. We and the convoy will emerge on schedule."

"Yes, sir. Four minutes, twenty-two seconds," his navigator confirmed.

Kyle ran through his mental checklist and the status reports of his ship's systems. Positron lances were charged. Missile launchers loaded, magazines full. The ready-magazine missile warheads had been charged with antimatter, one of the final steps before launch.

"Commodore Song?" he pinged the CAG. "What's the status of the group?"

"All fighters aboard are armed and ready," she confirmed instantly. "Alpha Wing is in the launch tubes; the rest are crewed and fueled, ready to go. With Echo off-ship, we should have a forty-five-second Alpha launch."

"Good. Hold most of that until we see the bastards," he ordered. "One squadron for CSP until then."

"I know, sir."

He chuckled.

"Fair," he conceded. "This is riskier than even I like, Song. Do you have a status on Williams's people?"

"She just checked in. All of her people are aboard the bombers and are ready to deploy. Engineers have checked over the torpedo warheads; the containment fields held up surprisingly well under the flight."

Like all starfighters, the Vulture didn't have large-enough zero-point cells to supply the antimatter for the warheads of its own missiles. Kyle would trust the long-term containment fields of the standard fighter missile—it had been tested for years now—but the torpedoes were new. It might be the same tech, but every part of the new torpedoes remained a potential problem.

"The bombers are good to go," Song concluded. "All of the Falcons are ready. If the Commonwealth wants to play, they're going to get a rude surprise."

"That, Vice Commodore, is what I wanted to hear. Emergence in thirty seconds. Hang tight."

———

EMERGENCE.

Eight ships shutting down their Alcubierre drives in sequence meant over thirty high-mass singularities collapsing within seconds of each other. Even with the Stetson stabilization fields, that made for a bumpy ride, and Kyle grimaced as the waves of shifting gravity rippled through his bridge.

The ships from what had been *Alexander's* convoy weren't as good at their station-keeping as the ones who'd flown with him. The seven freighters had been supposed to emerge separate from *Kodiak*, leaving an intentional vulnerability for the Terrans to try and exploit.

"Well, we definitely have a gap for our friends," Kyle said cheerfully, studying the bedraggled string of star freighters trailing behind his carrier. "CAG, feel free to launch a couple of extra squadrons and send them back to round up our loose sheep. I don't think anyone is going to question that today!"

"Understood. Alpha One through Alpha Three are launching," she replied. "Sending Two and Three back on lost-sheep duty."

Twenty-four new icons lit up on his tactical feed, the Falcon starfighters dropping back from the carrier as *Kodiak* began to accelerate toward Neverwinter. The sixty gravities the freighters could maintain was a casual lope for the old carrier, but it was enough that simply not accelerating allowed the fighters to close with the freighters.

"*Thoth* reports clear sailing," Jamison told him. "They've ceased acceleration and are waiting for us to catch up. Q-probe reports are clean throughout the system."

"And our blind spot?"

"Narrowing by the second," Sterling replied. "If they're here, they're ballistic and on a very specific line. Sixty seconds and I'll know, one way or another."

Kyle nodded silently, studying the feed.

Sixty seconds and they could be sure they were alone. But their blind spot would only be two million kilometers away from *Kodiak* at that point. A *Hercules* was a serious threat at that range.

Of course, the *bombers* would only be one point five million kilometers from the blind spot.

"Commander Trent," he pinged his engineer. "Do you have that special targeting package I asked for?"

"Ready to drop into any of the missiles Sterling wants," she confirmed. "It won't work perfectly, but you've got fifty-fifty odds that the missile will be able to identify the vulnerable side of the modular ship and adjust courses appropriately."

"Well done, Commander."

He waited, watching the feeds. The blind spot was now marked as a blinking red ovoid, shrinking as *Kodiak*'s probes shot out into space and the warship herself twisted to clear her own powerful sensor arrays.

"Got them!" Sterling declared, and the blind spot vanished, replaced by a set of flashing red icons. "No battlecruiser but... *Starless Void!*"

Kyle had been expecting the *Hercules* and the fifteen surviving raiders from *Alexander*'s encounter. They could take that, but it would be a fight. Without the Terran battlecruiser, he'd been confident they could take fifteen of the corsairs.

Instead, *twenty-eight* icons filled his feed as the pirates finally lit off their engines and charged for *Kodiak,* launching missiles as they accelerated.

"Target-rich environment, people," he barked cheerfully. "The order is go, get the bombers in space, full-deck launch. Close the trap, people.

"It isn't going to matter how much they've shoved in it."

———

"DESIGNATE TARGETS ONE THROUGH TWENTY-EIGHT," Michelle said as calmly as she could into her wing's tactical net. The *plan* had called for her throwing the payload of twenty-four bombers at one battlecruiser and leaving the raiders for the regular Falcons.

Given that the raiders had already put over a hundred missiles into space heading for *Kodiak,* that plan was now void and debris. She *could* throw the responsibility back up the ladder, but that wasn't what the Castle Federation Space Force expected of its Wing Commanders.

"Echo One, you've got one through eight. Echo Two, nine through sixteen. Echo three, seventeen through twenty-four. Dump your torps as soon as you're clear of your merchant ship, prep your Starfires for their fighters—because, believe me, we are going to have fighters coming our way."

The chorus of acknowledgements sounded nervous, but that was to be expected. Her pilots had never flown their bombers in action before, which made this the Federation—Void, the *Alliance's* first combat action for the new ships.

One bomber, one gunship sounded great in theory, but if they were more protected than Michelle thought, she was about to waste her wing's single punch.

"And...go!"

The structure attaching her bomber to the *Satie Dun* had taken fifteen minutes to set up and carefully assemble around both the starfighter and the freighter. It came apart in under five seconds as a series of explosive bolts detonated throughout its housing, blasting the Vulture away from the freighter with shocking force.

"We are clear!" her engineer snapped, the bomber's engines coming live as soon as they were pointed away from the freighter that had carried them there.

"Target One is at one point two million kilometers," her gunner, Vasil, chanted. "Fifteen thousand KPS relative velocity. Gemblades away, Gemblades away!"

The Vulture trembled as the four Gemblade torpedoes blasted free, their own engines lighting up at over a thousand gravities of acceleration as they happily charged toward immolation.

Twenty-three other sets of torpedoes joined them, ninety-eight brand-new weapons lighting up the empty space as they closed on the pirates.

"Seventy-seven-second flight time," Vasil announced.

"And there go their fighters," Michelle noted, watching as each of the raider ships launched ten Cobras into space. "Where the *hell* did they get that many of our fighters?"

"I don't know, but they just sent fifty of them our way," her engineer replied. "We got a plan for those?"

"That's why we have fighter missiles as well," Michelle pointed out. "And why there's three squadrons of Falcons *also* heading our way."

She was already setting up the salvos, leaving the torpedoes to her gunner as she laid in targeting parameters for the bomber's six fighter missile launchers. The pirate Cobras launched first, but only by a handful of seconds.

Three groups of starfighters were now closing on each other, the space between them rapidly filling with missiles as Falcons, Cobras and Vultures all launched—and in the middle of the chaotic mess, the torpedoes continued closing with the pirate gunships.

"Evasive maneuvers," Michelle ordered. "All bombers, vector for *Kodiak*; our role in this mess is done, so let's try to stay alive!"

"Impact in ten seconds," Vasil announced. "Gemblades going to full terminal ECM mode."

Entire sections of her feed disappeared into jamming as the torpedoes' jammers went to full strength, hashing their victims' sensors and defenses as they hit their final approach.

At the same time, the Starfires Michelle and her squadrons had launched collided with the Javelins the pirates had fired—and deto-nated, filling space with radiation and fire as her bombers made a hard vector change away from the fight.

For a few precious seconds, the entire battlespace was incompre-hensible. Even the q-probes outside the zone couldn't make sense of the mess, and the Vultures blasted clear of the danger zone for the incoming fighter's positron lances.

"We're clear, their salvo is down and *they're* not going to be as lucky with Alpha Wing's missiles," Michelle's engineer reported.

"And the motherships?" Michelle asked. "How'd we do?"

Her gunner was silent for a moment.

"Did we get them?" she insisted, refocusing her own feed on their targets.

"Twenty-two of twenty-four," her subordinate said softly. "Eternal Stars, that was a fucking *massacre*."

————

"MY GOD," Sterling breathed. "Ninety percent kills? The bastards weren't expecting capital-grade jammers, that's for sure."

"We might not run into quite as unprepared an opponent in the future," Kyle agreed, "but I think Commander Williams just handily demonstrated the bomber concept. CAG?"

"Alpha Wing is sweeping in to cover Echo," Song responded imme-diately. "Twenty-four of mine against fifty of these idiots? I'm not exactly worried.

"The rest of the group is closing on the remaining gunships. Some covering fire would be nice, sir."

"Understood. Sterling?"

"Missiles already on their way," the tactical officer reported.

"You're still outnumbered," Kyle warned Song. "Two hundred and thirty Cobras and six of those gunships against eighty Falcons?"

"Like I said, sir, covering fire would be *great*."

"*Thoth* is launching long-range salvos as well," Jamison reported. "ETI is almost twelve minutes, though."

"Wait, what are the raiders doing?" Kyle asked, watching his feed. The vectors for the six surviving gunships had suddenly twisted.

"Ninety-degree vector shift, jumped to Tier Three acceleration," Sterling responded after a moment. "They'll sweep by well clear of our lance range and likely dodge the fighter lances, too. They're running, sir."

"And there's no way they're going to be able to pick up their fighters," Song reported. "The *hell*? Did they just abandon almost three hundred starfighters?!"

Two hundred and eighty Cobras also meant over eight hundred flight crew. That was *cold*, though the raiders themselves probably had over five hundred crew apiece.

"What are the fighters doing?" Kyle demanded.

"Continuing on course," Sterling replied. "Like they don't even realize their bosses just cut and run."

Kyle shook his head.

"Focus missiles on the raiders," he ordered. "Use Trent's targeting algorithm; if we smash up the faces where they need to connect, they aren't going anywhere."

"And the fighters?"

He smiled grimly. "Take us right after Commodore Song, Houshian," he ordered. "Those are *Cobras*, people, which means even our secondary lances can take them out a hundred thousand kilometers before they can touch us.

"They're not winning this fight."

———

Kodiak slashed through space at two hundred gravities, her screen of starfighters spreading out in front of her at over twice her acceleration. The bombers happily ducked "under" that screen, hiding under the carrier's skirts as Alpha Wing collided with the starfighters sent after them.

That fight lasted two missile salvos, costing Alpha Wing two Falcons as they annihilated twice their number of older fighters, but it was a sideshow to the real battle taking place.

Whoever was in command of the Cobras clearly understood that the only way they were going to get out of this alive was if they took out *Kodiak* and enabled their motherships to pick them up. They formed the two hundred–plus starfighters they had left into a single massive hammer and threw it directly at the carrier.

Vice Commodore Song let them come, her own starfighters spreading out to leave the pirates a neat hole to dive into. They saw enough of the trap to lead the way with missiles, launching their Terran-built Javelins in a massive seven-hundred-missile-strong salvo through the opening.

The sheer scale of the salvos a full fighter force could launch was always intimidating. While the capital ship missiles that *Kodiak* carried were easily ten times as dangerous, the carrier only had eight launchers.

Of course, her *starfighters* had a lot more. Song's ships launched their own missiles, three hundred and twenty Starfires sweeping in on intercept courses even as *Kodiak*'s defensive lasers opened up at their maximum range.

Kodiak might only have eight launchers, and most of those missiles were targeted at the fleeing raiders, but Sterling had spared one. The single missile dove into the heart of the incoming missile swarm and triggered its ECM at full strength. Dozens of starfighter missiles were confused, losing track of their targets and pausing momentarily in their deadly hunt.

Few of those survived as the defending missiles smashed in. The carrier's lasers claimed more victims, the antimatter missiles dying in their dozens, *hundreds*.

Hundreds more were still coming.

Kyle watched grimly as they closed. *Kodiak* was a capable ship, but that was a *lot* of missiles—and a second, equally large salvo had just been launched from the starfighters. As that salvo launched, however, Song's fighters were closing in. Lances and missiles flashed in the void, and the pirate starfighters began to die.

"Lasers cycling," Sterling announced grimly. "Targets approaching optimal kill zone."

"Rededicate our launchers to self-defense," Kyle ordered. "We'll deal with Coati's survivors later. We need to make it through today first."

He'd underestimated the number of fighters he'd be facing, and *Kodiak* might be about to pay for that.

"Echo Wing is salvoing missiles in counter mode," Jamison reported.

Kyle chuckled grimly. He'd ordered the bombers back and had almost forgotten that each of the Vultures had six fighter missile launchers to go along with their torpedoes—and those launchers had four-missile magazines.

Williams's people put a hundred perfectly timed Starfires into the heart of the incoming salvo, firing early enough that their missiles had plenty of time to seek out individual targets and late enough that the launching fighters, already distracted by their own imminent demise, couldn't order their weapons to adjust.

With Song already having shattered the salvo, and the carrier's own missile defenses continuing to blow apart missile after missile, it was enough.

"First salvo down," Sterling reported, his voice calmer now. "Commander Williams is now linked into our defensive net. Coordinating her missiles with ours, targeting the edges with the lasers. She'll sweep, we'll clean."

More missiles exploded in the center of the incoming salvo, Jackhammers from *Kodiak* and Starfires from the bombers. Now the bombers' lasers joined in the fight as well, the new starfighters less capable in the role than Falcons were, but still a valuable addition to *Kodiak's* defenses in the face of the swarming missiles.

"We have lance range on the lead Cobras," Sterling reported. "Transferring missile defense to Commander Collinson; engaging starfighters myself."

Lieutenant Commander Collinson was Sterling's second, the junior tactical officer who'd already been helping run the carrier's defense. Ever so subtly, Kyle slipped into the tactical network himself, making sure the junior officer had everything covered.

He spent five seconds in the network, ready to leap in to back up Collinson if needed, then pulled back to his high-level tactical feed as the Lieutenant Commander smoothly linked up with Williamson and continued to annihilate the incoming missiles.

"Any chance we can bring down those raiders?" he asked his crew, confident that the pirate starfighters were handled. More than just the ships were inferior. The Cobra might be older, slower and more lightly armed than the Falcon, but it was still a capable ship. His pilots were veterans of the war against the Commonwealth, though, experienced pilots and combatants.

The pirate pilots…weren't.

"Negative," Sterling reported after a moment. "They're well clear and on their way. We can hit them with capital ship missiles, but they can handle the eight of those we can throw."

"Jamison," Kyle turned to his coms officer. "Send a surrender demand to the fighters. Their only way home is running the hell away; there's no point in them dying for nothing."

"Sending," she confirmed.

They waited in silence as the lances and starfighters ripped through the surviving pirates, hoping that at least one of them would choose to live. A prisoner would be *very* useful.

"Nothing," the coms officer finally concluded as the last starfighter came apart. "Not a peep. How the hell do you get pirates to fight like that?"

"I don't know," Kyle admitted, eyeing the surviving six pirate ships now attempting to merge together to go FTL. "I don't know," he repeated, "but by the Gods, we need to find out. Get search and rescue out there. Our people, their people, debris, data cores… I want it all.

"Anything that can get me some answers."

33

THE CARRIER SETTLED into orbit of Neverwinter with a general feeling of relief through the crew. Search-and-rescue craft continued to comb the wreckage of the fight they'd left behind, but the fighters were now converging on *Kodiak* and *Thoth*, though Kyle wasn't entirely sure where they were going to put *Alexander*'s surviving fighters.

"We lost six ships," Song told him from across the briefing room table. "SAR found two of the escape pods, but the crew of the other four are KIA."

Twelve lives was a small price to pay to shatter an entire pirate fleet, but that knowledge had never been a strong defense against the letters home for Kyle. From Song's tired expression, she felt much the same.

"We have sixty-five surviving fighters from *Alexander*," Kyle noted. "How many can we actually fit aboard?"

"Sixty-five fighters," Song confirmed, "but Neverwinter Control did search and rescue after the ambush. We have sixty-*eight* flight crews, and we have enough components aboard to fabricate new starfighters for the five crews, ours and *Alexander*'s, without ships.

"That gives us three squadrons of Vultures and twenty-one of Falcons. *Kodiak* is designed to carry sixteen squadrons...of ships that are smaller than our Falcons," she continued. "There was heavy refitting done to allow us to carry Falcons in a space that was originally designed for Typhoons, which are two-thirds the size."

"I'm guessing *Thoth* is in the same state?" Kyle asked of von Lambert, glancing at the screen mirroring the equivalent briefing room on the Imperial cruiser. All of the senior officers of both ships, plus Nebula, were present either physically or virtually.

"The names are different, but the generations and the size differential are roughly the same," he agreed. "*Thoth* is much the same vintage as *Kodiak*, after all. We have no spare hangar space aboard, but...we should be able to spot fighters on the deck as a temporary solution. CAG?"

"That...simply won't work," Horaček replied. "We need that open space; it exists for a reason. Without it, we can't transfer fighters, fuel fighters or retrieve fighters.

"What we *can* do," the Imperial Lieutenant Colonel continued, "is keep four squadrons in our launch tubes. They'll be a bitch to embark and disembark from, and it'll slow retrieval significantly, but that gets four more squadrons aboard *Thoth*."

"And we can do the same," Song agreed. "We could squeeze six squadrons into ours, we launch a full wing at once, but we're probably better off splitting the extra ships between us and *Thoth*."

"I agree," Kyle said instantly. "Get in touch with Vice Commodore Altena and sort it out; I want her birds aboard by this time tomorrow."

"Yes, sir," the CAG agreed.

"Nebula, anything with Neverwinter's government I need to worry about?" he asked the diplomat.

Nebula shook his head.

"Right now, your biggest problem if you went down to the surface would be not drowning in flower petals and booze," the old spy said cheerfully. "You just gutted the pirates who've been wrecking their lives for the last year. We may be the most popular people in the system right now."

"It was a nearer-run thing than I'd like," Kyle admitted. "And I'm damn glad that battlecruiser wasn't here. The Terrans are still here, people, and that's going to be a problem. Have we learned anything so far from the wrecks?"

"My assessment of the corsair's construction was accurate," Trent told him. "With the live data, I've refined the targeting program and passed it on to *Thoth* and the bombers. Physics and angles will have their part, but we now have a seventy-percent-plus chance of attacking a vulnerable side when we run into them again."

"They are not going to like that," Sterling said with satisfaction. "They weren't expecting the torpedoes, either. Those turned the tide."

"Our trick worked even better than expected," Kyle agreed, "but it's a one-shot deal. Not even pirates are stupid enough to try that twice. All they had to turn this into a fair fight was *not* try to cut us off from the freighters.

"Have we located their base yet?"

"No," Nebula said grimly. "The corsairs' computer cores wiped themselves. Extremely modern, extremely effective data security."

"That fits with most of what we've seen," Trent confirmed. "The corsairs were...weird. Some parts were extremely modern or even unique: the drive system, the stabilizers, the missiles. Others were a hodgepodge of stolen parts. The cores of their new modular systems were Class One manipulators stolen from merchant ships. The lances were twenty years out of date, the zero-point cells almost as bad."

"Their computers cores were old, but their software was top of the line," the spy added. "And the starfighters...well, those cores were even stranger. Almost no data on them. We managed to retrieve a couple intact, but..."

He shrugged.

"The data wasn't wiped from the cores," he said slowly. "It was never there. Everything they saw, everything they had aboard, was being fed live from their mothership. Every sensor system from the original design except for the actual targeting systems is missing."

"That's damned dangerous," Song pointed out.

"Yes. But it gave this Coati gentleman complete control over what his pilots saw," Nebula replied.

"What do you mean?" Kyle demanded.

"Did it seem strange that the fighters kept coming, even while the motherships died and fled?" the spy asked. "Strange that not one of them tried to surrender?"

"A little," Kyle admitted, "but the only way they were going to escape was if they took us out and allowed the remaining corsairs to pick them up."

"They didn't even know Coati was running," Nebula said flatly. "According to their tactical feeds and maps, the corsairs were right behind them. Hell, their sensors didn't even show the destruction of any ship they weren't directly communicating with. They weren't fanatics; they didn't even know they were fighting to the death!"

The meeting was silent as that sank in. Navy and Space Force officers alike relied on their sensors and communications. To see how badly the pilots they'd just fought had been lied to...

"The crews weren't properly trained, either," Song told them. "Hard to say for sure, but I'd be stunned if most of those flight crews had more than a hundred hours of training time. They were being treated like expendable cannon fodder."

"That makes no sense," von Lambert argued. "He just threw away almost three hundred sixth-generation starfighters. I didn't think there would *be* that many Cobras out here."

"There shouldn't be," Kyle replied. "We sold just over four hundred, total, to the various Free Trade Zone systems. Many of those have been confirmed destroyed and the remainder accounted for in various defensive platforms.

"I have no idea where the hell the bastard got that many of our fighters."

"I think I do," Taggart interjected. "Trent and I went over the data and there's a similar pattern to the one we saw in the corsairs also applies to the fighters. The *design* is that of the Cobra...but the components aren't."

"The components are an integral part of the design," Song objected.

"That's why we have stockpiles of the essential component to allow us to build replacement ships."

"To a point, yes," the XO replied. "You need certain power levels of mass manipulators and zero-point cells, but…if you have those, even if they're not quite the right ones, and the design…you can build something that's basically a Cobra.

"It's not as efficient or as effective, but it's cheaper and you can build it out of whatever components you have on hand—so long as they meet the requirements."

"He's building his own starfighters?" Kyle asked. "I know we can do that, but those fabricators and designs are even more restricted and controlled than the starfighters themselves!"

"We already established that the bastard has a shipyard somewhere that's building custom pocket warships," von Lambert said grimly. "Is it that much of a surprise that he has at least one starfighter fabricator?"

"No. But it's going to be a giant headache," Kyle admitted. "So, we have no idea where his bases are?"

"None," Nebula confirmed.

"We're working on analyzing the hull debris we've pulled in," Trent told them. "We may be able to narrow down a star system for the origin of the metal, but that's only likely if the supply is coming from a known source."

"Which it almost certainly isn't," Taggart agreed.

"What about prisoners?" Kyle asked.

"His fighters weren't equipped with such luxuries as escape pods," Song told him. "We've picked up a few lucky survivors in crippled ships."

"We're starting on interrogations," Nebula added, "but so far, they've been about as useful as mushrooms—kept in the dark and fed shit."

"Do they even have the bandwidth to be proper pilots?" Kyle demanded. "Given everything else he seems to have done with these fighters…"

"Your medical people say they're mostly borderline," the diplomat told him. "They probably stuffed a bunch of idiots who wanted to be starfighter crew more than they wanted to not be pirates into the ships and basically wrote them off immediately."

Kyle shook his head. Starfighter corps were generally regarded as the elite of most militaries, with high requirements in both neural bandwidth capacity and academic performance to even be considered. Planetary populations were large enough that the inherent losses were replaceable, and starfighter crew *had* to be somewhat expendable, but treating them like cannon fodder…

"What I'm hearing is that we're back at square one," he noted. "I was hoping for more."

"We gutted Coati's main force," Taggart pointed out. "We didn't think he even had that many ships, so losing twenty-two of them has to hurt. Even if he can replace the ships and the starfighters, that's thousands of crew he has to find again."

"There's twenty systems in the Free Trade Zone," Kyle said quietly. "Assuming he's only recruiting from them, that's still, what, thirteen billion people? You can find a lot of scum willing to rape and kill in thirteen billion people."

"What do we do now?" von Lambert asked.

"Continue the convoy escort," Kyle said with a sigh. "From here back to Antioch, then to Istanbul. See what intelligence we can pick up and if their losses make any kind of dent in their activities.

"If nothing else, people, there's at least one Terran battlecruiser out there, and I'm not willing to call this done until that ship is either taken or destroyed."

34

14:00 November 19, 2736 Earth Standard Meridian Date/Time
BC-305 Poseidon

JAMES TECUMSEH HAD half-expected never to see Coati again. In the safety of his own head, he could admit he was actually disappointed to see the six corsair ships limp back into the KDX-6657 System. There was a tiny flicker of hope that the pirate had not survived the damage his fleet had taken, but that was dashed when he was pinged a few moments after the pirate ships showed up on *Poseidon*'s sensors.

"Coati for you, sir," Amoto informed him. "Strange that we haven't heard from him since they reached Salvatore."

"It looks like it didn't go well, and our pirate friend is hardly willing to admit we told him so until he has to," James replied. "Put him through, Lieutenant."

In general, they hadn't heard from Coati except when the pirate was in the same system as them. From an operational standpoint, James would admit that was something of a problem. From a personal

255

standpoint, he was *delighted* not to have to talk to the scaled and brightly-haired pirate.

"Commodore Tecumseh," Coati greeted him as his unique visage settled onto the screen in James's office.

"Commodore Coati. You appear to be missing a few ships."

"Do you think I'm stupid, Commodore?" the pirate demanded.

James was taken aback.

"You walked into a trap you were warned about," he replied slowly. "It's certainly not the smartest thing I've ever seen anyone do, but I know you were convinced you could turn it on them.

"I take it that didn't work?"

"No," Coati hissed. "It did not, and I begin, Commodore Tecumseh, to wonder just how long ago I walked into this trap."

Now James was very confused. Coati had grounds to be angry, but with the loss of half of his ships, the pirate needed the Commonwealth ships more than ever.

Though, with all of the delays, James was currently wishing he hadn't sent *Chariot* to Amadeus. His second ship was finally on its way back but was still almost twenty-four hours out.

He let the silence linger, leaving it to Coati to either explain what he was going on about or move on.

"You were right," the pirate finally allowed. "I don't know who they turned, but they twisted my intelligence network against me. I have agents already in motion. I will learn who betrayed me, and they will all pay.

"Everyone who betrayed me will pay," Coati glowered at the screen. "And your Roberts…oh, his fate will be delicious."

"Be cautious in your vendettas," James warned. "Even the Commonwealth has problems with the Federation, and they will not blithely watch as you hunt down one of their most famous captains."

"You underestimate me, Commodore Tecumseh. You always have," the pirate noted. "But you were right, this time. Our losses against Roberts were significant."

"The Commonwealth stands ready to make certain our shared objectives are met," James said smoothly. "We can work together to make certain the Alliance force is…removed as a factor."

Of course, at this point, he would be perfectly willing to go after Roberts's remaining two ships with just *Poseidon* and *Chariot*. He no longer needed Coati...which meant he could feed the pirate's remaining ships into a meat grinder if it helped achieve his mission.

"We should meet in person," Coati finally replied. "It appears I will need to lean on you more in the immediate future than I would like, but this Roberts and his task group *must* be removed."

"I agree. I estimate you being able to come aboard around seventeen hundred hours?"

"It'll be nineteen hundred," the pirate told him firmly. "I have other affairs to arrange as well."

"Very well," James agreed.

Using the pirate and his ships as mobile ablative armor sounded better and better by the second.

———

IN THE END, not only did Coati refuse to show up on James's schedule, but he refused to even show up on time. His shuttle finally arrived just before twenty hundred hours, almost an hour late. James had waited ten minutes for the pirate to show up, and then returned to his office to get work done while Coati messed around.

"He's finally here," the dock officer informed James over the intercom. "Do you want to come down and meet him?"

"No," James said grouchily. "If he wants to be this late, let him deal with it. Have a pair of Marines bring him up to my office."

Coati could probably find his way to the Commodore's office by now, but there was no way that James was letting the pirate wander around *Poseidon* unescorted. The Marines were more of an honor guard than anything, but they'd stop the man from getting in *too* much trouble.

And making Coati come to him helped reinforce the necessary power dynamic—and let James finish the piece of paperwork he was working on, allowing him to have two cups of coffee waiting when the pirate finally arrived.

There was reinforcing power dynamics and there was being rude, after all.

Coati looked to have his own personal storm cloud as he entered the office, shaking off the Marines with a dismissive shake of his head as he dropped himself into the chair and glared across the table. He grabbed the coffee without a word and drank a massive gulp.

"I presume you're not trying to poison me," he concluded afterward. "Though I suppose I should know better than to trust one of Terra's Unity fanatics."

"I am a believer in unification, yes," James said slowly. "I am hardly a fanatic, though, despite what you've said before."

"Takes a blind fanatic to think that all of humanity can be ruled by one set of suits on Earth," Coati pointed out, his grouchiness fading somewhat. "Instant communication be damned, your theoretically elected rep would be four months' flight from here. There's no way she's going to be playing by the rules with all of the temptations of power to her fingertips."

"The system works," the Terran pointed out. "The Commonwealth is not the most powerful nation in human space by accident, after all."

"The system *has* worked," Coati replied. "As you expand, you will find the limits of your system, and your Commonwealth, like every empire in history, will break."

"No empire in history has ever had all of our advantages," James said. "What's your point, Coati?"

"I have to have a point?" the pirate said with a blatantly fake grin.

"You just got your ass kicked six ways to Sunday by the Alliance," James reminded him. "Is this really the time when you want to be discussing the virtues of quantum entanglement–based representative democracy?"

The fake grin disappeared and Coati leaned forward across the desk.

"It's related," he said flatly. "I do have a point, Commodore Tecumseh. My own assessment is that the Commonwealth is rapidly approaching the limits of its capacity. A two-front war against the second-largest polity in human space, however disorganized that polity is, and the largest coalition of nations ever assembled?

"Even *victory* will doom the Commonwealth now," the pirate continued. "Adding that many systems at once will break the annexation policies that have held it together. The nation you have sworn to serve, Commodore, is doomed."

"I think it's obvious I disagree," the Commodore said dryly. "And I am again left with my question: what is your *point*, Coati?"

"You are correct, Tecumseh, in that I need your ships if I am to complete my goals now," Coati admitted. "But I have no reason to trust the Commonwealth and many reasons not to. So, I have an offer for you, Commodore."

"And what is that?" James asked, though he suspected.

"Join me," the pirate offered. "Stand at my right hand while we forge a new empire here in this forgotten corner of the galaxy. I have resources and allies I have not yet revealed; the birth of a new nation, a new *dynasty* is within reach.

"I offered you a world once and I meant it," Coati reminded him. "Now I offer you the chance to help rule two dozen worlds. You can serve a nation that is doomed to fall and drag you down into the ashes with it, or you can stand at the right hand of an emperor. I reward those who give me honest service.

"Fight with me, Commodore Tecumseh, and you will be rich and powerful beyond your wildest dreams."

Coati's concept of riches and power were not James Tecumseh's, he suspected. Rulership of a world didn't appeal to him—it mostly sounded like work. A task group of three ships was enough work; a planet full of people? Especially a planet full of *resisting* people?

James would rather fight to save a dying civilization, not that he truly feared that fate for the Commonwealth.

"You really don't know what motivates men like me," he told Coati quietly. "I serve the Commonwealth for the greater good, not my own aggrandization. My mission calls for me to destroy the Free Trade Zone and undermine the influence of the Federation and Imperium out here.

"That requires me to work with you. You will get what you want, Commodore, but I will *never* betray the Commonwealth, and most certainly *not* to service you."

Coati sighed.

"I figured," he confessed. "But much as you have aggravated me, Commodore, you are also brave and useful and I need your ship.

"I wanted to see if you were part of the betrayal, to see if you ever had any attachment to my cause, and now I see you never did. I warned you, Commodore, that all who betrayed me would be punished."

James stared at the pirate.

"What are you talking about?"

"Do you think I'm *stupid*?" Coati demanded, echoing his earlier question. "Do you think I am blind? That squadrons of *Terran* starfighters stabbing me in the back would go unnoticed?"

A tiny voice in the back of James's head wondered how the pirate had got a gun aboard and past the Marines. Another realized that was why Coati had been late, so that the already-perfunctory check the guards would perform on a known, if not entirely trusted, ally would be rushed or skipped.

Now the pirate leveled the small gun he'd produced on James's head.

"I am familiar with Federation, Imperial, and Terran starfighter design, Commodore," he continued. "The fighters may have been new, but I recognize Terran designs when I see them. I know when I have been betrayed."

"You're insane," James replied. "Work *with* the Alliance? The whole point of this operation was to weaken them."

"You could barely bring yourself to sully your great presence with me," Coati spat. "I'm hardly surprised to see you turn like a dog at the leash. No, Commodore, I will have your ship—without you!"

"It doesn't work that way," the Terran officer replied, staring down the barrel of the gun. "You know that. This ship is full of Marines, soldiers, officers who the ship will look to for authority.

"Shoot me? You gain *nothing*."

Coati chuckled as he stepped forward to press the gun against James's forehead. It was a grating sound, terrifying in its certainty.

"I just pulled a gun, Commodore. Shouldn't your systems, your Marines, be doing *something*? Ask your ship. Give it an order."

James tried to trigger an alert, to call the Marines in from outside his door. *Poseidon* ignored him, kicking him out of the system as if he had no authorizations at all.

"It's fascinating," the pirate told him, "just how little attention everyone pays to the IT department. All of your security measures, all of your overrides and authority and power...Three guys in the tech team can undo almost all of it."

"What have you *done*?"

"Well, as we speak, the oxygen level on the entire ship outside certain rooms—including this one—is dropping rapidly and your crew is starting to pass out.

"Your ship's AI has already marked you and Sherazi as dead and locked out your command codes. The next in line, Captain Petrovsky? He was *so* much more amenable to the offer of a planet than you were. I think I'll give him Antioch. There's so many beautiful women on Antioch; he'll like it."

James was frozen in place. He was a naval officer, his training in hand-to-hand combat over forty years in the past. He had neither the skill nor the nerve to resist with a gun to his head.

"And now, my dear Commodore Tecumseh, you will pay for all of the petty power games you have so enjoyed," the pirate said sweetly.

Before James could say or do anything, Coati lowered the gun and fired, a frangible round smashing into the Terran's shoulder blade. At this range, James *felt* his bones fragment and his skin tear, pain ripping through as he crumpled backward, only to find the gun trained on his head again.

"Oh, yes, my dear Commodore, you'll bleed out from that," the pirate told him. "Eventually."

Another gunshot rang out and James's *other* shoulder blade shattered.

"I see no reason to kill you *quickly*," Coati pointed out. "This ship is mine now, and there's no one coming to save you."

"Go fuck yourself," James managed to hiss, but the pirate only laughed.

"I'm not my type, Tecumseh. Far too much of a sadist. I am, however, going to enjoy killing you slowly while I asphyxiate your entire crew. A horrible accident, Captain Petrovsky will tell Captain Modesitt. *Chariot* will join us, serving your Commonwealth loyally until the time is right."

James tried to take advantage of the gloating to crawl into something resembling cover—and another bullet smashed into his right hip, hammering him to the floor and crippling his leg.

"None of that. You and I have some quality time left."

Coati was raising the gun to cripple James's *other* leg when the door exploded inward to reveal a two-meter-tall demon of black ceramic, a massive rifle in its hands. Gunfire echoed in the confined space as the Marine tried to shoot the pirate, but Coati was already moving.

Whoever had decided to give the bastard scales and multicolored hair had done more than just that to his genome. The moment the room had an active threat, the pirate was moving with a speed matched by no human James had ever seen—*including* combat cyborgs.

He blurred under the combat rifle, knocking it aside as he opened fire on the power-armored soldier with his tiny gun.

There was no way the frangible rounds could penetrate, but that wasn't the pirate's intent. The bullets were a distraction, one that allowed him to duck around the soldier and dive into the hallway. By the time the Marine managed to turn around, Coati was long gone.

And James was already starting to have trouble breathing. The bastard really was asphyxiating everyone on the ship, though power armor would help.

"Dammit, sir, this is *way* outside my contingency plans," Barbados's voice rumbled from the suit as he pulled an oxygen mask from the power armor's emergency med kit. "The ship is running out of air and the shipboard emergency masks are uniformly fucked."

"He got to Petrovsky," James gasped. "We have to...get to *Stormcloud. Poseidon's* gone."

Blood loss and oxygen deprivation met somewhere in the middle, and Commodore James Tecumseh passed out.

35

KDX-6657 System
01:00 November 20, 2736 Earth Standard Meridian Date/Time
Terran Commonwealth Marine Corps Assault Transport Stormcloud

WAKING UP AGAIN HURT.

James Tecumseh's career had been aboard warships of the Terran Commonwealth Navy, vessels that outclassed the vast majority of their opposition. He'd never been seriously injured, never even so much as broken a limb in sports.

The sensation of his implants and medical nanite suite disabling his nerve receptors was new to him, enough that he tried to look down and see just what was going on with his limbs—only to discover that his head was immobilized.

"Shit, he's awake," a voice cursed. "Get Barbados in here; I am *not* briefing the Commodore."

"Where am I?" he demanded.

"Trauma Bay Alpha aboard *Stormcloud*," the voice told him. "Give me a second."

There was a faint whir, and James felt his body rise as the bed he was strapped to rotated, allowing him to look out over the largest shipboard medical facility he'd ever seen. Assault transports were equipped to handle major combat casualties or provide support in terms of natural disasters. Their trauma bays were larger and better equipped than most groundside hospitals.

"I'm Dr. MacDougall," the speaker told him, turning out to be a tall man with carefully cropped red hair and tanned skin, "senior trauma physician for *Stormcloud* and, if you'll allow me a moment of non-humility, the reason you're alive."

James closed his eyes, leaning back against the bed and breathing slowly. The trauma center was packed, every bed occupied.

"How bad?"

"The Colonel is on his way; he'll brief you," MacDougall immediately countered. "It's not my place; I'm just your doctor."

"All right, then, doctor, how bad am I?" James snapped.

MacDougall chuckled.

"Got me. You sure you want to know?"

"Doctor, my head is immobilized and I can't feel any of my limbs. How bad?"

"You took collateral damage to your upper spine and neck vertebrae," the doctor said flatly. "You're immobilized so that can heal; should take about another three hours. That's the part I can fix today."

"And the rest?"

"The good news is, you're a perfect candidate for standard regen," MacDougall told him.

"Doctor, stop it," James ordered. "How bad?"

"Under normal circumstances, we might have been able to save an arm," the doctor said slowly. "With the situation when you came aboard, we had no choice but to treat you as quickly as possible and move on to others in equally desperate need.

"We amputated and cauterized both arms and your left leg. You are a regen candidate, so my normal recommendation would be to ship you back to a fleet base and put you on medical leave for three months while we regrew your limbs."

"We're a long way from any fleet bases," James pointed out. "A long way from home, betrayed, and in serious trouble."

"And that is why the doctor called me to brief you," Barbados cut in. "Dr. MacDougall. Privacy screen?"

"Implant-activated. I'm watching the Commodore's vitals; I'll let you know if he needs to rest. He will," the doctor warned.

"I know," the Marine acknowledged. "Now give us the space."

James heard more than saw the privacy screen drop down around him and Barbados and coughed delicately.

"I can't even move my head, Colonel; I'd appreciate it if you'd stand where I can see you."

The Colonel stepped around to where James could see him, looking utterly exhausted.

"The doctor wouldn't tell me how bad."

"Our plans weren't built around this level of penetration of our security," Barbados told him bluntly. "We extracted four hundred and seven members of *Poseidon*'s crew, all of whom required major medical attention, and took over two hundred Marine casualties doing so.

"Less than half of those were fatal, thankfully, but that means MacDougall and his people are handling over five hundred cases of severe trauma."

"And over forty-five hundred people died on *Poseidon*," James half-whispered.

"I doubt Coati murdered the entire crew," the Marine said gruffly, "but outside of those he coopted...yeah. If we didn't get them off, they're either traitors or dead."

"Where are we right now?"

"Running," Barbados told him. "We got *Stormcloud* out of orbit running at Tier Three acceleration, but it cost us. We took several solid hits and it's going to be at least twelve hours before we have the Stetson stabilizers in sufficient order to warp space."

If they'd taken enough damage they couldn't warp space...

"How bad?"

"We're down over a thousand more casualties aboard *Stormcloud*," the Marine said grimly. "We burned ninety percent of our reaction mass getting clear of *l'Estación de Muerte*. *Stormcloud* isn't defenseless and we've blown all of Coati's remaining starfighters to hell, but he's still got eight corsairs...and, well, *Poseidon*."

"Even with Petrovsky, it'll take time for him to get *Poseidon* back online," James pointed out. "But we need to get out of here."

"Twelve hours for FTL," the Colonel repeated.

"Have we been in touch with *Chariot*?"

"I have. Captain Modesitt wants to speak to you."

"I don't even have *arms*," James snapped. "What the fuck does anyone expect me to do?"

Barbados looked around, as if making sure the privacy screen was working, then met James's gaze levelly.

"Command," he hissed. "You dragged us all out on this branch, and now Coati has cut it off behind us. I can't reassure the Navy personnel and I sure as hell can't give orders to Modesitt. The only thing *I* can do is take *Stormcloud* and head back to Commonwealth space...a trip I've already been warned she won't survive."

"Fuck."

"Your call, sir."

James closed his eyes again, breathing deeply and running through a meditation exercise as he prodded at his implant's self-check features.

Finally, he exhaled and opened his eyes, meeting Barbados's gaze.

"We're falling into the shit, all right," he conceded. "Start flapping, Colonel, then send Dr. MacDougall back in. It seems he and I need to talk emergency prostheses."

———

IN THE ERA of neural implants, being a triple amputee thankfully didn't render James completely incapable. Once he'd discussed his needs with MacDougall and sent the doctor on his way, he was able to close the privacy screen again himself and link into the q-com network to reach out to Captain Modesitt.

"Commodore, are you all right?" she asked the instant the channel connected. "Barbados wasn't willing to give me details of much, only that the situation was bad and I needed to change my emergence locus."

"That was what you needed to know and the Colonel's had a bad day," James told her. "We all have. Did all the problems get wrapped up at Amadeus?"

"Is that relevant right now?" she demanded. "Commodore…"

"Coati shattered my shoulders and one of my hips," he said flatly. "All three limbs had to be amputated. Commodore Sherazi is dead along with most of his crew. *Poseidon* is now in Coati's hands, and he's managed to buy Petrovsky, which means he'll have her online inside of forty-eight hours.

"*Stormcloud* is badly damaged and we've lost a huge chunk of the Marines. We need to get her Alcubierre drive online before they get *Poseidon* online, or Coati is going to finish the job. We need *Chariot* to make sure the bastard doesn't send his corsairs out before that."

Modesitt was silent for several seconds.

"Shit. Shit." She exhaled. "What do we do?"

"Right now, you come to that emergence locus that Barbados gave you and rendezvous with us," he ordered. "By then, we should be close to having *Stormcloud*'s drive online and we can all get the hell out of here."

"What about you? Even with implants, you can't do much without hands."

"I'm being fitted for emergency cybernetics by the Marines' surgeon," James admitted. "By the time you're here, I should at least be walking, if not…well."

There was a long silence.

"You know that wrecks your ability to take regen later, right?" Modesitt asked.

"I do," he agreed. Regeneration of nerves was the hardest part, and tying the nerves into the circuits of a cybernetic prosthesis caused even more damage—smaller, more complicated, harder-to-heal damage. By taking emergency cybernetics, he was drastically reducing the chances that he'd get his own legs back.

"I need to be fully functional," he continued. "I dragged us all into this mess and didn't see Coati coming. It's going to be up to me to get us out of it.

"What's your ETA?"

"We're still about eight hours out," Modesitt told him. "Please try to still be there when we arrive."

"Believe me, Captain Modesitt, it's high on my priority list."

36

KDX-6657 System
07:00 November 20, 2736 Earth Standard Meridian Date/Time
Terran Commonwealth Marine Corps Assault Transport Stormcloud

"I SUPPOSE that it was too much to hope for that he'd leave us alone," Captain Tabitha Colton, the fair-haired Navy commander of the TCMC transport *Stormcloud*, opined aloud on her bridge.

James swallowed the snippy response that came to mind. Trapped in a wheelchair with only somewhat-useful lumps of metal strapped to his shoulders and hip, his mood was aggravated by both his incapacity and a low level of pain his implants couldn't squash without preventing the cybernetics from bonding.

"What are we looking at?" he finally asked.

"Four of those modular corsairs are heading our way at two hundred gees," Colton told him, the officer throwing him a look that only barely concerned a level of worry that James wasn't entirely sure was appropriate. "Assuming they vector for a zero-velocity intercept somewhere close, their ETA should be somewhere around ninety minutes."

"Well before *Chariot* will get here," he concluded grimly. "How's *Stormcloud* doing, Captain?"

If he'd had any illusion that *Stormcloud* was a warship, her bridge would have wrecked it. It was smaller than a true warship's, with fewer stations, fewer crew, and fewer systems to control than a warship would have.

The assault transport carried no long-range weapons. Her entire arsenal consisted of light positron lances designed to take down fighters, and the launchers for specialized bombardment munitions designed to support her Marine landing forces.

Stormcloud wasn't intended to fight space battles. She was designed to enable four thousand Marines to take and hold a planet.

"About two solid hits from being debris and memories," Colton admitted. "We're down over sixty percent of our lances and half our missile defense. We killed every one of the bastard's starfighters, but we can't fight his corsairs."

"What about parasites?" James asked. "You have fighters, don't you?"

The Marine Colonel standing with them chuckled.

"Yeah. Marine Corps Piranhas. They're *atmospheric* fighters with a limited deep-space ability," Barbados pointed out. "Designed to drop from orbit into atmosphere to wreck the day of local defense aircraft. They're not designed or equipped for deep-space battle."

"But you can strap Javelins to them," the Navy Commodore pointed out. "Right? The atmospheric fuel pods are removable and can be replaced with a framework that holds starfighter missiles?"

The other two officers were silent.

"Yeah," Barbados admitted. "Hell, I'd forgotten we could do that. I'm not sure it's ever actually been done in a real fight."

"Well, Colonel, if we don't try *something*, those four corsairs are going to fly up to about half a million kilometers and start pumping half-megaton-a-second positron lances into us. We won't survive that," James pointed out.

"Do we even have that crap in storage?" the Colonel asked, looking at Colton.

She blinked, clearly checking her implants.

"Enough to arm forty Piranhas for one pass," she concluded. "Eighty Javelins, forty frameworks."

She shook her head.

"We'll have the flight crews strip the rest of the armament," Colton continued. "It's all atmospheric or extremely short-ranged by space standards. A five-hundred-KPS railgun is death in an atmosphere and deadly in low orbit, but it's not doing *anything* in this kind of fight."

"Just missile platforms," James agreed. "But that's more than the bastards think we have, so let's make it happen, people."

"I'll talk to my pilots," Barbados confirmed. "Oorah, sir."

———

STORMCLOUD DIDN'T HAVE enough fuel to try and evade the incoming corsairs. Burning at Tier Three acceleration for as long as they had had consumed well over ninety percent of the transport's reaction mass. Since she'd had half of her troop complement cut to fit her out as logistics support for the mission, she had the skimmer shuttles that could refill her tanks from an available gas giant, but that needed a gas giant and friendly space.

KDX-6657 was no longer friendly space.

The four ships heading their way were each barely a quarter of *Stormcloud*'s size, but they had missile launchers and heavy positron lances. The transport did not.

James and Colton waited on the bridge during the pirate's inexorable advance, watching the corsairs accelerate toward them and then make turnover, slowly reducing their velocity as they closed.

"The Piranhas are armed," she told him as the timers continued to tick down. "We only get one shot. What's the call, Commodore?"

"We can't let those corsairs reach half a million klicks, Captain," he replied. "Launch the Piranhas at a million kilometers and target for missile intercept while the bastards are still at least five fifty out."

"That leaves us almost no margin," she warned.

"Captain, we have one salvo," he said. "We already have no margin. We just have to trust Barbados's pilots."

And it was just pilots, too. Where a starfighter would have a crew of three, the Piranha was primarily an atmosphere fighter and carried only a pilot. Trading in the fighter's additional fuel tanks and atmosphere-based weapons for the rack with its two Javelins actually increased their mass.

By air-breathing standards, the three-hundred-ton Piranha was an immense, heavily armed and heavily armored behemoth. By space combat standards, it didn't even register as small. They were *tiny*.

And slow.

James watched as they labored their way out of *Stormcloud*'s hangar bays, the pilots clearly unused to operating in vacuum for more than brief periods, and light up their antimatter thrusters. Forty fighters was two-thirds of the complement intended to enforce air superiority for the landing battalions, but it was a small force compared to the numbers starfighters usually deployed in.

And those forty ships weighed less than a single squadron of starfighters would have.

"This can't work," he whispered. "They're *toys*."

Colton chuckled.

"Sir, I've watched those 'toys' destroy an entire planetary air force that outnumbered them ten to one in an afternoon. This might not be their native environment, but those are deadly fighters and experienced pilots. If this can work, those pilots will make it work."

"And they know the stakes," Barbados told James as he rejoined them at the heart of the bridge. "I let the pilots pick which of them flew this sortie. Their friends and their stuff are on this ship."

"They're still small and slow," the Commodore replied.

"You don't need more than Tier Two when the only purpose of your drives is to get you to atmosphere," the Marine agreed. "On the other hand, they're designed to circumnavigate a planet *inside* atmosphere, so even pulling the secondary fuel tanks, they've got a lot of delta-v to play with in deep space."

James nodded, continuing to watch the feed. The corsairs had almost certainly *noticed* the Piranhas, but they weren't changing their course or otherwise reacting. Presumably, they were at least considering them as potential threats, but *Stormcloud* was their target.

Seconds turned to minutes, timers in James's implant ticking away. *Chariot* was still forty minutes away, but if they survived this pass, the strike cruiser would be around before anyone else could reach them—and the only ship in the system fit to tangle with *Chariot* was *Poseidon* herself.

"Shoot straight, pilots," James murmured as the range figures drop. "I make it range in thirty seconds?"

"We're feeding them as much data as we can from the q-probes," Colton told him, "but the Piranhas don't have q-coms themselves. A lot of it has to be their sensors and their pilots' judgment."

By the time light reached the q-probes, the data was transferred to *Stormcloud* via entanglement, and then radioed to the Piranhas, it was easily three seconds old. The probes' sensors were significantly better than the atmospheric fighters' scanners, but that delay was everything in targeting.

"Missile launch! Confirm missile launch!" Colton's tactical officer snapped. "I have seventy-nine birds in the air; *Stormcloud* Delta Six reports launch failure on her second missile. She has ejected it as a dud."

"Those missiles were sitting in my magazines for *two years*," the Captain murmured. "I was expecting more failures."

James arched an eyebrow at his subordinate.

"And this wasn't worth mentioning?"

"It wasn't going to change anything," she replied. "So no, no, it wasn't."

He snorted but let that go. She was right, after all.

"Piranhas are now pulling back; range is opening," the tactical officer reported. "Time to impact, seventy seconds and count—

"We have lance fire!" he interrupted himself, *Stormcloud*'s computers drawing in the beams as simple white lines on the tactical feed. "Half-megaton beams; they're sweeping space to take out the Piranhas. Pilots are maneuvering to evade."

James heard Barbados's sharp inhalation as the icons began to drop off the plot. With that much antimatter in the beams and the Piranhas' miniscule size, even a near miss was deadly—and the Marines simply didn't have the experience for this threat environment.

Five of the Marine fighters died. Ten. Twenty. James forced himself to watch, realizing they weren't getting *any* of the Piranhas back and knowing that duty and honor alike required him to bear witness.

More of the fighters died, the icons dropping off the tactical like flies until there were none left.

"Semper fi," Barbados whispered. "Tell me we got the fuckers," he ground at Colton's tactical department.

"Impact in ten seconds. Fifty-plus missiles still inbound."

The missile icons were dropping too. The corsairs weren't nearly as well equipped for anti-missile defense as James would have made them, but they had enough lasers and light positron lances to carve massive swathes through the incoming salvo.

Just not enough to stop *all* the missiles.

"Impact, we have impact," the tactical officer declared as flashes of light lit up the tactical feed. "I'm reading eleven explosions; trying to identify targets."

Seconds ticked by as the radiation continued to hash the sensor data and then the tactical officer looked up at the senior officers and gave a satisfied nod.

"They did it, sirs," he announced grimly. "Three of the four are gone and the fourth is drifting, no power signature. We're clear."

James sighed in relief and returned the nod. They'd lost a lot of people today—but while the loss of the Marine pilots stung, they'd saved everybody.

"They could do the math before they went out," Barbados said quietly. "They could guess what was going to happen when atmosphere-trained pilots ran into anti-starfighter defenses. But like I said, they knew the stakes."

"Let me know if anything else in this goddamned system even *twitches*," James ordered Colton's people. "And keep me up to date on the repairs. I don't care if we can only jump for half a day; I want to be out of Coati's reach the moment we can be, understand?"

CHARIOT ARRIVED EXACTLY ON TIME, to the relief of everyone aboard *Stormcloud,* as the other four corsairs had now started moving in their direction. The arrival of the Terran strike cruiser put an immediate halt to that, the pirate ships turning tail almost instantly.

"Captain Modesitt, we're glad to see you," James told *Chariot's* commander. "Your presence seems to be having an appropriate effect on the junkyard hounds trying to dog us."

"I'd like to have a far more immediate effect on them all," she replied. "If I move in, I should be able to punch them out and retake *Poseidon,* sir."

James sighed.

"They have Petrovsky, Captain," he reminded her. "Right now, they're mixing his overrides and a team of hackers to take over systems one by one. It will take them days to have her fully functional, but if we present an immediate threat...they can have at least her missile launchers online inside an hour.

"No, Captain Modesitt, if you go in, you *will* end up fighting *Poseidon,* and even with her half-crippled, that's not a fight you can win."

"We can't just let them walk away with one of the Common-wealth's most advanced battlecruisers," Modesitt objected.

"We don't have a choice," James admitted. "We need to get the hell out of this system before they get *Poseidon* online, and then we need to come up with a plan. For now, however, all we can do is keep *Chariot* around as a watchdog while Captain Colton's people get her ship in motion."

"Where do we go from here?" Colton asked.

"Deep space," James told her. "Somewhere no one is going to think to look while we decide what we do about the fact that a two-bit pirate now has one of the Commonwealth's most advanced battlecruisers."

"Fuck," Modesitt snarled. "I hate this."

"Believe me, Captain, I hated being repeatedly shot and waking up a triple amputee more," James said dryly.

37

Antioch System
15:00 November 21, 2736 Earth Standard Meridian Date/Time
DSC-052 Kodiak

THOTH ONCE MORE LED THE way as the convoy arrived back at the Antioch system, erupting from warped space five minutes ahead of the rest of the ships and feeding data back to *Kodiak* and the other ships. Q-probes flew out from the cruiser, clearing a safe zone in front of the ship even as Houshian guided the rest of the convoy in behind her.

Unlike Salvatore, though, Antioch had its own network of q-com-enabled satellites and probes, which meant that Kyle had known what was waiting for him even before *Thoth* had emerged from warped space.

After the last few incidents, however, he didn't trust anything that suggested things were safe and normal, so out ahead the cruiser went.

Kodiak followed her out, her own scanners sweeping space as Song launched a two-squadron combat space patrol.

"Everything is clear," Taggart reported. "Nothing unexpected; two of Antioch's gunships are orbiting at one million kilometers, keeping an eye on our emergence locus."

"Good to see them," Kyle agreed. "Send them my regards by radio and let Admiral Belisarius know we're back. We've kept him updated, but if he has any questions, I'll be available."

"Yes, sir," Jamison replied.

"Any change in the status around Antioch?" Kyle asked.

"They're still clustering their ships and escorting the convoys from Orontes to Seleucus," Sterling told him. "Those escorts are lighter now, but they're still not letting things relax."

"That's for the best," Kyle reminded them. "We may have shattered the force that came after us, but we have no idea how many ships this Coati actually has, or just what the Commonwealth has sent out this way. They could still have that damn *Hercules* show up."

The tactical officer shook his head as he studied the system.

"If that *Hercules* shows up, they're screwed, sir," Sterling admitted. "Ten gunships, maybe three hundred fifth- and sixth-generation fighters? Unless their orbital platforms are better armed than they look, that one battlecruiser will walk right over everything Antioch has."

"I know," Kyle told him. "And if Belisarius doesn't know that, I'll make sure he realizes. We've dealt the pirates a body blow I doubt they'll recover from, but the Terran involvement adds a whole layer of bullshit."

"We got nothing from the debris and prisoners," Taggart complained. "So, what do we do?"

"Exactly what we are doing. Make sure shipping moves safely, watch for pirates, see if Nebula's people can track the ransoms back through Amadeus." Kyle shook his head. "We don't go home until the job is done, people. So, let's keep our eyes open for any scrap of data we find."

"Sir, I have Admiral Belisarius on the q-com for you," Jamison told you.

"I figured," Kyle agreed. "I'll take it in my office. Commander Taggart has the con."

———

ADMIRAL RECEP BELISARIUS looked far more relaxed today than he had any of the previous times Kyle had spoken with the man, his perpetual exhausted edge softened by the lessened threat.

"Captain Roberts," he greeted Kyle. "It seems we underestimated just how much you could achieve in a single month."

"We got lucky," Kyle demurred. "We were clever and we had advantages the pirates couldn't see coming, but we got lucky. And *Alexander* got crippled along the way."

"My Premier has instructed me to make certain that our condolences are passed on to the families of those lost in the battles your people have fought on our behalf," Belisarius told him. "Your victories have given the region our first true peace of mind in years, and the news arrived at a fortuitous time for Premier Yilmaz's government."

"Did it?" Kyle asked.

"Yes, the news of your victory over the pirates reached Orontes the morning of the election for the House," the Admiral replied. "Instead of losing much of their majority, the Premier's party increased their strength. We are better positioned than ever to sustain the Free Trade Zone through this difficult time."

"That's good to know," Kyle said slowly. "Because the difficulties are far from over."

"You crushed the pirates, Captain. Three quarters of their ships destroyed! How can they recover from that?!"

"Easily, Admiral, if they have more ships," the big officer pointed out carefully. "According to my intel, in the last two years alone, the pirates have taken more than fifteen freighters. Each of those ships had four Class One mass manipulators. If they had the resources—and we have no idea of the extent or limits of their resources—those ships alone could have provided the most expensive component for over *sixty* corsairs like the ones we fought."

From the silence and shocked expression on his screen, Belisarius hadn't thought that through.

"Plus, Admiral, we now know the Commonwealth has ships here," Kyle continued. "One of them a *Hercules*-class battlecruiser. That ship alone could conquer your star system, Admiral Belisarius. My guess would be that they brought two. This situation is not resolved, Admiral. The battle to save your Trade Zone has barely begun."

"Damn," the Admiral sighed. "I knew about the Terran ship, but my analysts hadn't dared suggest there were that many corsairs. I think..." He sighed again. "I think they were worried to hand the government news that was too bad. The worst-case estimate I was given was twenty of those ships, a number we now know was too low."

"Hopefully, the bastards don't have another thirty ships kicking around," Kyle agreed, "but we have to plan for the absolute worst-case scenario, which is that they can still field a force equivalent to the one we fought at Salvatore, *plus* two Commonwealth battlecruisers."

The Admiral looked pale and tired again now.

"What do we do, Captain?" he asked. "We bought our warships from you and the Imperium, neither of whom has ships to sell anymore. The Commonwealth would never have sold warships to us and that certainly won't change now!

"No system in this sector can stop the force you describe. Even your own task group would fail in the face of that strength. If they have that kind of fleet, we are doomed."

"And that, Admiral, is the surest sign that they don't have it," Kyle agreed. "If this Coati had another thirty ships, he'd have rolled over your systems by now. The Commonwealth doesn't *want* to conquer you right now; they want to use you to draw our forces out of position."

He sighed.

"Something we really no longer have a choice about doing," he admitted. "I have been offered reinforcements, but...there are no guarantees on timing or numbers. If we wait for them, this region may come apart at the seams before they arrive."

"So, what do we do?" Belisarius echoed.

"I need a target, Admiral," Kyle told him. "If we find a base, an anchorage, I can hit it hard enough that even the Terran battlecruisers won't stand a chance. But without a target, all I can do is guard your freighters."

"Then I will redouble our intelligence efforts," Belisarius promised.

"With the Premier's majority secure for at least two more years, there are options available we did not have before.

"We will find these bastards," he said grimly.

"If you find them for me, Admiral, I will blow them to hell for you," Kyle replied.

―――――

THEY'D COLLECTED full intelligence dumps from each of the star systems they'd passed through, and Serengeti and Antioch, at least, were continuing to update *Kodiak* with new information as they acquired it.

Kyle wasn't a data analyst by training and had left the work to CIC and Nebula, but there were aspects of it he did feel qualified to look over—mostly, trying to backtrack the exit and arrival vectors of the various pirate forces.

He had drawn them all onto a holographic representation of local space hovering above his desk, hoping to find at least *some* overlaps, some central point that would give them a target.

Of course, if it was that easy, the locals would have done it years before. There were overlaps, but they were of two or three courses at most, and there were *nine* of them, all in deep space. He wasn't surprised that Coati, a former military professional, had been too smart to make it that easy.

The lack of useful information was frustrating, though. Studying the vectors, there was information Kyle could interpolate, but it wasn't *useful* information. He could, for example, be certain that the pirates were dropping out of FTL some distance from the target systems and changing course.

He was also reasonably sure that there were at least two bases in play, and if he'd been coordinating the campaign, he'd have staging bases as intermediaries to protect the actual shipyard.

For a theoretically crazed pirate, this "Commodore Coati" was far too damned professional for Kyle's liking.

"Sir," Jamison interrupted his contemplation. "We have a q-com connection for you from *Napoleon*."

"*Napoleon*, Commander?" he asked. Another of the *Conqueror*-class ships; he thought she was assigned to Seventh Fleet, but he didn't know anyone aboard her.

"It's Captain Solace, sir," his coms officer told him after a moment. "The connection is live."

Mira contacting him from a ship other than *Camerone* was a bad sign.

"Put her through," he ordered, sending the hologram of the region away with a gesture and linking the channel to the big wallscreen.

His girlfriend looked shattered. Kyle had seen Mira tired, he'd seen her as an emotionless statute who didn't trust him...but he'd never seen her heartbroken and wavering even while sitting down.

"Mira, what happened?" he asked, before even considering that she might be able to tell him.

"Kyle," she replied, closing her eyes and breathing deeply. "Thank you. I...needed to see you. To know you were okay, at least."

"What *happened*?" he asked again. "I was briefed on the Via Somnia op..."

She exhaled and nodded.

"For the first time ever, a Commonwealth star system has been occupied by a foreign power," she told him in a leaden voice. "Via Somnia fell two days ago. The price was...high."

If the battle had been over for almost two days, the official loss announcements would be going out soon. From Mira's state, though, he could guess at least one.

"Miriam is dead," she told him softly and he winced. Vice Admiral Miriam Alstairs had been in command of Seventh Fleet, and Mira's ship had been her flagship. "*Camerone* was at the center of a fighter strike. We lost *Zheng He*, *Grizzly*, and *Horus* in ten minutes. *Camerone* survived, but we took too many hits. Flag deck was gone. We ejected half our damn zero-point cells."

"Gods," he murmured. He'd known the Captains and many of the officers of all three of the ships lost.

"Stars alone know how she made it through," Mira continued. "But we survived the battle. Shattered their defenses, landed troops on the station. More reinforcements are on the way, including *Avalon* and *Kronos.*"

Kyle managed to not wince at the realization that *Avalon* would be going back into action with a different captain. The surprise that *Kronos*, one of only two *Titan-class* battleships built with the new-generation hulls, was actually leaving the Castle system helped.

"*Camerone* isn't salvageable," the battlecruiser's captain said softly. "She'll be destroyed in place; she isn't even worth taking home for scrap. I lost half my crew to the Void, Kyle. I'm..." She swallowed. "I've been ordered to return to Castle for mandatory psych assessment and reassignment."

"You lost your ship," he reminded her. "That assessment is *necessary*, love. They're not going to ground you."

"We'll see," Mira half-whispered. "I lost the *Admiral*, Kyle."

"And saved half your crew. You know which Miriam would have wanted," he pointed out.

She choked down a sob and nodded. If Kyle had ever doubted that she trusted him, that she let him see her like this would have told him all he needed to know.

With that much damage to *Camerone*, he'd come perilously close to losing Mira, a thought that sent shivers of fear down his own spine, and he reached out to touch her face on the screen. The gesture earned him a strained smile, which he returned in full force.

"Trust the Fleet," he told her. "They've been through this before, they know the drill, they've a good idea of what you need."

At least with the ship being written off after a major battle, crippled facing the enemy with all guns blazing, there would be no need for a Board or other inquiry. Mira would get a new command, though; if JD-Personnel was as smart as he expected and he managed to deal with Coati in a "timely" manner, she'd likely still be on Castle when he returned.

"I do," Mira told him. "I do." She sighed deeply. "It's...not easy to lose a ship."

"No," he agreed. "So, listen to your doctors, my love," he ordered. "I don't know when I'll be back, but I'll be in touch as I can."

"I know," she said with an only somewhat-forced smile. "I needed to see you. Thank you."

"I'm fine," he told her with a grin. "The poor pirates out here, well, they're learning the errors of their ways."

Even more so than before, though, he desperately wanted a target he could hit to crush the pirates so he could take his people home.

38

STORMCLOUD'S main briefing area was designed to hold all the officers of a four-thousand-Marine assault brigade. Even with *Chariot*'s entire senior staff linked in by virtual conference, it seemed empty with just the senior officers of James Tecumseh's Task Group.

"*Stormcloud* is fucked," Commander Isaac Arsenault, the assault transport's chief engineer, told the gathering flatly. "We've almost no fuel, no weapons, nothing. Our stabilizer array is badly damaged, and I'm stunned we managed to sustain a warp bubble as long as we did."

"Is it repairable?" James asked.

"We'd have to cannibalize *Chariot*'s arrays," Commander Jillian Connor, *Chariot*'s chief engineer, told him. "Or get one or both ships to a system with an asteroid belt we can rip apart for resources. Out here?" The holographic projection of the petite engineer, which somehow perfectly reflected the grease stain on her face, shook its head.

"*Chariot* can fly and fight, but we don't have the life support to take on Colonel Barbados's Marines, let alone *Stormcloud's* crew and *Poseidon's* survivors," she continued.

"Life support is about all we've got left," Arsenault said bluntly. "I wouldn't want to risk even a short hop without replacing most of our stabilizer emitters, and we don't have the parts."

James sighed, carefully shifting the heavy weight of his new cybernetic limbs to try and find *some* comfort.

"I hesitate to rip apart our one functioning warship to rebuild an effectively unarmed ship, but I understand your point," he told them. "What alternative do we have?"

The engineers shared a glance.

"Depends on what you want us to do, sir," Connor finally said. "*Stormcloud* can easily carry all of our personnel back to the Commonwealth, and *Chariot*, much as I love her, is more expendable than the crew aboard."

"Can we get *Stormcloud* fitted for a journey back and keep *Chariot* at all FTL-capable?" James asked.

Arsenault looked to Connor, then shrugged.

"We have some spares between us," he admitted. "We could get *Stormcloud* fitted out for the journey home and keep *Chariot* somewhat functional, but..."

"We'd probably be able to hold the stabilizer fields together for about five days," Connor said flatly. "That's a seven-light-year range. More might be possible, but I wouldn't want to risk it."

"The only things inside seven light-years are KDX, Antioch and Istanbul," Modesitt pointed out. "All of those are hostile now and, well..."

"Intel says that Roberts is leaving Antioch for Istanbul in two days," James agreed. "We're not going to have much of a chance to repair and refit with a pair of Alliance warships in the system."

"We can't fight *Poseidon*, sir," *Chariot's* CO pointed out. "We had a small chance before, but now...she's twice our size and has the lances and missile launchers to match. If Petrovsky has her fully online, we can't fight her."

"They've disabled her q-coms," James told the others. "Likely, they've physically destroyed the entangled blocks to make sure we couldn't use any back doors to disable her. We have no data on her status, but given the skill their hackers already demonstrated, I would assume she is either fully online or will be within a day or two.

"Which means that a two-bit pirate psychopath now has one of Terra's most powerful battlecruisers."

He let that sink in, glancing around the room at his subordinates.

"Our mission was to draw Alliance forces out here, sir," Barbados pointed out slowly. "Much as I hate to say it, Coati having *Poseidon* means, well, we've achieved that mission. I hate the bastard, but he's damned good at what he does. He's going to give Roberts a run for his money and they'll need to send him reinforcements."

"That's one way to look at it," James agreed, hopefully not obviously unwillingly, "but there's another side to this we need to consider. Commander Arsenault, Commander Connor: given the demonstrated ability of Coati's hackers and Petrovsky's XO overrides, how much of *Poseidon*'s confidential and technical files do you think he'll be able to carve out for sale?"

He could see the sick look spread through his crew as the consequences sank home. The confidential files were bad enough. There was nothing truly damning or destructive in there, but he was certain the Alliance or the League could do a lot with the battlecruiser's copies of security codes and contingency plans, even though all of that changed regularly.

The technical files, though, included enough details that any half-decent yard would be able to *duplicate Poseidon*. And while James wasn't aware of any glaring hidden vulnerabilities to the cruiser's design, the Alliance would be certain to find *something* of value.

Something that would result in the deaths of their comrades.

"A lot," Connor finally replied. "Best-case scenario...given his demonstrated resources, he'll be able to produce crude but effective knockoffs of the Katana, same as he was doing with the Federation Cobras. Worst-case..."

"It's entirely possible he could produce a crude but effective knockoff of the *Hercules*-class battlecruiser," Arsenault finished the sentence for her. "Would take two, maybe three years. But nobody knows where his main base and shipyard are, and if he can build those damn corsairs, a *Hercules* is probably within his capabilities."

"That's what I was afraid of," James said. "He could lose *Poseidon* to the Alliance and still come back in five years and conquer this entire sector, creating a pocket empire we would have to suppress to make the Rimward Marches safe after their annexation."

He half-expected his subordinates to object, to challenge the argument. Only silence answered him.

"I don't believe," he continued after a moment, "that we can permit that to happen. That any naval officer worthy of their uniform could permit that to happen."

"Sir, we've already established that *Chariot* can't fight *Poseidon*," Modesitt pointed out. "Regardless of what we may want to permit, we can't stop him."

"We don't have the firepower," he agreed. "But there is a force here that does. A force that wants Coati as badly or worse than we do—and one that, once combined with *Chariot*, has more than enough firepower to take him down."

"The Alliance," Colton said aloud. "We can't work with the Alliance to destroy one of our own ships!"

"Why not?" James asked. "At this point, Captain Colton, we and Captain Roberts share an objective: the destruction of *Poseidon* and the elimination of Coati and his industrial base. They don't know where Coati is based, but we at least know about the KDX base."

He looked around.

"I will be honest, people. Every argument I have made is true and correct, but even if they weren't, I would be considering this. Commodore Coati murdered over three thousand Commonwealth personnel, most of the crew of a battlecruiser.

"I cannot—I *will not*—permit that to stand unpunished. Anyone who wants to remain will be covered by my orders, but anyone who is unwilling to commit to this can be transferred to *Stormcloud* untainted by my…actions."

Mutiny, after all, was such an ugly word.

"One condition, sir," Barbados told him.

"Conditions, Colonel?" James asked dryly.

"Just one, sir, and I'll have a battalion worth of volunteers ready to squeeze into wherever *Chariot* can put us," the Marine replied. "We kill Coati. No negotiations. No compromises. The son of a bitch swings."

"Yes," the Commodore said flatly. "I can promise that."

"Then I'm in," Modesitt told him. "I went through the academy with Daryush. He didn't deserve that. Petrovsky needs to swing alongside Coati."

"I *am* planning on vaporizing them," James pointed out. "There won't be any hangings."

"It'll do."

"So, what, we're going to trust the Alliance to refit *Chariot*'s stabilizers?" Connor demanded.

"Or at least to let us rip apart an asteroid in Istanbul," he confirmed. "There's not much choice, not if we want to send *Stormcloud* home."

She shook her head.

"This is insane. I'm out."

"I'm in," Arsenault said in immediate reply. "Want to switch places, Jessica?"

"If you want to write off your career, go ahead," she told him.

"I had friends in the boarding teams," he said flatly. "Too many didn't come back from *Poseidon* for me to walk away."

"Whatever needs to be done," James told them. "How long until both ships can fly?"

"Two, three days," Arsenault replied. "We'll have *Chariot* in Istanbul on December first, no problem."

"Make sure your crews and Marines know they can switch over to *Stormcloud*," the Commodore insisted. "With the survivors from *Poseidon*, I'm sure we can get enough to fight *Chariot*. I don't want anyone on this who doesn't want to be here."

39

Istanbul System
08:00 November 29, 2736 Earth Standard Meridian Date/Time
DSC-052 Kodiak

THE TRIP from Antioch to Istanbul had been quiet and calm. The freighters and warships had fallen into a rhythm now, with ten of the civilian ships following along with *Kodiak* and *Thoth* like well-behaved sheep.

Once again, *Thoth* led the way into the system, followed by *Kodiak*. The two warships tried to link in to the system sensor network, to make sure that Constantinople Control wasn't aware of any threats that they needed to keep an eye out for...but the tactical feeds didn't update.

"Sir," Jamison called Kyle over to her, the Lieutenant Commander's voice worried. "Constantinople Control isn't responding to q-com contact."

"Is the link broken?" he asked. If the entangled blocks linking Antioch to Castle or Constantinople Control to Antioch were damaged or destroyed, they wouldn't get through, and that would be an entirely different order of worries.

"No, I'm getting system responses confirming an active connection," Jamison replied. "There's just... nobody picking up."

"Houshian, what's our ETA?"

"Sixty seconds and counting," his navigator confirmed. "*Thoth* is in-system."

"Sterling, get me *Thoth*'s sensor feeds," Kyle ordered. He paused, looking around his bridge. He had his Alpha Shift on deck, half his senior officers and the most experienced NCOs, but...

"And take us to battle stations," he concluded. "Something is *not* right."

Silent alerts flashed throughout the bridge, and his implant informed him that the rest of the crew was getting the audio and implant alerts that would have them to their stations in under three minutes.

It wouldn't get everyone on station by the time they emerged, but the fact that they had an active link to *Thoth* suggested there was no immediate threat.

"Data is feeding from *Thoth*," Sterling confirmed. "Captain von Lambert has also gone to battle stations."

"Emergence in thirty seconds."

It was still theoretically possible to abort, stabilizing the warp bubble and swerving around the star system. Getting the entire convoy to do so, however, would be all but impossible.

Kyle studied the feed from *Thoth*. There didn't appear to be any immediate threats, but something was definitely wrong. The stream of ships between Constantinople and the gas giants appeared to have been cut off, all of them now headed away from the inhabited planet toward the skimmer stations that provided their cargos.

Constantinople orbit itself was quiet...too quiet. *Nothing* was moving.

"Emergence!" Houshian announced, and Kyle kept analyzing the feed as they erupted into reality, a the nervous feeling sinking into the base of his spine.

"Get Nebula up here," he ordered. "Then get me a widebeam transmission on the Istanbul Self Defense Force frequencies."

"You're on."

"ISDF units, this is Captain Kyle Roberts aboard the Castle Federation carrier *Kodiak*. We are not receiving responses on q-com channels and there appears to be some degree of uncertainty going on," he said calmly. "Please advise of your status and the status of Constantinople and its orbitals.

"We stand ready to provide humanitarian or defensive assistance as needed under the terms of our trade and security treaty. Please advise."

"Minimum four minutes for a response," Jamison told him. "Unless someone actually gets on the q-com, anyway."

Kyle nodded, studying the feed and looking for any clues.

"Energy signatures?" he asked Sterling.

"There have *definitely* been antimatter explosions in orbit in the last forty-eight hours," the tactical officer replied. "And remember those fighter platforms on the long transfer orbits? The one that would have been closest to Constantinople is *gone*, just debris now."

"What's going on?" Nebula asked, entering the bridge. "My implant paged me."

"I was wondering, Mr. Nebula, if you could answer that for me," Kyle admitted. "There's evidence of combat in Constantinople orbit and local space, but no sign of an invasion. Your estimate?"

The diplomat slash spy looked at the main screen. "May I link in to the tactical feed?" he asked.

"Go ahead."

The bridge systems happily allowed the man to connect in once Kyle gave his permission, though since he wasn't part of the bridge crew, they were tracking everything he did and reporting it to the Captain.

"I did tell you that the Sultanate has a tradition of assassination," Nebula warned. "I think…that's exactly what we're seeing here."

"Sir, incoming radio transmission," Jamison interjected. "I have Commodore Mataraci transmitting."

"Send it to me," Kyle ordered. For now, he suspected he might want to keep what was going on to himself.

"Captain Roberts." Mataraci's voice was significantly less aggressive than the first time they'd spoken. In fact, he sounded almost... embarrassed. "Your timing is, well, awkward. The political situation is in some flux, but Sultan Seleucus is dead.

"The...succession is being negotiated," he continued after a moment's pause. "It is mostly resolved at this point, but I am using the ISDF's orbital contingent to maintain order and security while the Scimitars sort it out.

"The arrival of multiple Alliance warships in orbit shouldn't affect that process, but it would still be a complicating factor. May I...*request* that you keep your ships at one light-minute for the next twenty-four hours?

"*Inshallah,* that should give us time to establish just who the new Sultan will be."

Kyle considered for a moment, then sighed and flipped the message to Nebula.

"Your thoughts, Mr. Nebula?"

The diplomat listened to the message and shrugged.

"We lose nothing by delaying a day," he pointed out. "And potentially gain goodwill from the next Sultan."

"Wonderful."

Kyle shook his head, but turned to Houshian.

"Orders to the convoy," he told her. "We are to decelerate to zero relative to Constantinople and hold for further notice from the surface."

TWO HOURS LATER, Kyle was sitting impatiently in his office, watching the continued slow, almost Brownian motion of sublight ships away from Constantinople. Now that they had time to study it, his people had picked out the civilian ships waiting in orbit...and the Needle starfighters launched from Mataraci's sublight carriers standing guard above everything left.

Rimward Stars

"Mataraci hasn't picked a side, if that's what you're wondering," Nebula said, the diplomat wandering into the office without much preamble. "From the data I'm getting on the ground, the only reason there's debris in orbit is because someone *did*, and that's not considered kosher in this kind of affair."

"This kind of affair is normal, is it?" Kyle asked.

"Oh, yes," Nebula said cheerfully. "This is a relatively normal transfer of power for the Sultanate. Someone tried to launch fighters from the closest platform, declaring themselves Sultan. Mataraci blew them to hell and ordered everyone in orbit to stay put until the new Sultan gave orders."

"And just what is going on on the surface?"

"Seleucus is dead and the Household Guards have secured the Palace, but Seleucus's brother apparently had a private army ready for just this event," Nebula reeled off quickly. "There's street fighting in Byzantium, but it shouldn't last too much longer. The Army won't tolerate it getting too bloody."

"The Household Guards," Kyle repeated. "Let me guess: is Colonel Osman involved?"

Nebula chuckled.

"Colonel Rembrandt, of the First Household Guards, died defending his Sultan," the diplomat explained. "Colonel Osman now holds the Sultan's Palace and, as the bearer of a Scimitar and the possessor of the Palace, will be Sultan once that situation has lasted for thirty-six hours."

"I see where Mataraci's time frame came from. What happens then?" Kyle asked, morbidly curious.

"At that point, *Sultan* Osman will command the loyalty of the Army and the ISDF," Nebula told him. "If the younger Seleucus concedes gracefully, he will be exiled to his family's estates and otherwise pardoned.

"If he does not, the Army will crush him."

"So, Osman will be Sultan," *Kodiak*'s Captain considered, studying the diplomat. "Didn't you meet with him for a while before we left? After you'd decided Sultan Seleucus was a threat?"

"Sultan Seleucus made himself an enemy of the Federation and was

295

looking to bring his system into the Commonwealth," Nebula said calmly.

"Did you assassinate him?" Kyle asked.

"I was not here," the spy pointed out. "I've been aboard *Kodiak* with you."

"That doesn't really answer my question," Kyle replied. "Did you arrange the assassination of the head of state of a gods-accursed *ally*?"

Nebula sighed.

"Do you want to know?" he asked flatly. "This is not the part of the job we give men like you. It's the job we give men like me."

"If someone under my authority is arranging assassinations, I need to know."

"I did not arrange Sultan Seleucus's assassination," Nebula said levelly. "I *did* discuss the situation in detail with Colonel Osman, make it clear to him that the Federation would welcome a friendlier Sultan, and arrange for him to receive funds and supplies from the embassy's black budget.

"We did not ask what he planned, nor provide direct assistance, but yes, we underwrote Osman's coup."

"We can't just go around assassinating heads of state!" Kyle snapped. "What the *hell* do you think you're doing?"

"My job," Nebula replied. "In another political structure, I would have arranged for us to fund the opposition political parties, possibly set up protests or forced a vote of no confidence. This is Istanbul's system, Captain Roberts, though usually, these affairs are significantly less bloody."

He sighed.

"If it makes you feel any better, I was *expecting* the usual targeted assassination and mostly ceremonial 'defense of the Palace,' not a goddamn street battle. Seleucus, it seemed, wanted to be certain his plans survived him."

"Did they?"

"Unless the younger Seleucus comes up with a miracle in the next twelve hours, no," Nebula said flatly. "We'll let Osman secure control, then I suggest we deliver the freighters and make sure we're properly coordinated with them.

"Everything else is…their internal affairs."

"Which we've already interfered in," Kyle pointed out.

"Yes. And now is the time to let the consequences of that run their course," Nebula agreed. "My job is done. I suggest doing yours as if you didn't know it had happened."

"This is *not* okay," the Captain snapped.

"No. But it is my job—just as it is your job to defend the Federation with starfighter and positron lance. And I do it damn well."

40

Istanbul System
22:00 November 29, 2736 Earth Standard Meridian Date/Time
DSC-052 Kodiak

"CAPTAIN, I have…Sultan Osman on the q-com for you," Jamison reported.

Kyle took a sip of his beer and nodded wordlessly, even though he knew she couldn't hear him. The last of the opposition to Osman had been driven from Byzantium before the deadline, though no one aboard *Kodiak* was quite certain what had happened to the younger Seleucus.

"Put him through," he ordered aloud. "Full visual."

He slid the beer into his desk. Irritating as the situation was, it was still not appropriate for even a friendly head of state to see the commander of a Federation capital ship drinking beer. He'd been expecting the call, sooner or later, so he was still wearing his full uniform.

Osman was still wearing his white-and-gold Household Guard uniform when he appeared on the screen, but he'd traded in the unostentatious Scimitar of a man in the line of succession for the Golden Scimitar of the Sultan of the Istanbul System.

"Captain Roberts," he greeted Kyle warmly. "Welcome back to Istanbul. I apologize for the confusion; the timing proved less optimal than I hoped—and the Seleucus clan less willing to concede than even my worst fears."

"I am led to understand street fighting in the capital isn't a normal part of your political changeovers," Kyle replied.

"No, but I freely admit that assassination is," Osman confirmed. "Fortunately, while this tradition doesn't require the Sultan to make transitions *easy*, I had some very qualified security professionals, and I've opened up my predecessor's files."

His face turned grim.

"You can imagine, Captain, how busy I am right now. So, you can guess just how bad what I've found is that I have made time for you this quickly."

Given that Kyle was in command of the only two capital ships in the man's star system, he wasn't actually surprised that Osman was speaking to him already. Phrased that way, though...

"The Federation stands ready to assist the Sultan of Istanbul per our treaties," he said calmly. "Though I'm sure you understand that your political transitions are...disconcerting for us."

"Stars know, they're disconcerting enough for us," Osman told him. "If I thought I could change the system, it would be among my highest priorities." He shook his head. "Send my extended family to the Void, though, if they'd be willing to run the planet any other way.

"Today, however, this is all to *your* advantage, Captain. I do not need the Federation's assistance beyond what you are already here to achieve, but I am afraid that it now falls to me to confess my predecessor's sins."

"What did he do?" Kyle asked. Osman's urgency suggested the answer, though, and it terrified him.

"Sultan David James Seleucus brokered the deal between Antonio Coati and Marshal Walkingstick," Osman said flatly. "He has been supplying Coati for over two years now, directing the pirates mostly at his competition."

"What about *Sultan*?" Kyle said. The ISDF's one starship had been destroyed by Coati's pirates.

"Collateral damage that Seleucus didn't know about in advance," Osman replied. "He was promised a modern Commonwealth ship to replace her, because, of course, the *ship* was more meaningful than the five thousand people aboard."

Osman's grip on the ceremonial scimitar was tight, his knuckles turning white.

"I wish," he continued, his voice slow and calm, "that I had known about more of this before. I apologize, Captain Roberts, on behalf of the Scimitars of Istanbul. It is our task to prevent Sultans from falling this far."

That made a certain degree of sense to Kyle, given his own problems with the Federation's Senators, though his own background suggested impeachment as a preferred option to assassination.

"How much have you learned?" he asked. "Have you found a base or something?"

"Not yet," Osman admitted. "My best people are tearing through the files, but there's a lot of information Seleucus kept locked down. I can tell you one thing: your opposite number is a Commodore James Tecumseh, and he arrived with a task group of two warships and a transport.

"There may be more details in the files, but like I said, we're still digging."

"James Tecumseh?" Kyle asked. "Are you sure?"

"Seleucus spoke with the man, it seems." Osman shook his head. "This is a mess, Captain Roberts, and it appears much of it is my world's fault. We will learn what we can."

"I've met Tecumseh," Kyle replied. "He seems an odd choice for this kind of operation."

Tecumseh, after all, had been the man who had chosen honor over his career and allowed Kyle to hunt down the Terran ship that had devastated an Alliance world.

"I can't speak to that," the Sultan admitted, "only to what I have learned, which is that he is in command."

"It's a starting point. I do have some expert software people aboard; we can assist if you wish."

Osman shook his head.

"While much of this is relevant to you, Captain, there is just as much that is our own affairs. Without knowing everything my predecessor locked away, I am hesitant to air his dirty laundry for the Alliance to see."

"I can appreciate that," Kyle accepted. "We'll be in orbit by morning ESMDT. Let me know what your people find, or if we can be of assistance in any way."

"So long as those freighters arrive intact, you're already being of great assistance," Osman told him. "Thank you, Captain."

———

"Go rest, Flight Commander," Michelle ordered her senior squadron leader. "Stand down the bombers; the situation is under control."

"What a fucked-up system," the man replied. "They seriously just *killed* the Sultan and everything just…goes on with the new boss?"

"Humans do all kinds of crazy shit," she agreed. "But we're not needed for now, and we might be in the morning. Go on, get."

"Yes, ma'am."

Michelle stepped off the Flight Deck into her office, her implants keeping her informed as the ready squadron of bombers slowly stood down, the crews disembarking and heading toward their bunks.

She was still surprised they'd made it this far without losing a single one of her twenty-four Vultures. JD-Tech had sent her some of the specifications for the intended final Vulture design, asking for her opinion, but the basic Terran design was perfectly functional.

The thought of having the Commonwealth spring them on the Alliance by surprise sent shivers down her spine. The countermeasure —regular starfighters—already existed, but the bomber was simply a more efficient ship-killer.

As she started pulling that in, a mental alert went off, letting her know she'd received a recorded communication from Angela via q-com. Given the later hour, she resisted leaving the schematic review until morning for roughly two seconds, then activated her girlfriend's message.

"Hey, love," the blonde nurse told her from the recording. "We're under a minor communication lockdown, so I can't talk live."

She looked tired, though that wasn't an uncommon look for senior nurses in the Navy.

"*Blacksmith* is in motion," she continued. "We got sent to back up… one of the other Fleets after a major action; we've been dealing with wounded Marines for days. It's been…rough."

Most space actions didn't leave a lot of wounded. Ground and boarding actions, however, often left many Marines in need of medical attention. Sometimes more than the available transports and Navy ships could provide, hence a ship like *Blacksmith.*

"I'm still here," Angela concluded with a smile. "We're shuttling a bunch of wounded back to Castle shortly, and my understanding is they'll be keeping us there for a bit. No idea how long, but I've been told I'll be able to get a few weeks' leave at least."

The smile twisted a bit, a sad turn that tore at Michelle's heart.

"By which I mean I've been ordered to take three weeks' leave, minimum," she admitted. "I'm hoping you'll be around before we head back out; I'd love a chance to see you. This whole Forces wi— girlfriend thing is hard enough when it isn't *both* of us out in danger.

"I've been thinking about us," she continued. "Stuff I don't think can be said over a com and definitely not over a recording. What I want, where I think we should go. Nothing bad, my love," Angela said determinedly, "but let's say I'm really looking forward to seeing you again.

"Fly safe and come back to me. I love you."

Michelle sat still for a long few seconds, looking at the frozen image of Angela. The nurse's slip of the tongue was meaningful, especially with how she'd *finished* the message.

"Wife" was the word she'd almost used, and the thought had sent Michelle's heart into pirouettes.

She wasn't entirely sure where she stood on the topic, even with the plan for a shared apartment back home, but the thought…was far from unwelcome.

41

Istanbul System
07:00 December 1, 2736 Earth Standard Meridian Date/Time
DSC-052 Kodiak

"Unscheduled Alcubierre emergence!"

The alert slammed into Kyle's implants like a war horn going off in his ear, instantly waking him from his slumber and jerking him bolt upright.

"Unscheduled Alcubierre emergence!" Sterling's voice repeated, the tactical officer's tone grim as he gave the warning, hesitating before giving the next order, the one he was fully authorized to give as the officer of the watch.

"Battle stations, all hands to battle stations," he snapped. "This is not a drill. We have an unscheduled Alcubierre emergence; all hands to battle stations, all flight crew to your fighters."

By the time Sterling had finished speaking, Kyle was on his feet and into his shipsuit, long years of practice making it a matter of seconds to get into the garment.

"Report," he ordered as he snapped its helmet-concealing collar around his neck. "What have we got?"

"Not much so far, sir," Sterling replied gratefully. "One ship emerged from Alcubierre at two light-minutes and lit off a flare of Cherenkov radiation so large, even a blind man could see it."

"That big a flare is unusual; any resolution on it?" Kyle asked.

"Working on it," the tactical officer told him. "What we've got for data marks it as a warship and we didn't get a notification in advance."

Which meant either someone local had a ship they hadn't known about or the Terrans were there.

"I'll be on the bridge in ninety seconds," the Captain told his subordinate. "Let me know the instant they do *anything*."

Two light-minutes was a long, long way for even a warship...but that was what starfighters and capital ship missiles had been invented for.

———

"YOUR DATA MAKES NO SENSE, COMMANDER," Ivy Trent snapped over the intercom as Kyle charged onto his bridge. "Are you certain there's no corruption?"

"I'm certain," Sterling ground out at the engineer. "CIC is feeding you the raw data, Commander Trent. You're seeing what we're seeing."

"Then it makes no sense," the engineer replied.

"What makes no sense?" Kyle demanded. "Commander Sterling, I have command."

"You have command," the tactical officer confirmed, clearing the command chair for his tactical station.

"The transition signature makes no sense," Trent clarified. "It's a warship signature, no question, but..."

"But?" Kyle prodded.

"It's like they had half of their stabilizers running at double strength and their stabilization fields burned out at emergence. From that Cherenkov flare, they *lost* the exterior field. No sane engineer would go FTL like that."

"If they had a choice," *Kodiak*'s Captain murmured. "What have we got on our mysterious guest?"

"She's Terran," Taggart answered, the XO cutting into the conversation from Secondary Control. "*Ocean*-class strike cruiser, thirty million cubic meters, sixty starfighters, six heavy lances and a dozen missile launchers. Old but not ancient."

"So, not our *Hercules* but still a threat to Istanbul. Or to us or *Thoth* alone, for that matter," Kyle concluded. According to the statistics running through his implant, the *Ocean* class was roughly equivalent to *Thoth*, in fact, a slightly bigger ship with fewer fighters and primary lances but more anti-fighter defenses and missile launchers.

"What's she doing? Has she launched anything?" he asked briskly. The biggest concern now was a long-range missile strike. Song's people could handle the cruiser's fighter wing, but if they dumped their missile magazines at the planet and then left, they could cause some serious headaches.

"Negative," his XO replied. "She hasn't even deployed a CSP; it's like—"

"It's like she had a shipwide electrical failure caused by the Stetson stabilizers overloading," Trent interrupted. "Unless there's something wrong with our data, that flare would have left her half-crippled. It won't last, she'll be back online in under thirty minutes, but somebody over there has had a bad, bad day."

"Why the hell would she even be flying with her stabilizers in that state?" Kyle asked. He shook his head. "It doesn't matter. What does matter is: can she go FTL?"

"Not a chance in Void," Trent replied. "I don't know why she was flying like that, or why she came here, sir, but that ship is not going anywhere."

"I see," Kyle murmured. "Get me Captain von Lambert," he ordered. "If they're not leaving and not heading inward, I think we should go ask why they're in Sultan Osman's system."

———

SC-153 Chariot

JAMES BLINKED against the unexpected darkness that suddenly filled his bridge. Every light had gone out simultaneously. Every screen, every feed, every computer link… and the gravity had gone with them. Most of the bridge was strapped in and no one had been trying to move, so everyone was staying put.

For now.

Emergency lighting finally began to flicker on, at least twenty seconds later than it should have, and James swallowed a sigh of relief as he saw that, whatever had happened, none of *Chariot*'s bridge crew were injured.

"Captain Modesitt?" he asked aloud, checking to see where the woman was.

Chariot had never been intended to act as a flagship. The *Ocean*-class had been designed to either operate independently or in concert with carriers or battleships that *would* have flag decks.

That left him in an observer chair at the back of Modesitt's bridge, watching to see what had happened…and with very little information when the bridge wasn't projecting its standard data feeds.

"We've lost power," she told him shortly. "Trying to get in touch with Arsenault, see what the *hell* happened."

As she spoke, a channel pinged James's implants, a direct com channel from the engineer to him and the Captain.

"Arsenault," Modesitt said dangerously, "what did you do to my ship?"

"I warned you we were running drastically under strength for the stabilizers," he noted. "Apparently, even I underestimated how badly we were straining them. The stabilization fields failed at shutdown. Even ten minutes earlier, and there'd have been enough energy in play to vaporize *Chariot*.

"As it is, we backloaded much of it into *Chariot*'s electrical systems and blew the primary busses."

"This ship has six primary power busses," Modesitt pointed out.

"And we blew all six of them," Arsenault said calmly. "Plus two thirds of the secondaries. We're dead in the water, sir, ma'am."

"Is it fixable?" James demanded.

"Give me time, and I have the parts and supplies to rebuild our entire power distribution net," the engineer replied. "But right now, I have barely enough power transfer systems in place to keep life support online. I suggest getting everyone to mag-boots. I can't prioritize gravity."

"We need coms, Commander," the Commodore pointed out. "If we can't talk to the Alliance, they may well blow us away before we can."

Arsenault shrugged helplessly.

"I'll prioritize," he promised, "but right now, we can't even open the damn flight deck. What do you want first?"

"Flight deck," Modesitt ordered.

"Coms," James replied simultaneously, then sighed.

"Your ship, Captain," he conceded. "If we get the flight deck open, I want a shuttle with long-range radio capability in space as soon as possible."

"Can we run?" *Chariot*'s Captain asked.

"This was going to be a one-way trip either way if the locals won't let us fix up," the engineer admitted. "Now…now it's just a lot more bloody obvious to *everybody*. The flare when the fields collapsed? Their engineer could read that from the other side of the system.

"We're helpless, sir, ma'am—and the Alliance *knows* it."

"Right," Modesitt said slowly, looking across the dimly lit bridge to meet James's gaze. "You win, Commodore. Communications it is, Commander."

———

DSC-052 Kodiak

"Bogey is still motionless," Sterling reported. "We could launch missiles and take her out…"

Kyle was tempted. However the Terran had screwed up, they'd screwed up badly. The strike cruiser was crippled, drifting. No major energy signatures, nothing. A single missile salvo would wipe a Commonwealth capital ship out of existence and turn the odds in his favor.

"No," he told Sterling with a sigh. "If she's in that bad a shape, we should have a decent chance of capturing her, which could tell us where Coati is based. Keep a salvo in the launchers, but hold for now."

"What about us?" Song asked, her image relaying from her command starfighter.

"Get Major Gonzalez on the line," Kyle ordered. The commander of *Kodiak*'s short Marine battalion linked into the channel instantly. She'd clearly been waiting for the call and was already in power armor.

"Yes, Captain?" she asked.

"Are your people ready to go?"

"Three companies, twelve shuttles, six hundred Marines," she reeled off crisply. "All locked, loaded and waiting for the word!"

"The word is go," Kyle told her with a smile. "Keep your eyes open; I want you to break off the instant it looks like she might have defenses online, but launch your strike.

"Song, she has sixty Katanas and she's more likely to get them into space than she is to get her defensive lances online," he continued. "Two wings, twelve squadrons. Cover the assault shuttles.

"You are authorized to destroy the cruiser to protect the shuttles, but we want her intact if at all possible," he told the CAG. "She might be the key to this whole mess. Fly safe, ladies."

"We'll get her for you," Gonzales promised. "We're Castle's damned Marines, after all."

Kyle could *hear* the answering wolf howl from behind the Major and shook his head at the woman.

"I have faith," he replied. "Go get them."

His Marines had been even more ready than Gonzales had implied. All twelve shuttles were drifting clear of *Kodiak* in under thirty seconds, joining the fighter wings that carefully took up escort formations.

A few more seconds for all of their computers to link together, and then all hundred-plus small craft took off for the drifting Terran cruiser at five hundred gravities.

Kodiak and *Thoth*, accompanied by even more starfighters, followed in their wake.

————

SC-153 Chariot

AFTER ALMOST AN HOUR, the dim lighting on *Chariot*'s bridge was starting to grow oppressive. The bridge had batteries to keep most of its systems online for twenty-four hours, but it defaulted to emergency lighting to conserve power.

"Please tell me you have good news," James told Arsenault as the engineer linked in.

"I wish," the junior man replied. "Three of the main busses are just plain gone, sir, ma'am. They're repairable, but we're talking complete rebuilding. The other three are fixable, but none of them are set up to easily run power to communications.

"I can get you the upper primary lances in twenty minutes, but it's going to take me another hour to get you coms," he concluded.

"Commander, they almost certainly launched starfighters within minutes of our arrival," Modesitt said harshly. "Which means that, right now, they would be barely forty minutes' flight from a zero-zero intercept."

"Probably longer," James suggested. "But only because they would have had to wait for the Marines to get into their shuttles.

"They'll board us, not destroy us. If they were going to kill us, a missile would have already hit us."

From Arsenault's uncomfortable expression, the engineer hadn't done that math.

"So, best-case scenario, Commander, you have roughly an hour before Federation Marines start cutting holes in our hull. I'd *really* like to talk to them before they do that," James told him. "I'd prefer to be in a position to *stop* them doing so as well, but I'll take talking first."

"I'll make it happen," Arsenault replied. "Fucked if I know *how*, sir, ma'am, but I'll make it happen."

The engineer dropped off the channel and Modesitt leveled an icy glare on James.

"Was that really necessary?" she demanded.

"Yes. Because it's true. What would you have rather I told him?" he asked.

Modesitt shook her head.

"At this point, sir, I'm not sure we're going to have a choice beyond unconditional surrender," she admitted softly. "Which will screw Coati, all right, but…"

"I do not intend to surrender this ship, Captain," James told her. "I want to work with the Alliance, not be imprisoned by them."

"How much choice do you expect to have?" *Chariot*'s Captain asked bluntly. "Even if Arsenault gets us our communications back, we'll still be defenseless."

"I'm hoping that Captain Roberts will be willing to repay a favor," the Commodore admitted softly. "But you're right; that's about the only hope we have left now."

———

"WE GOT IT!" Arsenault announced half an hour later. "You should have coms and scanners coming up right now. We're focusing on the flight deck next, unless…"

"Flight deck is your top priority now," Modesitt agreed without even looking at James.

He didn't argue. *Chariot* was her ship and she was right. She didn't need him backing her up.

"What are the sensors showing?" he asked as the systems began to come alive again, data feeds and tactical consoles lighting up with new data.

"Nothing good," Modesitt's tactical officer replied. "I've got over a hundred small craft accelerating toward intercept, mostly starfighters but at least some assault shuttles. ETA ten minutes or less."

"We have no defenses," *Chariot's* Captain said slowly. "Do we surrender, sir?"

The tactical feed was coming directly to James's implant now and he didn't disagree with anyone's assessment. Given the circumstances, the only *rational* option was surrender, except...

Once before, he and Captain Roberts had been in a position where the rational option was for one of them to surrender...but the *honorable* option had been something else entirely.

"Not yet," he replied. "Get me a radio channel; send it at those starfighters and on to the carrier."

———

DSC-052 Kodiak

"ASPECT CHANGE!" Sterling snapped. "Our friend's sensors just went live and she just pulsed the assault formation."

"Does she have them locked in?" Kyle demanded, a sinking feeling latching onto his chest.

"Pulse was over detection threshold...wait...pulse is not repeating," the tactical officer told him. "I do not, repeat, do not have recurring pulses. They know Song is there but they do *not* have a target lock."

"Song?" Kyle queried his CAG.

"Increasing evasive maneuvers," she confirmed grimly. "ETA is still eight minutes; none of my people are reading charged weapons. Her sensors are live, but I'm not reading any threats."

"Maintain approach," he ordered. "Stand by your lances, just in case. If she charges weapons, try to disable the weapons without destroying her, if possible."

"Understood."

The distance continued to drop, relative velocities dropping as well as the assault formation decelerated toward the cruiser. This was the most vulnerable part of the approach, when even the best evasive maneuvers didn't have much to work with in terms of distance or velocity.

"Captain Roberts," Song suddenly cut back in. "We're receiving a radio transmission from the cruiser—it's tagged for you by name!"

"Relay it," he ordered. They knew the Terrans had good intel, but this should be interesting...and then the image of Commodore James Tecumseh appeared on his screen. Apparently, the Earth-born Amerindian officer really was in charge out here—though if he was in charge, what was he doing on a crippled strike cruiser and not the *Hercules*?"

"Captain Kyle Roberts, I am Commodore James Tecumseh of the Terran Commonwealth Navy," Tecumseh greeted him. "We have matters of mutual interest and the security of both our nations and your local allies at stake to discuss.

"I propose a temporary cease-fire between the forces under our command to allow you and me to discuss this situation in person."

Tecumseh paused, allowing the shadows of the bridge he stood on, lit only by emergency lights, to play across his face.

"I'm sure you are considering the situation and perhaps think a cease-fire would be against your advantage. All I can do in that case is ask you to remember Barsoom.

"I await your reply, Captain Roberts."

The message ended and Kyle stared at the screen for several long seconds.

"Barsoom, sir?" Taggart asked. "Wasn't that where..."

"Where we caught the Butcher of Kematian and blew his ship to hell," Kyle confirmed. "And where a certain Commonwealth Commodore allowed us to do so, rather than picking a fight I couldn't have won."

"What are your orders, sir?" Song asked. "We're under five minutes from contact—she *might* get some defenses online by then, but it's not looking likely. If we give them more time..."

"Trent—will she be able to leave the system, given a few hours of repairs?" Kyle asked his engineer.

"No," Trent replied with a snort. "She'll need to build all-new stabilizer emitters, and while that doesn't need exotic matter like a mass manipulator, she still needs heavy elements she won't have enough of aboard. She needs to rip apart a bunch of convenient asteroids, at least."

"So, our Terran friend is trapped here unless we not only let him go but help him," *Kodiak's* Captain observed.

"Yes," Trent confirmed after a moment's thought.

"Break off, Vice Commodore," Kyle ordered as he made a decision. "Move to hold position at Starfire range. Have Williams prep the bomber wing for a second wave, but keep them aboard.

"I owe Mister Tecumseh one get-out-of-surrender-free card," he told his bridge crew with a grin. "Let's see what he has to say—he's *not* getting two chances."

42

Istanbul System
12:00 December 1, 2736 Earth Standard Meridian Date/Time
DSC-052 Kodiak

KYLE HADN'T EXPECTED to see a Commonwealth shuttle land on *Kodiak*'s deck in peace before he gave up command of her. He suspected his own tour of duty aboard the carrier would be short, under a year, and it would be years before the war was resolved.

The war continued with no sign of peace breaking out anytime soon...but an unarmed Commonwealth transfer shuttle, escorted the last several million kilometers by two of Vice Commodore Song's starfighters, coasted in to a soft landing on the deck regardless.

A full sixty-strong platoon of Marines in power armor, recalled from the aborted boarding action, stood ready around the exits from the flight deck. Kyle was prepared to meet with Tecumseh, but he was not putting his ship in danger to do so.

"Radiological scans are clean," the deck officer murmured over his implant. "No nukes, no antimatter bombs. Zero-point cell shut down on schedule. She's clean."

Kyle might have starfighters in position to destroy *Chariot* the instant something went wrong, but that was no reason not to be careful. He retained the upper hand, but he also planned on living through this meeting.

He stepped forward as the ramp descended, two Marines flanking him as he approached the spacecraft. Commodore Tecumseh emerged alone, his hands spread wide.

The Terran flag officer was tall and dark-skinned, his hair tied back in a single black braid that hung down his red-sashed black uniform as he politely ignored the Marines scanning him and offered Kyle a textbook salute.

He'd been badly injured recently, with obvious cybernetics replacing most of his limbs, but he held the salute without a tremor.

Despite their difference in titles, they were equals in rank, both O7s in their own nation's structure. The Federation had dropped the rank of Commodore and moved Captain up one to recognize the overwhelming authority of the commander of an interstellar capital ship, inserting the Senior Fleet Commander rank to fill the gap.

"Commodore Tecumseh." Kyle returned the salute. "I'll admit I didn't expect to actually meet the man commanding the Commonwealth's commerce raiding operations out this far. Nor did I expect to find you, in particular, in charge of such a mission."

"Duty is not always pleasant," the Terran replied stiffly. "We need to speak in private and in detail, Captain Roberts. I presume you have a space prepared?"

"You presume correctly," Kyle told him. "Captain von Lambert will meet with us via virtual conferencing. You'll understand, I hope, that I wasn't going to have us both on the same ship to meet you."

"I understand completely," Tecumseh said. "But I promise you, Captain, there is no deception here. We share an enemy now, and only together can we save this region from what he will unleash."

"The consequences of what the Commonwealth has unleashed," Kyle said softly, wondering just what the Terrans had done.

"Yes," the other man accepted levelly. "I would prefer to only explain this once, Captain."

"Very well. This way."

———

KODIAK'S DESIGNERS had considered many scenarios when they were laying the carrier out, and one of those scenarios was the need to have conferences with people you were willing to let aboard your ship but not willing to let see very much of it.

One of the carrier's several midsized conference rooms was just off the main corridor leading away from the flight deck. Three Marines escorted the two officers down the corridor, splitting off to stand guard outside the conference room as Kyle led the Terran officer in.

Von Lambert was already waiting, the holoprojector providing a reasonable facsimile of having the Imperial Captain sitting at the table, tapping his fingers on the cheap plastic.

"Commodore Tecumseh," von Lambert greeted the Terran. "I will note for the record that I feel this conversation should be taking place with you in cuffs as an official prisoner of war."

He hadn't told Kyle that beforehand. On the other hand, he hadn't really needed to. Kyle knew just how long of a limb he was going out on here—and the only reason he was willing to do it was because without starfighters, *Chariot* couldn't fight his task group and win… and the moment she tried to launch starfighters, Vice Commodore Song would blast the strike cruiser to hell.

Tecumseh wasn't a prisoner of war, but everyone in the room knew that was almost a formality.

"I can understand that," the flag officer replied calmly. "Our nations are at war, gentlemen, and I am out this far on a mission to make that war more difficult for yours."

"A process that has so far resulted in the capture or destruction of over a dozen neutral warships and civilian freighters," Kyle pointed out. "You have committed acts of war against at least six neutral nations and committed at least one serious war crime that I am aware of with the massacre aboard the ships in the Antioch system in September."

After Barsoom, he owed the Terran flag officer, but the mission the Terran had taken in this sector was the dirtiest of dirty ops, blacker in many ways than his own operation into Tau Ceti.

"I can't argue the acts of war," Tecumseh conceded. "My orders were clear and they were carried out. I did not have to like them. The Antioch massacre, however, we tried to prevent. We didn't realize just how far Coati would go.

"A pattern," he noted, "that we clearly did not break."

"You allied with and armed a psychopath," Kyle said flatly. "The last time I checked, enabling war crimes wasn't much better regarded than committing them directly."

"I don't believe that my superiors realized how far gone Coati was," Tecumseh replied. "Certainly, I was not briefed that the man was a mass murderer in waiting."

"Perhaps you should have done research of your own?" von Lambert snapped. "Asked Sultan Seleucus about the man when you met him? Coati's history in this region is rife with blood, and you blithely handed over a modern arsenal to the man."

The Commodore appeared taken aback that the Alliance officers knew of his meeting with the Sultan, but he sighed and nodded.

"We did," he admitted. "From a strategic perspective, it made sense. There are many who would say that Dictator Periklos was no better than Coati, but I doubt that will stop your Alliance courting and arming him, will it?"

Tecumseh had a point, though the fact that Periklos—correctly—blamed the Alliance for starting the war between the League and the Commonwealth had proven an effective barrier to working together so far.

"You asked for this meeting," Kyle noted. "I don't imagine it was to try and convince us that you and the Commonwealth were innocent in all of this. You said we had matters of mutual interest. Start talking, or those cuffs Captain von Lambert mentioned might still be an option."

"I did not come here to convince you we were innocent," Tecumseh agreed. "I came here to convince you that we share a common enemy: Commodore Coati."

"Who is your ally."

"Who *was* my ally," the Terran countered. "Until he ran his fleet into the meat grinder you so neatly trailed in front of him. After which he proceeded to blame us, on the basis of what he believed to be Commonwealth fighters in your formation."

Kyle considered that and concealed a truly evil smile. The Vulture was basically a straight copy of the Terran Longbow—and Williams's Vultures had *gutted* Coati's fleet. He could see the pirate assuming the Vultures were Terran starfighters.

"When I refused to join him on a more permanent basis, he revealed he'd bought the XO of my flagship," Tecumseh admitted. "Coati murdered the vast majority of the crew of *Poseidon* and stole the ship. My government's 'controlled' psychopath now commands a *Hercules*-class battlecruiser."

"That is…a problem," Kyle confessed. "Though, from my perspective, also a bonus: I know your crew would have been better than his people. What I don't see, Commodore, is why you are here."

"He co-opted the executive officer, Captain Roberts," the Terran told him. "That means he has the ship fully functional and has her tech files.

"You've seen his corsairs. He stole the Class Ones, but everything in them, he built from scratch and spare parts. I don't know where," Tecumseh admitted, "but he has a real shipyard, with a level of resources I find disturbing.

"Given that data and those resources, my staff believes that Coati can duplicate the *Hercules* class in two to three years. You don't want that," he said dryly. "This entire sector would fall; you wouldn't be able to defend your allies here against a fleet of a dozen or more *Hercules*es.

"If we succeeded in bringing the Marches into Unity, then that would become our problem," he continued. "Even if we don't, having a two-bit pirate psychopath in possession of one of our most powerful battlecruisers and the schematics for the same represents a major strategic danger to the Commonwealth.

"And an immediate and present danger to your allies here," he concluded. "Coati *must* be stopped. *Poseidon* must be destroyed. All of us can agree on this, I think."

"Yes," von Lambert said before Kyle could speak. "But if you don't know where his shipyard is, why does your warning give us any advantage that would be worth working with you, Commodore?"

"Firstly"—Tecumseh held up a finger—"one relatively straightforward set of repairs and *Chariot* is fully functional, the equal to your *Rameses*-class cruiser. I can't fight *Poseidon* alone, but our three ships combined are more than a match for her.

"Secondly"—he held up another finger—"I *know* Coati. I know the way he thinks, twisted as it is. More, I know Petrovsky, who is almost certainly commanding *Poseidon*. I have a far better idea of which way either of them is going to jump than you do.

"Thirdly"—he held up a third finger—"I may not know where his shipyard is, but I know where one of his main refueling stations is, and I have a battalion of Marines with a *serious* axe to grind. If we punch through *l'Estación de Muerte*'s defense, my people *will* find someone who knows where that yard is.

"Fourthly"—the last finger on his right hand went up—"I and my people want Coati's head. On a fucking pike. So long as you're helping us with that goal, we are no threat to you."

Kyle looked at the hologram of von Lambert, who shrugged.

"I will need to discuss with my staff and Sultan Osman," he told the Commodore. "I, after all, cannot allow you to mine asteroids for repairs in his system myself.

"Wait here."

———

THE REST of the senior officers had taken over the flight briefing room and were waiting for Kyle. Taggart was linking in via screen from the bridge where he held down command, and von Lambert's XO and CAG were virtually conferenced in as well.

Full as the room seemed, only Kyle, Sterling and Song were actually physically present. The other four members of the meeting were present by holographic or video avatar, and just about no one in the room looked happy.

"We can't seriously be considering this," Taggart snapped. "Snap cuffs on the bastard and either board *Chariot* or force her to surrender. He can give us the location of Coati's base in a proper interrogation and then we can deal with him ourselves."

"We could do that," Kyle agreed. "In fact, let's call that plan A. It's definitely the cleanest option, the one that raises the fewest dilemmas. I have a counterargument, but I want to hear everyone else's comments."

"I can't say I mind putting sixty Katanas between me and the pirates," Song pointed out. "That's a lot of extra firepower on our side if we trust them."

"We can't trust them," Taggart replied. "They're *Terrans*. They gave Coati his missiles, his tech—so he turned on them; excuse me while I weep."

"Oh, I don't think any of us have a great deal of sympathy for the Commonwealth here," Kyle told him. "I have some sympathy for Commodore Tecumseh's position, having apparently tried to carry out a clean commerce raiding mission while saddled with a lunatic, but this mess is entirely of their making."

"But we have to clean it up," von Lambert concluded. "And, frankly, I'm not sure we can afford to turn down an extra capital ship while going against a *Hercules*. The odds without *Chariot* are..."

"The odds are even without the bombers, in our favor including them," Kyle agreed. "We'd take her, especially manned by whatever crew Coati could pull together from his pirates, but we'd get hurt in the process. Add *Chariot* to our ranks, and it's far more of a sure thing."

"We also know there are at least six of those corsairs," Horaček pointed out. *Thoth*'s CAG looked uncomfortable with what he was saying, but he plowed on regardless. "And if Coati has kept his main base secret for this long, he almost certainly has more defenses and ships waiting there for whoever wanders in.

"The Commonwealth took my arm and my leg," the CAG continued. "I hate them for that, but this Tecumseh...if nothing else, he seems very angry."

"I'm guessing Coati had something to do with the Commodore's new collection of cyberware," von Lambert agreed. "And *Poseidon* was under his command. Tecumseh has one hell of a grudge; I'm willing to trust that, if not necessarily him."

"All we need from Tecumseh is the location of Coati's fueling base," Kyle admitted, "but that extra cruiser is worth the delay to repair her...and I owe Tecumseh *some* faith. He's the reason the Butcher of Kematian was brought to justice. They gave him a shit job, but the man has honor."

"I don't like it," Taggart replied, the XO glancing around at the rest. His gaze, however, lingered on Song. His girlfriend would be at the heart of any attack on *Poseidon*, and *Chariot*'s involvement could make the difference between her living or dying.

"I don't like it," he repeated, "but I see your point. I'm keeping a program in the banks to drop every weapon we have on his piece of crap and blow him to hell, though."

"Do it," Kyle ordered. "And Song?"

"Sir?"

"Williams and her wing are grounded," he ordered. "So far as I can tell, Tecumseh doesn't realize the bombers exist. Unless we absolutely need them, we do *not* deploy the Vultures where the Terrans can see. Understood?"

"Yes, sir. I'll tell Williams."

"Send her to me," Kyle told her. "No point in you taking that flak. I'll talk to her."

He glanced around the room.

"We all have our issues with this," he admitted, "but we need that ship if we're going to take out Coati. We play nice until Antonio Coati is dead."

"And then?" Taggart asked.

"Then we can reconsider the situation."

———

Tecumseh was doing a familiar set of physical rehabilitation exercises with his cybernetics when Kyle reentered the room, pausing in mid-motion to turn his attention to the Federation Captain.

"Those are new," Kyle observed.

"Coati decided he wanted to kill me slowly," the Terran told him. "He failed, but he took a few limbs with him in the attempt."

"Fucker," Kyle said calmly. "Your shuttle is waiting, Commodore Tecumseh. Sultan Osman has agreed to provide you with the parts and raw materials to repair your ship; an in-system clipper will be arriving in a few hours."

"What happened to Seleucus?" Tecumseh asked.

"He was replaced after his treason came to light," Kyle told him, his voice still calm. "As I said, your shuttle is waiting. The deck informs me she's been refueled and should be good to go."

"So, you are accepting my offer, then?"

"Until *Poseidon* is destroyed and Coati is dead, you have an agreement," Kyle confirmed. "Betray me or harm my people and I will burn you and yours to ash.

"Are we clear?"

"Perfectly, Captain Roberts."

43

Istanbul System
16:00 December 3, 2736 Earth Standard Meridian Date/Time
DSC-052 Kodiak

"THE REFUELING STATION known as *l'Estación de Muerte* is located in the KDX-6657 system," the image of Commodore Tecumseh on the screen informed Kyle's gathered officers. "It's an uninhabited system of basically no worth to anyone, even for mining.

"*L'Estación de Muerte* orbits the second planet, a lava-soaked ball of death that would kill an unprotected human seven ways in under ten seconds, starting with heat and toxic atmosphere," he continued. "It's an unpleasant rock, and the only decent gravitational anchorage in the system."

"What about defenses?" von Lambert asked.

"The station itself is quite heavily armed, with an assortment of missile launchers and heavy positron lances, but the main defense is her fighter wings," the Terran explained. "She has six fighter bays. My people have only been in two of them, but both of those bays contained thirty of your Cobra starfighters.

"If, as I expect, the others are the same, we'll be facing roughly one hundred and eighty Cobras. They'll be backed by about twenty missile launchers and a dozen megaton-range positron lances on the station."

"That is one tough nut to crack," Song noted. "Would be easier with…well, it would be easier with a battlecruiser, or at least *something* with better than six-hundred-kiloton guns."

Tecumseh hadn't handed over full specifications on *Chariot*, but he had given them enough that Kyle knew the ship had functionally the same guns as *Thoth*: six-hundred-kiloton-per-second positron lances, a mid-weight cannon for the last generation of starships.

"The station has a notable lack of decent anti-fighter guns," Tecumseh told them. "They do have a suite of fifty-kiloton guns, but it's heavily underweight for what any of our navies would have given a station like that. It's vulnerable to modern starfighters, hence its heavy defensive complements."

"Are you sure their fighters were Cobras?" Taggart demanded. "Those are a restricted export; I don't even begin to understand how Coati has so many."

"Easy: he's building them," the Terran snapped. "I won't even pretend I understand where he got the schematics, but he's using civilian-grade zero-point cells and mass manipulators to assemble his own replicas.

"It's not efficient, but I'm guessing he's got a crack team of engineers modifying the damn things," he continued. "They end up with a fighter that isn't quite as capable as your Cobra, but is more than close enough for their purposes."

"I'd really like to know where he got the schematics," Song muttered. "Someone back home is going to get strung up by their thumbnails."

"What's important today is that we know the Cobra," Kyle pointed out. "We know its capabilities; we know its weaknesses. It sounds like if we assume Coati's birds are fully Cobras, we might be pleasantly surprised—but let's not bet on the opposition fielding junkers, shall we?"

"I have full scans of the station and its surrounding platforms," Tecumseh told them. "There were never fewer than four of his corsairs there while we were there, but they might have been keeping an eye on us."

"I'll match two hundred–plus seventh-gen birds against a hundred and eighty sixth-gen," Song said confidently. "The corsairs are a bit of a headache, but I haven't been impressed with them as combat units."

"We'll clear any of them out with missiles," Kyle decided, "see if we can get the fighters to move out from the cover of the station's weapons. Once we've cleared the defending fighters, we'll need to *carefully* neutralize the station's defense to allow for the boarding strike."

"We'll need to make certain we have IFF links between the Marine forces," the pale-skinned Colonel Tecumseh had brought into the meeting said slowly. "We don't want any 'incidents' when our people are on the same station shooting."

"No tactical coordination," Major Gonzalez snapped. "I don't trust you in my networks."

"Nor do I trust you in mine," the Terran Colonel agreed. "But we must work together, and I have no interest in losing anyone we don't have to in this mess."

"Keep it civil," Kyle ordered. "This is uncomfortable for all of us, but stopping Coati is more important. I can understand not wanting to be in each other's networks, but have your EW people work out a solution. Clear?"

"Clear," Gonzalez agreed.

"Clear," the Terran confirmed. "I want Coati, Captain Roberts. Whatever it takes."

"Good. Then I think we all know what the plan is based on Commodore Tecumseh's data," Kyle said. "Let's make this happen. We leave Istanbul in two hours."

MICHELLE PAUSED outside the Captain's office, trying to marshal her arguments for the discussion ahead. Just because her wing was grounded hadn't kept her out of the whirlwind of preparation for the operation, but she could tell her people's morale was suffering.

Stars, *her* morale was suffering. They were about to finally go after Coati, and she'd been ordered to stay on the sidelines.

Steadying her nerves, she reached out to hit the buzzer for admittance, the door sliding open the moment she tapped it.

"Come in, Wing Commander," Captain Roberts ordered. "Have a seat. Coffee? Tea? Beer?"

She'd never met any senior officer as willing to feed their people not only beer but *expensive* beer while they were on duty, but she shook her head this time.

"Water, please, sir."

Michelle was certain that Captain Roberts *had* a steward—she was sure he didn't restock the fridge and drink dispensary himself—but she'd never seen them in his office. He poured her a glass of water himself as she took a seat in front of his desk.

"I can guess why you're here," he told her cheerfully, "so how about I run through the arguments for you?"

"You're our most powerful single starfighter formation; we may need you. Your people's morale has been impacted by being grounded. You want in on Coati's destruction; your people have lost friends fighting him.

"Oh," the Captain's smile widened, "and I forgot: 'It's just not fair!' Have I summed things up roughly correctly, Wing Commander?"

It was far too easy for even Michelle, who'd served under Roberts when he was in the Space Force, to forget that the Captain had been a starfighter pilot and a CAG before he'd been Navy.

"Roughly, sir," she admitted. "My people want—*need*—to be in on this, sir."

"I understand that," he agreed. "However, *I* need to keep the existence of the Vulture secret from the Commonwealth a little while longer. Your bombers represent a Sunday punch that may turn the tide of the next major campaign. I'm not giving up that advantage when we should have enough firepower to take down Coati without it."

"And what if we do end up needed?" Michelle countered.

"Then I expect that you and your people will have kept up your simulator regimen sufficiently that I will be able to deploy you to devastating effect," Roberts told her. "Make no mistake, Wing Commander, if I see the need for your wing, I *will* use you.

"But I also see a strategic imperative to keep the existence of our bomber wings quiet. I'm aware of the pressure that puts on you and your wing. It's not easy to sit back and watch your friends go into combat without you, but it is, in this case, absolutely necessary."

A tinge of something twisted the grin.

"You can consider it practice for higher command, Williams," he told her.

"I see, sir," she admitted. "I don't like it, but I understand."

"I know," Roberts said. "But it's the job. And if we couldn't take the joke…"

"We shouldn't have signed up," Michelle sighed, finishing the ancient cliché.

"Exactly. Is there anything else, Commander?" the Captain asked gently.

Michelle was about to rise to leave when a thought struck her.

"May I ask a personal question, sir?" she said slowly. "Advice, I suppose."

"While I don't think it's in my job description anywhere, personal advice to senior officers has been part of the Captain's job since time immemorial," Roberts replied. "I'm not the best at it, but I'll try."

"Vice Commodore Song specifically warned that her relationship judgment was compromised by her husband's death," Michelle pointed out.

"I know," the Captain agreed. "I take it this is another relationship question? You know my history, Wing Commander. I'm hardly qualified to give that advice!"

She chuckled. While he seemed to be doing better now, the rumors about the Captain's kid and how long it had taken him to see the boy were too detailed not to have *some* truth to them.

"It's a hypothetical question, I suppose," she conceded. "Would you consider getting married while the war was still on?"

Angela's slip of the tongue in her last message was still in Michelle's mind, like a loose tooth she couldn't stop prodding as she tried to wrap her brain around it. She wasn't sure if the thought made her happy or made her want to run away screaming.

From the Captain's thoughtful expression, it wasn't necessarily something he'd considered himself.

"Alvarez, I'm guessing?" he said softly.

"Yeah. She...implied she might be planning to ask," Michelle admitted. "With the war...I just don't know."

"Would you know if the war wasn't happening?" he asked. "Is it just that we're at war that scares you, or is there something else?"

"I've known wartime relationships that ended badly," he continued. "People who lost lovers in this war and the last. Whether or not you're married doesn't change how badly that hurts."

The Captain's voice had softened as he spoke, much of his usual cheer fading. There were clearly specific incidents and friends on his mind, but his point had weight.

"If we lose them, we lose them; is that what you mean?" Michelle asked. "So, we may as well take what we have?"

"Exactly," the Captain replied, his expression turning thoughtful again. "The war doesn't allow us much in terms of our own lives, but we shouldn't let it steal what little we are left. Find your joy where you can and don't let go."

"What about after the war?" she asked. "What if it turns out that being separated so much was the only reason the relationship could work?"

"It's always possible," he agreed. "But would you take happiness now or avoid it out of fear of a possibility?"

That laid it bare and Michelle found herself smiling, her decision suddenly made.

"Thank you, sir."

"Thank you, Wing Commander. I apparently needed to churn some thoughts of my own on the matter," Roberts told her, the grin returning to his face. "Now, it seems, we're definitely going to survive this mission."

"Why's that, sir?" Williams said slowly, barely concealing a cringe as he taunted fate.

"Because the last time I decided to take a leap like this, I flew a carrier through a battleship and lived," the Captain told her as his smile widened. "So, precedent says we'll be fine!"

44

KDX-6657 *System*
18:00 December 9, 2736 Earth Standard Meridian Date/Time
DSC-052 Kodiak

"EMERGENCE COMPLETE," Houshian reported. "All systems are green; engines are live."

"We are scanning the system," Sterling reported. "Confirming, *Thoth* and *Chariot* are in formation. Launching q-probes now."

"Anything that disagrees with Tecumseh's data?" Kyle asked.

"So far, the rocks line up," his tactical officer replied. "One chunk too far in for anything, one ugly mess, lots of asteroids and a gas giant that's too small to be of use to anyone." He paused. "It's not much of a system, skipper."

"Which is why there's nobody here. Do we have a bead on the station yet?"

"I've got a blip that might be artificial in orbit of the second rock," Sterling confirmed. "Probes are en route; I'll have more data in about thirty minutes as the first ones skim by."

"If there's something there, that's good enough for now," Kyle replied, linking through to Song. "Vice Commodore."

"Captain."

"Full-deck launch, if you please."

"Yes, sir."

Forty-eight starfighters flashed into space from *Kodiak*'s launch tubes, followed by more from both *Thoth* and *Chariot* as all three ships cleared their decks, getting the entirety of their fighter groups into space.

With the addition of *Alexander*'s fighters, it wasn't even obvious that *Kodiak* was holding back a half-strength wing. Hopefully, there was no way Tecumseh could tell that Kyle was holding anything back.

Over two hundred and fifty fighters took up formations in front of the warships, the Terran ships keeping distinctly clear of the Imperial and Federation starfighters.

"This is going to be awkward as Void," Taggart noted in Kyle's implant channel. "We have no q-coms with them; we're relaying through Song's fighters. Let's hope nobody gets too far apart, or relativity and time delays are going to start hashing our coms."

"I know," Kyle conceded. "But I'm not handing them Federation-entangled blocks and Tecumseh's not giving us Terran ones. So, we each keep a q-probe next to each other's ships, just in case, and relay through the starfighters. It's not efficient, but it will work."

And he'd rather have inefficiencies than hand a Commonwealth flag officer a link into the Alliance's communication networks, no matter how safeguarded.

"Tecumseh is sending us coordinates for the station," Jamison told him. "Your orders?"

The Terran Commodore seemed to be deferring to Kyle's overall command, a smart decision when the Alliance forces outgunned his two to one.

"Take us in," Kyle ordered. "Not much point in being subtle yet. Keep two squadrons from each ship as a reserve, everyone else goes in and the capital ships follow."

Right now, their biggest advantage was that no one here was expecting an attack. Shock and surprise could take them a long way. It would take almost forty-five minutes for the fighter strike to reach missile range of the station, so there wouldn't be *much* surprise by then…but he'd take what he could get.

And the pirates weren't going to like what he did with it at all.

———

"THERE YOU ARE," Sterling stage-whispered, the soft words still managing to project across most of *Kodiak*'s bridge as the tactical officer pulled the feeds from the first wave of q-probes, the ones that were blasting past *l'Estación de Muerte* without slowing down, and transferred the data to the main tactical display.

"The station is exactly where Tecumseh said it would be," he noted. "I'm not picking up any ships or deployed starfighters, though I do have a number of defensive satellites the Terrans didn't see."

"Didn't see or didn't tell us about?" Taggart demanded.

"I'd guess they weren't there," Sterling replied. "The orbits are unstable, and given their size, they won't be able to maintain them for long. These are a stopgap in case our Terran friend came back."

"Hardly enough of one," Kyle pointed out as he studied the data. "They're too small for capital ship missiles, so that's, what, one or two salvos of a hundred fighter missiles? *Chariot*'s fighters would eat that for breakfast."

"But it would help backstop their weakness against fighters," Sterling said. "If they used the satellite missiles to break Tecumseh's first fighter strike, their own fighters and on-board weapons would be enough to see off *Chariot*."

"Unfortunately for them, our Terran friend brought us," Kyle said with a chuckle. "Make sure Song has everything and remind her that we need that station intact. Much as I want to blow it to hell from maximum range, we need prisoners and data cores."

"She knows," Taggart replied. "Gonzalez and Barbados are launching shuttles now. They'll stick with us until the path is clear."

"Good. Any response from the station itself?"

"Nothing," Sterling said. "Which is weird. We've been in-system for thirty-five minutes and just buzzed them with high-speed q-probes.

Those probes are stealthy, but not *that* stealthy...so what are they doing?"

"Being clever," Kyle concluded. "Watch them, Commander. If they don't already have their starfighters in space, they've got something up their sleeve, and I *don't* want any surprises."

"I've got them dialed in with more waves of q-probes heading their way," his tactical officer replied. "If those bay doors open, we'll know before they even have the birds in space. But so far...it's quiet."

"Too quiet," the Captain agreed. "They're going to twitch, Commander. I need Song to know they're doing it before they do."

"We'll do what we can."

———

MINUTES CONTINUED to tick by and the distance between the fighter strike and the station dropped. The vectors put the range for both the Javelins and Starfires at just under two million kilometers, and the starfighters were rapidly approaching that line.

There was no way that the pirates could rely on a hundred missile-launching satellites to deal with the starfighter strike, let alone the capital ships following behind it. Every second that passed, Kyle grew more concerned.

"Son of a bitch," Sterling suddenly swore. "Missile launch, I have missile launch—twenty Stormwinds and a hundred Javelins outbound, targeted on the starfighters."

The starfighters' own acceleration worked against them, increasing the range at which the enemy could fire on them. The defenders had a hundred-thousand-kilometer range advantage, over fifteen seconds of flight time, and had used all of it.

"They're covering the fighter launch," Kyle snapped. "Get me details—where are their birds?"

"Jamming's come up as well," the tactical officer reported. "I can't get a clean sight line; maneuvering the probes."

"Get me details, Commander. There's a reason they're trying to hide."

Kyle didn't know what it was, but he knew it had to be there.

"And get our missiles in the air," he ordered. "Use their jammers to cover the starfighter wing and hold them for counter-fighter strikes. We can't use Jackhammers on that station and take it intact."

"On it," Taggart replied from secondary control. "Keep on those scans, Sterling. Missiles on their way."

Thoth was linked into Kyle's command network, and *Chariot's* commanders had clearly come to the same conclusion. Within seconds of the pirates' firing, all three capital ships had launched, sending thirty missiles back at the immobile station.

"*Son of a bitch!*" the tactical officer repeated, even more fervently. "Those aren't Cobras!"

"What?"

"Confirm, I have one hundred sixty, one six zero, Katanas on outbound flights," Sterling replied. "Repeat, *Katanas*, not Cobras."

"Fuck," Kyle swore. "Threat parameters? Give me the delta!"

"Fifty gees more accel, a fourth missile launcher, a sixty-kiloton lance instead of thirty-five, and a *Voids-cursed* powerful jamming module."

The Katana was a seventh-generation starfighter, and a hundred and sixty of them was a *very* different threat parameter than the same number of sixth-generation Cobras.

"Pass on everything we have to Song," Kyle ordered. "A third of the ships with her *are* Katanas; she should know the balance better than we do."

"How the *hell* do they have that many Katanas?" Taggart asked.

"We knew they could build starfighters," Kyle replied. "Now we know there's a maximum distance from here to Coati's main base: that's at *least* ten days' production for a fighter factory of significant size, and they've had the design since November twenty-second at the earliest.

"Their yard can't be more than eight, maybe ten light-years from here. That cuts down the possibilities a *lot*."

"They're using the corsairs to ferry them out here, figuring their biggest threat was Tecumseh either coming back or betraying the location to us," Taggart concluded. "So, if we live through this, we've *probably* punched out a good chunk of the Katanas available to them."

"Only probably," Kyle told him. "And we need to live through this mess *and* take that station intact."

"Song is launching missiles at the incoming starfighters," Sterling told them. "Our missiles are moving in to support."

With six squadrons, four of the Alliance's eight starfighters and two of the Commonwealth's ten fighters, held back to protect the warships, the strike's numerical edge was slimmer than Kyle would have liked. They'd counted on an individual superiority they weren't going to have—and the missiles from the station and its satellites were going to make up much of the numbers difference in the first salvos.

There were a *lot* of missiles in space. Even the neatly spaced salvos of capital ship missiles coming from the three warships were vanishing into the confusion of drive signatures and jamming, entire wings of starfighters easily lost in the confusion.

"Can we target any of the station's weapon systems?" Kyle demanded.

"Scans show her deflectors are weaker than expected, but not that weak," Sterling replied. "The satellites have shot themselves dry, too. Any missile we fired would have go through the fighters, and any lance beam will be deflected."

The station couldn't even maneuver and Kyle found himself wishing for one of the battleships they'd started the last war with—their massive railguns would have been perfect for this task.

Instead, he had modern ships with antimatter missiles and positron beams. Far deadlier warships overall, but completely incapable of a purely kinetic long-range strike.

"What are the Terrans *doing*?" Taggart suddenly demanded.

For a few seconds, icy fear gripped Kyle's heart as he thought his precautions against betrayal had been too few and Tecumseh had set them up…then he caught up with what the tactical feed was showing.

The Katanas under Tecumseh's command had used a burst acceleration capability he hadn't known the fighters had to charge out in front of the rest of the starfighter formation. Leading the way ahead of the Alliance spacecraft, their ECM sang a suddenly complex siren song, luring the incoming Javelins to them—and then hammering them with a clearly *perfectly* coded electronic warfare attack.

The Commonwealth might have handed Coati enough super-modern Javelin VII missiles to fight a war, but they hadn't done so without *any* precautions. Every missile in the first salvo detonated simultaneously, lighting up the uninhabited system with a wall of white fire.

"Getting out in front so they could hit the missiles with a directional transmission without interception, apparently," Kyle concluded. "Keep our missiles covering them. I'm betting that won't work twice."

The following salvo proved him mostly wrong. Some of the missiles in it were clearly, like the fighters launching them, Coati's home-built rip-offs. Those lacked whatever software or hardware mechanism the Commonwealth transmission was triggering, and survived as their brethren self-destructed.

Lasers and positron lances flared to life in anti-missile mode, but the Terrans had pushed themselves too far forward. The Alliance ships could support them, but their efficiency was degraded, and some, not many but some, of the missiles made it through.

"I make it six Katanas lost on our side," Sterling reported. "If Tecumseh's really are 'our' side."

"For now, yes," Kyle replied. "Coati's?"

"Our first two salvos have punched out over half of the Katanas; we've got one more salvo for both of us before lance range."

"I don't suppose we can get Tecumseh's people back in formation?" Kyle groused.

"Song's already ordered it once and they're ignoring her," Jamison reported. "Even with some of the missiles ignoring that code, they're clearing one hell of a path."

"Third salvo intercepting," Sterling said grimly. "Almost ten percent survived the self-destruct code, and they're hitting lance range...now."

Alliance doctrine now called for the missile-heavy Imperial Arrows to fall back at this stage, leaving the Falcons with their heavier lances to carry this part of the fight. That was even more true with the Katanas, whose lances were still more powerful.

With the Terran fighters already out in front, the Falcons closed the range as fast as they could, trying to bring Coati's fighters into their lance range before their "allied" Katanas died.

Antimatter flared across space as starfighters died, but the lack of training that Coati's pilots had always shown was aggravated by their new ships. In a direct duel with equivalent starfighters, they didn't stand a chance.

"Song reports a clean sweep," Jamison told Kyle. "They are beginning to decelerate to make a disabling pass of the station."

"Put me through," Kyle replied.

"Vice Commodore," he greeted her. "How bad?"

"The Terrans took the brunt of it," she answered, surprise in her tone. "Tecumseh's people lost twenty-two birds. We lost three. The pirates..." She sighed. "Coati's rip-offs didn't bother with such niceties as 'escape pods.' They're gone."

"And the station?"

"We'll clear the big guns as we pass and nail as many of the secondaries as we can," Song replied. "Compared to a hundred and sixty Katanas? This part is easy. Just make sure everything is clear before you send the Marines in; I kind of like Gonzalez."

"I have no intentions of sending them in until they've surrendered or we've cleared every positron lance off that station," Kyle replied calmly. "Well done, Vice Commodore."

"Well done, half-begun," she replied. "We'll finish the job for you, sir."

45

THE THREE WARSHIPS decelerated to a smooth halt three hundred thousand kilometers from *l'Estación de Muerte,* carefully orienting themselves to present the largest possible number of weapons, and then went to work.

James had provided his new allies with every scan of the station he had, and the q-probes were positioned barely five thousand kilometers away from it. The starfighters had removed all of the missile launchers and heavy lances, leaving the space station helpless beyond about a hundred thousand kilometers.

The Alliance and Terran ships were in much better shape.

"We've dialed in the deflector emitters and strength," Modesitt reported. "We should be able to land clean hits from here."

"Good," James replied. "Let Roberts call the shot. For now, this is his show."

The Terrans were very much here on sufferance, and they knew it. Debts of honor or not, James expected his new allies to turn on him as soon as Coati was defeated—if he was lucky, Roberts might give them a head start.

Of course, he had plans for that situation. For now, however, they were working together. Half of the shuttles waiting for the capital ships to clear away *l'Estación de Muerte*'s defenses were Terran, after all.

"We have their com codes," he reminded *Chariot*'s Captain. "Shall we see if they're willing to surrender?"

"Worth a shot," she said with a shrug, tapping a command on her chair.

"*L'Estación de Muerte*, this is Captain Modesitt aboard *Chariot*," she said sweetly. "You betrayed us, but we found some lovely new friends. We are now in a position to neutralize your defenses and take the station by force.

"I won't make promises at this point, but if you surrender, we will be *far* more positively disposed than we will be if you make us drag you out of your stinking hole."

James chuckled.

"I'm not sure how effective that's going to be," he admitted, "but damn, was listening to that cathartic."

"I'd *rather* let Barbados shoot them all," *Chariot*'s Captain replied. "I suspect he'd be pissed if we let them surrender."

"And I get the impression he and Gonzalez are on the same page," James agreed. "No one is going to mind too much if they surrender, but some of the Marines will definitely complain."

"No response from the station," Modesitt noted after a few moments. "Captain Roberts's people have informed they will commence firing in thirty seconds."

"Carry on, Captain," James ordered, settling into his observer's chair and making sure his tactical feed was updating properly.

Exactly on the deadline, all three warships opened fire. A carrier and two strike cruisers, none of them had particularly massive lance armaments, though *Kodiak*, while carrying lighter weapons than the two cruisers, actually carried as many as the two other ships combined.

Over forty medium positon lances lashed out into space, the computers happily drawing the invisible streams of antimatter into the feed as clean white lines. Where those lines collided with *l'Estación de Muerte*, however, they stopped being "clean."

Positron-lance and anti-missile-laser positions vaporized as beams of pure antimatter hammered home. Flash-boiled metal and exposed atmosphere blasted into space, short-lived gouts of flame lighting up the process as the three warships worked their way around the station's hull, disabling every weapon that could still threaten their Marines.

"I think we're good," James murmured, watching as the risk assessment continued to shift.

"Colonel Barbados, it's up to you and your Federation counterpart, but I think you're good to go."

"Thank you, sir," the Marine replied, leaving the channel open as he turned his attention to his people.

"All right, Marines, are you ready to go kill some pirates?!"

———

JAMES RODE on Barbados's virtual shoulder as the assault shuttles hammered home, laser cutters flaring to life to slice holes through hull already weakened by the craft's engines. Metal flashed to vapor, and the shuttle hammered a temporary lock into the hole.

"Go! Go! Go!" the Marine Colonel bellowed, waiting for his people to clear the shuttle before exiting.

James could see the same tactical map Barbados did, drawn from painstaking discussion and analysis of every visit his people had made to *l'Estación de Muerte*. The map they'd assembled covered over eighty percent of the station's volume but noticeably did not cover Engineering or the main command center.

Unfortunately for Coati's security, his people had so studiously kept the Terrans out of those areas that the attackers had a damned good idea of where they were, and the studiously split attack went in right next to the blanks on the map.

The Alliance Marines were going for what they thought was the control center, while the Terran Marines went for what they thought was Engineering. Splitting the objectives also meant keeping the two forces, who no one quite trusted not to shoot at each other, well apart.

"Clear!" a voice bellowed, and a wall that the Marines had suggested led into the engineering compartments disappeared in a series of explosions—and the Terrans charged through.

The image feed that James was getting from Barbados's helmet was hard for him to follow, all smoke and scanners and gunfire. The Colonel wasn't in the middle of the fight, but in this kind of corridor-to-corridor fight, no one was entirely out of the fight, either.

"Here!" one of the sergeants snapped. "I've got a primary ZP array."

"Second Company, move in to secure," Barbados snapped. "Third, swing around; we've got another pocket up and to your left. There's got to be at least one more array; let's lock them down before anyone gets clever."

"We've made contact with Alliance forces on Deck Six," another platoon commander reported. "Pirates are broken; falling back on all sides." Pause. "Alliance reports they've secured the command center and the primary computer cores."

"Report, is anyone still facing resistance?" Barbados demanded.

"Fourth Company, we've got at least half a battalion trying to launch a breakout from what I think is the armory! We're holding, but these are the first of the fuckers with real gear."

"First Company, move to relieve," the Colonel ordered. "Karlson, coordinate with the Alliance. If I'm reading this map right, they should be able to cut in behind those bastards and squeeze them up against First and Fourth."

Silence. James waited.

"Alliance confirms; they're moving Imperial Marines in," the platoon commander replied. "Watch your lines of fire, First and Fourth; let's not piss these people off today, eh?"

More gunfire echoed, but Barbados was finally out of the fight. The

Colonel paused, appearing to study the map as he stepped into the engineering chamber Second Company was securing.

"Zero-point cells are stable," he reported back to James after scanning the controls. "I'm reading three arrays, we hold two, the Feds have the third.

"Once that breakout is suppressed, we are in control of *l'Estación de Muerte.*"

46

KDX-6657 *System*
12:00 December 10, 2736 Earth Standard Meridian Date/Time
l'Estación de Muerte

"THIS IS STUPID."

"I know," Kyle agreed to Major Gonzalez's complaint genially. "The station is, however, almost entirely secure and represents a handy neutral meeting ground for us to discuss what happens next."

"This station is *not* secure," the Marine pointed out. "There are still pockets of resistance, even if they're a long way away from the computer cores and engineering bays. Fuck, I'm not sure this station is safe to *inhabit*; the maintenance of the atmospheric systems is better than the rest of the station, but still atrocious."

"I agree," Kyle acceded. "But the value of being able to meet somewhere neutral remains."

"Yes, because having all three capital ship commanders in one spot is a *great* idea. Why exactly couldn't this be a virtual conference?"

"So far as I can tell, because the analysts want to see our faces when they lay out just how amazing they are and how much information they extracted from this rusted-out piece of junk," the Captain replied. "But there is also a value in Captain von Lambert and myself being able to look Commodore Tecumseh in the eye while we plan the destruction of the ship he used to command.

"Plus, all of this information was pulled by a joint team of our analysts and spies and his. I think Nebula, if no one else, would blow a fuse at the thought of transmitting all of this over something as insecure as a radioed virtual conference."

"It's still dangerous," the Marine concluded, which was an improvement from *stupid*, at least.

"Which is why you and a dozen brave Marines in power armor are escorting me," Kyle replied, gesturing at the mobile wall of metal surrounding him. "Von Lambert and Tecumseh have similar escorts, and the location we're going to has been well secured by both Alliance and Commonwealth troops."

"I don't trust the Terrans."

"Which would be the other reason no one is traveling anywhere on this station alone," Kyle agreed. "But we need this meeting, Major. We need to know just what Coati was up to and how we stop it."

"What happens after that, sir?"

"I don't know yet," *Kodiak's* Captain admitted. He was leaning toward "give Tecumseh a one-hour head start and kick him out," but that wasn't something he'd admit just yet.

———

DESPITE THE DECREPIT nature of most of *l'Estación de Muerte*, the area around the main control center was perfectly clean. That area, thankfully, included a decently equipped conference room linked into the pirate station's computers.

At the front of the conference room, dressed in an Intelligence Senior Fleet Commander's uniform that Kyle suspected he had every right to wear, was Karl Nebula. He was sitting on the table on the presentation dais, four Terran, three Imperial and two Federation intelligence specialists sitting behind him in the actual chairs.

"Ah, good," he greeted Kyle. "Now that Captain Roberts is here, we can begin."

The intelligence officers outnumbered everyone else in the room. With the Marines outside, only the three Captains and Commodore Tecumseh were waiting to hear what they had to say.

Kyle took a seat next to von Lambert, wishing he'd had the foresight to pack a thermos of coffee or something. He wouldn't trust anything the pirate station produced to drink, and from the lack of coffee mugs or water glasses in the room, everyone else felt the same way.

"This has been an unusual and likely educational process for us all," Nebula told the officers. "We spend most of our careers trying to block each other's intrusion software, not assigning responsibility based on whose software is better at certain tasks.

"And, well"—the spy grinned—"making sure none of us are watching over each other's shoulder or trying to copy said software. While this was a pile of fun for us spies, I'm not sure you four have any interest in anything except what we found out."

"And what have you found out?" Kyle asked. "Do we know where Coati is now?"

Nebula jumped down off the table and gestured theatrically, turning on a holoprojector to create a rotating globe of a green-and-blue world. The green was off, darker and yellower than usual, with splotches of black that spread across both land and water. The planet looked almost sick.

"This, for those of us whose records were wiped by an isolationist racist trillionaire three hundred years ago, is Quebecois Bien," Nebula told them. "Fourth planet of the KDX-6647 system. The system was never officially named, and all records from the survey expedition were modified at the order of the man who bought the survey, a Jean Saint-Lacroix, to conceal that there was ever a habitable planet."

"They hid a *planet*?" Tecumseh asked. "A habitable planet?"

"Saint-Lacroix intercepted the report before it made it into any general databases, from what I can tell," Nebula replied. "He wanted a planet to set up his perfect society of atheist free-thinkers, a definition that appears to have excluded anyone who didn't match his ideal skin tone.

"And since he didn't want any foreign thought in his paradise, he buried the records and didn't take the technology to build A-S drives with him," the spy continued. "They had their original colony ship for a bit, but that was long gone by the time Giorgio Coati was scouting the region for potential mining locations.

"Imagine his surprise when, instead of an uninhabited star system he could grab minerals from with no one realizing his source, he found a somewhat backward but intact colony of over a hundred million souls."

That would have been a shock. Somehow, Kyle didn't think that the elder Coati had done what he would have done in his place.

"At the time, Antonio Coati was a gunship commander with the Serengeti fleet. He managed to funnel resources, money and men to his father, but they needed transport. His father's one ship wasn't enough.

"So, when Coati was promoted to command the detachment in the Soledad System, they felt out his subordinates and launched a quiet campaign of piracy. Once they had four ships, they launched their invasion and conquered Quebecois Bien.

"That was twenty years ago, in which time they have assembled a full, mostly modern shipyard sufficient to assemble their corsair ships, and built an entire starfighter manufacturing facility from scratch."

"That's more than most of the star systems out here *have*," von Lambert pointed out.

"Stolen goods are never sold at a loss, Captain," the senior Imperial analyst pointed out. "Most of what they needed, they stole. What they couldn't steal, they had the money to buy."

"Giorgio Coati died ten years ago, making Antonio Coati, our dear Commodore, the dictator of a planet he uses for conscripted slave labor and crews to build and man his ships and starfighters. He uses recruited mercenaries to stiffen their ranks, and it appears that all of our prisoners prior to this came from that group rather than Quebecois Bien.

"While the shipyard isn't currently capable of building battlecruisers, given the possession of *Hercules* and her technical files, that's something he can relatively quickly fix."

"Where is *Poseidon*?" Tecumseh demanded, his voice grim.

"Quebecois Bien," Nebula replied. "All of Coati's mobile units have been recalled to have their fighters swapped out for Katanas under *Poseidon*'s protection. The yards themselves are heavily fortified, surrounded by fighter platforms, corsairs, and missile bases."

"What about the planet?" Kyle asked.

"It appears they mostly let them go on as they choose, but with orbital bombardment platforms and drop squads to keep order and make sure the labor drafts are supplied on schedule. Those platforms are controlled from the primary station at the shipyard.

"If we capture or destroy the shipyard, Quebecois Bien will be safe," Nebula told them.

"But the shipyard is fortified and guarded by *Poseidon*—backed by an unknown number of corsairs and Katanas?" Kyle asked.

"We don't know how many Katanas, but we do know how many corsairs," the spy replied. "He only has twelve left after the losses they took against us and against Commodore Tecumseh. All of them were at Quebecois Bien before we lost q-com connection to the planet.

"I can't see Coati being likely to send them anywhere else when he has to *know* we'll be coming for him."

"And we will be," Tecumseh said grimly. "I didn't know the son of a bitch had enslaved a planet. No wonder he was so cavalier with his starfighter pilots. He could replace people almost as easily as he could replace ships—and he could replace both easier than we thought."

"He plans to make this region his empire," Nebula warned. "If he defeats us, he may well succeed. He'll be waiting for you."

Kyle studied the projection of the planet and the shipyard.

"Waiting for us, yes," he agreed. "But he has no idea what's coming."

47

"AT THIS POINT, it appears that all of Coati's forces have concentrated in the KDX-6647 system," Kyle told the three heads of state on his wallscreens. "The resources now present in that system represent a major leap forward for this sector, and it is the official position of the Alliance that those resources properly belong to the people of Quebecois Bien."

Translation: we'll take out Coati and liberate the planet, but then you're going to have to negotiate with whoever ends up in charge there.

"What about KDX-6657?" Premier Yilmaz asked. "The facility that Coati's people have set up there is of some value."

"It was built with stolen resources," Sultan Osman pointed out. "And sits halfway between our systems, used as a base to raid us both."

"I am leaving a small detachment of Alliance Marines to guard the prisoners and secure the station," Kyle told them. "The ultimate disposition of the system and the station is up to you."

"I would suggest," President Fatima Johansson, the leader of Serengeti, cut in, "that we arrange a mutual ownership of the station. It is a refueling platform, after all, that all of us may find useful. If we take it over as a joint facility under the Free Trade Zone rules, it also will not become a threat to any of us."

"That...makes sense," Osman agreed.

Yilmaz didn't look happy, but he nodded his acquiescence. Right now, none of the three core powers of the Free Trade Zone had the military strength to force their desires on the others.

Or on any of their neighbors, which was going to have consequences for the FTZ going forward. Consequences, thankfully, which weren't going to be Kyle's problem.

"What do we know about Quebecois Bien?" Johansson asked. "I find the concept of an entire world in our region that none of us knew about disturbing, to say the least."

"We don't have much," Kyle admitted. "Our intelligence people pulled a lot of data and historical information about the system from *l'Estación de Muerte*'s computers, but...there was nothing close to a full archive here.

"We'll learn more once we have liberated the system, I'm sure. Until then, all we really know is that they were founded by a trillionaire who wanted to set up his own 'perfect society' and that they didn't have the technology to stop the Coatis' mercenaries when they decided to set up shop as planetary dictators."

"We owe them our assistance," Johansson insisted. "Coati was ours, Serengeti's specifically. We will do what we can to help."

"First, Coati needs to be removed," Osman pointed out. "Do you have a plan, Captain?"

"We have some information on the system and the positioning of his forces, but we are six days' travel away and expect all of that to be obsolete upon arrival," Kyle told the leaders. "Captain von Lambert, Commodore Tecumseh, and I will establish a better strategy on our trip there, but it will be necessary for us to scout the system before finalizing our plans."

"How can you trust this Tecumseh?" Yilmaz demanded. "The blood of our soldiers and citizens is on his hands!"

"And the blood of his crew is on Coati's," Johansson reminded him. "I would not trust him to guard my system against the horrors of the Void, but he will pursue Coati to the end of the Stars for his revenge and his honor."

"I know his type," the woman finished.

"As do I," Kyle agreed. "We can trust Tecumseh against Coati, I think. Past that... I intend to permit him to leave your space in exchange for his assistance, but that is all. The Commonwealth remains the enemy of the Alliance."

"They have committed acts of war and treachery in our space as well," Osman told him. "Istanbul will speak to the leaders of the Alliance, to see what aid we can provide in this war. The Commonwealth will find they have only broadened the scope of this war they have begun."

"My Councils will be voting in the morning," Johansson told them. "A declaration of war against Terra and a measure to join the Alliance of Free Stars is on the agenda. We will not permit the Commonwealth's actions here to go without response."

Yilmaz sighed. The pudgy leader of Antioch looked unhappy, but he nodded slowly.

"Similar measures have been suggested in my own Parliament," he admitted. "If my fellows in the Trade Zone are walking this path, then I find myself unable to stand against them."

"The Alliance will welcome your aid and your support," Kyle told them. He wasn't sure if the three systems, now completely lacking in the ability to project force, would actually be *useful* members of the Alliance, but they wouldn't turn aside anyone at this point.

If nothing else, the morale benefit to the Alliance's populations of new systems signing up in the middle of a war with the most powerful nation in human space could not be understated.

"We must deal with Coati first," he continued. "All of this depends on removing the specter of his plans from this region and liberating Quebecois Bien."

"I suggest that we all send troop detachments to KDX-6657 to take over security of the station," Osman said. "While they're en route, we can come to some agreement on the judicial fate of the prisoners, but that is not a conversation we need Captain Roberts for."

"You have a liberation to plan, Captain," Johansson agreed. "Know that our hopes and thoughts are with you. If there is any aid any of us can give, let us know.

"Much as we would rather save ourselves, it seems the future of our systems now rests on you. May the Eternal Stars watch your path."

———

"I'VE SEEN EASIER targets in the Imperial War College's *Kobayashi Maru* scenario list," von Lambert observed, the Imperial officer linked into the conference aboard *Kodiak* by q-com. His XO and CAG shared the wallscreen with him, the two Wing Commanders under Horaček in the room with them currently offscreen.

"We have a similar list," Kyle agreed. "And this place puts most of those to shame."

"*Kobayashi Maru*" scenarios were suicide missions used in training exercises. Generally, their purpose was to teach prospective officers to recognize when to cut their losses, though some of them were set up so that clever thinking *could* win the day.

Most of the offensive scenarios in that list, however, were designed to force officers to accept lesser victories rather than lose ships and lives trying to actually succeed at the official objective.

The defenses around Quebecois Bien put most of those to shame. The Coatis had clearly been determined to make sure that no one took their little corner of the galaxy away from them, and the addition of *Poseidon* to the defenders didn't help.

Layered networks of manned and automated platforms surrounded both the planet and the high-orbital shipyards. The defenses of any major Alliance system would be more modern, but few systems Kyle had seen had defenses this dense.

The battlecruiser and twelve corsairs had been orbiting with the shipyards when the q-com connection to KDX-6657 had been cut. Any of them might have moved, but it wasn't going to make too much difference.

"The good news," Nebula pointed out, "is that I don't think Coati will have expected us to get quite so much information out of the computers here. In all honesty, we wouldn't have on our own—and neither would the Terrans. Combined, however, we got everything.

"And they had a *lot* of data in here on those defenses," he continued. "More than was wise, really."

"Thankfully, pirates have a horrible sense of information security," Taggart agreed.

"Given that they have an entire *planet*, are these people really pirates?" Song asked. "That's a lot more resources and firepower than a pirate fleet would normally command. There are almost two thousand defensive platforms in orbit!"

"And they're all obsolete garbage," Sterling pointed out. "None of them have lances over the three-hundred-kiloton range. The missile launchers were loaded with home-built eight-hundred-gravity weapons. They might have updated some of them, but it's unlikely they reloaded *four hundred* platforms."

"The Terrans didn't give them that many missiles."

"They'll have been building their own," Kyle replied. "We have to assume that those platforms are carrying modern Stormwinds or a near equivalent. The truth, however, is that we can deal with the platforms. Immobile defenses are critically vulnerable to long-range missile fire, and the intel suggests a far lower proportion of manned control stations than we would have accepted."

"But we can't do it while twelve raiders, a battlecruiser, and an ungodly number of Katanas swarm us," Song concluded.

"We know we can take out the raiders in one pass with Williams's bombers," Taggart pointed out. "Can we really justify keeping them secret at this point?"

Kyle glanced over at Williams, the Wing Commander sitting quietly with her fellows but looking eager.

"Commander Williams, how would you stack your ships up against *Poseidon*?" he asked her.

"It…depends," she admitted slowly. "At maximum range, she has ten minutes to respond to our launch. That's more than enough time to fire missiles and get fighters into space for missile defense."

"A Commonwealth group would be in space, even completely surprised, in three minutes," von Lambert pointed out. "But these aren't Commonwealth pilots. They're conscripts—and conscripts who are so ill-trusted, their computers are programmed to *lie* to them."

"Let's be generous and say it would take five minutes for them to deploy," Kyle suggested. "They'd still have thirty starfighters in space to block Williams's salvo. Coati has seen torpedoes in action now; he's going to expect capital-ship-grade jammers and brains.

"We might still take her out, but then we also have to protect the bombers from *Poseidon*'s fighters."

"So, we fire at five minutes' flight time instead of ten," Michelle replied. "We take out the cruiser before she can launch fighters."

"And how exactly are going to sneak twenty-four bombers to half a million kilometers away from her?" Song asked.

"We don't. We go in with a base velocity, at least two thousand KPS," Michelle told her boss. "That gives us over a million-kilometer range at five minutes' flight time."

"We can come out of Alcubierre with that," Kyle told the others. "But to get within even a million kilometers of *Poseidon*, we need to know *exactly* where she is—and we will be at risk from her lances at that range."

"You need her looking somewhere else," von Lambert said slowly. "And we need live data. There's only one way to manage both."

48

KDX-6647
04:00 December 17, 2736 Earth Standard Meridian Date/Time
SC-153 Chariot

As THE AIR itself in *Chariot*'s bridge started to tear apart and scream, James Tecumseh concluded that Kyle Roberts was possibly the craziest bastard he'd ever met. At no point in the Commodore's entire career had he ever attempted to "thread the needle" and ride the careful balance of stabilizers and mass-singularity-balancing necessary to emerge from Alcubierre drive inside the generally designated gravity well of a planet or star.

From the intel reports he'd read, it was starting to become the Stellar Fox's default tactic, and James had allowed himself to be talked into it.

"We can't hold this together much longer," Arsenault said over the channel. "We only just replaced the stabilizers and we're going to lose them!"

"Sixty more seconds," Modesitt told him. "You've got to hold it together for sixty more seconds, Commander!"

James winced as the screaming noise edged up another octave, his implants automatically shielding his ears to prevent damage.

"Why the *hell* did we agree to this?" he demanded.

"Because we've all got a guilty conscience over helping Coati?" *Chariot*'s Captain suggested. "And because the whole scheme is insane, what's one more crazy stunt?"

"It's very Stellar Fox," James agreed.

"Hang on!" Arsenault suddenly snapped. "We've lost too many stabilizers; I'm dropping the warp and this is going to *hurt*!"

The universe broke around James Tecumseh. He felt his own flesh twisting as reality tried to object to the sudden re-intrusion of *Chariot*'s bulk and presence, and swallowed something resembling a scream...

Then it was over, the screens and tactical feeds lighting to life as *Chariot* emerged into real-space, barely one point five million kilometers from Quebecois Bien.

"Targets on all screens!" Modesitt snapped. "If it's armed, take it out! Fire at will!"

The emergence had been hell, but it had left them with a significant base velocity as they hurtled into the planet's orbit, *Chariot*'s positron lances flaring to life as they entered range of the orbital platforms. Antimatter tore through empty space, and the missile and lance platforms started to come apart, dozens of the satellites vaporizing as *Chariot* charged.

"Q-probes deployed," the tactical officer announced. "Relaying data to the one in our cargo bay."

The solution to the lack of trust between the Alliance and Terran forces had been simple in the end: a single Alliance q-probe, modified with a tamper-proof self-destruct device, sat inside one of *Chariot*'s cargo bays. A similar probe sat inside *Kodiak*'s bays. All of the data from *Chariot*'s probes was retransmitted at that probe, which then sent it over to *Kodiak* and *Thoth*.

"Shit! We've got four corsairs, dead ahead!" Modesitt announced. "Scramble fighters, scramble fighters!"

Twenty of the tiny craft blasted into space instantly, but the next two squadrons were still loading as *Chariot* careened into lance range of the three pirate ships.

Missiles came with her, launched as soon as the probes and sensors had identified the ships, but the raiders had been more awake than many of the defensive platforms. Their own missiles blazed into space and their lances lit up.

"Hitting the missiles with the override codes." *Chariot*'s tactical officer paused. "Got barely half; I think they're running out of the missiles we gave them."

Chariot's defense could take nine missiles, and the raiders hadn't even launched fighters. It was a lance duel now, and that wasn't an environment the strike cruiser was built for. A raider came apart as the Terran ship's heavier beams hammered them on approach, and then the strike cruiser lurched as a beam struck home.

"We got the second wave of fighters out—son of a *bitch*!"

"What?" Modesitt demanded.

"We lost the starboard launch tubes," her XO said in a sick voice. "They took all of Fifth Squadron with them."

Chariot lurched again, but the second raider was gone now and their missiles were closing in on the last two, which were now focused on their own defense, desperately firing everything at the missiles. They barely managed to wipe the salvo out, but unfortunately for them, *Chariot*'s fighters were right behind the missiles.

Their lances were lighter, but forty of them made short work of the modular warship.

"Status report," James demanded as they blasted past the wreckage of the pirate squadron.

"Fighter launch tubes are gone," Modesitt reported grimly. "We have four squadrons in space and that's all we're getting. Most of our missile launchers are gone. Arsenault!"

"Ma'am?"

"Please tell me we can go FTL."

"Not yet," the engineer said grimly. "We're clear enough to begin repairs, at least until their fighters start catching up."

James was watching. The space station was starting to spew fighters like a broken gumball machine. Most were Cobras, but there were plenty of freshly built Katanas in the mix.

"We've got *Poseidon*," the tactical officer announced. "Relaying to the Alliance."

"All right, Roberts," the Terran Commodore said softly. "I know you weren't telling me everything. Show me what you had up your sleeve."

It had *better* be enough. *Poseidon* was moving away from the shipyard, heading in pursuit of *Chariot*. She was newer, bigger, and faster. If the Stellar Fox didn't take her out, James Tecumseh had just doomed his people.

———

Vulture Bomber Kodiak *Echo Actual*

MICHELLE WILLIAMS HAD BEEN aboard the old *Avalon* when they'd ridden the needle into Tranquility to save the day at the start of the war. She had never done it before then and hadn't done it since, until today.

A starfighter was about the worst place to be during this kind of flight, with limited air supply and tight spaces that were extremely vulnerable to the warping and twisting inevitable to the process. Theory and her experience alike said that everything would "snap" back into place once the drive field went down, but that didn't make the actual flight any less painful or terrifying.

"We have the target coordinates," Song announced over her implants, the keening of the air around her ripping apart echoing alongside her voice. "Houshian is adjusting to bring us in at a million klicks and two thousand KPS.

"This is going to get rougher," the CAG said grimly. "Hang on."

Michelle's personal universe turned inside out, and for several moments, all she saw was light, as if flying into the heart of a sun. When the light faded, the *pain* began, making the previous discomfort seem almost gentle.

Even if light was traveling normally to her eyes, which it wasn't, there'd have been nothing to see with her bomber inside *Kodiak*'s fighter launch tubes. She hung on to the arms of her pilot's chair with grim determination as her body tried to tear itself apart and reassemble several times a second for what felt like eternity.

Then a brick wall slammed into her face, she grabbed a moment's breath, and her tactical feed updated with their surroundings.

"Launch! Launch! Launch!" echoed into her ear, the deck officer slamming in the commands to throw her bombers into space, even as she processed that *Kodiak* had overshot her intended emergence point by a full light-second.

Forty-eight starfighters, half of them Vulture bombers, blasted into space barely seven hundred thousand kilometers from *Poseidon*, the battlecruiser in hot pursuit of *Chariot* and seeming to miss the new threat for several critical seconds.

"Echo Wing, Fox Three all, Fox Three all!" Michelle snapped as her bombers swung clear of *Kodiak*. She spun the little ship in space, aligning the four torpedoes on her launch frameworks with the battlecruiser and triggering the launch sequence.

It wasn't a perfectly coordinated launch, but between her bombers and *Kodiak* herself, over a hundred missiles lunged toward *Poseidon* in under six seconds.

"Clean launch," Michelle reported back to Song as the data filtered in. "I have ninety-six, repeat, nine six torpedoes on course, three-minute-forty-second flight time."

"All right, Williams," the CAG responded. "Alpha Wing is launching, Bravo is loading in and Charlie is prepping. Fall back behind Delta Wing and return to *Kodiak* to rearm. We're going to need you again before this is done."

"Yes, ma'am."

As they spoke, another set of forty-eight starfighters blasted into space. With the extra birds from *Alexander*, it would take two more full launches before all of *Kodiak*'s fighters were in space, and it wasn't going to be safe for the bombers to try and land until the launches were complete.

"Echo Wing, form up on *Kodiak* and prepare your landing runs," she ordered. "Keep an eye on your birds, guide them in. We'll stay out until impact."

If nothing else, she wanted to watch the son of a bitch burn with her own eyes.

———

MICHELLE HAD FOUGHT TERRAN WARSHIPS. *Poseidon* was the fourth *Hercules*-class battlecruiser she'd gone up against since the war began, and her new crews' reactions were pathetic. Any of the *Herculeses* she'd faced before would have already had their fighters out before *Kodiak* jumped in-system and would have turned to face the carrier and the bombers the moment they arrived.

It might not have saved them, though thirty Katanas would have made one hell of a dent in the torpedoes, but it would still have been *competent*.

Almost sixty seconds elapsed before *Poseidon* even began to adjust course, turning to bring her heavy positron lances to bear on *Kodiak*. The carrier's half-megaton-a-second lances couldn't penetrate the battlecruiser's deflectors at this range.

The reverse was *not* true of *Poseidon*'s one-point-five-megaton beams, and the fact that it took over two minutes for *Poseidon* to even start shooting was a damning tale of the conscripts Coati had crewed her with.

There should have been starfighters in the launch tubes, ready to go the moment there was a threat. There might have been a delay getting the crews for more than the ready squadron up and into space, but that ready squadron should have deployed at *least* by the time the cruiser opened fire.

Instead, the torpedoes were less than a minute from impact when the launch tubes flared, throwing two squadrons of Katanas into space...far too late to change the battlecruiser's fate.

Beams of positrons flashed past the bombers, reaching out for the carrier that was their way home, but Houshian demonstrated the difference between a veteran of the vicious war with the Commonwealth and a raw recruit with practiced ease.

Again and again the battlecruiser fired, cycling through all of her massive primary beams as she tried to take down the carrier...and again and again, she missed.

Then the crescendo of death crashed down over *Poseidon*, with dozens of torpedoes surviving the desperate attempts by the starfighters and the cruiser herself to turn back the tide.

Poseidon was a massive, well-built ship. She would have survived one direct hit, possibly even two or three, or half a dozen near-misses. Over thirty missiles struck home in five seconds, and one of Terra's most modern battlecruisers disappeared in a ball of matter-antimatter annihilation.

"Echo Actual, this is *Kodiak* Flight Control," a voice said in Michelle's implants as the light from the explosion washed over them. "Starfighter launch is complete; we're ready to bring your bombers home.

"Well done, Commander."

———

SC-153 Chariot

"What. The fuck. Was that?" Modesitt demanded in the stunned silence of *Chariot*'s bridge.

James studied the data on the strange fighters a moment longer, noting patterns, manipulator balancing, the many minor details that could be discerned at this distance and used to identify manufacturer.

"Those, Captain, are why Coati thought we betrayed him," he said quietly. "I don't know exactly what kind of missile they fired, but the design is ours. A few modifications, enough to make it easy for *me* to say they aren't ours, but close enough to confuse anyone who isn't from us or the Alliance."

"Those missiles had capital-ship warheads and penetrators," the tactical officer told them. "Launched from a starfighter? This is bad news."

"Or would be," James replied dryly, "if the design wasn't so blatantly stolen I'm perfectly confident we have something similar. It appears the Alliance has solved our biggest problem for us. Now, I suggest we all focus on staying intact enough that we can still run, seeing as how my last count was, what, two hundred starfighters heading our way?"

"I'm reading two hundred and ten," Modesitt said grimly. "Our birds are in the air in defensive formation, but they've got sixty Katanas of their own, plus a hundred and fifty Cobras. Arsenault, how are those systems coming?"

"You'll have missiles in ten minutes. Every secondary lance we've got left around the same time," the engineer replied. "You're not getting the big guns back. The power surge from firing the damn things would overload the network."

A positron lance was a modified zero-point cell. For every positron it sent into space, an electron went into the ship's power systems. There was a series of capacitors, distributing busses and smart systems designed to use that power effectively, but with the damage *Chariot* had taken in this operation, half those systems were held together with duct tape.

And the last few hits had knocked the duct tape loose.

"Anti-fighter guns are what I need," Modesitt told him. "Ten minutes will have to do. We're all depending on you, Commander. Don't disappoint me."

"I like not being vaporized as much as the next engineer, Skipper. You'll have those guns."

The Captain stepped over next to James, watching the incoming fighters. More starfighters were being launched now, but these were coalescing around the last eight raiders and heading for *Kodiak*.

"What about the planet, Commodore?" she asked softly.

"CIC ran the analysis," he told her. "We killed almost all of the bombardment platforms. Once his ships are gone, Coati can't threaten them with annihilation anymore. But..." He shrugged. "We did our part and there's not much more we can do. Let's live through this mess.

"Quebecois Bien's fate now lies with the Alliance."

49

KDX-6647
04:30 December 17, 2736 Earth Standard Meridian Date/Time
DSC-052 Kodiak

"TARGET DESTROYED," Sterling announced with satisfaction. "Bombers are rearming for the next strike; the rest of the starfighters are in space."

"Rearming will take at least ten minutes," Taggart warned. "We don't have the infrastructure in place for a rapid turnaround on them. The torpedoes don't fit in the arming systems."

"We're going to have to fix that," Kyle said. "They're too damned effective for us to wait on that kind of turnaround. What have we still got on the board?"

"Orbital defenses have been decimated but remain dangerous," Sterling noted. "*Chariot* focused on the bombardment platforms, so most of the defense platforms remain. The planet is safe. Us...not so much.

"All of that appears to be automated, though, with the majority of the manned platforms all around the shipyard, which is still fortified to *hell* and back," he continued. "I'm reading upward of two hundred starfighters going after *Chariot*, but that leaves another two hundred—a quarter of them Katanas—playing watchdog over the shipyard.

"They've pulled the last of the corsairs in close and have the yard locked down tight. We've got them contained, but..."

"But that is one hell of a tough nut to crack," Kyle agreed. "Houshian, keep us moving; I don't want them having clever ideas about long-range missile fire."

He studied the tactical feed. The planet was almost a secondary concern; if they took control of the shipyard, the planet would fall into their hands by default. The shipyard, however...

"What's *Thoth*'s ETA?" he asked softly.

"Five minutes," Taggart replied. "You have a plan?"

"More like a thought," Kyle admitted. "These folks know how many ships we have. They're going to be watching for her and half-expecting a sucker punch."

"Show them what they're expecting and punch them in the back of the head while they're looking that way?" Taggart suggested.

"Something like that. Get me von Lambert on the com."

———

COATI REACHED out before von Lambert arrived, an omnidirectional radio transmission of the strange pirate broadcast to the entire star system. The pirate sat on the edge of a command chair, his strangely scaled skin and gemlike eyes glittering in the harsh light, his hair a folded-over mohawk glittering in rainbow hues as he glared at the camera.

"I know who you are, Captain Roberts," he hissed. "You must think you have struck a grand blow for freedom here, but you have no idea. No idea of what the worlds you have allied with have done to this sector, of the lifeblood they have drained from world after world to fuel their greed.

"And now you come to crush our hopes for freedom. You shall not succeed! The defenders of this world stand ready to throw back your pathetic ships. The destruction of *Poseidon* is a setback, but make no mistake: my people stand ready to duplicate her a dozen times over.

"You shall not conquer here!"

The image faded and Kyle snorted.

"Anyone buy that pile of bullshit?" he asked. Chuckles from around his bridge were the answer. The Free Trade Zone was far from perfect and the Alliance knew damn well there'd been abuses, but Coati was no liberator.

"Record to send back to him, if you please, Jamison," he instructed, then leaned into the camera.

"I know who *you* are, Antonio Coati, son of Giorgio Coati," he told the pirate. "I know what blood drips from your hands and what violence you have wrought on the systems around us and on the world beneath us.

"Your day ends here. The punishment for your crimes is due. Surrender, Commodore Coati, and spare the poor bastards you have forced to fight for you."

"Ready to go," Jamison reported.

"Send it."

A timer on Kyle's tactical feed counted down the seconds until *Thoth*'s arrival. Unless Coati responded quickly, the Imperial cruiser would arrive before the pirate's response did.

"Missile launch!" Sterling announced. "I have Terran Stormwinds on the scopes, minimum two hundred inbound."

Kyle whistled silently. It seemed Coati was responding quickly, after all.

"Pass the targets to Song and spin up the defense lasers," he ordered. "We'll weather the storm; hopefully, *Thoth* won't have to."

"What about our strike?" Song demanded.

"Wait to see how they respond," Kyle replied. "We have to live before we can attack."

The starfighters were moving, spreading out in a defensive formation that would give them the best angles on the incoming missiles. Beyond them, a sudden blue streak of Cherenkov radiation backlit the entire shipyard and its fortifications—and then resolved into the kilometer-long mass of the Coraline Imperium strike cruiser *Thoth*.

Fighters blasted clear of the cruiser the moment it exited warped space, followed seconds later by missiles, pre-targeted based on the data from *Kodiak*'s q-probes. They needed to be, as *Thoth* had misjudged the jump and emerged *between Kodiak* and the shipyards.

And in front of the missiles Coati had just launched at *Kodiak*. The presence of the strike cruiser triggered a second salvo, this one from the smaller—but far more numerous—fighter missile launchers.

Two hundred capital ship missiles swarmed toward the strike cruiser, followed by over a *thousand* fighter missiles.

Thirty seconds later, a combined salvo of twelve hundred missiles launched into space, and Kyle knew *Thoth* was doomed. They'd tried to be clever, but a combination of the missed emergence point and the shipyard having even more firepower than they'd allowed for had just doomed von Lambert's ship.

The Imperial Captain clearly recognized that, a q-com channel opening to Kyle's implant a moment later.

"We can both do the math, Captain Roberts," the junior man told him, the conversation taking place at the speed of thought. On the screen, *Thoth*'s missile launchers went to maximum-rate fire, throwing their desperate handful of capital ship missiles back into the salvo's teeth.

"We'll have all of our starfighters clear before the first salvo hits, and I'm ordering nonessential personnel to life pods," von Lambert continued calmly. "Promise me you'll get my people home."

"I promise, Yann," Kyle told him. The nature of the implant channel made a mockery of both of their attempts to be calm and cover their fear. They could turn off those channels, but here and now, with the other Captain, they didn't. "I'll get them all home."

"Right, then," von Lambert replied. "You're a reliable man, Roberts. Transfer control of your missiles to my tac department?"

"Done," the senior man replied, a few mental commands making the switch. "What are you going to do?"

"The only thing I can. I'm going to fly right down their throats with every missile and electronic-warfare trick I can muster and blow a giant hole in the outer defenses. You know what you need to do with it."

Kyle nodded, knowing the emotion channels would carry his understanding and determination to the other man.

"It has been an honor, Captain Elector von Lambert," he sent softly across the link. "Go with the Gods."

"To the only place men like us ever end," von Lambert said levelly. "Into the fire. I'll see you on the other side, Captain Roberts. It's been an honor and a privilege."

The channel dropped and Kyle's heart sank as he watched the cruiser accelerate, shedding escape pods as it went. A capital ship could match a starfighter's acceleration, but not for long.

Thoth didn't have very long left.

———

Michelle linked into the cameras on the flight deck through her implant, watching and trying not to worry as *Kodiak*'s deck crews went through the dangerous dance of loading the torpedoes onto her bombers. There should have been robots and machinery to handle this aspect of the job, but those hadn't been designed for the Gemblade torpedoes yet.

None of the work required actual human hands, but without the carefully designed custom systems and automation software, it required human eyes. Missiles were being moved with manual forklifts and jacks, loaded into mass-reducing collars and carried by robots designed for weapons a tenth of the size.

Each of those missiles had enough antimatter in their warhead and fuel tanks to vaporize the entire carrier if they went off in the flight deck. There wasn't anything the Wing Commander could do to make the process safer except watch and worry.

"Williams, what's the status of your reloading?" Roberts suddenly barked in her mental "ear".

"Echo One is fully armed and Echo Two's birds have about two torps apiece," she reeled off instantly. "Echo Three's just moving in for rearming now."

"Anything that has a torpedo aboard needs to be in space *now*," the

Captain ordered. "I need every torpedo we can deploy in the next thirty seconds. Go."

The Captain knew just how jury-rigged the loading process for the torpedoes was. He had to know how dangerous what he was asking for was…and he was asking for it anyway.

"Deck officer, abort all loading and clear the decks," Michelle ordered through her link to the flight deck. "Get Echo One and Echo Two in the launch tubes; we have thirty seconds to be in space. *Move.*"

She had faith in the skill of *Kodiak*'s deck staff, and it was proven justified in spades. Even before her orders had been officially relayed, the lifts with the torpedoes were already swinging back and people were moving away from the starfighters.

Automated tugs locked into place on her armed bombers within ten seconds of the order's being given, the ships lurching into motion toward the tubes that would fire them into space.

With everything in motion, Michelle turned her attention to the main tactical feed to see what in Void was going on—and saw *Thoth*'s suicide charge begin.

"Eternal Stars, sir," she sent Roberts. "What do we do?"

"We can't do anything for *Thoth*," the Captain replied grimly. "But we're going to ram every starfighter, every missile and every torpedo through the hole von Lambert's about to blast for us."

"I thought we were taking the shipyard intact."

"Not anymore."

———

QUEBECOIS BIEN and the rest of the region would benefit from taking Coati's shipyard intact, but with one ship already crippled and a second about to be destroyed, Kyle was no longer able or willing to pay the price it would take.

A third of his attention was on the starfighter assault formation Song was rapidly pulling together in the wake of *Thoth*'s charge, starfighters from both ships assembling into a single hammer of firepower anchored on Williams's two squadrons of bombers and their half-load of torpedoes.

Another chunk was on *Thoth*'s escape pods, their engines already burning hard to clear the battlespace and get away from the shipyard's defenses. From the sheer number of pods, von Lambert had used an extremely generous definition of "nonessential"—if there were two hundred of the cruiser's four thousand crew left aboard, Kyle would be surprised.

The rest of his attention was entirely on *Thoth* herself and the missiles swarming toward her.

The third salvo of mixed missiles was the most dangerous, but the lead salvo of capital ship missiles was the next worst. Starfighter missiles relied on speed and numbers to penetrate defenses; capital ship missiles used terrifyingly smart suicidal AIs and incredibly powerful electronic warfare to do the same job.

None of that, however, was prepared for the strike cruiser to charge *into* the missile salvo at six hundred gravities of acceleration and rising.

Thoth was well past Tier Three acceleration and into the inefficiency spike leading to Tier Four, and the missiles simply weren't programmed for capital ships to accelerate that fast.

Her own missiles hammered into the center of the salvo, explosions ripping a hole the cruiser slid into, her lasers and lances widening it as she tore through the wall of missiles, somehow making it out the other side unscathed.

Many of the missiles tried to follow her, twisting and decelerating —but that made them vulnerable to the starfighters following in *Thoth*'s wake, and Song's people ripped them to pieces.

The same trick wouldn't work on the starfighter missiles. There were just too many of them, and Kyle inhaled sharply as he saw von Lambert's plan. The Imperial cruiser *ignored* the missiles as she entered her range of the defenses.

Heavy and light lances alike tore into the defensive platforms, with *Thoth*'s own missiles charging in their wake as the cruiser disregarded her own already-forfeit survival to clear a path for the starfighters following her.

The cruiser's ECM reached out to the missiles swarming her,

beguiling them, luring them in, showing a clear target and creating a point for them all to converge on—*Thoth* herself.

Dozens of platforms had died but dozens more remained in the cruiser's path as the missiles struck home. Weapon after weapon slammed into the ship, lighting up the shipyard and its defenses with brilliant white light as she transformed into a glowing fireball.

A glowing fireball still charging toward the station at over a thousand kilometers a second.

Thoth's remains hammered into the missile salvo still charging toward her, shattering the core of the salvo and expanding as more antimatter was added to the inferno. The superheated debris field kept expanding and hammered into the corsairs coming out to meet her. Half of the smaller ships spun away, crippled by the impact.

The other half simply came apart, their debris adding to the cloud that swept onward and over the station and its defensive platforms. Too diffuse by then to destroy the defense stations, the storm blinded their sensors, stripped away deflector emitters and rendered a small but significant number of them completely helpless.

"You see the hole, Vice Commodore," Kyle told Song softly. "You know what it cost. Go!"

———

Vulture Bomber **Kodiak** *Echo Actual*

STARFIGHTERS SWIRLED IN SPACE, closing in the wake of the sacrificial battlecruiser and making sure to cover the life pods.

Sixteen Vultures shot down the center, Williams straining her people's scanners to try and get a clean shot for her torpedoes and fighter missiles.

"Williams, I'm attaching you to Horaček's command," Song told her, linking the Imperial Colonel into the channel. "Stick with the Arrows; you're clear to fire torpedoes on your discretion, but I want you and Horaček to hold your Starfires until you have a clear shot at the yard itself.

"You're our Hail Mary punch, and the Falcons will cover you all the way in. That yard is a big damned target and we don't know where the command center is." The CAG paused, then sighed. "Only one choice. Spread your fire; vaporize anything big enough to have a transmitter. Won't leave much for the locals to use afterward, but we have to be sure we get a clean sweep."

The Falcons lunged forward, the Vulture bombers and missile-heavy Arrows falling back as the Federation starfighters took the lead, daring the defenses to aim at them.

The remnants of the last missile salvo aimed at *Thoth* hammered into them first, lasers and lances filling space as the starfighter formation charged into the cruiser's radioactive wake. The scattered and half-blinded missiles didn't stand a chance, but sheer numbers meant some of them hit home.

Starfighters died, the Falcons throwing themselves into the fire to cover the missile ships following behind. The survivors launched their own weapons, hundreds of missiles lighting up Michelle's feed as the Falcons opened fire on the defending platforms.

The radiation from *Thoth*'s destruction was clearing…and there was the shipyard.

"All Vultures, Fox Three all," Michelle snapped. "Hit the central structure, every torp and a full salvo of Starfires!"

That would leave each of her ships with two salvos of six fighter missiles apiece and give the barely fifty torpedoes additional cover on their flight. Jamming from the Falcons and Arrows helped, but those torpedoes weren't going to make it all the way on their own, high-powered jammers or not.

With over a hundred of the lighter missiles to escort them, they had a chance. Enough of one that the defenders recognized them as the main threat, focusing their fire on the incoming torpedoes.

The missiles from the Falcons swept in at the same time, forcing the defenders to choose: defend the shipyard or protect the defensive platforms themselves. There were clearly multiple controllers, deciding for different platforms…and they didn't make the same choice.

There were enough defenses that the space around the shipyard lit up with fire as dozens—hundreds!—of the incoming missiles blew apart. Counter-fire cut through the radiation cloud *Thoth*'s destruction had left behind, missiles and positron lances alike reaching out to target the incoming starfighters.

Michelle rode her torpedoes in via her implant and couldn't help feeling a stab of disappointment as the last of that salvo died ten thousand kilometers short of the station. The split in the defenses, however, had left the platforms themselves vulnerable to the Falcons' strike, and the gap *Thoth*'s suicide run had opened up was widening, clearing a path all the way through.

"You see it," Horaček said via her implant. "Let the Falcons burn it wider, hold for my signal, then fire everything you've got and break off."

"I see it," she confirmed. The defense web was weakening, but there still wasn't a hole they could actually slip missiles through. There never would be, not while any of the platforms still existed, but there was a gap between the surviving platforms and it was getting wider.

"Last salvo," Song reported. "We're not going to survive to lance range if we don't make a bigger hole. Hit 'em hard!"

The surviving Falcons sent over five hundred missiles blasting forward, and the defenses focused on them...and Michelle and Horaček saw the same moment.

"Now!" the Colonel snapped.

Sixty Arrows and twelve Vultures launched over four hundred Starfire missiles. Ten seconds later, another four hundred blazed into space, and then all seventy-two fighters flipped to burn away from the yards.

Unlike the Vultures, the Arrows at least *had* a positron lance, but it was weaker than the Falcons'...and the Falcons were pulling the same flip, with capital ship missiles from *Kodiak* blazing in to help cover their retreat as they broke off. Side vectors began to build, rapidly increasing the starfighters' closest approach distance, trying to pull them out of reach of the lances of Coati's station.

The station and its defending platforms had more immediate concerns as over a thousand starfighter missiles crashed down on them in a single immense wave. Their own missiles slashed out in defensive mode, their numbers vastly reduced by the damage they'd already taken.

The damage wasn't enough to leave even the bombers' salvo unopposed, but fewer weapons could angle on them, leaving it almost entirely to the missiles to protect the weak spot.

It wasn't enough. Many of the defensive missiles intercepted missiles from the Falcon's slightly earlier salvo. There were still enough for hundreds of the salvo Horaček and Michelle's people had launched to die, covering their entire view of the station in fire.

Hundreds of missiles were destroyed…but there *were* hundreds of missiles. Some made it through, and the defense finally collapsed under the weight of fire.

Their second salvo slipped through already-overwhelmed defenses and struck home in a carefully dispersed pattern. Fireballs lit up critical structural components, working stations, the half-complete hulls of two corsairs, and any piece of the station that had looked big enough to be a command center.

Michelle waited, watching as the radiation cleared and the q-probes swept in for a closer look. Parts of the station had survived, but almost nothing of significant size.

"Targets destroyed," Song said softly. "Captain Roberts, Quebecois Bien LaGrange points are secure."

50

KDX-6647
05:00 December 17, 2736 Earth Standard Meridian Date/Time
SC-153 Chariot

THERE WAS a point in any engagement at which there was nothing left that the flag officer in command could do. Commodore James Tecumseh hated that moment. He sat on *Chariot*'s bridge and watched the Alliance's suicide strike run at the shipyard and the starfighters heading his way at the same time, knowing there was nothing he could do to change the outcome of either.

Modesitt's starfighters were tucked in close to the cruiser, extended less than ten thousand kilometers in the direction of the incoming pirate ship to form a screen to defend against their missiles.

"Arsenault?" the Captain asked as the range continued to drop. "We're going to get a close introduction to their missiles in about two minutes. Please tell me I'm going to have something."

James's feeds flickered, a brownout cutting through the bridge, and then new data began to drop onto the feed as systems came back online.

"All right!" the engineer announced. "You have missiles, lasers and secondary lances on the starboard and upper broadsides. That's all you're getting anytime soon," he finished grimly.

"It'll have to do," Modesitt snapped. "Guns?"

"We're live. Missiles launching."

Only half of *Chariot*'s launchers were online, but six capital ship missiles were more useful than none. They lanced past the defending starfighters, charging out to meet the incoming enemy. A second salvo followed before any of the fighters reached range.

And then the starfighters reached their own weapons range, the defending Katanas hurling a hundred and sixty missiles out into space. The vectors gave them a few extra seconds of range, enough to get their salvo well into space before the pirates launched.

James closed his eyes as the tsunami of icons lit up the feed. Seven hundred missiles made a mockery of their own salvos, the two-hundred-fighter strike heading their way enough to threaten even a fully functional modern warship.

Chariot was neither.

"Hayden, what the *hell* are you doing?" Modesitt demanded.

Even with his eyes closed, the Commodore was still receiving the tactical feed routed directly to his optic nerve. Closing his eyes couldn't stop him seeing what Colonel Zack Hayden was doing.

The Katanas were leaving *Chariot* behind, the neatly organized formation of cruiser and starfighters coming apart as the fighters lunged toward the enemy, their ECM lighting up at full power...and making the starfighters easier to target.

Hayden didn't reply, his starfighters making a suicide charge into the teeth of the pirate formation as their ECM sang a suicidal siren song to the enemy missiles. Their own weapons spoke, missile after missile hurtling at an incoming formation that had no idea how to deal with this.

More experienced gunners and pilots could have compensated, used their own ECM to avoid Hayden's missiles or to compensate for the starfighters' determination to lure the missiles away from *Chariot*.

384

The conscripts Coati had shoved into his ships didn't have the training, didn't have the experience, didn't have the skill—and didn't stand a chance. Seven hundred–plus missiles lunged in at a mere forty targets, confused and deceived systems resulting in dozens of fratricidal collisions.

Hayden had fired fewer missiles, but he'd launched first and his people knew *exactly* what they were doing. Every single pirate Katana died in the first salvo, but there was nothing to save the Commonwealth starfighters. Both sides had launched their missiles, and now all the Terran ships could do was force those missiles to come for them instead of *Chariot*.

The Colonel and his people never replied to Modesitt's demands to respond, to explain themselves. They just threw themselves into the fire and gutted the incoming starfighters and their missiles in an orgy of explosions and missiles.

"Report," James said as the explosions died. *Please let it be over.*

"I'm reading at least eighty missiles and twenty starfighters still headed our way," *Chariot's* tactical officer replied. "Engaging with positron lances and missiles."

James gripped the arms of his chair as the enemy kept coming. Missiles flashed into the defensive perimeter and died. They had the speed to penetrate his defenses but lacked the numbers. The last died barely five kilometers from *Chariot's* hull, washing over the ship with radiation, but they died before impact.

"Starfighters closing," Modesitt noted calmly. "I want them the fuck out of my sky!"

James realized he was holding his breath, watching as the starfighters lunged toward *Chariot*, the numbers attached to their icons dropping—and wondering why the cruiser hadn't fired yet.

"Guns?" the Captain said, her voice no longer calm.

"Making certain," the tactical officer replied, his voice distracted. "And...now."

At fifty thousand kilometers, still outside the range of the lances the older starfighter design carried, twenty-four secondary positron lances, every one of the ones that Arsenault had arranged power for, fired at twenty targets.

Thirteen died instantly, but the beams were already sweeping, a lethal pattern that wiped starfighter after starfighter from space...and then cut out as the entire cruiser *lurched* and the lights died.

Again.

———

THE FACT that they were all still breathing was a positive sign, and James leveled his best "Grumpy Commodore" gaze on the tactical officer as the emergency lighting kicked back in.

"Please tell me you got them all."

"I'm..." The commander swallowed. "I *think* so. I was half-expecting something like this from Arsenault's complaints, so I waited until I had the best shot I was going to get."

"Computers are back up on batteries, but there's nothing feeding them," Modesitt told James. "Arsenault isn't responding to implant messages."

James waved his hand experimentally.

"Gravity is gone again," he noted. "I suggest everyone stay still except for whoever is closest to the emergency supplies. That lucky person gets to start passing out mag-boots."

Magnetic boots were a mediocre solution at best to zero gravity, but they were better than having crews used to artificial gravity floating around like loose balloons.

By the time the tactical petty officer who'd been closest had passed boots to James, he was feeling more confident that they, at least, had survived the battle. Though, of course, if the Alliance's attack had failed, they were going to end up dead in short order.

On the other hand, if the Alliance's attack had *succeeded*, then Coati was dead and they were going to be in serious trouble when Roberts came to check on them.

"Is anyone getting responses from outside the bridge on implant coms?" Modesitt asked.

"I'm getting most of the ship, ma'am. Aren't you?" her tactical officer replied.

The Captain looked perplexed, then sighed.

"Self-diagnostic says everything but the shortest-range transceivers are done," she admitted. "Backlash from the link failure. Commodore, can you reach out to Arsenault?"

James nodded and pinged the engineer. There was no response for a moment, so he tried again.

"Would you like sensors or me to spend time gabbing at you?" the engineer snapped after a moment. "Right now, we are blind, deaf, dumb and crippled. I can't fix any of that if you lot don't leave me alone."

"An update would be nice, Commander," James said dryly. "Status?"

"We blew the primary power busses again," the engineer replied. "Half the distribution network went down with it. The other half just went...away."

"That's not a technical term I'm used to," James told him.

"We vaporized the fuck out of half of our wiring, transformers and junction boxes. Technical enough for you?"

The Commodore winced.

"Any time estimate on repairs?"

"I can have *some* systems online soon-ish," Arsenault told him. "Short-range coms, maybe some sensors. Enough for us to talk to that q-probe in our hold. Not much more."

"FTL?"

The engineer sighed.

"Not today," he said quietly. "Probably not tomorrow. Forty-eight to seventy-two hours, minimum."

"Commander, this system has a high likelihood of *remaining* hostile space, even if it is now in Alliance control," James pointed out. "If we're sitting dead in the water for two or three days, we are quite possibly simply *dead*."

The channel was silent for several seconds.

"I can't do the impossible, sir," Arsenault finally said. "Forty-eight hours minimum to get the Alcubierre drive back online. I... We're not going to have weapons before that." He coughed. "We're, ah, not going to have weapons before a very long shipyard visit. If ever."

"Get me coms," James said with a sigh. "One way or another, it seems I need to talk to Captain Roberts, and I'd rather not have to do that by flashing our *running lights* at him."

"Ten minutes," Arsenault promised. "For short-range coms that can talk to their q-probe, that is. I'm not sure if the running lights are working and I don't plan on taking the time to check."

————

THE ENGINEER WAS as good as his word. Just under ten minutes by the clock in James's implant later, the short-range coms came back up, linking them into both the q-probe they'd kept close against just this endeavor and the Alliance probe they'd tucked inside their hold to allow for communications with Roberts's force.

James was unsurprised to discover that the Alliance probe was no longer feeding him any sensor data. There was still an active channel there, but it wasn't carrying any live information. Just…waiting.

They had their own probes scattered around the KDX-6647, though, and those told him what he needed to know.

The shipyard was gone. The cloud of debris was settling into orbit of Quebecois Bien and would eventually give the planet a new set of temporary rings formed of chunks of solidified metal vapor and loose debris.

Thoth was gone with it. So were the corsairs and most of the defensive platforms that had been guarding the shipyard. A network of platforms still orbited Quebecois Bien, some of them still active, but *Kodiak* was well outside their range. It wouldn't take the Federation crew long to isolate the remaining manned platforms and either destroy them or force their surrender.

Coati's empire was broken. The pirate had presumably died with his shipyard. The planet he'd conquered would be liberated within hours. The deal James had agreed to with Roberts was complete—and the q-probes warned him of the inevitable next stage from that.

"I've got what looks like two wings of fighters heading our way," the tactical officer announced grimly. "They're all Falcons, none of whatever they killed *Poseidon* with, and it looks like they just finished rearming aboard *Kodiak*.

388

"What do we do?"

There weren't a lot of choices. *Chariot* wasn't combat-capable, and Colonel Hayden and his people had died keeping her as intact as she was. James was mildly surprised that there weren't any assault shuttles in the formation sweeping toward them.

"I'd say we can't surrender," Modesitt told him, "except that they already know what we were doing in the Free Trade Zone." She sighed. "I don't see any other choice, sir. Two wings of Falcons is overkill against *Chariot*'s current state."

"Link in to that q-probe and get me a channel to Roberts," James ordered. "Let's see just how this ends."

From the speed of the response, the Federation commander had been waiting to hear from him.

"Commodore Tecumseh."

"Captain Roberts. It seems our arrangement has come to an end," James said.

"So it seems," the big Captain replied. "I'm not a fan of what duty requires of me, Commodore Tecumseh, but your ship is crippled and in an area under the Alliance's protection."

"It seems poor recompense for fighting by your side against Coati," the Terran pointed out. "I won't say I'm surprised, but one might have expected better."

"We might have expected you not to commit acts of war against neutral parties," Roberts said, a strange twist to his grin. "Perhaps more relevant, Commodore, is that there is no way I can justify providing technical or medical assistance to a Commonwealth vessel that has not surrendered."

"*Chariot* is helpless, Captain Roberts," James admitted, the words ashes on his tongue. "I request that you allow us to evacuate and destroy her before we surrender ourselves as your prisoners."

The Federation officer looked uncomfortable, then sighed.

"You have fought by our side," he conceded. "Is *Chariot* repairable? I'm guessing she'll never be combat-capable again."

"Her A-S drive may be fixed, but she'll never fight again," James said. No ship whose power systems had failed as completely—and repeatedly!—as *Chariot*'s would ever be sent into action.

"Are you prepared to offer your parole and the parole of your crew and officers, that you will never take up arms against the Alliance again?"

That wasn't a question James had been expecting. It was a question normally asked of an enemy *after* they'd surrendered—which, James supposed, he effectively had. They both knew it. Everything from here was a formality.

"I was not under the impression that much repatriation of prisoners was going on," James said slowly.

"I am a Federation capital ship commander on an independent deployment, authorized to act as both the military and political representative of my nation," Captain Roberts stated firmly. "Exceptions can be made. Are you prepared to offer parole?"

"I am," James rushed out before he could think about it.

"Your parole is granted. You will be repatriated aboard *Chariot*," Roberts told him. "You may repair her and leave this system. If you are seen in Alliance-protected space again, your parole is void and you will be destroyed on sight.

"Do you understand the conditions of your surrender, Commodore Tecumseh?"

"I do. And thank you."

"Don't thank me," the younger man replied. "Your career won't survive this."

"No," James agreed. "But my crew will."

51

KDX-6647

12:00 December 17, 2736 Earth Standard Meridian Date/Time

DSC-052 Kodiak

WITH ALL OF his starfighters finally retrieved and rearmed, Kyle was almost relaxed as *Kodiak* slotted neatly into a trailing orbit of Quebecois Bien.

"We've identified three manned control platforms," Sterling told him. "Without starfighters or multi-layered defenses, it'll be child's play to drop a missile into each of them on a ballistic course. On your order, Captain."

"Today is a day for last chances," Kyle replied, eyeing the icon of the still-ballistic *Chariot* on her way out-system. "Set up a transmission, Jamison. Make sure both the surface and the orbitals get it."

"Yes, sir. Recording at your order."

Kodiak's Captain inhaled deeply, letting as much as possible of the stress of the morning and its battles fade. He'd lost friends today, subordinates, people he'd respected—but that was war and the last thing he could do was let those losses be in vain.

Nodding to Jamison, he settled himself facing the camera.

"This message is for the forces under the command of 'Commodore' Antonio Coati," he said cheerfully. "My name is Captain Kyle Roberts of the Castle Federation Space Navy and I am now in control of this star system.

"You retain forces on the planetary surface and some orbital platforms. You may think this is sufficient to resist, but allow me to disabuse you of that notion.

"If you fight me, I will crush you. If you surrender, you will face fair trials for any crimes you have committed against the people of Quebecois Bien, but I will guarantee that there will be no arbitrary reprisals.

"I am in a position to begin the liberation of Quebecois Bien in one hour. Any combat formation that has not surrendered by that time will be destroyed.

"The choice is yours."

A mental command ended the recording and sent it on its way.

"So, we wait?" Taggart asked from CIC.

"We wait. We'll stay at Condition Two, but make sure food gets to everyone still on station," Kyle ordered. "And tell Gonzalez to meet me in my office. Even if these bastards surrender, we're going to need to install some kind of peacekeeping force."

———

KYLE AND GONZALEZ were reviewing the orbital photos of what they were *reasonably* certain was Quebecois Bien's capital city when Jamison linked into his office.

"We have a transmission from the surface directed to you, Captain. Looks like one of Coati's people."

"What's the time delay?" Kyle asked. "Can we talk live?"

"Four and a half seconds. You should be fine."

"All right. Put them through. Cut Gonzalez from our feed, but I want her to listen in."

"Yes, sir."

Jamison linked the camera to his implant for a moment, letting him make sure that they had the right angle to exclude the Marine Major without being obvious about it, then connected the call.

A heavily muscled man with pitch-black skin and gemlike eyes similar to those sported by Coati himself stood in the middle of what appeared to be a stone-paved courtyard, wearing a simple white uniform.

"This is Captain Roberts," Kyle told him. "To whom am I speaking?"

"I am General Joseph Nkrumah," the man said nine seconds later. "I command the ground forces responsible for security on Quebecois Bien. You should know that most of my forces were in orbit and are now dead.

"Riots are spreading through the cities. I have recalled my remaining men to our central barracks in the capital. From here, we can stand off the rioters for weeks, if not months, and any sustained siege will result in a massive loss of life.

"The orbital platform commanders answer to me and I am prepared to negotiate terms."

Kyle smiled coldly.

"You know my terms, General," he told the man. "I will not promise better ones. Don't think that your barracks will hold against orbital bombardment. Only my desire to minimize loss of life gives you any leverage at all here."

Nine seconds later, some of the stiffness seemed to drain from Nkrumah's spine.

"A man has to try," he said simply. "We appear to have underestimated the Princess, Captain Roberts. I offer the immediate surrender of my men and the orbital platforms, under the sole condition that we be evacuated from Quebecois Bien within six hours.

"I do not believe that Maria Duarte intends to leave any remnant of the Coati regime alive in her wake."

If this Duarte was the descendant of the rulers that the Coatis had murdered to take control, Kyle had a great deal of sympathy for her... but it was also his duty to prevent an atrocity.

"Stand down the orbital platforms, General, and I will have shuttles on the ground inside an hour. You understand that you and your men will still face trials for crimes you have committed?"

"I'll face a court, Roberts, if you'll promise it will be a fair one," the General snapped. "I wouldn't trust the same promise from Duarte."

"Then we have a deal."

Kyle cut the channel and looked to Gonzalez.

"Major?"

"I'm guessing I should assume he's going to stab us in the back?"

"Probably. I'm almost more concerned about this Maria Duarte," Kyle admitted. "They've surrendered to us. Let's make sure the locals don't massacre them, please."

It took less than ninety minutes after getting Federation boots on the ground and *Kodiak* in orbit for the call Kyle expected to arrive.

"Sir, we're receiving a call from a woman who refuses to identify herself but insists on speaking to you in person," Jamison told him. "They're bouncing it through some relays to try and confuse things, but she's in an old armored personnel carrier in the force that's moving into the capital city."

"Ah," Kyle allowed. Shaking his head, he rose from his command chair. "I'll take Her Highness's call in my office."

He left the bridge, dropped into his chair, and then linked the communication channel.

"I presume I am speaking to Her Highness Maria Duarte, Princess of Quebecois Bien and sole surviving daughter of Pierre III, King of Quebecois Bien?" he asked as an attractive young woman in unmarked dark green fatigues appeared on his screen.

There'd been a *lot* of data on Quebecois Bien in the files at *l'Estación de Muerte*. Once the name had been mentioned, he'd made sure to do his research.

The woman jerked as if stung.

"I am," she admitted after a moment. "I see you have the advantage of me."

"You know my name," Kyle replied. "While I imagine little information on the Federation has made it here, even less on Quebecois Bien has made it to the rest of the galaxy."

"That was how our founders wanted it," she snapped. "The rest of us were stuck living with it after the idiots died."

"As is often the case. How may I assist you, Your Highness?"

"You can turn over the murderers and scum you're protecting in New Montreal," she snapped.

"Princess Duarte, I will happily do so...once Quebecois Bien has a functioning judiciary in place to try them."

"The final court was always the King," Duarte said sweetly.

"That will not be acceptable," he told her. "I will not turn my prisoners over unless I am certain they will face a fair trial. I think it would be wiser for us all if we allowed, say, Serengeti to carry out the trials. From what I understand, most of Coati's personnel were from his home system."

"And I am to trust Coati's home world?"

"Given that I am here and have liberated your world because they asked me to, I would suggest so, yes," Kyle replied. "I will not permit atrocities or reprisals, Your Highness, but I would be delighted to offer my Marines and my diplomatic aide to assist you in restoring order and establishing a stable government on your world.

"We are here to help."

"And what is your price, Captain Roberts?"

"My price, Princess Duarte, is that the piracy of the systems my government swore to protect stops," Kyle told her. "That price was paid by Antonio Coati in fire and blood. Any assistance I provide you can be considered charged to his account."

Duarte closed her eyes and sighed, almost sagging against the clearly uncomfortable chair in her APC.

"I am...hesitant to trust an outsider," she admitted, "but I have little choice. I will send an unarmed messenger with a radio to meet with your ground commander. We will coordinate from there.

"Thank you, Captain Roberts," she said softly. "I do not know if we would ever have been free of Coati's grip without you, and yet we had never dared to dream that help would come from the stars."

08:00 December 19, 2736 ESMDT

"Not everyone, Captain Roberts, is going to be entirely okay with your allowing Commodore Tecumseh to repair his ship and leave," Meredith Blake, Chairwoman of the Castle Federation Joint Chiefs of Staff, told Kyle calmly. "He remains our enemy."

"I trust him to honor his parole, ma'am," Kyle replied. "And…he'd earned it, Admiral. *Chariot*'s crew fought and died by our side to defeat Coati and liberate Quebecois Bien."

"Indeed. I have already decided to endorse your actions," Blake said. "If anything, Tecumseh's actions once again give us hope that there is some sanity in the Commonwealth's military. Though, if they keep him in uniform, they'll just send him to fight Periklos."

"They have many uses for soldiers."

"There is only so far they can stretch their resources, ma'am. We must show ourselves to act with honor, or we are no better than the fanatics who burned Kematian."

"I agree. Others won't. What is *Kodiak*'s status?"

"We managed to avoid damage to *Kodiak* herself, somehow," Kyle said, managing to keep the bitterness out of his voice. "*Thoth* is gone, *Alexander* went home crippled, and out of the fighter groups of three starships, we don't have enough fighters left to fill *Kodiak*'s hangar deck, but she remains unharmed."

"We weren't certain, so additional forces are already en route," she told him. "With the Free Trade Zone's core systems signing on to the Alliance, we've managed to break free several ships from our other allies. The Trade Factor is sending *Breslau*, one of their *Principality*-class carriers, and it turns out we still have one of our old *Invictus*-class carriers doing back-system security duty.

"They're old carriers, but they'll do the job. Once they arrive, you are to bring *Kodiak* back to Castle and report to Central Command in person."

"Yes, ma'am."

"And, Roberts?"

"Ma'am?"

"The bombers?" she asked. "I've seen the reports; they seem impressive. Your thoughts?"

"I've been on both ends of a bomber strike now, Admiral," he admitted. "They're not perfect. There are countermeasures and vulnerabilities, but they are an extremely valuable addition to our capabilities. I'll have a formal recommendation before we're home, but I would suggest that we move toward replacing at least one wing on every carrier with a bomber force."

"That useful?" Blake questioned.

"That useful, ma'am," he confirmed. "We killed a *Hercules* with a single bomber strike. Yes, we took her by surprise, but she didn't stand a chance. That's not a weapon I'd turn aside lightly."

"I look forward to your recommendation," she told him. "By the time you return, we should actually have a final bomber design of our own to deploy, one with a few tricks and advantages the Terrans don't have."

"I look forward to seeing it, Admiral."

52

Niagara System—Commonwealth Space
08:00 January 30, 2737 Earth Standard Meridian Date/Time
BB-285 Saint Michael*—Marshal Walkingstick's Office*

COMMODORE JAMES TECUMSEH stood in front of the desk belonging to the man charged with the annexation of the systems known to the Terran Commonwealth as the Rimward Marches and their occupants as the Alliance of Free Stars and waited patiently for his fate to be dictated to him.

He would once have called himself Marshal James Calvin Walkingstick's protégé, the two of them bonding over a shared name and cultural background.

He had no illusions that relationship would spare him the consequences of what he had done. Which left him standing, without a seat even being offered, while Walkingstick reviewed the fully detailed report he'd provided.

"I must ask, Commodore Tecumseh," Walkingstick finally said, "was there something wrong with *Chariot*'s q-com array?"

"No, sir."

"And yet. And yet," the Marshal repeated. "At no point between Coati's betrayal, your deciding to ally with Roberts against him, the assault on his bases or the liberation of the world he had conquered, did you feel it necessary to advise me of the events and decisions taking place?"

"I felt..." James swallowed. "I felt that what I did was necessary for the honor of the Commonwealth. I also felt that the blame and consequences of what I did should fall only on me and spill neither up nor down."

"Noble of you. You realize that, as your commanding officer, I am responsible for your actions regardless of whether I am properly informed of them, correct?"

"Yes, sir."

"You threw away a carefully planned operation to lure Alliance forces out of position on a matter of honor," Walkingstick said slowly. "I've read all of your justifications, Commodore, and while I recognize the truth to them, I also recognize excuses when I see them."

"Sir," James acknowledged levelly.

"Fortunately for you, there is enough weight to your excuses to help cover this mess up," the Marshal snapped. "Useful as Coati was as a distraction for the Alliance, he was also more dangerous than we predicted, and there was no way we could have permitted him to retain the use and schematics of a *Hercules*-class battlecruiser.

"Plus, the confirmation of the deployment of bombers by the Alliance has value all on its own.

"Nonetheless, you should have phoned home, Commodore. There would have been options that weren't technically *treason*."

James winced but retained his parade rest.

"And this parole bullshit. What were you thinking?"

"That it was an alternative to the surrender or destruction of a capital ship of the Terran Commonwealth Space Navy," James said swiftly. "I could protect my crew and officers. I understood then and accept now the price for my actions."

"Prepared once more to sacrifice your career on the altar of Terra's honor, are you?" Walkingstick asked. "I would not be so swift in your choices. Your fate this time is not mine to decide, Commodore. Your parole means you can no longer be assigned to my command—and therefore I can do nothing with you.

"*Chariot* will need to undergo repairs here in Niagara. You, Captain Modesitt, and Colonel Barbados will be shipped back to Sol on the next transport liner. The three of you will have the opportunity to plead your case to Central Command."

James wavered, swallowing hard, but nodded.

"I understand, sir."

"I'm not certain, Commodore, whether you are truly as determinedly honorable as you seem or are just bloody-mindedly stupid," Walkingstick snapped. "But, either way, I cannot save you from the path you've set your feet on. I hope, for my sake more than yours at this point, that your protestations of honor and necessity find fertile ground in Sol, Commodore.

"I won't wish you luck," he concluded. "You've used up any good-will of mine you had. But safe travels, Commodore Tecumseh.

"I do not expect us to meet again."

————

Castle System
18:00 February 5, 2737 ESMDT
New Cardiff

"ADMIRAL KANE IS WAITING for you, Captain Roberts," the aide informed Kyle. "Go right in."

Kyle had been rushed down to the Castle Federation Joint Command Center within minutes of *Kodiak* entering orbit. He'd barely had time to pack an overnight bag, so he'd assumed the Admiral wanted to see him with urgency.

It still wasn't an entirely positive sign that Kane, the man responsible for the carefully balanced personnel needs of the entire Federation military, was *waiting* for him.

"Come in, Roberts, come in," the Admiral ordered as he stepped through the door. "Have a seat. Beer?"

"That's usually my line," Kyle said with a grin. "Sure."

"Your habits are in your file," Kane told him with a smile of his own, sliding a cold bottle from Kyle's favorite Anston microbrewery across the desk. "Though I'll confess I tried one of these after acquiring them for this meeting, and I was impressed."

"Thank you, sir. I'm not sure what I'm getting beer for."

"You short-stopped a pirate campaign that was on the edge of birthing a new empire on our Rimward frontier," the Admiral pointed out. "Doing so, as per usual, with style and skill."

"And sacrifice," Kyle replied. "Von Lambert was a good man. Sarka's crew deserved better than the beating they took, too."

"But you are victorious regardless. *Alexander* returned to duty a week ago," Kane told him. "The rewards of victory will be widespread, though the most immediately important one is for Senior Fleet Commander Taggart."

"Sir?"

"He'll be receiving the formal orders within the hour, but he is being promoted to Captain and will be taking command of *Kodiak* in your place," the turbaned Admiral explained. "Which is well deserved but does leave you at loose ends."

"I serve at the Federation's pleasure," Kyle said carefully. The last time they'd taken a ship out from under him, he'd ended up on a black op deep in Commonwealth space.

"Don't worry, Roberts; I have *plans* for you this time," Kane told him with a smile. "I apologize for rushing you down so quickly; I wanted to let you know in person what was going on before Taggart got his Captain's planet."

"I appreciate that, sir. You'll want to transfer Vice Commodore Song," Kyle warned softly. "She and Taggart are in a relationship. With myself in command, they were extremely professional and it caused no problems, but she cannot continue as his CAG."

"No, she cannot," the head of JD-Personnel agreed. "Thank you, Roberts. It shouldn't be a problem, but I appreciate the heads-up.

"You had leave booked for your arrival here," he continued. "Did you have any particular plans?"

"I mostly was intending to look up Captain Solace; she hadn't left the planet, the last I'd heard," Kyle admitted.

"She was placed on mandatory counseling leave," Kane told him gently. "That's over now, but she's been assigned here at Joint Command as XO for Project Armada's battlecruiser design team. It's a desk job, but one where she will gain some much-needed staff seasoning, and the Federation will benefit from her knowledge."

"So, she will have some time available," Kyle concluded.

"She will," Kane confirmed. "May I suggest Markham and Sons, Roberts?"

"Admiral?" Kyle blinked. He wasn't quite sure what Kane meant.

"They're a jeweler in New Cardiff, near the Joint Command Center," the Admiral told him with a chuckle. "They give a discount for Navy officers and do fine work. If I misjudged and was presumptuous…"

"No, sir, you did not," the younger man admitted. "Am I that obvious?"

"There is a reason I head JD-Personnel, Roberts. Now, I apologize, but I am going to have to cancel your leave," he continued.

"Sir, I…"

"It won't interfere with you and Captain Solace's time together, I promise," Kane assured him. "Much as I know you're going to hate it, I have a desk job for you. Have you heard of the Joint Strategic Options Command?"

"No, sir," Kyle said, hesitantly.

"Good," the Admiral said with a laugh. "It's as classified a desk job as exists. JSOC is a team we are gathering over the next few weeks, made up of thirty or so of the best tacticians and worst mavericks we could find in four fleets, *none* of which are going to be happy about being pulled from combat duty."

Kyle winced.

"That sounds like it's going to be unpleasant, sir," he admitted. He could understand why Kane was including him in that list. "I'm guessing at least some of them will have a problem with my reputation."

"There won't be a problem, Roberts," Kane said with a grin. "Or if there is, you'll be able to deal with it. You misunderstand why I asked, and I need you to understand just what JSOC is for.

"All logical assessment says we cannot win this war. The Joint Strategic Options Command is where we plan to put together the most unconventional brainpower we have and try and find options to do the impossible and defeat the Commonwealth."

A small velvet jewelry box appeared in Kane's hands as if by magic, the type the Navy used for rank insignia. Kyle found himself staring at it in shocked silence as Kane concluded.

"It will be your responsibility to make sure that JSOC works together and succeeds—*Admiral* Roberts."

JOIN THE MAILING LIST

Love Glynn Stewart's books? Join the mailing list at

GLYNNSTEWART.COM/MAILING-LIST/

to know as soon as new books are released, special announcements, and a chance to win free paperbacks.

ABOUT THE AUTHOR

Glynn Stewart is the author of *Starship's Mage*, a bestselling science fiction and fantasy series where faster-than-light travel is possible–but only because of magic. His other works include science fiction series *Duchy of Terra, Castle Federation* and *Vigilante*, as well as the urban fantasy series *ONSET* and *Changeling Blood*.

Writing managed to liberate Glynn from a bleak future as an accountant. With his personality and hope for a high-tech future intact, he lives in Kitchener, Ontario with his partner, their cats, and an unstoppable writing habit.

VISIT GLYNNSTEWART.COM FOR NEW RELEASE UPDATES

facebook.com/glynnstewartauthor

OTHER BOOKS BY GLYNN STEWART

For release announcements join the mailing list or visit **GlynnStewart.com**

STARSHIP'S MAGE
Starship's Mage
Hand of Mars
Voice of Mars
Alien Arcana
Judgment of Mars
UnArcana Stars
Sword of Mars
Mountain of Mars
The Service of Mars
A Darker Magic
Mage-Commander (upcoming)

Starship's Mage: Red Falcon
Interstellar Mage
Mage-Provocateur
Agents of Mars

Pulsar Race: A Starship's Mage Universe Novella

DUCHY OF TERRA
The Terran Privateer
Duchess of Terra
Terra and Imperium
Darkness Beyond
Shield of Terra
Imperium Defiant
Relics of Eternity
Shadows of the Fall
Eyes of Tomorrow

VIGILANTE
(WITH TERRY MIXON)
Heart of Vengeance
Oath of Vengeance

Bound By Stars: A Vigilante Series
(With Terry Mixon)
Bound By Law
Bound by Honor
Bound by Blood

TEER AND KARD
Wardtown
Blood Ward

CHANGELING BLOOD
Changeling's Fealty
Hunter's Oath
Noble's Honor
Fae, Flames & Fedoras: A Changeling Blood Novella

ONSET
ONSET: To Serve and Protect
ONSET: My Enemy's Enemy
ONSET: Blood of the Innocent
ONSET: Stay of Execution
Murder by Magic: An ONSET Novella

FANTASY STAND ALONE NOVELS
Children of Prophecy
City in the Sky

Printed in Great Britain
by Amazon

48460713R00239